RAENE
AND THE THREE BEARS
BEARS

RS MCCOY

Copyright © 2016 by RS McCoy
www.rsmccoyauthor.com
Cover Art by Kit Foster Design
© 2016 * http://www.kitfosterdesign.com/
Edited by Courtney Whittamore
www.themoralofourstories.com

ISBN 978-1537394480

For my boys

GONE

RAENE'S STOMACH continued to twist in useless circles as it had for the last week. Something was wrong—so, so wrong. It hung over her like a dense cloud of smoke, choking the air and obscuring her vision.

But until Kaide agreed to see her, there was nothing she could do.

Her fingers skipped over the closetful of silk gowns and shawls, black Pyro pants, and short scarlet tops. So many luxurious pieces, yet nothing to wear and nothing to do. Endless waiting.

Something had happened with Blossom. That much she knew. It couldn't be a coincidence that her uncle shut her out the day of Blossom's transformation.

Or, maybe, he was angry at Raene herself. Tomorrow, for her own transformation, she would travel to the capital and earn her totem animal—a tiger, no doubt. She would finally be a fierce predator like the mother she never knew.

Maybe Kaide hated that she would get her mother's tiger when he got only a monster.

Or maybe his silence was for something else entirely. Tomorrow, with her tiger totem secured, Raene would be in prime position for a marriage arrangement. She'd spent the last two years researching good families with influence and connections—and with eligible, attractive sons, of course. For any young woman of her class and pedigree, a trade was inevitable, and Raene wanted her alignment to benefit Kaide in his political career. After all he'd done to keep her safe, agreeing to a favorable arrangement was the least she could do for him.

For the thousandth time, Raene thought over the short list of suitors she'd presented to Kaide only months ago. There was the Porsten Clan with their son Corson. Poor guy. Corson Porsten. But he had a lion totem, and his parents were both involved with the security training facility. They held an annual gala to raise money for new equipment and uniforms. An alignment with their family would give Kaide sway over the use and distribution of Pyro security details across the realm.

The Ignala Clan was a viable option as well. Their youngest son, Armis, was more than ten years her senior, but he seemed kind and pleasant enough when she met him a few months ago at a formality course. His obscene wealth and position as Pyro Commissioner of Interrealm Affairs didn't hurt, either.

But Raene knew which candidate Kaide would pick. Emile Lagrada was the obvious choice. He was classically handsome with dark eyes and hair as sleek as a raven's wing. He was only twenty-two, but he had a cheetah totem, a respectable position as Syndicate Liaison, and was known for the finest and most-selective parties in the branch. As his wife, Raene would wear stunning gowns and attend the most lavish events. Emile Lagrada was perfectly aligned to help Kaide while also offering her everything she could want in a husband.

She couldn't stand waiting to start the rest of her life— a new home, a new role in society, a new family. She would no longer be held under Kaide's protective wing. So much would change in the next few days. The anticipation was enough to make her fidget, snaking her fingers through her hair over and over again.

Raene only wished Kaide would let her know what he'd decided. She was confident his selection would maximize her safety and happiness. She had no greater faith in anyone.

But until she knew for certain, she was stuck in this nothing. Only waiting for a call that never came and a transformation that couldn't come soon enough.

Raene sat on the edge of her modest bed and ran her hands through her lengths of blonde hair, mindlessly tucking strands into a sloppy braid. Afternoon light shone in through the narrow-slit window, casting a yellow rectangle on her rug. She traced its outline with her toe two, three times, when she heard a noise.

"Rain Drop?" Her father's rough voice sounded from deep within the stone house.

Raene abandoned her musings and set out in search of him, more than eager for a distraction. "Yes, Papa?" Trotting through Naiden's lava stone home, her expensive crimson shoes picked their way around the meager furnishings: a low crimson sofa with matching chair, porous stone floor covered with threadbare rugs, a maple wood table cluttered with glasses and mostly empty bottles of strawberry wine. The whole place stunk with the sweetness of old wine, but it had been that way all her life. It was the smell of home.

While Kaide showered Raene with dresses, jewelry, fine linens, and all manner of luxuries, he refused to share his wealth with Naiden. She didn't know why her entire family—even her estranged grandparents—so detested her father, but Raene could guess it had to do with her mother's death some seventeen years before. Whatever the reason, it put Raene's life in a strange split between Kaide's extravagance and her father's poverty.

Before she found him, Raene heard the beep of her panel—the sleek handheld device that could connect her to the world but only connected her to Kaide. Raene's heart leapt to her throat, and she broke into a desperate jog. "Papa?" she called out just as she found him in the kitchen, his feet shuffling to find her.

Raene grabbed the device and answered it in a single motion. Naiden tried to look disinterested, but he stood only steps away, watching as she held out the panel and waited for Kaide's face to fill the screen.

But it was only Norsa. Kaide's head housekeeper let a weak smile play with the corners of her mouth. "He's asked to see you."

"Why didn't he call me himself?" Raene asked. It didn't make any sense. Up until the last week, she and Kaide had been as close as siblings. They had no secrets. They hid nothing from each other. Why this sudden chasm between them?

Had she done something wrong?

Raene rubbed at the lines that creased her brow. After this week, she'd have a wrinkle for sure.

"He didn't say. Just wants you to pack a bag and bring enough clothes for a few days. Can you get here in an hour?"

Raene couldn't fight the smile that spread across her cheeks. "A few days?" she squealed. He wanted to see her. He wanted her to stay over, like she had several days a week for her entire life. Whatever had grown between them, it was over. "I'll be right there."

Raene ended the transmission and clutched her panel between her hands with glee.

"Everything all right?" Naiden asked. A low-bred Pyro with a python totem, Naiden was the opposite of Kaide— small, nervous, quiet. For the thousandth time, Raene wondered what her mother had seen in him. Or had she seen someone else entirely? Maybe before her death, Raene's mother had known a different Naiden Randal.

Now, his hands were clasped before him, a motion he used to try to hide the uncontrollable shaking. His eyes were clear, and his jaw trembled in a rare moment of sobriety. Raene would have asked if he could manage on his own for a few days, but she didn't want to know the answer. It was selfish, she knew, but Raene didn't want to be delayed by yet another of her father's habitual breakdowns.

"Everything's fine, Papa. I'm going over to Kaide's for a few days. You'll let me know if you need anything?" She leaned forward and kissed his cheek. Naiden Randal was almost a full head shorter than her—clearly she'd gotten her height from her mother's side—and he looked up at her with those sad, empty eyes he always had.

Raene didn't know what had happened to her father, what had made him this empty shell of a person who could only be filled with drink, but she knew no amount of sitting by his side or watching over him would change anything. She'd tried that for years and years. He would drink himself sick and spend his night on the couch like he always did.

So she was going to see Kaide. After only a week away, she missed him. She didn't even care why he pushed her away anymore, as long as he let her back in—not just into the manor, but back into his life, his confidence.

And she'd get to see Blossom. With her own transformation on the horizon, Raene was eager to see her new sister and hear about the process first hand.

While her father lingered in the living room and searched through his pile of bottles to see which was the most full, Raene darted to her room and pulled out a small bag from under her bed. Then, she filled it with three sets of the wide-legged pants and scarlet tops, the colors all Pyros wore. After that, her night clothes: a thin-strapped top and silken shorts, always black. At the last minute, while wondering about the possibility of a big surprise party or an intimate wedding ceremony to her selected husband, Raene collected her newest gown—a floor-length scarlet dream with a low-cut bodice covered in elegant, shimmering beads. Her mind raced to think who she would wear it for.

As she left her room, Raene pulled the bag over her shoulder and adjusted her waist-length hair so it wasn't tangled in the strap. She kissed her father's warm cheek one last time before she jogged out the door and started up the hill toward Kaide's manor.

Her feet couldn't carry her fast enough. She'd walked the short path between her father's modest home and Kaide's considerable estate so many times, she could do it with her eyes closed. As always, she kept off the streets and wove through the dense wood, as Kaide insisted. It was safer there, away from the crowds of Pyros, prone to anger and violence as they were.

Raene would be one of them tomorrow.

She would have a predator's blood flowing in her veins. All her life, she'd known she would be a tiger—like her mother—but now that it was only a day away, her nerves were on edge. What would it be like to be so volatile? Would she be able to control it?

Afternoon light peeked between the towering alders and blossoming fruit trees. The hot summer air had yet to permeate the cool shade of the woods, and for that she was thankful. Heat only made everything worse.

Raene raced along faster than usual. But even at such a pace, her ears perked to the sound of boots in the distance. She stopped and scanned with eyes and ears, searching for the source.

"It's only me," Olin called.

Raene's reflexes quieted when she saw his dark hair and rough features as he approached "Did he send you after me?"

Olin shook his head. "Norsa said you were on your way."

When she was close enough, Olin pulled her against his chest and kissed her head, a fatherly gesture he'd adopted long ago. While her own father was lost in drink for most of her life, Olin had filled that role—for her and Kaide. He was the steady rock in their racing rivers.

"How is he?" Raene asked as they continued toward the manor, walking under the alder and peach and cherry trees weighed down with flowers and fruit.

Again, Olin shook his head, his eyes cast down. A sullen cloud loomed over them.

"What happened?" She searched his face for any sign but there was only the heaviness of worry and fatigue.

"You'll see," he said, leaving it at that as they climbed the last hill, the one that rose up to the west of the manor. When at last they had the manor in view, Norsa already stood waiting on the front step.

Her features were downcast, her skin dull where usually it was vibrant. Her grey-streaked hair looked even lighter, like she'd aged years in the last week.

At the sight, Raene's stomach sank and twisted, consumed with a nervous knot.

It was then Raene ran. Fear and worry propelled her across the clearing and toward the woman who was closer to a mother than any Raene had ever known. "What is it? What happened?" Raene begged for answers when she was close enough to get them.

Norsa put a comforting arm around Raene's shoulders, though Raene had outgrown her years ago. "Come in, child. I'll tell you what we know." In her late fifties, her hair having already turned grey, Norsa looked like a sweet little grandmother, but Raene knew better.

She let Norsa walk her down the guest wing and push

her toward a stool at the island in the kitchen, a steaming cup of tea already waiting, filling the air with a soft, sweet aroma.

Violet berry tea. For calming.

Raene was scared just at the sight of it. "What's that for?" She jabbed a pointed finger toward the little metal cup.

"Thought you could use it. Sit, child."

"What happened? Why won't anyone tell me what's going on?" Raene sat tall and voiced a week's worth of concerns in a single breath. Her chest couldn't take much more of this nervous pounding.

"I'm going to tell you. Now sit and drink your tea." Norsa glared with piercing eyes until Raene conceded. Only when she had taken three sips of tea did Norsa begin. "She never came back."

Those four words were all it took.

Blossom was gone. *She never came back.* Raene's heart sank like a rock thrown from a cliff's ledge. She knew Kaide better than anyone. She saw how he was with Blossom, how they were together. If Raene knew anything in the world, she knew Kaide cared for Blossom with an intensity that rivaled the volcano legends.

And she knew he would never recover from this. Not in a hundred lifetimes.

"What do you mean, she never came back?" Raene asked, failing to keep the desperation from her voice.

"She left with Druma for her transformation. They arrived in the capital. Druma's sure she made it there. She went up to earn her totem, but no one has seen her since." Norsa's eyes darkened, and she shook her head to banish such thoughts.

"But—" Raene stammered. Druma had been Kaide's serviceman for years. They both trusted him greatly, but Raene couldn't make sense of it. "But people don't just vanish. She has to be somewhere. Did she get her totem? She has to be in the databases!" Raene launched from her chair, encouraged by the sudden realization. "We can go check to see what her totem was and where—"

Norsa sighed with disappointment. "He already checked. She's not there."

"Not there?" Raene was slow to grapple such news. She couldn't fathom what would keep a person from being in the database after transformation. They were kept up to date and used for all sorts of reports, like those for Kaide's work.

There could only be one possibility. Raene felt the shocking realization as if it was a barrel of cold water dumped over her head. "She didn't go to transformation."

Norsa shook her head with a solemnity Raene had never seen from her. "She ran home would be my guess."

Raene's brow creased but she didn't have energy to rub it away. Her thoughts were too scattered. It didn't make any sense. Blossom wouldn't have left—not like that. Raene remembered the look on her face when she saw Kaide's transmission not two weeks ago. There was something strong between them that couldn't be thrown away so easily.

But she had no other explanation.

Blossom had used her transformation as a means to leave Kaide and go home. Something made her leave, and Raene knew it wasn't Kaide himself. Of that she was certain.

Raene had to concede to the horrible truth of it.

The last time she'd seen Blossom—headed toward an alder tree on the outskirts of the clearing that surrounded the manor—they'd spent the day in the market discussing totems and transformation. Blossom had asked about Raene's tiger totem and how she got the scars—the ones Kaide had given her after his own transformation.

Raene couldn't help but question every word of their conversation, examining her memories under the light of Blossom's departure. And the more she remembered, Raene knew it was her fault Blossom was gone.

She hadn't meant it. She had only tried to be a good sister, to be honest as Kaide had asked, and she could never have predicted how those words would prompt such a reaction, but the events spoke for themselves.

Despite her intentions, Raene had pushed Blossom away. A black pit of guilt took root in her chest.

And the more Norsa talked, the worse it was. "We were supposed to have a wedding. Not a big thing, but he ordered flowers and picked out all the meals. Planned to take her to the Hydra Gardens to celebrate. Did it all himself. I suppose he thought—"

"He's totally destroyed, isn't he?" Raene withered at the thought of Kaide attempting to put together a wedding for a bride who'd gone missing. How desperate he must have been.

"I've never seen him like this. He sent Druma away. Valenta was scared, left a few days ago. Just me and Olin now. That uncle of yours got a dark look in his eye. His temper—" Norsa poured herself a cup of tea from the kettle and blew away the wisps of steam before she took a sip. "At least he's asked to see you. Maybe he's coming round."

"He's in his office?"

Norsa nodded, her gaze fixed on her tea, staring as if she saw a whole world in that little cup.

Raene couldn't wait any longer. She bolted for the formal sitting room, sailing right through it and toward the stairs that led to the upper floors. Raene flew up the steps like she had a thousand times, though never had she had such anxiety about what she would find at the top.

This was worse than even Kaide's transformation— when she hadn't known to be scared. She hadn't known the monster that was his totem. She hadn't known the fierce flames of anger raging within him.

But now, she knew. And she knew Blossom's disappearance had lit that fire into a strong, enduring blaze.

When she reached his office, he stood motionless facing the wall-length window, gazing out with his back to her. He wore the floor-length cloak required of his position. Today, it was a sleek black, and even without seeing his front, she knew there were embroidered filigrees in scarlet thread.

Despite the noise she'd made on the steps, Kaide didn't move. He stood frozen, locked in place.

"I'm so sorry, Kaide." The apology sounded weak even to her, but what else could she say? His wounds were evident from across the room.

At last, he turned toward her, but she hated the sight. His face was gaunt, and his skin was pale. He looked even thinner than usual, like he hadn't eaten in a week. His usually bright blue eyes were dim and dark, just as Norsa had said.

It made Raene's eyes prick with tears.

"Did you bring your panel?" Kaide asked, ignoring her words.

Raene dipped her hand into her pocket and held it out to show him, and when Kaide motioned for it, she stepped forward to place it in his hand. She could think of no reason he would take it, but she was not in the habit of disobeying him.

Kaide walked to his desk and deposited her panel in one of its drawers. A second later, he produced a document, stamped and sealed with his official mark—a black griffin. "I've traded you to an Alderwood clan. You'll find all the arrangements have been made." He held the folded paper out toward her.

But Raene didn't move. "You're sending me away?"

The tears in her eyes dried in an instant as her sadness turned to anger.

Kaide remained stone-solid with his arm extended, waiting for her to accept the document. "You're old enough to marry. Olin will accompany you." His voice had all the warmth of an ice block.

Raene could hardly believe he was the same uncle she'd known all her life. He had the capacity to be cold and callous, but never to her, and never when they were alone. It was like he'd forgotten who she was.

Like he knew what she'd done, and this was her punishment. "But Kaide—"

"This is your duty."

Raene took two steps forward and accepted the official marriage arrangements, or so he said. She couldn't open it to see for herself. There was only the crisp white paper and black wax seal.

Behind her, she heard Olin's heavy steps on the stairs, but all her attention was on Kaide.

"Don't do this," she pleaded. When she looked up at him, she saw his ice-cold stare and the tension in his jaw. Something inside him had broken—maybe forever—and sending her away was easier than facing it.

Raene couldn't let her life be ruined over an innocent mistake. "Please, I swear. I didn't say anything. We just talked. I don't know what I could have said to make Blossom—"

At the sound of her name, Kaide winced as if she'd struck him, but he regained his bearings a moment after. "Now you must leave."

"Kaide!" she screamed in shock and hurt and grief. "I didn't mean to—"

But he only put up his hand to stop her. With a low voice laced with calculating coldness, his eyes dark and empty, he said, "You will leave, and you will never come back."

Raene's knees became weak, and despite her anger, a tear slipped down her cheek. From behind her, Olin tugged her toward the stairs. She stood dazed—her breaths loud in her ears and her feet couldn't feel the floor. As she was led away, she turned to see him, the Vice Syndicate Kaide Landel, the man who was more her brother and friend than anyone in this world.

Now that was gone.

He was a stranger.

And he was sending her away.

Blossom crouched with her back against the wall of the narrow, concrete room. The miserably cold air hurt to breathe and made her shiver constantly.

A single, circular light shone too bright from the center of the ceiling. The space held a small wooden bed with a single white blanket, though it was more dingy grey than anything. Beside it, a desk of shining metal that startled her with its chill each time she touched it. Across the room, a metal wardrobe held simple white shirts and pants she'd refused to wear. On the not-so-far side, the door to the perfunctory washroom where she washed her Pyro clothes—the ones she'd been wearing since the day of her transformation.

Otherwise, there were only the grey stone walls, and grey stone floors. Not a single window.

And she thought the Alderwood had been a prison.

She'd thought Kaide's manor had been a prison.

She thought the carriage had been a prison.

So many times her freedom had been infringed, and she'd rebelled. Now, it all seemed like silliness. Now that she was here, in an *actual* prison, she knew how wrong she'd been.

Eton called the space 'her personal quarters' but he made it clear she wasn't free to come and go as she pleased. The door was always locked. And worst of all, he put that horrible silver device around her wrist.

Like everything in Aerona, it was cold. No matter how she held it or pressed it against her skin, it was nothing but a cold, metal bracelet, so unlike the warm alder wood ring on her fourth finger, the one that said *Beauty* in small, carved letters.

A knock sounded. It would be Eton, of course. No one else came to see her. No one else could open the door.

When she didn't answer, he pushed in. His platinum-blond hair was shaved on both sides so only a strip of shoulder-length hair grew down the center. It was perfectly straight and slicked back, never a single strand out of place. On his neck, the word AERO was tattooed into the slender shape of a crane. His mouth was pierced with a hoop in the corner, matching the one at the tip of his eyebrow. His diamond-white suit was pressed and crisp. He looked more businessman than kidnapper.

"Syndicate Mercer has agreed to meet with you." When she didn't move or even look at him, he asked, "What *are* you doing?" His tone was one of confusion mixed with disgust, as if she was a rat that had snuck into his dinner party.

Blossom stood tall, her eyes locked on the man who'd taken everything from her. "I'm waiting for the day I'm no longer your prisoner."

Eton's ultra-light blue eyes stared at her like they could see right through her. "We've been over this. You're not my prisoner. I'm your liason until you're cleared for full duty."

Blossom tilted her head to display the tattoo on her neck, the sky-blue letters in the shape of bird, the one that marked her as Aero, the one he'd given her. A week ago, she'd gone to transformation to learn her true totem, and instead, Eton had altered it, robbing her of ever knowing what she should have been and trapping her in Aerona for the rest of her life.

Blossom was his prisoner in every sense.

When Eton didn't respond, she lifted her arm and rattled the metal device he'd placed there.

"It's for your own good. You don't know how to control your totem, and you're a flight risk." His tone was so dry, he sounded like he was reciting the Alder Mother's prayers. She wondered how many times he'd given that particular speech.

"That's kind of the point of being Aero, isn't it?" Blossom eyed him with all the disdain she possessed. Her totem, a peregrine falcon, marked her as Aero, the branch of society that contained all aerial totems. After he sabotaged her totem to make her a bird, she found it more than a little ironic he kept her grounded, afraid she'd fly away.

Eton's pale features became pinched. "Stop acting like a child. Do you want to fight with me, or do you want to bring your argument to the Syndicate? She won't wait long."

"Fine." With several quick steps, Blossom rushed out the door, and for a moment it was possible to feel like she'd wasn't under his control, though of course they both knew better. The second she was out of sight, Eton would activate the electric mechanism within her bracelet, the one that would ignite her body with jolts so painful she would collapse and convulse. Not once had she been able to withstand that pain—not once in her six attempts.

Blossom knew how useless it was to complain to Eton—her jailor no matter how he denied the role. And despite how he glared disapprovingly at her Pyro clothes, she was determined to see the Syndicate. Blossom continued to rush down the corridor, eager to get her answers.

"I trust you won't run again," he droned, guessing her thoughts.

"Why would I run when there's *so much* here? How could I *live* without a little grey room to be locked in all day?" Blossom looked back to glare at him as she let her sarcasm run away with her.

Eton didn't bother to reply.

In another life—another situation—she and Eton might not have been enemies. He was callous to her, as if she was beneath him, but he never harmed her or mistreated her, other than activating the totem-control device. He simply did his job. But Blossom hated that it was his job to keep her trapped, and he did it without question—without hesitation. Eton was a mindless tool only to be used at the bidding of someone else.

Blossom had no respect for that.

Side by side, they walked the length of plain, white corridor that held the inductee quarters. As a transfer from another branch, Aero was required to offer her housing until she could arrange her own. Blossom didn't remember captivity being part of the arrangement, but no one had asked her, either.

On and on they walked, until the crisp corridors opened, exposing raw stone and frigid caverns.

The lava tubes.

Contrary to their name, the lava tubes were enduringly cold. She tucked her arms across her chest but couldn't combat the permanent chill in the air. No one else seemed to notice, though. Blossom was alone in her misery.

Only a few weeks ago, she'd been in the warm Pyro market, listening to Druma describe the volcanoes and the tubes beneath them. He'd told her the Aero tubes had been dormant for centuries, and Aeros lived inside them. Even then, she'd wanted to see the tubes.

Now she was here and it was the last place she wanted to be.

Despite her newfound hatred of everything Aero, she couldn't deny the lava tubes were magnificent. The cavern ceilings stretched so high the lights couldn't find them. The darkness simply consumed anything more than ten stories up. In the air, in the space between the foot traffic and the darkness, there were hundreds of birds.

The aerial totems of Aero were on display, all different sizes and shapes and colors. Some were slow, like the hulking albatross, a seabird with milk-white wings spanning longer than three grown men. Others were fast, like the muddy-brown finches and fiery cardinals. It was a canvas splattered with wings and beaks and screeching calls.

Blossom looked up at them with envy. What she wouldn't give to let loose her wings and join them. But even here, trapped within the confines of the lava tubes, Eton wouldn't let her free. Only days after her transformation, the urge to fly made her more desperate than ever.

Her feet felt doubled in weight. She struggled to move her heavy human form when she could be light, could ride the air like the birds of Aeros. Eton rushed her along, tugging on her arm to break her from her reverie, but her eyes remained upward and her feet dragged on the stone floor.

"Let me go," she fussed when she grew tired of his incessant pulling.

Eton stopped and glared. "If you miss this appointment, you'll have to wait another two weeks. I imagine you'd like to be rid of me before then." Beneath his words was his undeniable desire to be free of her as well.

Blossom allowed herself a wan smile. She'd made him miserable, too. There was a sort of satisfaction to that, but she knew it was petty. How dark did a person become when they relished the misery of others?

One week locked in a stone room had made her just that dark. One week with her feet on the ground and the sun hidden from her eyes. One week away from Kaide, wondering what he thought of her disappearance, knowing what kind of hatred he harbored for Aeros. Her heart hoped, but her mind knew Kaide would never forgive her for this.

Blossom had wallowed in darkness long enough to get consumed in it.

"Will she take this off?" Blossom asked, lifting her arm and shaking her metal bracelet.

Eton looked at her from the corner of his eye. His tone remained frigid as he replied, "No one can predict what the Syndicate will do, but no. I don't think she will."

"Why? Because I ran?" Blossom glowered at him, though she knew it was useless.

"Yes, and she wants you here. It's an easy means of accomplishing that." Brusquely, he added, "Can we go now?" His mask of calm was beginning to crack as she tried his patience.

"Fine," she grumbled. If nothing else, at least she'd be free of Eton after this. Once she was formally a Vice Syndicate of the Aero branch, she wouldn't need a liason.

With her eyes down, Blossom could only hear the beating of wings and the calls of the birds over their heads. She tried to concentrate on the ground and the crowd of people walking down the tunnel.

Whoever heard of such a thing? Walking when you could fly?

She would never understand. Anger and unfairness kept her company as they walked deeper into Aerona, the tubes widening and the crowds thickening.

Blossom didn't know where they were going, but she didn't expect Eton to pull her off into a narrow side passage and push open a hidden door.

"What is this?" she asked as she followed him.

"A short-cut reserved for the high class and such."

"But you're not high class," she reminded him. Eton was little more than a servant, and she was not about to let him forget that.

His jaw clenched. "You are."

Blossom recoiled, appalled that he would have the gall to use her position—and all its benefits—while keeping her confined as he did. She was still gaping in disgust as they filed into a glass elevator.

"You're using my credentials?" Blossom finally seethed, ignoring the layered stone flying past them as they ascended.

"We *could* have gone the long way if you weren't so slow. It's like you're trying to be difficult. Or maybe you just don't know any better." Eton crossed his arms and faced the corner of the glass box like a child being punished for stealing candies.

Blossom was about to laugh at his petulance when a wave of white light flooded the elevator. Her hand flew to shield it from her eyes, but even then it was still too bright. As they climbed higher and higher, she blinked through the light, until at last, she could see the landscape slowly shrinking below them.

Like a white blanket, snow covered everything. The terrain sloped up into mountains and down into valleys. Trees occupied the narrow paths between peaks; even those were dusted in white.

Blossom stood so close to the glass her nose pressed against it. The chill crept in, but she didn't pull away. Her eyes were too focused on the view. Despite her hatred of everything Aero, Blossom gasped.

She'd never seen anything like it.

Behind her, Eton leaned on the glass wall with a satisfied smirk. "Welcome to Aerona."

Her eyes absorbed the awesome sight—the endless white ground and grey-clouded sky. Now, she could see farther, could see sharper. Blossom had stood at such vantages hundreds of times before her transformation, but her vision was clearer than ever before. Like Kaide's smell or Parson's strength or Gemini's hearing, Blossom's totem left its mark on her human form. She could see everything from up here.

Only the thin tower beside them blocked the view.

There was so much space. So much air to carry her and trees to hold her if she grew tired. Her hand moved to the device on her wrist and tugged, hoping one last pull might be enough to set her free, but of course, it wasn't. She was still trapped.

Trapped in this human form.

Trapped in this glass box.

Trapped in Aerona.

"Stop," Eton demanded behind her, but she paid him no mind. Her hand worked at the device, and her eyes drank in the air she desperately wanted—*needed*—to feel beneath her wings.

"Just because you never transition doesn't mean I don't want to," she growled as she continued tugging on the uncompromising metal bracelet.

Eton's hands landed over the top of hers, and she froze in place. In a hushed tone, as if divulging a secret, he told her, "The more you fight it, the longer you'll have to wear it. Convince her you're here to stay. Quit trying to run. Play this game by her rules, and she'll give you what you want."

Blossom couldn't figure out why he'd suddenly given up his surliness, but nonetheless, she wanted to believe him.

She wanted to believe there was a way out of here. Tentatively, she asked, "She'll let me go back to Pyrona?" Back to Kaide—back to her beast? Blossom looked up into Eton's too-light eyes and knew the answer before he said it.

"Never. But, if you're smart, you can convince her to let you use your totem. If you show her you're an ally, she'll give you a place by her side."

"I don't want a place at her side," Blossom screeched.

"It's the only place you have left."

Eton's hands were still on hers when the elevator slowed and slipped into darkness. He stepped back to the opposite side just as the doors opened to reveal another crisp white corridor. She was starting to think this was all a trick, some endless white corridor she was doomed to walk on repeat for the rest of her life. Didn't they have any other colors?

"Where are we?" Blossom whispered. Even that little sound echoed off the walls.

Eton regained his clinical tone. "Each branch has a symbolic structure. In the capital, it's the Syndicate Building. In Pyrona—"

"The Pyro Building," she answered. How could she forget it? For the rest of her life, it would be etched into her memory, burned into the deep places no one else could see.

"And in Aerona, we have this, the Aero Tower. The tallest building in the realm. It's rather impressive, don't you think?" When the corridor revealed a long windowed wall, Eton allowed her to stop. He stood at her side and gazed out over the land. The tower stretched so high over the alder trees, they looked like dark specks in the snow-filled expanse.

Again, Blossom was struck with the urge to flee. Only this piece of glass and the metal bracelet kept her trapped here. Without them, the world was open air and space and freedom.

Her heart sank again as the word echoed in her ears. *Never.*

"Remember. Show her you're on her side, and you'll get what you want," Eton said as he continued to face the glass, his voice so soft Blossom struggled to hear him.

Then, without another word, they resumed down the corridor and arrived at a pair of wide double doors, both shimmering white and blue, as if made of ice.

Eton placed his hand on a device on the wall and let it be scanned. After a brief pause and a beep, the double doors gave way to a massive crystalline space. The alabaster floors gleamed. Windows wrapped around three sides, broken only by a series of decorative marble pillars, each depicting an aerial scene of eagles or gulls or hawks.

Standing at the window was Jurra Mercer, husband to now-Syndicate Audra Mercer. He was a lithe man with platinum-blond hair and face full of piercings. Jurra turned and grinned when he saw her enter. "My love, looks who's come," he said to his wife seated at the oversized desk.

At his words, Audra Mercer looked up from her work. "My dear Ms. Frane!" She gushed as she sailed forward with arms wide. Blossom could do little more than blink as the new Aero Syndicate squeezed her in a loving embrace. "What a pleasure to see you again," she purred.

Unlike the rest of their branch, with their light skin and eyes, Audra Mercer stood out, much like Blossom. Only her snow owl totem tattoo marked her as Aero. She had dark brown hair, cascading down one side of her head; the other was shaved clean. Her blood-red lips curled into a luscious smile as she eyed Blossom's Pyro outfit from top to bottom.

Nasty retorts were the first to find Blossom's tongue, but she pushed them back just in time. *Show her you're on her side, and you'll get what you want.*

Instead of being curt, she tried to emulate Eton's tone.

"Thank you, and congratulations on your appointment as Syndicate. I can think of no one more deserving." The words tasted worse than Norsa's dreadful tea. But to get back to Kaide, she would endure this and much more.

"How sweet you are, dear." The Syndicate left a hand on Blossom's shoulder long enough to offer her a friendly squeeze. "Eton's told me how you wanted to see me, but I'm afraid I've just been so busy with this new position. Moving my office. Planning the official ceremony. Jurra's already sick of my tiresome schedule. It's all so tedious. Can you forgive me?" Her warm smile was effortless.

Blossom smiled, matching the Syndicate's ease. "Of course, I completely understand." Her eyes darted to Eton, uncertain if she should press on. When he nodded, she continued, "I just wanted to ask what it is I'm supposed to do here."

"What do you mean? You're not happy here?" Audra's brow furrowed with dire concern.

"No, I'm happy here. Of course, it's wonderful here." Blossom could almost hear Eton roll his eyes. "I just thought, maybe I could do something more useful. Is there anything I can do to help you?"

When Audra's frown melted into a stunning smile, Blossom knew she had won. "I would love that. Really, I would. Which reminds me—we haven't even had a moment for you to accept your position. Could you go ahead and sign the official form? You could be so much help to me that way." The Syndicate floated to her desk and returned with a small device and metal pen.

On the screen, there was only a line awaiting Blossom's signature. She looked to Eton, but he offered no supportive nod. His mouth was pinched, a tell-tale sign of his anger, though at what she could only guess.

But Blossom didn't care what he thought she'd done wrong. She signed her name on the line and handed the pen back.

Syndicate Mercer snatched the device and grinned. "There. That's better, isn't it? I'm afraid since you're a transfer, you'll have to remain under Eton's advisement until you you're approved for full duty. Still, you're one of us now. At the Appointment Ceremony, you'll be introduced as my newest Vice Syndicate." She made it sound like the title was anything Blossom cared about.

"Thank you, Syndicate. Does that mean you'll give me something to do?" The sooner she was in the good graces of the Syndicate, the sooner she could reach out to Kaide and explain.

"Of course, dear! I'll send over some files for you." Then to Eton, she added, "You're her advisor now. Get her set up with a panel."

Blossom choked back a gleeful squeal. A panel? Just for her? She knew Kaide's transmission code, that he carried his panel with him always. It would be easy to contact him, to hear his voice again.

"Yes, Syndicate Mercer." Eton's reply was so quick and monotone, Blossom knew he'd said it a hundred times over.

With that, Eton approached Blossom and escorted her to the door with one hand around her upper arm. The Syndicate returned to the humungous desk and the large screen that faced her.

But there was one more thing Blossom had to ask.

She wriggled from Eton's grip and managed to hold up her bound wrist as she said, "Syndicate Mercer, is there any way—"

The Aero Syndicate didn't even look up. In a tone as cold as ice, she said, "It's for your own good."

TRANSFORMATION

R AENE SAT on the front steps of Kaide's manor and sobbed into her arms like a child. She wasn't much of a crier, but today, the tears came easily.

Behind her, Olin shifted uncomfortably, trying to sort out what to do with her.

But he already knew what he had to do. He had to take her to the Alderwood and leave her there, never to return. She'd been cast off like a criminal. Like a piece of garbage.

Kaide could have chosen from a number of suitable offers. He could have traded her to a dozen Pyro clans—the Lagradas with their cheetah son and fine parties, the Ignalas with their connections. She'd even take Corson Porsten.

But Kaide chose a Terra clan on the far side of the realm. It wasn't a mistake. It wasn't an oversight. He wanted her out of his life. He was angry with her. He was punishing her.

The sun had already begun to set by the time the last person arrived. Raene looked up at Norsa through her water-logged eyes. She knew her cheeks were puffed and red, and that the sheen of sweat made her hair stick to her brow, but she didn't care about any of that. Not anymore.

After today, she would never see Norsa again.

It was too unfair. Whatever it was Raene had said to

make Blossom leave had been unintentional. When she brought her future sister to the market that day, Raene answered all her questions openly and honestly, as Kaide had asked. She'd never done anything else. She'd been a good niece, helping him when he needed it and stepping back when he didn't. She'd entertained all his important guests and kept from asking questions when he didn't want her to be involved. She attended countless courses on dance or dining or conversation to make herself into the best possible bride.

Raene had done nothing to deserve such exile. It was all a horrible mistake.

Norsa crouched down and pulled Raene against her chest as she had hundreds of times in their years together. The comforting motion only served to renew Raene's cries.

"Come now, hush up, child." Norsa's low voice was as soft as velvet. Her hands stroked through Raene's mess of hair.

"I didn't mean to make her leave," Raene squeaked.

"I know, child. The Mother knows I know it. One's got nothing to do with the other. You'll be married, that's all. This is the way for all young women. And fine ones such as yourself will be the first to find their place. That's the way of it. Always has been."

"No, it's not. He's exiling me, but I didn't do anything!" She knew she was being petulant, but she didn't care. Raene had little more than anger and grief inside her.

Norsa pulled away, leveling her gaze with Raene's as she did. "You listen here, my Rain Drop. That uncle of yours is many things. Twisted and cruel and darker than any of us want to think, but I know for a fact that he's not capable of what you're thinking. He couldn't do it, not even now." Norsa's thumb skated across Raene's cheek and intercepted a falling tear. "So you quit your crying, get your bag, and go and do as he says. And you just know—"

Norsa's voice caught in her throat. "You know that we'll miss you—"

A fresh wave of sobs racked Raene's chest to see Norsa so upset she could hardly speak. She threw her arms around the woman's shoulders and accepted one last lingering embrace. Then, with more strength than she knew she possessed, Raene let go.

She pushed to standing and wiped at her face, determined not to look such a mess in their last moments together. With one last sorrowful glance at Norsa, Raene said her last goodbyes and started down the driveway with Olin, her bag on his shoulder. A transport already waited at the end, ready to take her away.

"Love you!" Norsa shouted across the drive.

Raene turned and smiled, but she couldn't quite manage a sound. Her voice was just as broken as the rest of her.

The world felt heavier now, and a part of her knew it would never really be the same.

It was then she noticed the man in the second-floor window. He stood tall with his shoulders back and arms clasped behind him. Dark hair haloed his face so she could see him clearly even with the greenery reflected in the glass.

And despite how angry she was, despite the sadness and grief she felt, Raene hated that this was the last time she would see Kaide. Only three years older than her, he wasn't the typical uncle. He cared for her like only a brother could when they were children, and even after, he'd always been protective over her. She'd been closer to him than anyone.

So ignoring everything else, she reached up a hand and waved goodbye to him. It wasn't much, a sad twist of the wrist, but when he waved back, she smiled, and her heart hurt a little less. That was enough to get her the rest of the way to the transport.

After that, it was too late to turn back.

Raene clutched the document in her hand and waited for Olin to maneuver the metal transport from the ground. A low cloth seat wrapped around the rectangular space, and the walls were all clear glass. She could see everything.

Kaide's manor fell away as they rose into the sky. The transparent cylinder had been a second home to her—where she'd spent her nights and evenings as a child, when her grandparents were at parties and her father was too drunk to care for her.

At the memory, Raene remembered her father.

"Olin?" Raene called out, surprised her voice was as clear as it was.

"Rain Drop?" he answered from the nav station.

"Can you check in on my father when you get back? I told him I'd be gone a couple days, but he doesn't know—"

"Of course. Do you want to stop and see him before we leave?"

"No. Take me to the portals." Her father had been sober a few hours ago. He was likely drunk on his couch by now, wasting away the night as he always did. She didn't want to remember him that way. Her father wasn't a great man, or even a good one, but she wanted her last vision of him to be the sober version, not the drunk one.

And despite Kaide's treatment of her over the last week, she wouldn't go against his wishes. Somehow, against her best efforts, Raene had made Blossom leave. If satisfying this marriage arrangement compensated for that mistake, in even the smallest way, she would do it. A thousand times over, she would do it for him.

Olin didn't press her, and she was glad for that. She didn't know how much fight she had left in her today. So, she gazed out over the towering volcanoes and their spires of steam and ash that punctured the sky. Sprawled between them, the low stone buildings that made up Pyrona. Lit streets curved between them like veins.

The last glimpse of her home.

Raene threaded her fingers into her hair, and by the time the transport landed at the steps of the Pyro Building, a neat braid fell across her shoulders. She pressed her cool hands to her face in a last, desperate attempt to limit the mess she'd made of herself.

Suddenly, she remembered why she wasn't a fan of crying. Raene wasn't one of those pretty girls prone to a delicate tear. When she cried, it was in earnest, and it ruined her face for the whole rest of the day. Not exactly compatible with her desire to always look presentable.

Olin opened the transport door, and she was struck with a wave of hot city air. It smelled of exhaust from the transport, but beneath that, the savory aroma of blood drying on the streets. Pyrona was home to no small amount of violence, but she'd never known anything else.

After her transformation, she would be one of them—a predator, a violent animal. Only she wouldn't be here in the haven of Pyros. Kaide had denied her the only place her kind could live.

What would become of her then?

Raene climbed the onyx steps, lost in thought. Olin trailed behind her, and before they were halfway across the lobby, he presented her with a copper coin, her passage across the realm.

"Thank you," she said as she accepted the coin. She'd forgotten all about the toll. Then, she realized Kaide must have given Olin the coin before telling Raene of the marriage arrangement. Olin had known she was leaving before she had.

"Why didn't you tell me?" She made no attempt to hide the wound he'd inflicted.

"You know why, it's not my place."

"You could have warned me."

"He would have killed me." Olin didn't carry any trace of doubt. Whatever Kaide had done in her absence, it had scared even Olin into silence.

While Raene understood his need for self-preservation, it did little to lessen her anger. She marched toward the portal wing and selected a door. Somewhere deeper in the building, Olin would use the service portal—the one reserved for anyone of lower status who had clearance for portal use.

But not Raene. As Kaide's niece, she had access to the fastest method of transport across the realm, but this would be the last time. After her transformation, she was promised to someone else. It would be her new husband who decided her fate—her station, her position, everything.

Alone in the narrow portal room, Raene inserted the coin in the wall slot and heard the brief clinking of metal before it started. Like she was in an elevator rising up, her eyes detected no movement, but her body knew. It felt her spinning, careening through space, until she landed once more. There was nothing to indicate she'd arrived except the sudden stillness in her ears.

Raene opened the door and returned to the lobby. Where before, the Pyro lobby had been all onyx floors, low-burning braziers, and Pyro attendants in scarlet tops, now the room stood transformed.

The lobby of the Syndicate Building was stark white and gleamed with the reflected city beyond the glass doors. The attendants were all Aero, their crisp, white suits and artistically-shaved heads. Each of them wore metal punched in their ears or lips or brows.

It was exactly the same yet entirely different.

In the brief moment Raene spent taking in her new surroundings, Olin found her again. "They'll have temporary quarters for you. All upcoming trans—"

"I know." Everyone knew the realm offered safe housing for anyone undergoing transformation within three days. It was an accommodation for the poor who couldn't precisely plan their travel. Raene had never thought to have need, but now that she was no longer in the care of her uncle, she had no other choice. It was yet one more injustice inflicted upon her—he could have easily sent her to transformation tomorrow and saved her this humiliation.

Raene walked to the row of attendants at their high-tech displays. While Pyros exhibited dark hair and skin, Aeros were notorious for their fair skin and creepy eyes. Raene could hardly stand to look at the young woman at the console, the one with the bat totem tattoo.

"Welcome to the Syndicate Building. How can I help you?" The woman's smile was warm and welcoming, a stark contrast to her severe look.

Raene swallowed and said, "I'm Raene Randal. I'm here for transformation tomorrow."

"A pleasure to have you with us. Will you be seeking quarters in preparation for your interview?"

Raene nodded, refusing to let this woman make her feel ashamed. She fingered the ends of her braid as the woman made several quick motions on her screen.

Then, the attendant placed another copper coin on the countertop, this one smaller than the last. "You'll be on the ninth floor. Room 984. Once you're off the elevator, take a left. You'll see it."

Raene collected the coin and headed for the elevator, pretending she didn't notice Olin shadowing her. He followed her all the way to her room, not a word passing between them.

Only when she put the coin in the slot did he say, "I'll keep watch from here." With the weight of a hundred years, he leaned his back against the wall and slid to the floor.

Raene's anger sizzled when she saw him sitting there,

his head hanging low. "You don't need to watch me. I'm no one anymore."

"You're someone to me. I should have told you what he was up to." Olin pressed his head against the wall like it was the only thing holding him up. "Besides, I only have a few days left with you."

Raene's anger softened, if only a little. "Thank you, Olin," she said, though she knew he was wrong. Raene Randal was a high-class Pyro woman with a bright future ahead of her. But that was all gone, and now she didn't know who she was.

She shut the door before he could say more.

The room was small and modest, all silvery metal and smooth, white stone. It was undoubtedly Aero, and Raene couldn't help but wonder why. Didn't they know people of all branches used these rooms?

Raene sat on the edge of the narrow bed. She was far from uncertain of her totem. She would be Pyro. She would be a tiger, like her mother.

But up until this afternoon, she'd been confident in Kaide, too. Never could she have predicted his sudden shift, his ice-cold demeanor that shattered their relationship in a single blow.

Maybe she'd be wrong about her totem, too. Maybe she'd be a snake like her father or a wolf like her grandfather. Maybe they'd turn her into something unnatural like Kaide's monster. Maybe she wouldn't even make it there like Blossom.

Doubt and confusion muddled her thoughts

Raene lay across the stiff bed, drifting between concern and fitful sleep—between dreams of her totem and nightmares of Kaide and what he'd done.

Blossom wasn't sure she could accurately convey how tired she was of being dragged around, but she was sure the right hook to Eton's face did a pretty good job.

He released her immediately.

"By the *Mother*—" he hissed. His fingers delicately turned the metal stud in his lip—the one Blossom had managed to strike dead on.

Beyond the closed doors of the Syndicate's office, Eton had no reason to hold his tongue. "You're the most difficult person alive, you know that?"

"Yes." Blossom only grinned. "So, what happens now? You drag me around some more?"

"We run some errands," Eton replied, rubbing his cheek as he walked back to the elevator, quickly reigning in his anger.

Blossom was forced to trot after him. "We?"

"I'm your advisor now. As much as you don't like it, we both just got a major promotion. I'm stuck with you, and you're stuck with me. And now we have a lot of work to do." Eton leaned against the wall of the elevator and crossed his arms.

"Like what?"

Eton looked at the ceiling as if the answers were written there. "Fitted suits, a cloak, your Vice Syndicate quarters. I'm sure she'll have sent you a few documents to sign by now. And your hair, of course."

Blossom's lip curled. "That's it? I had to come here to be some all-important Vice Syndicate so you could dress me up and sign my name on a few forms?"

Eton shook his head, and his gaze shot to the marble floor of the elevator. There was something he wasn't telling her.

Blossom took up residence in the same corner as she had during their trip up—her nose pressed to the glass as they descended toward the ice-covered landscape, the whole world spread before her like an open book. "I hate dressing up," she grumbled. Her heated breath fogged the glass, and for a moment, it was possible to believe she was falling through a cloud.

"Get used to it. That's half your job."

"Do I want to know what the other half is?"

"Probably not."

Blossom would have pressed him further, but the elevator landed and released them back into the lava tubes. Eton took a sharp right and started down the northern corridor and toward a part of Aerona Blossom had yet to see. Then, again, she'd been locked in her 'personal quarters' for almost a week.

As before, the lava tubes were split between on-foot traffic navigating the uneven, pitted surface of the stone floor, and the aerial, gliding traffic sailing overhead. Blossom couldn't help but watch the graceful motions in awe.

This time, Eton was less pushy about her slow speed. When he thought he was too far ahead, he stopped and waited. He didn't rush her, and he didn't grab her again. At least he was learning.

For the few minutes they walked, the birds became gradually larger and slower. The sweeping circles and racing arcs of finches were replaced with the steady glide of eagles. The bouncing tunes of song birds became infrequent screeches of owls or falcons.

Falcons.

Blossom was a falcon. Her shackled hand moved to the tattoo on her neck, trying to remember if it was even real.

She hadn't been a falcon since the day of her transformation. She'd flown high over Seraphine City, looked out over the wide markets and buildings that sat in neat rows. Her wings had easily ridden the currents of air that raked across the sky.

Her falcon eyes had looked east, toward the tower and the beast and the man she'd left there. But Blossom had balked. Too afraid of her own ability, afraid she wouldn't make it so far, afraid she'd get lost, Blossom landed on the steps of the Syndicate Building and transitioned to her human form. She only made it halfway across the lobby—halfway to the portals—before Eton materialized from thin air and slapped the metal cuff on her wrist.

Seven days had gone by since then.

The memory faded into dream, and Blossom couldn't help but wonder if it had ever really happened at all.

The tattoo on her neck was the only proof, but she couldn't see it. At first, it had been bandaged, and after that, scabby and rough. But now, the skin was smooth to the touch, like it had never been inked.

"Come on. We have a lot to do." Eton's voice was kinder than it had been since their meeting with the Syndicate. Blossom realized she'd stopped walking, and at the sound of his voice, she forced herself into motion.

"Is your neck bothering you?" Eton asked, noting the hand cupped over her tattoo, his voice in total control. When she shook her head, he continued, "Sometimes they itch. I can get you a cream if you like."

"No." It would take more than a bit of cream to fix what ailed her.

And while Eton was never cruel to her, he was far from thoughtful. His offer had to be a test or a trick. Blossom was weary of kind strangers with promises. She wouldn't fall for it so easily this time.

After that, they both walked in silence, her eyes cast up at the slow-gliding birds. Within minutes, they arrived at another elevator. Rather than afford her another glimpse of the world, this one stayed within the ground, though it took them up at least six or seven floors. Blossom wondered how close they were to the surface—how far underground they really were. Never in her life had she gone so long without seeing the sun.

The elevator doors opened and revealed yet another white corridor. "We call this the Halo. These are the main homes and offices for the Aero branch. The Syndicate lives in the tower, but everyone else is here." As something of an afterthought, he added, "Your apartment is here."

A pair of glass doors slid apart as they approached, revealing an intersection where the corridor split in two. "It's a loop, so technically you can go either way, but your apartment is on this side." Eton pointed to the first door on the left. It was made of stone and looked to weigh more than ten men could lift, but Eton's hand on a wall scanner made it slide away, as if it was as light as rain.

Blossom's eyes went wide when she saw the space. It was the same crisp, sterile whiteness of the rest of Aerona. The walls were so opalescent white they looked to made of diamonds or ice. Frosted-glass sconces gleamed off the polished alabaster floors.

The only color in the room was the furniture: a frost-white seating set arranged around a low aluminum table complete with metal serving tray.

Acting as nothing more than her guide, Eton motioned around the room as he described the amenities—shower with water purification system, full kitchen stocked with fresh meat and fish daily, programmable air circulation system, door security with fingerprint scanner—punctuating the details with a motion toward each feature. "It should have everything you need, but if you have any requests, just let me know. Your room is over that way. This is mine." Blossom looked where he pointed to a pair of doors but didn't bother to voice her complaints about living in such close proximity to one another. It wouldn't do any good.

Instead, Blossom approached the doors to her bedroom, and in it she found yet another luxurious space. A stone-grey comforter was spread over the enormous bed— large enough to sleep a dozen people. Blossom didn't know what she would do with so much bed, but as soon as she sat and felt the softness of it, she knew she would never sleep on it.

Then she noticed the plush rug on the floor. White, of course, but when she lay across it and spread her arms wide, it almost felt like the rug in Raene's room in the manor. If she closed her eyes, she could picture the woven tiger image and the greenery, the colored lights shining on the ceiling, the blonde girl kicking her feet on the bed and pestering her with a hundred questions.

Blossom's thoughts were interrupted by Eton. "What *are* you doing?" he asked in that way of his, as if she'd licked the bottom of her foot.

"You wouldn't understand," Blossom answered with a sigh as she propped herself up on her elbows.

He shot a disapproving glance at her Pyro clothes before he admitted, "You're right. Ready to go?"

"Go where?" Blossom was entirely sure she didn't want to know the answer.

Eton's lips twisted into something like a smile. "To make you Aero."

By morning, Raene's neck was stiff, and her eyes were mildly puffy from the all her crying. A night without sleep didn't help, either. She smoothed out her hair and re-braided it, taking extra care to make sure it was neat. She wanted to look good today.

It was her eighteenth birthday, after all.

This should have been a good day—a happy day when

she attained her mother's totem. This wasn't anything like she imagined this day would be.

From her bag, she pulled out a fresh scarlet top and wide-legged pants—the clothes that marked her as Pyro. She made easy work of the many straps that held her top in place, and within minutes, she was ready.

When she opened the door, she found Olin fighting sleep, his head pressed back against the wall and his eyes squeezed shut. He didn't move until she said, "I'm going down now. Are you going to wait here?"

Olin pushed to standing with all the heaviness of the night before. "I can go with you as far as the interview."

"No, that's all right. You should lie down for a while." No use in them both being exhausted. Raene pushed open the door to her little room and pointed to the still-made bed on the far side.

Olin protested a while longer, but eventually her stern voice and his fatigue sent him shuffling into the room. As she pulled the door shut, she heard the bed shift under his weight.

It was then Raene felt alone. She didn't want Olin to go with her, not really. She wanted to do this on her own. But Olin was her last connection to her old life. Moving forward alone felt like the beginning of the end.

Transformation marked the start of her new life, one in which she was alone.

Raene reminded herself she'd be back in a few hours, and hopefully, she'd have her tiger totem to show him.

Holding her head high, Raene marched to the elevator and followed the posted instructions to the third floor. There, she found a tall, cavernous corridor with a small desk positioned in the center. Four others already stood in line. Two were Hydra, based on their clothes, likely twins. One was a Terra youth with bouncing brown curls that made him look younger than his eighteen years. And the last was an Aero boy with shimmering-white hair shaved on the right side.

Raene took her place behind them.

Her heart sped up when the line moved forward. The twins walked to the end of the hall and disappeared behind a white door.

"Are you literate?" The Aero attendant asked the Terra boy. When he only shook his head, she proceeded to ask him a series of questions and fill in his answers. Raene's heart softened for him. A child of the Alderwood, he was likely poor, uneducated, and far from the comforts of home.

Raene pictured Blossom here, standing in line, intimidated by the Aero woman. Maybe it had been the pressure of upcoming transformation that made Blossom flee.

But Raene knew better. Blossom wasn't one to be scared away so easily. And neither was Raene.

A minute later, the attendant motioned the Terra boy through the door, and without question, he trotted to the end of the hall and disappeared.

"Welcome, Master Nalla," the attendant said to the boy in front of Raene. He only scanned his fingerprint before moving forward.

When Raene approached the screen, she lifted her finger over the scanner as the Aero boy had done, but nothing happened.

"Are you literate?" the woman asked.

No name. No welcome. No warmth.

Raene looked up at her, torn between confusion and shock. "Of course I am. Why can't I scan my finger like the last one?"

"He's Aero. You are not." She made it sound like the most obvious thing in the world.

Raene narrowed her eyes at the girl as she filled out the questions. Her birth branch. Her mother's totem. Her birth date. All in all, she thought there would have been more questions, rather than just these basics. Regardless, she filled in her answers on the screen.

Then, the woman pointed her toward the door. Raene was more than happy to leave the company of the attendant but soon found she wasn't going to be left alone for very long. A pale-eyed woman met her on the other side.

"Welcome, Ms. Randal. I'm Orsa Yuman, and I'll be administering your interview. Follow me right this way." She grinned and started down the hall.

Raene wasn't sure she could tell one Aero apart from another. This one, while friendly enough, wore the same white suit fitted to her narrow figure, and she had the same pale blonde hair shaved on one side and the same fair complexion as any other Aero she had seen.

The same look, and the same untrustworthy nature as all Aeros.

But Raene had no choice but to follow her down a long, crooked corridor until they entered a small room. It was as white as the woman's suit and contained only a small table with two chairs.

With the cold of the metal chair against her skin, Raene waited for the interview to begin. Fatigue gave way to excitement. It was here her nerves finally registered the momentous occasion. She was minutes away from receiving her totem. Only this woman and a few questions separated her from her tiger.

"Your birth branch was Pyro?" the woman began.

"Yes, I answered that before."

After typing Raene's answer into a small, screened device, the woman continued, "And your mother was a tiger?"

"Yes, I already said that as well." Raene clenched her jaw in frustration. Why were they stuck on these generic questions? Why didn't they ask her about her strengths, her personality, her passions?

"Do you have a pending marriage arrangement?"

Raene's ears perked at the mention of a new question. "Oh, yes—" For a half-second, she thought she might have left the document in her room, but she found it deep in her pocket a moment later. She slid it across the table.

Like it was nothing, the woman popped the wax seal and read over the document, telling Raene nothing of its contents as she typed the information into the device. Raene was tempted to ask what it said, but a part of her didn't want to know. Not yet.

She didn't expect the woman to keep it. "At this time, I'm going to take you to the transformation chamber. You'll be injected with a serum, and you will undergo the transformation process. After that, I'll take you to receive your tattoo, and you'll be free to go. Ready?" The woman's smile was soft and warm, and Raene couldn't help but nod and follow her out of the room.

By the time they arrived at the transformation chamber, Raene's heart pounded hard as she tried to swallow down her nerves. The metal walls were a patchwork of scratches. Tufts of hair clung to the edge of the circular floor, and the ceiling stretched high above her.

"It's for the Aero totems," the woman explained though Raene hadn't asked. "For those with flight, the height is comforting. You won't need it, though."

"Oh," was all she could manage.

The woman moved behind her. "You'll feel a pinch."

While Raene's eyes were still pointed up at the ceiling, the needle punctured her neck. It was little more than a prick, but then, as if someone had doused her in hot tar, her whole body burned. She was nothing but pain embodied in physical form. Raene clutched at her stomach and doubled over, but not even the smallest sound could escape her locked-up throat.

When she could take it no more, Raene collapsed on all fours—only her hands were no longer her own. Her warm, summer skin was covered in rusty-orange fur tipped with white. Sharp, pointed claws emerged and scratched the floor, producing a shrill, metallic sound.

Raene stretched her paws out before her and marveled at the length of them—at the sheer size of her tiger form.

She was a *tiger*.

Not a mouse or monster, but a tiger. The totem she was always meant to have. It was too good to be true.

The space was impossibly small, but Raene trotted around the perimeter in tiger form. Her new legs carried her easily. She was strong and quick and, when the idea struck her, she bounded up the side of the wall, climbing two, three times higher until she fell back onto her paws with the grace of a gazelle.

This was going to be fun.

The rightness of it consumed her. She'd been wrong about Kaide and Blossom, and so many things. But this— this tiger was her.

She threw up her head and growled in satisfaction.

In the metallic chamber, her tiger ears easily caught the echo of her own voice as her deep, feline growl faded into the laughter of a young woman.

When she looked down, she was herself again—her human self, at least. Tiger-Raene was gone, and the tall, blonde girl she'd always been stood in her place.

And now, in her human form, she couldn't make sense of anything. Her ears pricked at every little sound—the whirring of moving air, the clink of stiff shoes on the white stone corridor, the pumping of blood in her own veins.

The door swung open with a tired groan and Orsa Yuman appeared in the doorway. "Right this way, Ms. Randal."

Even Raene's own footsteps sounded loud as she

followed the woman—and her audible pulse—to another sterile white room. Her thoughts felt thick as mud. The loudness of each sound drowned out everything else.

"You can have a seat here. Vernesta will administer your tattoo, then you're free to head home. Best of luck on your upcoming marriage, Ms. Randal." The woman's voice was a song in the cacophony of the space—a mixture of low-humming machinery, slow breaths, and a tapping, impatient foot.

Raene sank into the chair. She tried to listen as the woman—whose name she couldn't remember—told her to look over her shoulder, to be still, that this might hurt, but the brightness of the lights and the loudness of her voice made it difficult to concentrate.

The tiny needles in her neck produced a scraping-burning sensation that was definitely uncomfortable, but in way, Raene liked it. She'd have to make tattoos a regular occurrence in her life. The pain helped silence to the other sounds, to thin out the sludge that clogged her thoughts, to remind her she was human once more.

Little by little, her mind cleared and the feral, predatory edge of instinct gave way to more collected thoughts. By the time the woman was done, Raene felt almost right again. Better than right. She was a tiger, and becoming the tiger was the best she'd felt in a long, long while.

VENGEANCE

R AENE'S STOMACH growled by the time she arrived back at her room. Her transformation felt like it lasted only seconds, but the corridor attendant assured her she'd been gone more than three hours.

No wonder she was so hungry.

Olin was already seated at the foot of the bed when she appeared in the doorway. His black hair was messed and only half-raked through with his fingers. He still looked tired, but he managed to look up at her with relief-filled eyes.

"I'm fine," Raene said before he gave in to worry. Remembering the bandage covering her tattoo, she shrugged and added, "Tiger."

Olin's tired lips formed a fervent smile. "You deserve nothing less, Rain Drop." Then, without pretense, he collected her bag, pulling the strap over his shoulder, and headed out the door.

"We're leaving already?" Raene stood anchored in the doorway.

"We have no reason to stay."

"But you don't even know where we're going," she protested. Only Kaide and the Aero woman knew her destination. And in her excitement, Raene had forgotten the document entirely.

Olin paused and let out a long, low breath. When he looked up at her, his dark eyes were even dimmer than usual.

"You knew that, too, didn't you?" Raene shoved her way past him. When she reached the elevator, she smacked the call button so hard she made a web of cracks across it. Raene stared incredulously for only a second before her anger completely took over. "You should just go back to the manor. Tell me where to go. I'll make my own way."

"I'm supposed to deliver you." Olin climbed into the elevator when it arrived, and Raene had no choice but to join him.

"How long have you known?" She wasn't sure she wanted that answer, but she was too angry—too hurt—not to know. She wanted the truth.

"My Rain Drop—"

"How long?!" she screamed.

"Since he made the arrangements." Olin's shoulders sagged low and he refused to look at her. He was saturated with his guilt and regret, but that didn't change the fact he'd known and kept it from her. For the first time in her life, Raene had no one she could trust.

A quiet beep signaled the elevator's arrival in the lobby, and it was just in time. Anger finally won out, forcing Raene to shed her weak, human exterior and burst into tiger form. She spilled out of the elevator and across the smooth stone lobby and grappled for purchase, sliding around to face the black-haired man.

He looked familiar, he *smelled* familiar, but tiger-Raene couldn't remember anything. There was nothing but the urge to kill him.

The man shouted something from within the elevator, but the sound of his voice carried no meaning. It was as empty as a birdcall or a frog song. She heard it, but it meant nothing to her.

Tiger-Raene growled to silence him, urging him out of the safety of the metal box, circling in wait. Betrayal and frustration swam through her veins, liquid fuel to spur her on. The man's refusal to engage only reignited the blaze.

She felt all eyes on her from every direction. There was chatting and murmurs and screams from the growing crowd, but she didn't slow. Her stomach ached for the flavor of his flesh. Tiger-Raene scraped her claws across the floor and leapt at the man, desperate to sink her teeth into him. In an instant, she had his leg clamped square between her teeth as she dragged him from the safety of the metal box.

She was so focused on the feel of his leg in her mouth—on the staggering weakness of him as he tried to fight her off—she didn't notice the second man.

Behind her, he transitioned from human form to a hulking elephant, but it wasn't until his thunderous feet stampeded across the white, stone floor and his truck sent her flying that she knew he was there.

Tiger-Raene was only aware of the leg no longer gripped between her teeth. She landed with feline precision on all fours and slid across the slick stone to face both her prey and her new attacker.

Seeing the elephant's huge, curved back and his four gargantuan feet that could crush her with ease, tiger-Raene's anger stewed. She wanted to eat—she wanted to eat the man—but now, this huge creature stood between them.

And for a moment, she hesitated, sizing them up, determining if her claws and speed would be enough to subdue such an oversized animal.

The elephant didn't hesitate. It spread its ears into huge flapping sails. It thrust up its trunk and trumpeted before charging straight toward her.

Tiger-Raene only stared, terrified into stillness as the hulking beast stampeded across the lobby. At the last second, she darted out of the elephant's path. Fear overtook anger. Her will to live trumped her will to fight.

That was all it took for her to let go of her anger, for a calm breath to fill her lungs. As fast as it had come, the urge to kill was gone. Her tiger paws dissolved into a flurry of rusty hairs, and before she knew it, Raene was in her human form, crouched on the ground, one knee tucked up against her chest. Her blonde hair cascaded around her in a curtain, guarding her face from the crowd.

As soon as she looked up, she saw with fresh eyes what she'd done. A Hydra man—who she assumed had the elephant totem—knelt beside Olin, both hands placed firmly on the bleeding wounds of his calf. Already, a pool of crimson widened over the alabaster floors, and even from across the room, Raene could see he was seriously injured.

Guilt struck her like a knife. She'd hurt Olin for nothing more than her stupid, childish tantrum, and had it not been for the elephant, she might have killed him— would have killed him, she was certain.

Raene collapsed and pressed her shaking hands to her face. What had she done?

"Come here," Olin called from across the lobby, his voice echoing above the gathered crowd and commotion.

But Raene was too afraid to move. She was just like Kaide—a monster that lashed out, injuring those around her without thought. She had no control over her aggression or rage. Raene was just another Pyro animal—wild, angry, dangerous.

"Rain Drop, you get over here." It was the tone of Olin's voice that made her move—that voice he used when she'd snuck out or disobeyed and gotten herself in trouble. It was the voice of a father, a real one, and she knew better than to keep him waiting.

With head low and eyes on her feet, Raene shuffled toward him. The crowd gave her a wide berth.

Raene had never been more ashamed. She didn't want to see them. She didn't want them to see her. When she reached Olin, Raene sat beside him but still looked away.

"It's just a bite, nothing more." Raene felt Olin's fingers under her chin, and when he pulled her face toward him, she didn't fight. His head was propped-up in the lap of a Hydra woman, her cerulean skirt spread out around them. The Hydra man, maybe her husband, had both hands clasped around Olin's leg while another woman tied several strips of fabric around the wounds, cinched tight to slow the bleeding.

But his eyes were bright. Where before there had been guilt, now there was relief. "Just a bite, and it's only me. And I deserve it, and much more. Don't worry, Rain Drop."

"I'm so sorry," she whispered. In a single motion, she slid along his side and laid with him while the strangers dressed the wound. Olin's strong arm around her shoulders kept her pinned against his chest, and Raene couldn't help but question how he could forgive her after what she'd done.

"Why didn't you transition? You could have fought me off—" Olin's lynx totem was nothing compared to her tiger, but he was small and quick enough to put up a defense against her.

But that would have put her at risk, and Olin would never allow that. He'd spent the last eighteen years protecting her. He didn't have it in him to hurt her, even if it would save his life.

Raene lay beside him on the floor and let her mind spin with all that had happened. She could taste his blood in her mouth. She could feel the muscle fibers snapping as she sunk her teeth into his flesh. She remembered the fire in her veins and how easily her anger had consumed her. She remembered how it felt to want to kill him.

She remembered how much she loved it.

That, more than anything, made her afraid.

Raene clung tight to Olin, feeling comfort from the very man she'd tried to kill.

After what felt like an hour, the Hydra man said, "That's as good as it's going to get. Do you want to try to stand?"

Raene sat up and watched Olin accept the man's outstretched hand. Together, they managed to get him to his feet, but he immediately shifted his weight from his wounded leg. Raene cringed at the sight of the damage she'd caused.

"Thank you," Olin said and smiled to the stranger. And then, like it nothing at all, he started limping across the lobby.

Raene was up and beside him a half-second later. "Let me help you." She put her shoulders under his arm and was grateful for her height; at least she could take some of his weight.

"We don't have far to go. Just down the block. To the stables." Olin tried to look like he was fine, but his stern grimace and clenched teeth told otherwise.

"Stables? You can't ride a horse like this." Raene was amazed he could even walk.

"I'll not have you arriving late on my account." Olin limped on, refusing to slow or rest, and when at last they reached the stables, two black stallions were already drawn and waiting. Raene helped Olin into his saddle as best she could before she climbed into hers.

They worked the horses through the commotion of the city—past a pair of jaguars circling in a fight, row after row of Hydra tables, and hundreds of Seraphinians all roaming the capital on various business. Each crackle of roasting fires, each herding animal or rolling cart sounded new and loud and sharp in her ears as she'd never heard before.

Olin and Raene were among the few in the city on horseback, picking their way through the crowds that lined the busy streets, but they moved quickly. Within minutes, they arrived at the stone wall that separated the city from the rest of the realm.

It was as far from home as Raene had ever been. She'd only been to Seraphine City a handful of times, and always with Kaide. He'd brought her here to sign the documents that made him her official guardian when she was fifteen. Other times, he'd taken her to events—a conference about totems, an exhibit of the four branches, her grandmother's funeral.

But never had she ventured outside the walls of the city. Raene paused under the stone archway and wondered if she'd ever come back. Behind her, the familiar sights of the capital, the Syndicate Building, the portal to Pyrona. Ahead of her, a wide meadow of low grasses blew in the spring breeze, and beyond that, the long, dark edge of a forest.

The Alderwood.

"Ready?" Olin's voice brought her back from her daydreaming. "We've got a hard ride ahead for a few hours. Let me know if you need to rest." With that, Olin spurred his horse forward.

Raene was only a half-second behind him. She squeezed her heels into the flanks of her borrowed stallion and leaned forward, aligning her torso with its neck. Pressed so close to the horse's flesh, Raene had no trouble making out its strong, steady heartbeat over the sound of pounding hooves. To her dismay, the scent of horsemeat filled her nose for every second of the ride.

The grasses shone as green as emeralds in the afternoon sun, and only minutes later, they passed the first trees. Young and scattered alder trees gave way to massive trees close enough to block out the sun. Flower-filled canopies hovered over them so high and thick they formed a looming, ominous ceiling that made Raene feel trapped. As if the forest itself was pressing down on her.

It was nothing like Pyrona.

But Raene wouldn't slow. An expert rider since she was young, Raene relished the wind flying across her face and the heavy pounding of hooves beneath her. A part of her wanted to stop and take in the novelty of the landscape. The other part of her wanted to keep moving and never stop.

Traveling to the Alderwood had never been her plan. It wasn't her decision, and deep in her heart, she couldn't help but rebel against it. This wasn't what she wanted.

But it was what she deserved. Raene earned this life when she interfered with Kaide's relationship with Blossom, intentionally or otherwise. Raene was serving a life-sentence for a crime she hadn't even known she was committing.

So Raene raced her horse further into the dark Alderwood, keeping close behind Olin and trusting he knew where he was going.

But moving at such a pace only made her itch to transition again. Her tiger paws could move just as fast as her horse, if not faster. Her ears would prick with each little sound, and her nose would smell every animal in their vicinity. In tiger form, she could have full use of her senses. Now, as her human self, she felt blind, like someone had pulled a mask over her eyes, dulling what once was sharp.

Only the memory of Olin's leg in her mouth stayed her transition. When she'd last been a tiger, she'd nearly killed someone she loved, the only person she had left.

So Raene rode her horse through the gloom of the Alderwood in human form. She ignored her hunger, remembering the sight of Olin's bleeding wound. She tried to forget how her tongue savored the taste of blood. She pushed back her selfish desire to kill.

Even then, in the corners of her mind, Raene knew it was only a matter of time.

Kaide stood at the windowed wall of his office and sipped strawberry wine as he watched the sun fall behind the distant mountains. The blue afternoon sky had given way to violets and ambers, and eventually, the indigo of night.

It was finally time.

The air was charged with excitement. He had waited for this day for as long as he could remember. He'd dreamt of it hundreds of times—each scenario filled with different details, different methods, different words—but in the end, he would get his revenge.

Raene was gone, and with her, his only reason to keep Naiden alive was gone as well. For seventeen years, Naiden had lived against Kaide's wishes, protected by his father's refusal to shame the family name. Raping his sister wasn't enough. Murdering her wasn't enough. Kaide's own father was so determined to protect the reputation of his family, he worked to deny such crimes had ever occurred.

Kaide was eighteen when Raene signed the documents that made him her guardian, and with that one stroke of the pen, Kaide inadvertently freed himself from his family. His parents disowned both of them, and Kaide could finally seek justice for his sister.

But by then, Raene knew her father—and loved him. It was for her that Kaide let Naiden live.

And now she was gone. Another woman he cherished pulled from his life never to be seen again. Letting her go hurt worse than he thought it would. He'd known it was coming, but in the wake of Blossom's departure, sending Raene to the Alderwood was unbearable. It was the alcohol to an already festering wound.

Kaide would likely never forgive himself for not telling Raene the true motivations for her trade to the Alderwood, but in that moment, he couldn't bring himself to voice the words. He couldn't tell her he'd traded her to the Bear Clan in exchange for the woman who'd left with his heart.

When Raene arrived in her new home, Blossom would be there to explain it to her. Kaide could only hope that would be enough to keep her from hating him forever.

There was nothing he could do about it now.

That couldn't be said for his sister's murderer. Tonight, Naiden Randal would finally meet justice.

Norsa must have known. She labored up the stairs, her portly-figure huffing hard by the time she reached the top. "I've got a—lovely elk steak—with cranberry glaze," she told him between breaths.

"I have other plans for dinner." Already, Kaide could taste the metallic flavor of blood on his lips. He'd gone out every night this week, seeking to satisfy that hunger but never succeeding.

Maybe this would be the night.

Eager to temper his rage and unable to take action against Naiden Randal for the past week, Kaide had sought solace with others. The murderers, rapists, wife-beaters, and child molesters of Pyrona had begun to disappear, one by one, as Kaide moved down his list of criminals, but none had quieted the fire within him.

Norsa wasn't satisfied either. "You've gone out enough. Maybe it's a good night for staying in. I made you some of that peach cake you like."

Kaide didn't want to think of peaches or anything else that reminded him of his lost bride. "If you mean to use a cake to—"

"It was worth a shot," she answered with a sigh.

Kaide swirled the last sip of wine in his antique glass as he watched the indigo creep further across the sky, smothering the last of sunset.

"You don't have to do this. What'll Raene say when she finds out?" Norsa asked as she made her way beside him, looking up at him with hands on her hips, but Kaide didn't look back.

He couldn't be talked out of this. He was going to kill the man who murdered his sister.

A sister who, to his great shame, he couldn't remember a thing about. Kaide had been robbed of the chance to get to know her because Naiden Randal thought it best to kill her. Alia would have been thirty-five now had Naiden not stolen the life from her.

Kaide shot back the last of his wine and turned away from Norsa.

"Haven't you done enough?" she screamed, her voice shrill. "First Druma, then Valenta. You sent our Rain Drop away. How many people will it take before you're done? She's not coming back, Kaide. She's gone. Blossom is *gone*."

Already holding back that beast within, Kaide didn't last even a second before his transitional energy coursed through him. Muscles expanded and fur sprouted and covered his skin. Even faster than usual, Kaide's beast paws hit the carpeted floor of his office as he let out a bloodthirsty howl.

He had to get out.

As her head barely met his shoulders, it was easy to knock the old woman out of his way as he darted down the stairs and out the door. In the warm evening air, beast-Kaide swelled with the power in his veins. Hunger bubbled up like magma, white hot and relentless.

He needed to eat. He needed to hunt. He needed to kill.

And he knew just the blood he wanted to taste tonight.

As he had rarely had cause to do before, beast-Kaide raced down the mountain to the west. He kept off the roads and loped between the trees, using his capable night eyes and impeccable sense of smell to find his path. His long legs carried him to the stone house in minutes.

Beast-Kaide's shoulders were as tall as the flimsy wooden door, so that even after he sent it crashing to the ground with an impressive *boom*, he still had to work to wriggle his hulking body through the frame.

So consumed with the moment, beast-Kaide struggled to stay focused, to hold his human thoughts inside his beast mind. He forced the man's name through his thoughts. *Naiden Randal. Snake. Killer.*

The house was dark, utterly pitch black, but beast-Kaide knew his target was close. His sense of smell was too keen, and from the first day he picked up the scent of Naiden Randal, Kaide had dreamt of this moment. A growl of excitement sounded in his throat.

A moment later, the faint glow from a lamp cast the room in dingy, yellow light. Naiden stood beside it, his clothes soiled and his eyes glassed over with drink.

Beast-Kaide was almost too disgusted to eat him. He stank of wine and filth and spoil, but it was the man himself who smelled the worst. At his core, Naiden was rotten.

Naiden pulled a half-empty wine bottle to his lips and took a long swig before he spoke. On and on he went, rambling in words beast-Kaide couldn't understand. Naiden had always had a serpent's tongue.

Beast-Kaide let loose a low, rumbling growl to silence him. Nothing could stop him now.

The pathetic excuse for a man dropped the half-empty bottle to the ground and remained motionless as it shattered at his feet. Then, he closed his eyes and whispered yet more words.

Beast-Kaide growled again. He didn't understand. Human words were so difficult in totem form. It was too hard to concentrate when he was so hungry, so eager to kill.

When beast-Kaide didn't move, the words continued.

Nothing made sense. Naiden didn't run or flee or transition to fight him off. He only stood there, speaking but not moving. Beast-Kaide grew tired of hearing his voice and his breath and his heartbeat. It was finally time to rid the realm of Naiden Randal.

Beast-Kaide lunged forward in a flash and gripped Naiden's torso in his jaws. It was easy to crush him, to feel the crunching, snapping bones as he smothered the life right out of him. Blood poured from a dozen different wounds, and beast-Kaide was rewarded with the bitter flavor, still hot and delicious.

He had no doubt the man was dead, but he wasn't satisfied. The wolf in his blood made him shake his victim, swinging his head wildly from side to side, causing more bones to snap and blood to splatter the walls.

But still he hadn't had enough. Beast-Kaide dropped Naiden's body to the floor in a lifeless heap and worked to free his organs from his body. Intestines, stomach, esophagus—he pulled them all out.

As a last desperate measure, beast-Kaide gripped the head between his canines and crunched it clean through, leaving nothing more than a bloody pink splatter where the brain had once been.

Nothing worked. Nothing quieted that rage within him. Frustrated and well beyond furious, beast-Kaide tilted back his monstrous head and howled through his anger.

At a loss for what to do next, beast-Kaide wriggled his way back out of the stone house and made his way up the slope, leaving the catastrophic scene in his wake. What started as a desperate, full-speed run slowed to an easy jog, and finally the trudge of defeat. Only halfway to the manor, he transitioned back. He didn't have enough energy to maintain his totem any longer.

He didn't have enough *anything*. Whatever had been inside him before was gone now. She was gone. She wasn't coming back.

She saw an opportunity to run and she took it.

Nothing between them was real.

And in his human form, Kaide could process what he'd done. Naiden hadn't run. He hadn't transitioned to fight. He'd merely stood there, probably begging for his life or making a final apology. Naiden had known Kaide would kill him, and he didn't try to stop it.

He let Kaide end his life. He knew it was what he deserved.

The knowledge that Naiden and Kaide agreed on something—even this—made Kaide wonder if he'd ever really understood the man. After ridding the world of such a snake, Kaide thought he'd feel vindicated, but instead, there was only this cloud of confusion and something that bordered on guilt. He couldn't help but wonder if he'd made the right decision.

But it was too late now. Naiden Randal was dead. No one would go looking for him. No one would notice he was missing—save maybe his wine vendor. Otherwise, Naiden would simply be another Pyro to disappear and never surface again.

Kaide stumbled up the front steps of the manor and found Norsa sitting on the entryway stairs, wiping at the tears on her cheeks.

"You did it, didn't you?" she cried when she saw him.

He could only smear a hand across his beard and try to lessen the blood he knew was there.

But Norsa only cried harder. She stood and cupped his cheeks in her hands, ignoring the gore still stuck to his face.

If it had been anyone else, Kaide would have pulled away. But he couldn't. He was a sail without wind, empty and stuck. He stood and endured her tear-filled eyes as she said, "I know it hurts. It hurts something awful. It cut you deep, don't the Alder Mother know it did. But this? This is not you. And this has got to stop. I'm not going nowhere, no matter what you do or who you do it to, but please. Please, boy. Don't make me watch this. I don't want to see no more of this from you. I raised you better than that."

And with that, Kaide knew for good and certain he was a monster—not just his totem, not just his murderous behavior—he was a true monster in every sense of the word.

He had become beast he'd fought so hard against.

Kaide placed his hands over both of hers and closed his eyes, threatening to spill tears as he hadn't dared in years. With nothing more than breath, he told her, "I don't know what to do."

Norsa squeezed his face in her hands. "We'll figure it out, boy. We always do."

The last light of evening disappeared between the trees as Raene and Olin pulled their horses into the stables behind the Mother's Inn. Raene was more than ready for a soft bed and a hot meal. On this day that started with transformation and ended in the Alderwood, Raene had yet to taste anything other than Olin's leg. As she thought of food and her growling stomach, her totem urged to let loose yet again. Her hands tightened into fists, eager to unleash their claws.

She couldn't be around horses another moment.

Raene climbed down first so she could help Olin. His bandages were remarkably intact; the stain of blood hadn't spread much since they left the city hours ago. The Hydra man's skill with wrapping wounds had prevented Olin from bleeding out, but that didn't keep him from gripping Raene's shoulder as he struggled to regain his balance. They both handed their reins to the stableman and together they slowly walked toward the inn and the comforts that waited within.

"It's only a half-day's ride from here," Olin said, though she hadn't asked. He let her help him up the worn wooden steps into the fire-lit warmth of the inn's central room. A spinning staircase led to the upper floors and to sitting rooms on either side, though only the one nearest to the kitchen was occupied. A dozen Terra patrons already sat eating and engaging in low conversation.

But all chatter stopped when Raene and Olin entered. Both in Pyro clothes and weary from a full day of travel, they stood out like candles in the night.

Raene had never felt more out of place.

Olin, however, didn't seem to mind. He motioned toward an empty table and limped his way to the nearest chair. Both were maple wood, well-worn by decades of rough hands and tired feet.

"Don't you want to get a room first?" Raene asked.

"You need to eat." As he said it, Olin raised his hand and signaled a Terra woman. Under her cream-colored apron, she had a large moss-green tunic top and loose honey-brown pants. All in all, she looked to be drowning in so much fabric, but she managed easily enough as she neared.

Standing across from him, Raene protested. "I'm fine. Really, we can get—"

Olin huffed a breath out his nose and shook his head. "You need to eat, Rain Drop. I know the appetite of a cat better than anyone, though I suspect yours is worse. Sit down and eat. Then we'll worry about the room." He looked up at the woman, who was now standing at the tableside, and asked, "What meat do you have?"

The woman's mouth twisted into a frown, as if she suddenly disliked speaking to them entirely. "Roast badger and a turtle soup," she offered.

Raene cringed at both as she sat.

Olin ignored her and said, "We'll have three plates of badger."

"There's only two of you," the woman fussed.

The coins he put on the table were answer enough. She slid them into her hand and spun back toward the kitchen a moment later.

"You're really that hungry?" Raene asked as she untied what was left of her braid, combing between the strands with her fingers.

"It's for you. Trust me. It's better to do it this way." Raene didn't know what he meant, but she wasn't in the mood to ask. Instead, she occupied herself untangling her hair and braiding it until their dinners arrived.

Just the smell of it made her mouth water. Raene was sure she'd never eaten a badger before, but the savory scent that filled her nose made her want nothing else.

She dove in as soon as the plate hit the table. Her teeth ripped through the meat with ease, shredding whole sections off as she barely chewed them down. Oil coated her face, and juices slicked her fingers, but she wouldn't slow, couldn't slow.

Before she knew it, only the slender arm bones of the badger remained on her plate.

Without a word, Olin slid over a second helping.

Raene dug in and stripped the bones in minutes. Never had she enjoyed meat that way—the feel of muscle tearing between her teeth, the heat and juice and flavor of the animal in her mouth.

And then, like a crashing wave retreating back to the

ocean, the urge was gone—at least for now. Raene sucked a few breaths into her lungs and felt the emptiness in her chest. After an afternoon of continuous struggle, it felt strange to have it gone now.

"Feel better?" Olin shot her an amused smile as he continued to eat his own portion, working each bite from the bone slowly and carefully. Like any civilized person would do.

Suddenly conscious of her behavior, Raene wiped a hand across her face and tried to remove the evidence of what she'd done. "I'm sorry," she told him, embarrassed at her barbaric performance.

"Don't be. It takes a while to get used to it."

"Was it like this for you?"

"It's like that for all Pyros, Rain Drop. Some more than others. Yours will be some of the worst, but like him, you'll learn to control it." Olin hadn't even said his name but Raene felt the impact of it.

She was like Kaide. More than she'd ever wanted to be.

Her finger found the beginning of the faded scar on her temple and mindlessly traced it down her cheek to her jaw and on past to the other side of her neck.

Raene remembered the chilling look in his eye when he reached out with his massive claw and gave her that scar. He'd been angry with her, and she'd been scared of him, but once he learned to keep that rage inside, they'd been closer than ever.

Like Kaide, she just had to figure out how to keep in control of her totem.

With her stomach full and the warmth of the nearby fire, it almost felt possible, but Raene knew she was far from in control. On her neck, her fingertips found the edge of the bandage and pulled, cleanly removing it in one motion.

Less than a day after earning her tattoo, the skin was still raw and sore. She grazed the tender skin with her hand and wondered if it would ever really feel the same—if *she* would ever feel the same.

This was a new Raene. She was no longer the elegant niece of a leading political figure. Now, she was a predator and the future bride of some Terra man in the Alderwood.

She clung to the hope that, at least, whoever her husband would be, he would make her feel like this was all worth it. Kaide had had a glimpse of it with Blossom. The prospect of a future with love and happiness was the only light in the dark had become her life.

On the far wall of the central room, Raene noticed the alder tree engraved in the wood, so massive its branches spanned the entire room. From the sweeping boughs hung the symbols of the branches, a raindrop for Hydra, a flame for Pyro, a gust of wind for Aero, and an alder leaf for Terra.

The Alder Mother and her four branches.

"They're quite religious, aren't they?" Raene asked with her eyes still on the carving.

"Terras? That's what they say. Devotion to the Mother and such." Olin shrugged like it didn't matter, but a moment later, he leaned in and asked, "Sure you want to go through with this?"

"What choice do I have?" Raene wished she had the marriage document to throw at him. "It's all in writing. He traded me to a clan. In the *Alderwood*. There's nothing I can do about it." Raene would have been so much less angry if everything had happened differently. He could have traded her to another clan in Pyrona. He could have told her when he made the arrangements rather than blindsiding her. He could have delivered her himself. He could have been sorry to see her go.

"You're already out. You could run. I could take you

anywhere you want, except Pyrona of course." Olin made it sound like choosing a restaurant for lunch rather than the whole rest of her life.

"I'm not going to do that. I'm not a coward." Raene realized as soon as she said it. Raene was no coward, but Blossom was. She'd run the first chance she got. She'd run away and ruined everything.

Raene pressed her hands to her face and exhaled a long, slow breath. What was happening to her? How could she harbor so much hate and anger for people she loved? Nothing made sense.

Maybe she *should* run. With her tiger totem, she could make her own way. She could go anywhere, do anything. She would never be in danger.

But it would be a betrayal to Kaide. And so Raene would never do it. She was stuck here in the Alderwood for the rest of her life.

Then, Raene looked up at Olin and said the words she knew must be true. "He traded me to Blossom's clan, didn't he? The Bear Clan of the Alderwood? In exchange for Blossom?" She didn't need to see the document to know. It was the only way that made sense.

Olin nodded with a cheek full of badger meat. "There were a few other contingencies, but yes. They stayed in this very inn on their way to Pyrona."

Raene's head spun. Kaide didn't send her away as punishment. It was arranged even before Blossom arrived in Pyrona. Maybe he'd done it to secure his bride, but even so, he hadn't done it out of spite or misery. Raene was a pawn in his game, but at least he didn't hate her.

And she was going to Blossom's clan. Where Blossom likely went instead of transformation. Maybe this whole mess could be salvaged. Maybe she could get Blossom to go back to Kaide.

Maybe Raene would lose her all over again.

The selfish desire to have Blossom in her life once more crept up like a thief. Living in the Bear Clan as Blossom's sister wouldn't be so bad.

But she couldn't do that to Kaide. He needed Blossom, and if Raene had even the smallest say in the matter, Blossom would go back to him.

Raene was on her own no matter what.

Overwhelmed by the revelation, Raene pushed out of the wooden chair so hard and fast it fell to the floor with a crash, earning the attention of every person in the room. Only Olin would speak. "Give it some time, Rain Drop. You'll learn to quiet it. It just takes time," he offered, incorrectly guessing the source of her renewed anguish.

But she didn't want to explain it. Raene barked at the woman by the door. "Show me to my room."

As she was told, the Terra woman darted up the stairs, taking them two at a time as Raene jogged up behind her. Then, in a room that was all her own, Raene closed the door and sealed herself away from the rest of the world.

INTRODUCTIONS

PARSON RAISED the axe high over his head and brought it down with all his might. The blade hit the wood with a thud and cleaved off the slender branch in a single motion.

Again, he lifted the axe and sent it sailing into the next limb. One by one, he worked his way down the length of the branch, removing the pieces too small to be useful. Heat coursed through his muscles, and his lungs worked to get enough air, but Parson wouldn't stop.

It felt too good to hit something, even if it was just this dead tree.

Sunlight streamed through the new hole in the canopy and baked him in spring heat. Sweat slicked his fingers until his two-dozen rings slid with every swing. His moss-green tunic clung to his sweat-coated skin, suffocating him.

Parson stopped swinging his axe long enough to peel off his tunic and toss it on a nearby limb. Then, he collected his tool and resumed, relishing the cooling breeze across his torso.

He'd only cut three more branches when he heard Da's whistle, the usual call.

Da wasn't a large man, and his totem was even smaller—a red fox—but somehow, within the confines of the Alderwood, he could whistle louder than anyone.

Parson groaned and fought to get his shirt back over his sticky shoulders. Of course Da had seen him take off his tunic. Forbidden, he knew. Sacrilegious to the Alder Mother and all that.

But it was hot, and Parson was beyond caring.

He'd been that way for a while now.

It took him ten minutes to get himself covered and to find Da on the far side of the cut. Prepared for a lecture, Parson was more than a little surprised to find Hale there as well. The youngest Frane son stood stoic as he waited, cool and collected compared to Parson's agitation.

"Where's Lathan?" Da asked as his eyes scanned the cut. A dozen men from the clan all worked to process their most recent claim, a ninety-eight year old alder tree—the perfect age to be felled and cleaned for distribution. Completely illegal to harvest, of course, but that's what made them so valuable.

"What's going on?" Parson asked his father, but no answer came. He only continued to whistle for Lathan across the cut.

It was Hale who stepped beside Parson and said, "Something he wants to show us. Won't say a word about it until we're all here."

"Da, get on with it. I've got work to do," Parson said, interrupting his father's whistles. Technically, stripping such useless limbs was the work of one of the younger men in the clan working their way through the process of felling an alder tree, but Parson couldn't sit still. So while some of the others rested, Parson had taken it upon himself to start stripping the branches. No one would miss him if he didn't return to finish the branch, but nevertheless, he didn't want to stand around all afternoon.

"Just hold tight." Da turned to face them, his eyes gleaming with mischief. He was up to something, but

Parson was in no mood to play along.

He clenched his fists and groaned out his impatience.

"It must be important," Hale continued. "He hasn't asked for all of us since—"

Since he sold their little sister to a monster. No, not sold. *Gave her away.* Surely Da thought he was making a fair trade—not even Parson could deny him that—but whatever it was that had been decided between Da and the Vice Syndicate, Da had been cheated. No horses nor grain nor barrels of wine had arrived in exchange for her. Blossom was simply gone, and there was nothing Parson could do about it.

As if shaken by an earthquake, a chasm had split across his chest as he watched his little sister walk away with a stranger that day, never to return. And no matter what he did in the days since, he couldn't feel any better about it. There was only pain and anger and the gaping hole in her place.

Just as he turned to head back to his work, Lathan arrived. "Can it wait?" he asked. Parson knew his oldest brother harbored the same anger over Blossom's departure, but Lathan would never say it. He was too quiet, too private in his emotions.

And then there was Hale, who acted like he didn't even care—like he didn't even notice she was gone. There was no little sister for Hale to chase, but even so, Parson expected more from him.

"I have a surprise for you three. Come on." Da put a hand on Lathan's shoulder and beamed with whatever it was he had in store for them.

Parson tried not to groan as he followed his da and brothers through the woods. It was a good twenty-minute walk between the camp and the cut, a security measure in case one was ever discovered by agents of the Alderai. Today, it felt like a waste of time.

The rays of mid-afternoon sun peeking through the canopy and the birdsongs echoing between the trees did little to settle his mind. He'd rather be doing a hundred different things. Indulging Da's game only made him more agitated.

Then, his bear nose detected a new scent mixed in with the familiar ones. Along with the lesser totems—the deer and the elk, the rabbits and the beavers—there was something else. Something smoky, like ash, but with a bouquet of scents he'd never encountered. A new person was in their camp—a stranger

And blood. Parson was sure he smelled blood.

Minutes later, the three brothers and Da arrived in the clearing across from Da's tent. It was the largest in camp, the same moss-green as everything Terra, and was painted with the silhouette of his fox totem above the flap.

Today, a man waited for them there, his feet together and his hands behind his back. Parson knew immediately he was Pyro. His dark hair and skin would have been enough even had he not been wearing the red-and-black of his branch.

And even if Parson hadn't noticed how the Pyro man stood favoring one leg, he would have had no doubt the man was injured. He reeked of blood.

Something was wrong. Parson knew it as much as anything. The man didn't cross the realm with his damaged leg and deep-set scowl to deliver good news.

Parson could think of only one reason a Pyro would come to see them.

Blossom was dead.

At his sides, Parson clenched his fists. His blood raced through his veins as his totem form took hold. Hair had already begun to sprout across his shoulders and down his back when Lathan appeared, placing his massive hand on Parson's chest and shouting something. Parson couldn't understand his words clearly, but they were enough.

They were just enough to stay his transition.

The momentary distraction brought Parson's mind back to the clearing, to the Pyro man, to his sister he'd already lost. At the thought of her, grief bubbled up anew until Parson could scarcely breathe.

Da turned to offer Parson a glare over his shoulder before he said, "Sons, may I present Olin Cox of the Lynx Clan of Mount Huntari. Master Olin, these are my sons, Lathan, Parson, and Hale Frane of the Bear Clan of the Alderwood. Welcome." Da stepped forward and clasped the man's shoulders, grinning ear to ear.

At least the stranger seemed as disappointed as Parson. Still wearing a frown, he clasped Da's shoulder in return and bowed his head in respect. "Thank you, Master Frane."

"She's inside?" Da sounded like a giddy little girl.

For the first time in weeks, Parson's pulse raced from something other than anger. She? Could it be? Had this Pyro man brought Blossom home?

The circumstances must have been dire, she'd probably had a horrible time, she may even have been harmed, but she was home.

Somehow, against all odds, Blossom was back where she belonged.

Parson almost knocked Da aside as he crossed the clearing in a few racing steps and barreled into the tent.

But it wasn't her.

Parson could only stare at the girl who wasn't his sister. She was tall—probably the tallest girl he'd ever seen—and she had straw-colored hair that hung clear down to her waist. Candlelight bounced off her sapphire eyes staring wide at him. She, too, wore Pyro clothes, revealing her arms, her collarbones, her waist.

She was nothing like his sister.

She wasn't Blossom.

No sooner was he inside than Da, Lathan, and finally Hale appeared behind him.

And that was all Parson could take. He pushed Hale aside and stomped back into the sunlight of the clearing. Someone shouted behind him, but he didn't have it in him to care.

Chestnut fur already sprung across his shoulders. His face elongated and his clenched fists grew into massive paws. When his form became too heavy, he fell forward at a full run. Parson darted between the trees with no desire to ever come back.

Raene choked back her apprehension and nervous excitement. This was it.

She'd meet her future husband. She'd see Blossom, and convince her to go back to Kaide. All Raene had to do was wait. Her already-simmering tiger's blood felt ready to explode.

For a full minute, Raene heard the voices outside the tent. One of them was Olin's—she'd know it anywhere. The others, she had no idea.

Olin had merely sent her in to wait in silence. She'd been standing there for at least half an hour, though with only the light of the flickering candle, it was impossible to know for sure. The conical tent was nothing more than a large piece of heavy green canvas hanging from a tree. A patchwork of mismatched fabrics—all green and brown and golden yellow—covered the floor.

It was a far cry from the grandeur of the manor.

Waiting in such a dull space with no one to talk to and nothing to do had seemed boring at first, but now that she could hear the voices outside, she could barely contain herself.

In a flash, Raene lightly pinched her cheeks to ensure a lovely pink color flushed her face. She soothed down her hair, already re-braided since her travels, and made sure her clothes were as perfect as possible. When she was satisfied she'd done all she could given the circumstances, Raene forced her hands to her sides.

With each passing second, her heart thumped faster and louder, her mounting anticipation and nerves saturating the air around her.

She was here in an Alderwood clan to be married, honoring Kaide's arrangement. Raene was all too aware the next few moments would determine the rest of her life. She tried to think back to what Blossom had mentioned of her clan—three brothers, all bears—that much Raene remembered.

But she didn't know which brother Kaide had chosen for her husband.

Then, a man ran into the tent and stopped short, staring at her.

Handsome, mid-twenties. Just right for her.

Raene held back a nervous smile as she measured her future husband. He had broad shoulders and his dark-chestnut hair had fallen into his startling green eyes, the rest of it tied low just off his neck. Several days of growth coated his chin and cheeks, not unlike Kaide's usual look. Even in the dimness, she could see how he examined her in turn, searching for something.

For several eternal seconds, they stood locked in place, gazing, staring, evaluating each other. Raene made sure to stand tall to show him her height, and when he didn't move, she swept her braid over her shoulder to give him a better look. But he only continued to stare, gaping. By the narrowing of his eyes, Raene got the distinct feeling she didn't measure up to his expectations in some way. It was a stab through the heart.

A moment later, three others pushed in behind him, though it was too dark to see much other than their silhouettes against the sunlight outside. One was massively huge with a full beard, one was smaller and clean-shaven, and one was much older than the other two, his thick beard streaked with grey. Beyond that, she couldn't tell.

Then, finding her unsuitable in some way, the first peeled his green eyes away, pushed his way out of the tent, and disappeared.

Somehow, Raene had managed to disappoint him in a matter of seconds without saying a word. She steeled herself against whatever else the others might find wrong with her.

In all the ways she'd considered this moment might go, never had she thought the family of her future husband would be disappointed in her. In Pyrona, she was wealthy and elite. But here in the Alderwood, she was no one.

Raene stood tall on display for the three Terra men still crowded at the tent's entrance. She wouldn't let them make her feel inadequate. Ignoring the ache in her chest, she held her head high, waiting for their assessment, determined they should find her suitable.

"My sons," began the one to the right, the oldest one with dark brown hair turning grey above his ears. "May I present Raene Randal of the Tiger Clan of Mount Huntari?" He stepped forward and clutched her hands between both of his, which were so full of rings she could hardly see his skin. In a warm voice dripping in paternal love, he said, "Welcome to the Frane Clan, the Bear Clan of the Alderwood, my dear. We are so very pleased to have you with us."

For a moment, Raene was calmed. Then, her eyes darted back to the two young men on the far side of the tent. They stood frozen, eyes wide in shock.

They hadn't known she was coming.

It seemed Kaide had left everyone ignorant of his plan.

Forcing back her tiger's instinct to fight, she grasped the edge of her loose black pants and bowed her head low, as she'd been taught. "Thank you, Master Frane," she said with all the elegance she could muster.

When her braid fell in front of her shoulder, the clan leader pushed it back and eyed the fresh tattoo on her neck, still scaly as it healed. Satisfied, he added, "And happy birthday, as well."

"Thank you, Master Frane," she repeated. Raene was determined to put on her best airs—to show them she had all the class and decorum expected from her family.

But he only replied, "Please, call me Da. Everyone does. And these are my sons, Lathan," he said as he pointed to the first, the one with the full beard, a huge specimen of a man even by Pyro standards. "And my youngest son, Hale." The smaller man nodded at the mention of his name. Like the first, and Blossom herself, the Frane sons shared the same stunning green eyes—each of slightly different shades—and chestnut hair with a bit of wave. In the dimness of the tent and silhouetted by sunlight streaming through the flap, the sons were impossible to see clearly, but Raene's heart raced at their presence.

"I'm sorry you missed Parson. He hasn't been himself lately. I'm sure he'll be back shortly." Da's weak smile suggested he had no confidence in such an assertion.

Apparently, Kaide had traded her to an Alderwood clan of heathens, living in dirt-floor tents and running about disrespecting their clan leader. What was he thinking?

What little excitement Raene had held for the day quickly dissolved. It was as bad as she feared. Kaide had either intentionally sabotaged her future, or been too negligent to notice. Either way, Raene's hopes unraveled into confusion and anger.

It only heightened her urge to transition.

"Did you say Huntari?" Raene's eyes darted up toward the youngest one—the one named Hale. He had the same chestnut-brown hair the Franes all shared, but unlike Lathan's considerable beard or Parson's short-cut stubble, Hale was clean-shaven, revealing the square line of his jaw.

Raene admired the bright green color of his eyes as she answered. "Yes, sir. My family has lived there for generations."

"You're with the Vice Syndicate, aren't you? That was the deal you made," he asked of the man called Da. "You traded Blossom for this girl, didn't you?"

Da puffed his chest proudly. "That's why they call it a trade, son. Clans trade for things, in this case, daughters."

"I'm his niece," Raene said, though she wasn't even sure why.

The three stared up at her confused, but it was Raene who felt lost. Where was Blossom?

Da motioned his sons closer, and when they were near enough he said, "We agreed to a trade, a tiger for a bear. Since none of my sons had ever met Raene, we determined that it should be her choice as to who she will marry." Then, with eyes on Raene, he added, "Unfortunately, I didn't think to tell the Vice Syndicate that Lathan has already taken a wife. Nonetheless, you'll have your choice, as agreed. Hale," he said, his hand pointed toward his youngest son. "Or Parson." Da thrust a double-ringed thumb toward the tent flap.

Toward the one who'd run at the sight of her.

On the surface, Raene maintained her calm expression, but inside, she felt close to bursting. It didn't make any sense. Marriage agreements were designed to prohibit such a thing. Raene was never meant to choose her husband. That was Kaide's role, not hers. How could he burden her with this?

Raene looked back and forth between the three men,

completely at a loss. Her chest felt like it might cave in at any second. Surely he didn't mean for her to choose now…

"She's only just arrived. Let her get settled. I'm sure she's tired after so much traveling." It was Hale who spoke up for her. Perhaps he too felt pressured into something none of them wanted.

They'd only met two minutes ago, after all.

"Yes, I'm quite tired," Raene admitted. It wasn't a lie. She was exhausted from the ride, and anticipation kept her from sleep at the inn, but really, fatigue was just an excuse. She simply didn't want to face the horrible decision—not now or ever.

An excuse would have to work for the time being.

Da frowned through his thick beard. "I'm afraid our arrangement is quite clear. She is to stay with the son of her choosing, for her safety and protection, as Blossom is with the Vice Syndicate for hers." In the low candlelight, it was hard to tell if Da was really as concerned as he let on, but Raene knew it didn't matter.

She was going to have to choose now. A man who'd spoken only a few sentences to her or another who'd run at the mere sight of her.

Neither seemed a good option.

Never mind the fact Da had just admitted he thought Blossom was still in Pyrona with Kaide.

She wasn't in the Bear Clan.

The reality of it shocked Raene further into silence. She could only stare and gape in abject horror.

"She can stay with me." Raene's looked to the largest son, the one who hadn't yet said a word. Lathan, she remembered. "You'll be honoring the agreement, and Tasia will watch her as she settles in. When she's ready, she can make her choice. Can we agree to allow her one month?"

Raene didn't know who Tasia was, but as she wasn't a son Raene might someday have to marry, she seemed the obvious choice. Raene nodded eagerly, but it wasn't up to her.

"It's not a direct violation—" Da had barely gotten started before Lathan, Hale, and Raene all agreed. He put up a few more minutes of fight, but it was clear Lathan's words weren't taken lightly. With both sons on her side, Da caved with a long sigh. "All right, get her home. Maybe when Parson gets back—"

Raene didn't hear the rest as Lathan placed one of his massive hands on the middle of her back and propelled her toward the tent's flap. She didn't know him in the slightest, but he was the best option she had. He was the only one she might not have to marry.

So, despite her reservations and fears and discomfort, Raene walked beside him as they emerged into the sunlit clearing. "Go ahead and take a few minutes to say goodbye."

Raene was momentarily confused, looking at Lathan for an answer.

Then she remembered Olin. He'd done his job. He'd brought her to the Alderwood clan. And now, he had no further reason to stay.

Olin stood at attention, waiting for her one last time. Despite his proud smile, his eyes dimmed with regret. She knew he didn't want to leave her.

The realization of his departure hit her like a boulder falling from the sky. Raene felt empty, flattened by the prospect of saying goodbye to the only person she had left. She threw her arms around his neck and squeezed him tight. "Take care of him for me," she whispered, biting back the tears that stung her eyes.

Olin held her tight, clinging to her embrace one last time. "You take care of yourself, Rain Drop. You've got your mother's blood and your uncle's charm. You just make sure and use it if you need to." When he stepped away, Olin's eyes glistened in a way she'd never seen from him. That, more than anything, made her heart ache.

First Kaide, then Norsa. Now Olin. This was really happening. She was really going to stay here. As Olin took his first steps back toward the horses, Raene struggled to find the words to tell him goodbye.

Da stepped in to fill the silence. "Thank you, Master Olin, for delivering our daughter to us. Please tell the Vice Syndicate she'll be well looked after, as our Blossom is with him."

The reminder of Blossom's absence was heavy enough to crush her.

"Olin—" she called after him. She wanted to make sure Kaide got the news, but her voice lost its strength.

Kaide's serviceman only turned and nodded. "I'll tell him." He understood her, as he always had. Raene breathed easier, but still the confusion and dread settled into her gut.

Then, with nothing left to say, Olin walked to the horses, and with a last lingering glance back, he disappeared into the Alderwood. It felt so wrong to watch him leave that way, to know she'd never see him again, that he'd go back to Pyrona and live his life without her.

Raene could only stare after him in shocked silence. Cut off from everyone she'd ever known, Raene would never learn Blossom's fate—for better or worse. She was trapped alone in the forest with this endless guilt and regret. Already, it filled her with a suffocating heaviness. Her tiger blood bubbled to the surface, her totem desperate to get out and run.

Lathan reappeared at her side and pressed a gentle hand on her back. "Our tent is just over here." His voice was quiet, and he spoke with such care that Raene couldn't help but follow him. Lathan's touch, his deep voice, was all that kept her grounded in the chaos of the day.

It was all so much. It was all so fast. In two days she'd

earned her tiger totem, crossed the realm, and met the men who could be her future husband. And if that wasn't enough, she was plagued with the new knowledge that Blossom had never come home.

Her mind spun with the possibilities. Did she run home only to be killed by a street gang along the way? Was she collected as a favor for the Prentis? Did she go somewhere else entirely? Raene didn't even know if Blossom was still alive.

Raene was so mixed up she couldn't even see straight. Had it not been for Lathan's guiding hand, Raene would have simply stopped and collapsed in the clearing. She couldn't bear the weight of so many decisions, so many secrets. They were too heavy.

Like a phantom, she let Lathan lead her to a tent on the far side of the clearing. It had a bear silhouette painted over the flap and was slightly smaller, but otherwise, it was identical to Da's. He lifted the flap and let her in.

Inside, the space was perfectly dark until Lathan pinned open the flap. Scattered rays of afternoon sun streamed in and revealed a floor of vibrant carpets and colorful pillows. The perimeter was lined with a series of low cabinets, stacks of fabrics—all Terra green and brown—and in the center, a wide bowl of still-smoldering ashes.

Without a word, Lathan strode through the tent and sank onto one of the pillows, sitting tall with his legs crossed. His shoulders were impossibly wide, and his arms looked powerful enough to strangle a lion. He had a strong jaw and quiet eyes of the darkest pine green, almost black. In the quiet that hung between them, he breathed easily. He was comfortable without words, satisfied in his silence.

Raene couldn't decide if she liked that or not.

When Raene remained standing, he motioned to the pillow beside him. As soon as she thought about sitting comfortably on the cushion, she wanted to do nothing else. Exhaustion pulled her down beside the stranger. She would have loved to curl up in the dark space, clutch her knees to her chest, and waste away her days, but Raene would suffer no such breach in decorum. Instead, she crossed her legs in front of her and mirrored Lathan's stoic calm, working to even her breaths in spite of the storm in her chest.

For the time being, she was content sitting in a dark tent in silence. The quiet soothed her restless totem, and she felt a little less like she was going to explode.

Until two forms filled the tent entrance.

At first, Raene could only see the shapes of a man and a woman, but after a moment, she recognized one of them as Hale.

Just the sight of him made her stiffen. He was handsome, surely, and he seemed reasonable and respectful, but the pressure of her decision made her nervous to even be in his presence. Raene did her best to look as calm as Lathan.

"Sorry we took so long. She was out at the Connor gardens," Hale explained.

The woman ignored him and stepped into the tent. Her large brown eyes were focused on Raene as she neared and sank to a pillow. "You must be Raene."

Lathan cleared his throat and said, "Raene Randal of the Tiger Clan of Mount Huntari. And this," he motioned to the woman, "is Tasia Frane of the Bear Clan of the Alderwood. My wife," he added, as if Raene hadn't figured it out.

Then, deciding his introductions were done, Lathan pushed to standing and lovingly kissed Tasia's cheek. They exchanged a long look, rich with emotion and meaning Raene couldn't begin to understand. Then, without another word, Lathan left, taking Hale with him.

Whatever peace Raene had earned with Lathan was

gone as soon as he was. She remained with his wife and her disapproving stare. For someone with a deer-totem tattoo, Tasia looked less like a woodland doe and more like an angry jackal. Raene no longer felt welcome, though she wasn't entirely sure why.

Tasia and Raene sat in heavy silence for several minutes until, without warning, Tasia rose and began tending to the various items around the tent's perimeter. Raene watched as Tasia collected a pair of wooden goblets and a thin metal plate. Only when the goblets were filled with wine and the plate piled high with fruit did Tasia take her seat again.

"Go on. You must be hungry."

In fact, Raene was starving, but she wasn't in the mood for peaches or cherries or whatever those little green ones were. Her mouth watered for something else. Something breathing.

So Raene collected a goblet and drank the wine instead. It was horribly bitter compared to the sweet strawberry wine of Pyrona, but all in all, it was drinkable. All too soon, she'd emptied the goblet, and Tasia hadn't said another word.

When she did speak, Raene wished she hadn't. Tasia clutched a berry in her fingers, biting it in half as she asked, "You met Blossom in Pyrona?"

Raene swallowed hard and nodded.

"I'm not going to ask. I'm not sure I want to know. I don't trust Pyros." She munched on the rest of the berry and ate a few more before she continued, "But if anything happened to her—anything at all—you keep it to yourself, you understand?"

Raene froze, unsure what that was supposed to mean. Did Tasia know something about Blossom's disappearance? "Kaide would never hurt—"

"I don't want to know." Tasia sighed and wiped her

hands on her pants. "Bears are dangerous. I'm sure you're used to that, but out here, there's no one to stop them. If any Frane, including my husband, was to learn that Blossom had been harmed, it would be very dangerous for the rest of us. No matter what you know, you keep it to yourself."

"All right," Raene replied, not really sure how to take such advice. Her thoughts were a mess; she didn't want to argue about things she couldn't help. Instead, she extended her goblet for more wine.

Tasia's lip curled into a smile. "Get it yourself. You're not a Pyro princess anymore, remember?"

Raene's mouth fell open, not at the words—those she knew were true—but that this woman would be so callous as to remind her. "I meant no disrespect," Raene managed to say.

But Tasia only smiled, like this was all so amusing. Raene felt like the butt of a joke no one had bothered to tell her. "If you don't screw it up, you could be a Terra princess. The Franes are as famous as the Alderwood itself. It's not all bad."

"I'm not Terra. I'm Pyro." Raene stretched her neck to show the red-and-black tiger tattoo, all too aware how the woman hated her for it.

Tasia shrugged. "Even so, there are worse families to be traded to. Get to know them a little. You'll see."

"I don't have to get to know them. I have to marry one, and that's as far as my obligations go." After her days of grief and her less-than-warm welcome to the Bear Clan, Raene's enthusiasm was all but gone.

But Tasia only laughed. "Suit yourself. No one can make you get to know them. But that will make for an awkward evening for you." She laughed so hard she had to cover her mouth to keep from spewing half-chewed berries across the tent.

"What do you mean?" Raene rubbed at the wrinkle in her brow.

"Da's organizing a celebration for you. For your arrival and your birthday. The whole clan is gathering as we speak." Tasia collected both goblets and refilled them before sitting down again.

Raene accepted hers and continued to drink, wondering what sparked the change in Tasia's attitude. "Can I tell him I don't want a celebration?"

Tasia clutched at her ribs in hearty laughter. "Oh, you can try, but it won't do any good. You'll see. Da gets his heart set and that's that."

"Everyone really calls him Da?" Raene had never heard of a clan that used such an informal title for their leader. She'd never been particularly close to her actual father, and now she was supposed to call someone else Da?

"That's what he wants." Then, Tasia dusted her hands on her pants and stood. "Come on. We'll get you ready, and then I'll show you around."

Raene sighed and downed the last of her wine. She knew she couldn't stay in the tent all day, but she didn't know if she was ready to see the whole clan. It was all too surreal.

At least she'd be spared seeing them while she freshened up. Getting ready for an event with Norsa and Valenta had been one of her favorite activities at the manor.

But Raene never expected the dismal reality Tasia showed her. The dirt floors and rudimentary candles were nothing compared to the lack of running water. No sink to wash her face. No washroom to handle personal business. No tub to soak away the stresses of the day.

Instead, Tasia presented Raene with a copper basin of water. It had been warmed slightly over a fire, but it was far from hot. Between that and the simple rag, Raene had scarcely felt less clean after a wash. How did people live this way?

When she was as fresh as she could manage, Tasia gave her a salve to run through her hair. It smelled nice enough and removed the grease, but Raene still didn't feel like it was clean. She braided her hair once more and donned fresh Pyro clothes before she pushed past the tent flap and found Tasia waiting in the cleaning.

"I didn't mean to kick you out of your own home." Raene offered, at a loss as to why the woman hadn't stayed in the first place.

"Modesty for the Mother," Tasia replied with her gaze on the slit of exposed skin between Raene's scarlet shirt and black pants.

Raene forced herself not to roll her eyes. "So what do you want to show me?" She was eager to avoid the celebration and the Frane brothers as long as possible.

Tasia pointed back at the tent and said, "This is Lathan's tent, and mine, of course. He has the stronger totem, so it's marked here above the flap. He's the first son of the clan leader, so his tent is larger than most."

At the mention of totems, Raene remembered Tasia's deer. "Do you miss your family?" Raene asked, surprised by her own question.

Tasia's gaze remained even on the bear over the flap. "I've been with the Franes for five years now. I love my husband, and I love his family, but yes, there are times I miss my home." At that, Tasia started along the worn path between tents.

Raene slipped her hands into her pockets and fell in step beside her. "How did it happen for you? Did you know the Franes wanted to trade for you?" If anyone knew how it felt to be in Raene's place, it was surely Tasia.

And after she'd taken the time to help Raene freshen up—as limited as it had been—Raene found she didn't dislike the woman as much as she had initially. Raene hung on her every word.

Tasia's laughter rang between the tents and trees. "The Franes aren't the wealthiest clan, but they have three bear sons. Every clan in the Alderwood has offered to trade a daughter at one point or another. When Lathan came of age, he had two dozen offers. The Ape Clan offered all three of their daughters. The Raccoon Clan to the north offered a daughter and enough alders to fund the camp for a decade. Even a pair of Hydra clans offered daughters for trade."

Raene's eyebrows shot up at the extensive list. She'd known bears were valuable in the Alderwood—Blossom had told her as much—but Raene would never have guessed there was so much competition for one.

"That's impressive," Raene admitted, "that Lathan picked you out of so many offers."

"Oh, he didn't. It was Da. They were pretty close to making a trade with the Fox Clan to the south, but when my father offered me, Da accepted. No one really knows why." She pointed to the next tent, a small one with some sort of horned deer over the flap. "That's Asla Brimmen's tent. He only recently came of age and earned his own. He'll get a larger tent when he takes a wife."

"Do I get my own tent?" Raene asked, but she already knew the answer.

"Technically, yes. You're a woman of age. But you have to abide by the restrictions of the arrangement. You can stay with me and Lathan until you make your choice. Lathan said you have a month, so there's no rush." Tasia waved it off, as if a couple weeks was some interminable length of time. But Raene felt the opposite; the deadline for her decision loomed over her, pressing down more desperately than the ever-present alder trees.

Tasia and Raene continued around the camp as Tasia pointed to tents and named people Raene didn't know. Each person gawked at her like she was a new babe. They studied her hair, her clothes, her skin, her height. "Why are they looking at me like that?" Raene dared to ask Tasia.

"Aside from your uncle, they've never seen a Pyro. And you're—your clothes are, shall we say, *unorthodox*?" Tasia smiled to show she didn't mean offense.

Raene was glad for the honesty. And she was curious about them, too. They all had the same walnut-brown hair and eyes the color of chocolate or hazel. Their skin was milky white, a stark contrast to Raene's bronzed complexion. She marveled at how similar they all looked to one another, yet so different from her.

Minutes into Tasia's tour, they passed a small tent lacking a totem. When Raene paused, Tasia named it as Blossom's tent. No one had the heart to take it down.

Just the sight of it made her chest ache. Raene fought to breathe as they hurried past, but it only got worse from there. After yet another dozen tents of strangers, Raene found a face she knew.

The man she'd only seen for a few seconds in Da's tent.

Parson Frane.

The son who ran from her.

He stood tall in front of his tent—larger than most and marked with his bear totem—with his hands in his pockets and his gaze focused on the trees on the far side of the clearing.

"Ah, there you are," Tasia teased him as she stopped in front of him. "Raene, I don't believe you got the chance to meet Parson, second son of the Bear Clan. Parson, I'm sure you're delighted to meet Raene Randal."

"Delighted," Parson repeated, his voice cold and monotone. If Raene had to guess, she'd think someone put him up to it. Probably Lathan.

Tasia was having too much fun. She couldn't even manage to conceal her smile as she said, "Parson here is the best dancer in the clan—in any clan, it's said. Perhaps you'll be lucky enough to earn a dance with him at the celebration tonight."

Parson only flared his nostrils and continued staring at the trees. Waves of anger rolled off him hard enough to force Raene to take a step back.

But Tasia would have none of it. She cupped Raene's elbow and pushed her in front of Parson, despite his refusal to look at her. If she hadn't seen his emerald eyes in Da's tent, she'd have no idea what color they were. He was determined to stay away from her, only she didn't know why. Her thoughts raced with self-conscious doubt. Was her hair a mess? Was her face too plain? Was her skin too dark?

She hated that he had unnerved her so completely in only seconds.

Raene could think of no better revenge than to show him up with her elegance. While Parson pouted over whatever unnamed crime she'd committed, Raene clutched the side of her wide-legged pants and bowed low as she said, "An honor to meet you, Master Parson."

When Raene righted, his eyes were on her at last, narrowed and indignant. His lip curled into something like a snarl just before Tasia burst into laugher and said, "See you tonight!" as she quickly led Raene away.

"What is so funny?" Raene complained when they were well away from him and Tasia continued to laugh.

"That look on his face. Did you see it?" she asked through more chuckles.

"Uh, yes. I did. It looks like he hates me." Raene sulked, a rare show of displeasure from her. Just the idea that she wasn't in control of her emotions made her angry, and she sulked more. Raene massaged the lines from her face as she waited for Tasia to regain her composure.

At last, Tasia sobered, but the smile never left her

features. "He's always in a foul mood. Don't take it personally."

"Excellent. I'll be sure to remember that next time." At the moment, she was most certainly taking it personally.

"Come on," Tasia said when Raene remained locked in her pout. "Only a little ways more. Then we can head back to the celebration. They should be getting started soon." She wiggled her eyebrows and beamed. "The Franes are far more fun when they've had a few drinks."

Raene rolled her eyes and followed along, wondering if the Franes could possibly be any *less* fun. She didn't want to dance or talk or celebrate. She wanted to crawl into a hole and disappear.

After all her years of training, Raene didn't have it in her to pretend to be happy.

Not today.

When Eton said he was going to make her Aero, Blossom hadn't quite grasped the misery he intended for her. She'd already been subjected to signing upwards of fifty documents related to her new duties, and a tour of the political offices, though none of the other Vice Syndicates were present.

Now, she stood on a raised platform getting fitted for her new clothes. It was hardly her ideal way to spend the day.

Blossom had never been good at standing still or staying put. She had no interest in frilly dresses or sequined gowns. Her skin didn't delight at luxurious fabrics.

Her interests were far simpler. She would always prefer being outside in the sunlight, the earth under her feet.

Blossom felt like a wine bottle turned upside-down. Everything that had once made her full was now gone. All that remained was a fragile shell.

Waiting for the tailor to finish his measurements, Blossom wondered if there was anything she was less suited for. Presently, nothing came to mind. She hated standing for so long. She hated being so cold. And she hated being so naked.

A mirror covered the opposing wall, showing Blossom her own figure in all its bareness. Weeks ago, she would have shied from such a sight, but now, it didn't seem to matter. Blossom just wanted to be done standing like a spectacle.

But if letting this shaking old man fit her for those dreadful white suits meant she could see Kaide, even for a moment, then she would do it one hundred times over.

She could think of nothing but him. What he was doing. What he was thinking. How he would react when he found out where she'd gone. No one mentioned him, and Eton pretended he didn't know, but Blossom felt Kaide like the undercurrent of a river—never visible, never on the surface, but always pulling at her thoughts. Every conversation, every new experience, was filtered through the lens of Kaide and what he would think of it.

Every time she closed her eyes, she imagined he was there with her, but of course, as soon as she opened them, he never was.

Instead, there was only the ancient man and her trusty advisor.

Eton hovered like a hawk in the corner, watching her, making sure she didn't try to leave—not that she could. Yet his gaze was always on her, unashamed to see her so bare.

"What torture do you have planned for me next?" she asked Eton's reflection.

Eton glared back. "We've been over this. Just stand still, and let him finish."

Blossom sighed her annoyance and pressed her eyes

shut, trying to pretend it was Paloma making her a gown to show to Kaide. That it was Raene standing beside her, filling her ear with stories of the past and questions of the future. That she was merely in the washroom with Norsa and Valenta.

"All finished," the old man said, interrupting her thoughts. He took three steps back and bowed low as he continued. "We'll have your suits sewn and pressed by tomorrow, Vice Syndicate Frane."

Blossom was sure she'd never get used to the sound of her new title. *Vice Syndicate Frane.*

She hopped down from the stand and rushed to gather her clothes piled in a nearby chair, desperate for what little bit of warmth they would provide. With speed and deftness, she pulled her Pyro pants up to her waist and tied them before slipping her scarlet top over her shoulders. Within seconds, she was covered and out the door, eager to be moving again.

As always, Eton fell in step behind her. "It's appropriate to say *thank you.* Even Pyros have manners."

Blossom didn't miss how he referred to her as Pyro. "I'm not wearing *that,*" she said, her lip curled up at his crisp, white suit.

"Well, you can't wear Pyro clothes here. Dressing Aero is the least of your concerns."

"Good, then no one will care if I don't—"

"Yes, they will. It'll only serve to piss her off." He didn't need to mention the Syndicate by name to fill Blossom with burning disgust.

Eton ran a hand through the strip of hair along the top of his head. He marched forward, gaining several steps on her before turning back to face her. "Don't you get it? I'm your *advisor.* I'm trying to *help* you."

Blossom stood taken aback at his sudden display of anger.

"Quit fighting this stuff. *This* is the stupid stuff. Fight when it's worth it. I'll tell you when fighting will make a difference. But this? Wearing a different color shirt? *That's* what you're bent out of shape about?"

Eton looked like he could have gone on for a while, but a pair of Aeros appeared at the end of the corridor and turned toward them. For several long moments, Eton and Blossom stood frozen, waiting for them to pass. When they'd finally turned the far corner, he resumed, "I get it. This is new. But you have an important position here, and it requires you have more decorum than this."

"I don't want the position. I want to—"

"Go home," he finished for her. "I know. But you can't. If you're not going to accept the role of Vice Syndicate, say the word and I'll take you to the Criminal Unit for processing. But if you are, then do it. Don't do this halfway nonsense. Do it all the way, or don't. But make your choice."

Blossom crossed her arms over her chest and glared her frustrations at him. "That's not much of a choice."

As Eton shook his head, he pressed his mouth into a line, his lip piercing flaring with the motion. "No, it's not. But it's the best you have. So put on a brave face, and get it done. I saw you with the Syndicate, telling her what she wanted to hear. You can turn it on and off. You can play this game."

Blossom started to argue but caught herself. She didn't know what had marked this change in her advisor, but she knew Eton wasn't her enemy here. He was only a pawn. And he was right. Her energies would be better spent on things that mattered.

Things like getting back to Kaide.

Blossom closed her eyes. *You'll have to pretend to be someone else sometimes,* Kaide whispered in her ear. *You'll have to be nice to people you hate, and you'll have to wear clothes you don't like and say things you don't mean, because being with me means looking and acting a part, even if that part isn't you.*

When she opened her eyes, only Eton was there with her. Blossom sighed, knowing what she had to do. "All right. I'll put on a brave face."

Eton returned to his stoic calmness. "Good. We're almost done for today. Can you hold out for one more stop?"

Blossom relinquished her fight with a terse, "Fine." A second later, she darted back down the hall in the direction they'd come. There in the room, the ancient tailor stood before a dress form with an armful of the shimmering-white fabric every Aero wore. "Excuse me, sir?" she called from the doorway

The man turned with the speed of sloth, rotating until his pale eyes found her in the doorway.

"I'm sorry to bother you. I wanted to say thank you for your patience. I look forward to seeing the suits tomorrow." With all the respect she could manage, Blossom bowed to the tailor.

The man nodded with reverence. "The honor is mine, Vice Syndicate Frane."

After that, it was easier to follow Eton down the corridor to wherever they were going. She was sure he'd told her a half-dozen times already, but she hadn't bothered to remember.

Blossom told herself no matter whatever they were doing, she would do it with grace—well, maybe not *grace*, but at least she wouldn't be so difficult. Kaide had asked her to pretend, and she'd promised him she could do it.

And so she would. She would pretend to be Aero as long as it took for her to get out.

Blossom didn't argue as they passed block after block of shops and stores, various facilities with symbols on the doors and others that were blank. Birds and people shopped and strolled, always with their white suits and platinum hair. Only Blossom stood out in her Pyro clothes and Terra complexion.

"Why aren't there people from other branches?" In Pyrona, she'd seen Hydras and Terras—not many, but a few—while here in Aerona, it was a sea of white and pale blue.

Eton tilted his head as he thought of how to explain it. After a long, considerate pause, he said, "Aero is different than the other branches. We value investigation and discovery through science and research, rather than devotion to the Alder Mother. Non-Aeros don't live here because it compromises their beliefs."

"And Aeros don't leave because you like all your fancy gadgets." Blossom said it as fact. She knew Eton would never survive in the Bear Clan. Living in an open air tent on the ground? He'd beg for an air circulation system the first night.

Eton bit his lip in an obvious attempt to hide a smile. "Something like that," he admitted.

At last, they arrived at some sort of salon. Blossom saw the space and remembered where they'd been headed all along: to get her head shaved.

A middle-aged woman motioned to a chair in the center of the room. She was tall and thin, save for the soft belly her children had left behind. Her skin was light, and, where it wasn't shaved, her blonde hair had a honey warmth. She wasn't always Aero, Blossom realized.

When Blossom was seated, the woman put both hands on her shoulders. "What code?"

"Code?" Blossom looked to Eton for an explanation.

Instead of answering her, he spoke only to the woman. "Transfer. Falcon. Unmarried."

Based on the way the woman spurred into motion,

Blossom guessed she knew what that meant, but Blossom was lost.

Eton appeared before her and leaned against the wall, his hands resting casually in his pockets. "The skull patterns convey basic information about each Aero."

Behind her, the woman gripped Blossom's head and tilted it so the left side of her head was exposed. Then, out of the corner of her eye, Blossom saw a long blade in the woman's hand—the kind Hale used to shave his face baby smooth.

Blossom swallowed hard but otherwise kept perfectly still.

"Your left side will be bare. That marks you as a transfer from another branch," Eton continued. As he spoke, the blade scraped across her scalp. Hair rained down her shoulder, and a few pieces slipped into her lap. Blossom couldn't help but pick up a lost curl and hold it in front of her.

There was no going back now.

"The center line is for Aero," Eton said and pointed to his own narrow stripe. "It signifies devotion to branch and Syndicate, which is why every Aero wears it."

With each passing moment, the woman scraped off more of Blossom's curls, sending them onto her shoulder or into her lap. Her hands filled with the cast-off bits.

"On the right, you'll have two spikes shaved above your ear. These are for aerial totems."

"All Aeros have aerial totems," she reminded him.

"Not all of us. Some totems are flightless—penguins, ostriches, rheas—that sort of thing. Others are aerial, but aren't birds. There's a large butterfly clan on the west side. There's a small, but notable, population of Arctic totems. Bears and foxes mostly. And then there's Bat Clan, of course. Each category has its own marks. Since you're a falcon, you get two spikes."

Sure enough, the woman tilted Blossom's head the other way. There, she scraped at her head in slow, careful strokes, her eyes narrow in concentration.

"And what do I get for being not being married?" Blossom wasn't sure she wanted to know the answer.

"Caught that?" Eton half-smiled before he recovered. "You don't get anything. When you take a husband, you'll wear his mark, whatever that might be."

Blossom imagined asking Kaide what kind of stripes he'd like shaved into her head when they were married, and for a brief moment, it brought a smile to her lips. But of course, it faded a moment later. She couldn't marry him— not anymore. And even if she could, she knew he wouldn't have her. She was Aero now.

She was everything he hated.

A sharp pain above her ear pulled her thoughts back to the present. "I'm terribly sorry, Vice Syndicate Frane," the woman started. "I didn't expect you to move—"

Eton jumped to his feet and pulled a white cloth from his pocket. In a second, he was in front of her, pressing it to her head, and when he pulled it away, there was a tiny smear of fresh blood.

"I'm so sorry, Advisor Samina. I've never cut anyone before—" The woman's voice turned frantic as she tried to explain it away, but Eton stopped her soon enough.

"You don't have to apologize. We won't say a word." Then, he looked to Blossom. "Are you all right?" he asked her quietly, his eyes intent on hers.

"I'm fine. It's just a cut." Not even Hale would have fussed so much over so little an injury.

"I mean—you looked like you were going to faint. You stopped talking, and your head fell against the blade."

"You were talking to me about the skull patterns. I remember."

Eton shook his head. "No, I was discussing the

Syndicate's requirements for taking a husband. The time frame. The suitor requirements. Do you remember that?"

"No," she admitted.

Eton pulled back the cloth and took note of the tiny pricks of blood that remained. "Will you be all right to let her finish?"

"I'm fine." Blossom settled back in her chair bristling with humiliation. She hadn't meant to get lost in her head. Even when he wasn't with her, Kaide was a distraction.

Blossom did her best to stay focused and still as the woman finished the second spike. Then, the woman smeared some sort of cool liquid into her hair, starting at the tips and working up through the roots until her scalp burned from the cold.

"Does it hurt?" Eton asked when she winced.

Blossom didn't answer, instead focusing on her breathing and outlasting whatever it was on her head. Like the serum for transformation, it burned without heat, searing her flesh as she sat, trapped in agony. She bit her cheek to keep from screaming.

"Get it off," he demanded, his tone suddenly distraught.

"Less than a minute left," the woman argued.

"I said, get it off. You're going to give her scars. Rinse it out *now*."

A second later, Blossom's shoulders were pulled back, and her head was dipped into a bowl of warm water. The burning sensation subsided as soon as the water touched her head.

For several minutes, the Aero woman worked to clean the cool liquid from her hair and then dry it. Only when the woman was finished did Blossom realize what happened.

Her hair hung well past her shoulders. It was still a warm, chestnut brown, but it held not even a hint of its natural curl. Her hair was perfectly straight like she'd never seen it. She looked to Eton for an explanation, though she already knew it was too late.

"Aeros prefer straight, clean lines." He made it sound so easy. Like it was nothing to give up her curls.

But it wasn't nothing. Blossom didn't realize how much she'd loved her curls, that little silent rebellion, until they were gone.

"That's all for today. Ready to go home?" Eton held out a hand to help her from the chair, but Blossom pushed up on her own. She thanked the woman and started back toward her apartment, though it was anything but home.

When they were alone in the hallway, Blossom said, "I don't want to be surprised like that again. If something is going to happen to me, I want you to tell me. Even if I don't like it."

"That's fair," Eton replied. A moment later he added, "At least I let you keep the color."

Blossom's mouth fell open. "You would dye my hair? Like yours?" She tried to reel in her disgust. Ghost-white hair? For Blossom? It would look hideous, she was sure.

Eton rolled his eyes. "It's not that bad. Most Aeros prefer this coloring. The lighter the skin and hair, the purer the bloodline. For the transfers who can afford it, lighter hair reduces discrimination against them. Your position ensures your fair treatment, but you have the option to go lighter at any time."

As Eton held open the door to the lava tube and ushered her down the corridor, Blossom tried to think of what her Aero experience would be like without her title. She wouldn't be a target for Mercer or anyone else, but she would have to navigate this new life—her clothes, her apartment, her hair—without Eton's assistance, and as unfriendly as it was, she had to admit that he made the transition less difficult than what it could have been.

For a brief moment, Blossom was thankful to have his

guidance, though that didn't quiet her distrust toward her advisor. During her transformation, Eton altered her totem, the most grievous of crimes. Not only had he robbed Blossom of her life with Kaide in Pyrona, he'd eliminated her only chance of finding out her real totem.

So no matter what Eton did to help her now, it couldn't wash away her hatred of what he'd already done. Someday, there would come a time Blossom no longer needed Eton, when their futures were no longer entwined. Then, Blossom would cut him from her life.

Until then, she was stuck at his side, following his lead through Aerona's frozen tunnels.

As always, birds sailed overhead, but now there were less. It must be close to nightfall, she decided, though without view of the sun, she'd never really know.

Blossom despised watching them fly when she was confined to her human form. Out of reflex, her hand fell to the metal cuff. How long would she have to pretend before she could be free again?

Thoughts ricocheted through her mind like echoes in the cavern. She hated that she was still so far from Kaide, that she couldn't tell him where she was. She hated that he'd been right, that her totem had been altered, and she never should have gone to transformation that day.

And she hated that he would hate her for this. Blossom had no doubt her new status within the Aero branch was all it would take to earn the full extent of his fury.

Blossom had nowhere else to go. She had no one left. As much as she hated this new life in Aero, it was the only one she had.

So she'd have to pretend to be Aero until she meant it, or until she saw Kaide again. She knew she'd see him eventually, that much was sure. They were both Vice Syndicates. At the very least, he'd be at the Summer Ceremony in a few months. In the meantime, she could only bide her time and wait.

Blossom filed into the elevator with Eton and relished the idea of being done for the day. Already, she felt like a boat adrift on a wide sea, spinning with no hope of finding land again.

Only a few more minutes.

Except they were intercepted.

"Is this her?" squealed a small voice as soon as the elevator doors opened. Blossom was rushed by a tiny girl in a snowy cloak. Her hair and skin were perfectly white, and her eyes were the lightest blue Blossom had ever seen. And despite how she stood a half-head shorter than Blossom, there was no doubt she was a stunning beauty.

"You're the Vice Syndicate Frane, aren't you?" the girl fussed. A moment later, her hands were on the ends of Blossom's newly straightened hair. "Such gorgeous color. I'm insanely envious."

"Thank you—" Blossom started, until she remembered she had no idea who this girl was.

"My apologies. I'm Yveline Dodd," she replied with a low bow.

Blossom wondered if she was supposed to know the name and looked to Eton for help.

"Vice Syndicate Frane, this is the Vice Syndicate Apprentice Yveline Dodd." Eton, too, bowed low in respect.

"Oh! You're the third Vice Syndicate." Blossom had met the first, Crin Peppers, at the Spring Ceremony, though she'd done little more than shake the woman's hand before Kaide whisked her off to mingle with the next person.

But this Yveline Dodd was new to her.

"I'm an Apprentice," Yveline corrected. "I'll earn my full Vice Syndicate title upon transformation. Only two more years," she said, an annoyed smile playing at her lips as if it were a question she was asked too often. "I was just headed down to my sitting room for some tea. I'd be very grateful if you'd join me." The sprightly young girl smiled up at Blossom.

Blossom smiled back. "Thank you, Vice Syndicate Apprentice Dodd," she replied, careful to annunciate the mouthful of a title. "But I'm afraid I won't be much company today. Let's plan another time in the future. I'm sure there's a lot you can teach me about life in Aerona." Blossom bowed her head in respect.

"That would be lovely. I'll have Adviser Herson make the arrangements." She motioned to the Aero man behind her.

After the usual parting pleasantries, Blossom and Eton were free to continue on to her chambers. It was still a boring white cavern with too-shiny furnishings, but at least she didn't have to pretend anymore. No sooner were the doors shut than Blossom collapsed on the nearest rug and threw her arms out wide.

With her eyes closed, Blossom listened to Eton's footsteps move toward his room and the door shut behind him. At last, she was alone. In the quiet of her Aero apartment, surrounded by Aero furniture and dressed in Aero finery, Blossom lay on the plush rug and remembered the Pyro girl she used to be.

PUNISHMENT

DEEP IN THE POCKET of his honey-brown pants, Hale fingered his alder wood coin. Over and over again he'd asked the Sacred Mother for her wisdom and guidance, and she'd never led him astray.

But as he watched the Pyro girl sit at the central fire pit, Hale couldn't help but wonder if the Mother wasn't playing some kind of trick on him.

A beautiful girl with a strong totem had arrived in the Bear Clan. His first question to the Mother had been, of course, who she would marry. When he flipped his coin to learn her answer, it had shown his bear.

Raene would be his wife, by the will of the Mother.

The other pieces fell into place easily enough. Da had always reserved Hale for a leadership role while he sent Lathan and Parson to the cut for physical work. They all knew Hale would be clan leader one day, and with a tiger for a bride, there would be no doubt.

The Bear Clan would become the Tiger Clan as their children grew. They'd be the strongest Terra clan in the Alderwood.

Hale would have fortune and family and purpose. Surely, the Mother didn't mean to give him *all* her gifts.

Then again, only Hale offered his full devotion to the

sacred tree. Lathan worshiped silently and Parson not at all. Who should receive the Mother's bounty if not Hale?

So even though the idea of talking to—much less marrying—such a beautiful young woman filled him with utter panic, his confidence in the Mother's course allowed him to push it aside.

Hale squeezed the coin tight in his palm for one last moment before he summoned up the courage to leave the shadows and claim the seat beside her.

Raene's stunning sapphire eyes acknowledged him for only a moment before she returned to watching the flames eagerly lapping at the sky. If it hadn't been for that brief moment, he might have thought she hadn't noticed his arrival.

Hale allowed himself only a handful of seconds to admire her handsome features—the lovely light yellow of her hair, the way the amber glow danced across her exotic brown skin. "I hope you know we're all very glad to have you here," he began, not sure what he would say next but elated he'd managed to get the words out in the first place.

"Thank you," she replied with a wan smile. An automatic response, he suspected.

"Have you had anything to eat?" When she shook her head, Hale offered, "There's some bread from Hydra, corn-based and sweetened with honey. Would you like to try it?"

Again, that smile. "Yes, thank you."

Hale pushed up and breathed easier as he put distance between them. Damn, she made him nervous. From the baskets of food, Hale made her a plate—two bits of bread and a handful of summer berries—all the while wondering what to say to her.

Then, he remembered he didn't need to be nervous. The Alder Mother intended for them to be together, and there was nothing Hale could do to thwart her plan.

When Hale returned to Raene's side, he felt the

rightness of it. He handed her the plate and smiled to show her he wasn't afraid.

"I'm sure it's nothing compared to the finery you're used to. In a few minutes, we'll have music, once Thersa and Fornen have eaten. And Cresta will bring us some amberwine. The Mother knows Da likes to throw a party." He didn't mention Da would celebrate a cloud in the sky if they'd let him get away with it. But this celebration was for Raene, his future wife, and he wouldn't spoil it for her. "And happy birthday," Hale added.

But she didn't say anything in reply. Instead, she stared at the fire with glassy eyes, mindlessly munching a bite of bread.

"We have a convoy headed to trade with Hydra this week. We'll get a fresh supply of grains and spices." Again, she only stared ahead, like she hadn't heard him.

Hale understood the Mother's intention well enough.

Raene would need time. She'd only been in camp for a few hours, and she thought she had a choice to make. Hale would have to wait until Parson and Raene were no longer an option.

Hale offered her a quiet 'goodnight' before slipping back to his tent.

He was just going to have to bide his time.

Parson leaned against an alder tree and watched the clan celebrate the arrival of their new daughter. From such a distance, he couldn't make out individual faces, but their general excitement was clear.

The large fire of the central pit illuminated the entire area against the dark, early evening sky. Parson had run to his heart's content, and when he thought he was in better control of himself, he'd come back. He hadn't expected

Tasia to bring her to his tent only minutes after returning.

He hadn't expected a celebration.

The wine flowed. The music played. And no one remembered Blossom was gone.

Their apathy disgusted him.

They celebrated the arrival of this Pyro girl like she could replace his sister.

Parson thrust his hands into his pant pockets and sulked. The merriment of his clan only furthered his resentment. He couldn't pretend he wasn't still angry. He *wouldn't* pretend.

"Are you going to hide out here and pout all night?"

Parson looked over to discover his oldest brother hiding in the shadows. "How'd you know I was here?"

"There's music playing. I thought you'd be back hours ago. Never known you to miss a chance to show off." Lathan stepped beside Parson and put his hands in his pockets. For a while, the two brothers stood watching their clan silhouetted against the flames.

Couples danced, and others chatted while some ate. Somewhere in the crowd was the Pyro girl, but it was impossible to see her from so far away. Parson was glad he couldn't make her out in the group.

"You know Da set this up for you."

Parson rolled his eyes and allowed himself to chuckle at such nonsense. The last thing he needed from Da was a pretty, pampered princess from a rival branch. He wanted nothing to do with such a dainty girl.

"You're the oldest unmarried son. You're twenty-five. Twenty-six in a few months. The contract gives her the choice, but Da arranged this for you," Lathan continued, though he must have known Parson wanted to hear none of it.

Parson spun the pair of rings on his index finger. It had been so long since he'd worn the third, he couldn't even remember the weight of it anymore. Out of all the rings he wore, it was the one he didn't have that bothered him most.

After Da turned refused to make a reasonable offer for the only girl he'd ever asked for, Parson lost interest in the prospect of marriage in general. He'd received offers from nearly every Terra clan over the last seven years, but after he was denied Darsa's hand, Parson flatly rejected each and every one.

If Da meant to rectify his mistakes, the Pyro girl was the worst possible attempt. Every sight of her was a reminder Blossom was gone.

"You can go back." Parson tilted his head toward Lathan's tent. "I'm sure Tasia wants you home by now."

"I'm sure she does, but I'd feel better if I saw you home first."

"What?" Parson shot him a horrified glare but was sure it was lost in the dark. "Go mind your new pet. *I* don't need you to watch me." Disgusted he had to say such words, he spat on the ground in front of him.

Lathan shook his head like he'd received bad news. "You've been reckless. You're not focused. I know—"

"You don't know anything!" Parson screamed.

With that, he marched away, distancing himself from the happy clan and the brother who thought he needed supervision. It wasn't his fault this trade had been made. If left up to him, he would have killed the Pyro politician and removed the problem entirely.

Instead, he had to watch his clan dance and drink to welcome a new daughter to replace the one that was gone.

Parson was the only sane person in camp. The rest of them had lost it.

Refusing to return so soon, Parson took the long way home. He let the night winds quiet his anger, if only a little, before he made his way back to his tent.

With the flap closed, it was perfectly dark, just as he

liked. Parson collapsed onto the pile of sheets with a heavy flop, but no sooner was he spread across the tent floor than Fig appeared. His ferret feet climbed up Parson's side, tickling his ribs, before the fidgety pet settled down along the midline of his chest.

Parson stroked Fig's soft fur carefully, always weary of hurting such a small creature. Fig had been Blossom's, raised since he was a little hairless thing she found in the woods. One of the dozens she'd collected over the years.

She got that from their mother.

Parson had been only eight years old when he pushed his ear to his mother's swollen belly and felt the kicks of the baby inside. He'd marveled at the whole affair—that his mother could get so big, that a real baby could be in there, that he would have a new sister. Ma had always known Blossom was different.

"You'll love her more than anyone," she'd said.

"Not more than you." Parson beamed, his beautiful mother glowing as she sat in the candlelight in their family tent.

But Ma had only laughed, running her hands through his hair. "Love always grows—like the sacred alders always growing larger. When one dies, a bigger one takes its place."

She'd always been in love with the trees, always honoring the sacred alders. She was a true believer if he ever saw one. And when she'd told him love was like an alder, Parson didn't believe her. Even as a boy, he dismissed it as romantic nonsense.

But then she died. In the span of a week, Parson lost his mother and gained a sister. They named her after the most beautiful part of the trees their mother so loved.

Parson was angry then. For a long time, he couldn't understand it. Lathan was old enough to cope, and Hale was too young to fully grasp it, but Parson was lost. He knew his mother was gone, but he couldn't figure out why.

The obvious answer was Blossom. He tried his best to hate her, but it was impossible. The little girl who looked so much like their mother, with her chestnut curls and freckled cheeks. She had that fire and passion and energy. Of all the Franes, Blossom never fussed at him to relax or quiet his totem. Only once had she intervened when he and Lathan fought, but even then, she'd only stood between them. She'd always been brave that way.

Parson loved her more than anyone, as his mother had said he would.

But now she was gone, and some Pyro girl had come to take her place.

With celebratory music filling his tent, Parson continued stroking the soft fur of the ferret on his chest, but he couldn't get his pulse to quiet.

Something inside him was broken.

Raene couldn't sleep that first night, or the next, or any night that first week.

Curled into a tiny ball in Lathan's tent, Raene knew for certain she was being punished. Nights in the Alderwood were miserably cold. Raene refused to give up the comforting familiarity of her Pyro clothes—her right as a Pyro—but she was left shivering on a thin pallet.

When Raene asked Tasia for an extra blanket, she was rewarded with yet another disapproving speech about the length of her sleep clothes. Apparently, black shorts and a slender top didn't qualify as appropriate sleep wear for the future wife of a Frane son.

On the second night, Tasia set up a cotton partition. It separated the tent into two sides so Raene could keep her immodest self on one side while the more conservative

Tasia and Lathan shared the other. Raene tried not to let it get to her. She tried to think of it as an amenity, an unexpected privilege of privacy, but it burned her up inside.

And the Alderwood was surprisingly loud at night. Or maybe it was her newly sensitive tiger ears. Either way, Raene was kept awake by the sounds of alder branches swaying in the breeze, the animals scurrying in the greenery, and the sweet whispers between Tasia and Lathan even after they finished their infuriating prayers. It was enough to make her go mad. Trapped in a tent with a couple so obviously in love—that was her real punishment. She'd taken Kaide's chance at happiness with Blossom, and now she was subjected to Lathan's quiet laugh, Tasia's hands roaming through his thick beard, and the two sleeping curled together night after night.

What Raene wouldn't give for a night back in the manor. She would even settle for the wine-filled stink of her father's home.

Maybe there she'd be able to sleep.

Or maybe her totem was enough to keep her awake all on its own. With each passing day and each sleepless night, anxiety filled her like a flagon. Her hands shook from more than the cold. Her legs were restless to run. Her mouth watered for more blood.

Except for the brief outings to answer nature's call— holding the small, humiliating shovel—Raene declined to leave the tent. She refused to be the cause of bloodshed. She couldn't risk losing control and harming someone again.

So Raene remained in hiding, both from the clan and her totem, and that was fine with her.

Others didn't seem to agree.

After Lathan and Tasia said their morning prayers, Lathan left for the work day. Tasia and Raene remained inside alone until someone joined them.

"Ms. Randal?" a voice called from outside the tent.

Raene nearly choked on the fruit in her mouth as Tasia answered, "Come in, Hale."

Before Raene had fully swallowed, Hale pushed in and stood just inside the flap. Beams of morning light illuminated the tent. Raene and her host each sat on a moss-green pillow, munching on bits of fruit—their usual morning fare—and staring up at their unexpected guest.

"Good morning, Tasia," Hale said with a nod. "Ms. Randal," he continued. "I thought I might offer you a tour of the cut."

"What did Da say about it?" Tasia replied for her.

"It's not his decision." Hale's chestnut hair fell into his eyes, giving him an ominous sort of look, but he didn't push it back. Instead, he only stood tall and waited for Tasia's argument.

Raene felt the tension in the tent rise like morning steam off a volcano. She had no idea what they were talking about, but the disagreement was clear. She promptly shoved another bit of too-sweet fruit in her mouth. It wasn't what she wanted—not even close—but juicy bites of apples and peaches were all Lathan and Tasia offered her. Still, at least she didn't have to figure out what to say to him with her mouth full.

"He might have reservations," Tasia continued.

"*He* may, but *I* don't. It's the Mother's will. If I wanted to argue, I would have gone to Parson." Hale shot her a silencing look, and that appeared to be the end of it. He turned his attention back to Raene and reached out a hand. "Would you like to see the cut?"

Raene looked back and forth between Hale and Tasia for several seconds before Tasia finally nodded. "Go on. But if Da finds out, I had nothing to do with it." She shook her head with an amused smile.

But Raene didn't want to go. She didn't want to leave

the temporary safety of Lathan's tent. She didn't want to risk losing control again.

Not that she could tell him that.

All at once, Raene realized she would be alone with Hale Frane, the youngest son of the Bear Clan and her potential future husband. She had a month to decide and she'd foolishly wasted an entire week with her sulking. Her whole body seemed to hum with nerves and excitement and consuming, gut-wrenching fear.

What if he didn't find her suitable? What if she was simply too different from Terra girls? What if she didn't like him? It probably didn't help that the only time he'd ever spoken to her, she'd been too in shock to even converse properly.

Sitting on the floor of Lathan's tent and eating breakfast with his wife seemed so much safer than going anywhere with Hale. For several seconds, Raene sat in stunned silence, her cheek full of fruit she couldn't remember to swallow down.

"Ms. Randal?" Hale prompted.

Only then was Raene spurred into action. She set down her half-full plate of fruit and let Hale help her to her feet. Standing before him, she was reminded he wasn't quite as tall as her.

Raene nodded respectfully with the force of habit. "Thank you, Master Frane."

"Please, it's just Hale." His face lit with a pleasant smile.

When they were outside and moving, Raene asked, "So where are we going, exactly?" Out in the open, it was easier to breath. She hadn't realized how smothered she felt until she had space to move again.

Walking beside her with a full step between them, Hale answered, "To the cut."

"What is that?" Raene was desperate to keep talking,

to prevent some sort of horrible awkward silence. If she asked him endless questions, he'd keep talking, and she wouldn't have a chance to think of how much she hated the whole situation.

Hale offered her a sweet smile and oozed a calmness she couldn't begin to fathom. "The Bear Clan is best known for its bears, but we've made another mark on the world. We harvest alder trees throughout the Alderwood and sell the lumber. The cut is the site of our current tree in process."

"And you do that as well? You cut down alder trees?" Away from camp, and with only the sacred trees to keep them company, there was no escaping his presence.

"No, not usually. I work with Da managing the clan and finding our next site. Lathan and Parson manage the cut." Hale rubbed his hands together for a moment before he stopped short and turned to face her.

Raene's pulse fluttered at the base of her throat, pounding so hard she couldn't make a sound. She twisted her hands together in hopes of staying her transformation. She was so close to the edge.

Hale sighed and said, "I am sorry about Parson's behavior. He doesn't take loss well. It should be him that shows you the cut."

"I don't mind. I don't think he likes me very much." It was all Raene could think to say.

"It's not that he doesn't like you. He just doesn't handle change very well. He'll warm up to you eventually." When Raene didn't respond, Hale continued toward the cut.

As she'd dreaded, a silence grew between them. Raene didn't know what to say, what to ask him. She didn't want to talk about Pyrona or Kaide or Blossom. She didn't want to know why Parson hated her or why Hale had asked her out here today.

So instead, she kept her gaze on the surrounding

forest. The alder trees loomed high above, and her tiger ears caught more sounds than her human ears ever could. Small mammals clung to the branches high above—squirrels and birds and the like. In the distance, some sort of hooved creatures made their way to the east. Frogs drummed and crickets sang.

And Raene could only think of how each one would taste—how easy it would be to race through the forest on her tiger paws and crush an animal in her jaw.

They walked for only a few more minutes before she caught sight of sunlight streaming to the forest floor ahead. The sounds of axes and men yelling filled the air, growing louder as they neared. At last, when they were close enough, Raene saw a dozen men working at the base of a fallen alder tree.

"Welcome to the cut," Hale offered with a proud smile.

Raene gazed at the clearing in awe. Never had she seen such a massive tree on its side. The trunk alone was tall enough to hide the manor behind, and it stretched so far ahead she couldn't see more than a tangle of branches at the other end. Men worked at the closest end to remove the roots, stripping them off with large saws that took three men on each side. The warm-honey wood shone where several roots had already been removed.

Rather than the ashy-grey of the cut trees they had passed at the edge of the Alderwood, this tree retained its warm-honey color. "It was still alive when it was cut down," Raene said, the realization striking her like a stone.

"Yes, ours is a highly illegal operation, but it offers the best wood and the highest prices at market." His eyes studied her features, searching for her reaction, but Raene declined to give any.

Hale and Raene walked along the length of the trunk, watching the men work and marveling at the process.

Everyone moved together, shouting commands that made no sense to her, but they seemed to know exactly what they were doing.

"What do you think?" Hale asked when the first branches were within view.

Raene shrugged and smiled. "I'm a little relieved."

"Relieved?"

"I thought Terras were quite religious. I was preparing myself for a life of devotion to a tree I don't believe in. But seeing as how you're illegally cutting them down, I'm guessing that won't be the case." Raene looked up at the youngest Frane brother and found her answer written across his face.

She had been so, so wrong.

"I'm sorry, I thought—"

Hale straightened and shook his head. "A sensible conclusion, Ms. Randal. However, devotion to the Mother and utilization of her gifts are not mutually exclusive. We honor the Mother by harvesting her trees at their peak." Raene heard shades of Kaide's business voice in Hale, masking his disappointment.

"Of course, how silly of me." Raene slipped into her familiar innocent-girl routine and played it off like she'd simply had a daft moment. She didn't let him know the depth of her own disappointment.

Hale was kind enough to smile, though he didn't seem convinced. "Not all Terras share my devotion. Every person makes their own relationship with the Mother. Maybe someday you'll come to be close to her."

Raene tried not to roll her eyes and gag. Instead, she offered a girlish smile and said, "Yes, maybe someday." Thankfully, she was saved from saying more when Parson and Lathan appeared among the nearest group of working men.

Lathan lowered his axe when he saw them and headed

in their direction. Parson only offered them a cold look before continuing to strike a branch.

"You shouldn't have brought her here," Lathan began as soon as he was near enough.

"She deserves to know," Hale answered.

Raene could feel the same argument rise up again, and as with the first time, she didn't want to be involved. She took a half-step back and let the brothers discuss it.

"We have security measures for a reason. You know better than this," Lathan continued, his voice its usual booming echo, though today it was tinged with anger or protectiveness.

"She's one of us now. There's no reason to keep this from her."

Lathan sighed and glared at Hale for only a moment more. "You're right, but you should have discussed this with us first." Then, without warning, Lathan spun and shouted, "Parson! Get down here!"

Raene cringed. She didn't want to see the hateful brother. He clearly wanted nothing to do with her. Bringing him down would only force them both into an unpleasant situation.

Parson, too, seemed to think better of it. His axe swings didn't so much as slow in response to his brother's call. For all Raene knew, he hadn't even heard.

So Lathan called out again, louder and sterner this time. Only then did Parson lower his axe and turn to look at them.

Lathan had to shout several more times before Parson started toward them. They all watched as he approached, his disapproval set deep into his features.

"It's time you were properly introduced," Lathan said.

"We met," Parson answered, his gaze remaining on the trees on the far side of the clearing.

"Da's tent doesn't count—" Hale started.

Parson gaze locked on his younger brother. "I said, *we met*."

Raene stepped forward to end the uncomfortable exchange. "We did. Outside his tent. Tasia introduced us." Hale and Lathan both stared, mouths half-open in surprise.

Parson seized the moment. "If there's nothing else—"

"There is," Lathan cut him off. "You have a duty and obligation to let Ms. Randal choose between you two—"

Parson stepped forward and filled the space directly in front of Raene. He was the same height as her, but she felt like a child standing before him. His voice was low, and his eyes were intense and serious as he said, "Let me make this easy for you. I don't want some Pyro princess. Choose Hale." Then, he turned to his younger brother. "You can have her." With that, he spun on his heel and started back toward the tree.

"Excuse me?!" Raene screamed, her voice echoing across the clearing. She could feel every man looking at her, but she was past caring. White-hot anger exploded out of her like a geyser.

Even Parson turned to look at her.

Raene marched to where he stopped and pointed an angry finger in his face. "I'm not a toy to be passed around. I'm not a piece of garbage to be tossed aside. You don't know the first thing about me. How dare you. How *dare* you."

And then, it happened. Raene felt it begin even before she saw the rust-orange fur erupt over her hand. Transition rolled through her like a wave. Her shoulders widened, and her legs filled with muscle. Human hands gripped her. Someone shouted in her ear. But it was too late. The release was too powerful, the build-up too long.

Being in tiger form felt far too good.

Raene's tiger paw lashed for the closest victim, but he dodged too soon. She missed and fell to the ground on all fours. Refusing to give up this taste of freedom, tiger-Raene bolted for the cover of trees.

LOST

K AIDE SMOOTHED a hand over the front of his cloak before he reached up, rapping his knuckle on the massive door. The sound echoed through the corridor and a moment later, a small voice bid him entry.

"You needn't knock," Syndicate Mora seethed from her chair, unpleasant as usual.

"I only meant to be respectful." Kaide approached his customary position on the far side of her desk and held his hands clasped behind his back.

In an enormous black chair at a matching desk, Syndicate Mora looked tiny and harmless. Of course, Kaide knew better. She had a water monitor totem, a sneaking, slithering lizard. She was ruthless. She was one of the most formidable Syndicates in decades, but time had gotten the better of her. Arthritis left her crippled and slow. Most of her hair had fallen out some years ago. These days, she opted for a short-cropped wig of black-and-grey horse hair.

Her time was over. To Kaide, her fate was clearer than the cloudless summer sky.

"You called this meeting. Even claimed it was an emergency. So by all means, Landel, tell me what I can do to help you." She tilted back in her chair and gazed up at him with that sly little smile she so often wore.

Kaide swallowed down his apprehension. "First, I'd like your support in arranging a meeting of the realms regarding the spread of the Prentis and the resurgence of the Milton's collections within Pyrona." Kaide had made eliminating the sex-trafficking ring his primary focus. He lifted his chin and awaited her response, more resigned to this task than ever.

As was her habit, Syndicate Mora stroked her chin with her knobbed fingers, finding some measure of thoughtfulness from the gesture. "I'll support you informing the Alderai and Syndicates. It's too early to call a full meeting. For all we know, this is a Pyro problem—"

"It's not a Pyro problem, Syndicate Mora." Kaide struggled to keep his composure when she made such erroneous decisions. The Prentis were getting out of hand, collecting more women in recent weeks than they had in the past year. At current, none of their victims had been located. They weren't in Pyrona. They were in another branch, and someone knew it. Gathering the Syndicates and their Vice Syndicates in a single location would force someone to take responsibility—or at least inform the branches that Kaide was aware of their activities without leveling specific allegations.

And after they attempted to kidnap Blossom and sell her to their leader, the Milton, Kaide decided he'd had enough. Blossom was far stronger and more capable than he ever imagined, but he didn't want to think about what might have happened had he not shown up to the warehouse when he did. The idea that they were still out there, pulling women off the streets, selling them into service, using their bodies without remorse—it made Kaide ill to even consider it.

Mora clearly didn't suffer the same affliction.

She shot him a terse gaze. "Send word to the Alderai and the Syndicates. We will reassess at a later date if necessary." And then remembering, she added, "The second item?"

Kaide cleared his throat and prepared to say the words he'd wanted to speak for so long. "I seek your endorsement to ascend the Syndicate Office of the Pyro Branch."

"Ah, yes. I supposed as much." Her eyes drifted down, and her smile faded. It was then Kaide knew she would deny him.

"You have no cause to prevent my ascension," he argued. "You named me your successor before the Spring Ceremony—"

Syndicate Mora pushed up from her chair and speared him with her intense regard. For so small a person, she carried great presence. Even with her slowness, Kaide could feel her every step as she rounded the desk and arrived in front of him, reaching no higher than the middle of his chest. "Yes, Landel. I named you my successor. But that was when you held my confidence. In the weeks since, you've allowed yourself to be swayed. You've given in to your enemies. Look at you. You're falling apart. I cannot in good conscience leave the Pyro branch in your hands. Not anymore."

If he hadn't just been accused of falling apart, Kaide would have transitioned and shredded her in a heartbeat. Even her oversized-lizard totem was nothing compared to the strength of his beast.

But since she'd named his lack of control, he knew transitioning was the last thing he could do. Kaide sucked in a calming breath and worked to remain in his human form. "I am the best candidate, and you know it. The time has come. Name me Syndicate."

Syndicate Mora looked up at him. For the first time in the years he'd served her, she didn't offer him a serious glare or a vicious grin. Instead, there was something else. "Tell me what happened to your bride," she asked in a low voice.

Kaide closed his eyes and clenched his teeth. He didn't want to discuss it. He wanted to forget Blossom had ever lived, but at the same time, he was desperate to know if she was safe and why she'd left him. He hated her and loved her with every breath.

If it had been anyone else, Kaide would have ignored the question and talked his way out of it. But this was Reva Mora, Pyro Syndicate. She wouldn't let it go until she had her answers.

So, Kaide told her. "She left my protection under the guise of transformation. She neither underwent her transformation nor returned to Pyrona. I can only guess her current whereabouts."

Syndicate Mora nodded like she'd known all along. "Even so, I cannot endorse your ascension at this time. Prove to me you are still the dedicated, vigilant politician I know you to be. Then we'll discuss it further."

"As you wish, Syndicate Mora." Kaide kept his tone level despite his anger. It was the right decision, he knew, but that didn't quell his frustration.

Once he was named Syndicate, Kaide would be fully occupied carrying out his plan to destroy Aero and unify the branches. Without the title, there was nothing he could do but return to the manor and simmer in the disaster his life had become.

Parson saw it in her eyes—the bright blue ones that suddenly turned gold. He knew she would transition, probably before she knew it herself. He had only a half-second to grip her by the shoulders and shout her name, but it wasn't enough. She was too angry. Her totem was too strong.

Her totem claimed her while he still gripped her tight. Parson had barely stepped to the side before she landed on all four paws in her full tiger form.

Admittedly, she was impressive. There was no denying it. Her size and strength and the sound of that growl echoing through the trees were like nothing he'd experienced before.

But then she was gone.

"Nice going. I swear by the Mother—" Hale snapped before he started after her.

Parson intercepted him and put a hand on his chest. "Let her go."

"She doesn't know where she is. She's pissed off and—"

"And she's not going to calm down with a bear chasing her." Parson knew better than anyone. Sometimes you just had to go get it out of your system.

"And you don't want her, remember?"

Parson felt the words like a slap across the face. He reeled and stepped back. "I don't. But I know she won't come back with you chasing after her."

Hale glared at Parson for a second more before moving around him and continuing toward the clearing's edge.

"Parson is right." Lathan's voice boomed and stopped Hale in his tracks.

"So what would you suggest? Just leave her out there? Just leave my future wife in the Alderwood and hope she decides to come back someday?" Hale's words dripped with venom and anger. Parson had never seen him so unnerved—not even the day Blossom was taken.

Lathan nodded. "There's nothing else you can do. Go back to camp and wait there. We'll keep an eye out here. She'll come back."

Hale started to protest, but they all knew there was no

arguing with Lathan, especially when he wore that stern look of his. They'd have it out about this later, Parson knew, but for now, he was satisfied to return to his axe and swing it into fresh alder wood.

The day wore on like so many did. The sun rose higher and higher in the sky, and heat filled the clearing by midday. Parson's axe made quick work of several dozen branches, stripping them clean and cleaving them off to be cut into smaller and smaller portions for sale.

There was nothing remarkable about the day, but still Parson found his gaze skirting the edge of the clearing every few minutes. He satisfied himself with the reminder she'd probably followed her nose back to camp, but then he'd worry tigers couldn't smell as well as bears. Maybe he'd made the wrong call. Maybe Hale should have gone to fetch her.

Then, Parson would remember he didn't care. He'd swing his axe high in the air and bring it down hard into the next limb. Then he'd scan the clearing's edge and start all over again.

The afternoon turned later, and the sun fell behind the canopy, casting long shadows across the cut, and still Parson was stuck scanning and worrying and scanning some more. With each passing hour, his anxiety increased until he spent more time looking for her than he did working.

When he heard the evening whistle to head back to camp, he still hadn't seen her.

"Come on. You heard it," Lathan said as he passed by with his axe in hand.

"I'm coming. Just going to finish this one," he replied. In truth, Parson hated to quit with a branch half-cleaned, but even more than that, it didn't feel right to leave—not yet. The rest of the work crew replaced their tools in the out-of-sight storage container and headed back to camp for the night. Only Parson remained.

Parson was wedged between two branches well off the ground, clearing the base of the last branch when a bit of red caught his eye. Sure enough, a girl in Pyro clothes emerged from the dark Alderwood. Even at the distance, he could see she was covered in blood.

He dropped his axe immediately.

Parson jumped down and trotted over to where she walked in a daze, her eyes on the ground. Blood coated her mouth and chin and her entire front of her shirt.

"Are you all right?" he asked, his frantic eyes searching over her.

Raene looked up at him and took three steps back, tears streaming down her face. When she moved to wipe them, she only smeared fresh blood across her cheek. "I killed it," she squeaked between quiet sobs.

Parson froze in place. "Killed what?"

Her gaze fell to the ground. "I don't know," she cried. "A deer with horns." Again, she wiped at her cheek and left yet more blood smeared across her face.

"An elk?"

Raene only shrugged.

"Are you hurt?" he asked, referring to the blood covering her hands and chest. It wouldn't be the first time an elk speared a predator with a horn. He had a considerable scar on his leg to prove it.

When she bowed her head, her hair hanging over her face, Parson took a single step toward her, refusing to acknowledge how the sight of so much blood left him itching to hunt. Now wasn't the time to get lost to his indulgences.

"Get away from me!" she screamed and lunged back a step.

Parson threw up his hands to show he meant no harm.

As she wiped at her cheek again, Parson chanced

another a step toward her.

"Leave me alone," she cried. "I'm not safe."

Parson stopped, and this time he laughed. "That's what you're worried about?"

At last, she looked up at him. "I killed a deer. Or an elk. Or whatever it was. I ripped it open," she said as her eyes fell to her blood-soaked hands. So quiet he could barely hear, she whispered, "I couldn't stop."

"Don't take this the wrong way, but you're a *tiger*." When she only shot him a confused look, Parson explained, "If you *weren't* killing things, I'd be worried. That's what tigers do. When's the last time you had any meat?"

"A week," she admitted.

It was then Parson knew he'd been in the wrong. She'd been fighting against a strong totem without any meat to quiet her hunger, and he'd goaded her on until she erupted. It had been his fault, not hers.

She deserved better, even from him.

Parson sighed and took one last step toward her. "I'm sorry for what I said. I don't like this situation, but it isn't your fault."

"Thank you," she replied and wiped at the last of her tears. "I'm sorry I cried. I hate crying. I'm sure I look awful." A half-second later, she seemed to realize what she'd said. She looked like she wanted to say something more, but she didn't.

"Depends on who you ask," he teased. Parson enjoyed the sight of her covered in blood, but he wouldn't tell her that. Gone was the dainty princess, replaced with this ferocious, predatory young woman. Even Parson couldn't deny the allure of such strength.

When she didn't smile in the slightest, he told her, "You smeared blood on your cheeks." He didn't mention her braid of golden hair was so disheveled it looked more like a bird's nest.

With the back of her hand, Raene wiped at her cheek, but it was too late.

"There's a stream nearby," he offered.

"Yes, thank you."

Parson didn't mention how ridiculous she sounded in her coy, demure voice with drying blood on her cheeks. She looked aggressive and powerful and dangerous, but she sounded like a shy girl. He couldn't help but wonder which was the real Raene.

The closest stream was a fifteen minute walk south of the cut. The last traces of evening light were long gone, but Raene's tiger eyes had no trouble seeing in the dark. Parson, too, seemed to make his way well enough.

When they arrived at the modest creek bed, Raene was all too eager to kneel by the water's edge and rinse the stickiness from her hands. The idea that she was covered in blood made her stomach churn. But when she thought of getting sick, she remembered the contents of her stomach—the undigested meat of the elk she had killed—and she choked down her disgust. That was one particular meal she didn't want to see again.

Raene splashed cool water on her hands and arms, but it took a good bit of scrubbing to get the drying blood to come off. Even with her cat eyes, it was hard to tell if she'd gotten it all. Then Raene started on her cheeks, scrubbing them over and over again, never knowing if they were clean.

Then she remembered her shirt. It was soaked through, so badly stained it would likely never be scarlet again. But she had brought only a handful of Pyro tops to the Alderwood. She couldn't let one go to waste.

Raene looked around to find Parson sitting on a nearby

rock jutting from the creek bed, his animal eyes glowing a faint green.

Raene's wet hands made the straps of her shirt trickier to remove than usual, but she managed. The drying blood caused the fabric stick to her front, producing a vile sucking sound as she pulled it free.

Parson stood and walked a dozen steps away, keeping his back turned toward her. Only then did Raene remember Terra rules on modesty.

She was so very far from home.

The reality of her situation struck her. She'd killed an innocent animal for no reason other than she wanted a taste of it. Raene Randal, former Pyro elite, was now nothing more than a common criminal, a murderer, a monster.

Alone in the Alderwood with a man who hated her, scrubbing her blood-soaked shirt in a creek, she couldn't help but feel her life had gotten away from her.

"Did you mean it?" she called out to him over her bare shoulder.

"Mean what?" he shouted back.

"That I should choose Hale."

An eternity passed before he answered. "Yes."

Even now, the truth of it pained her. Raene had never been so casually dismissed in all her life.

"Is there someone else?" she asked, hopeful. She could live with that—if his rejection stemmed from a connection with another woman.

But Parson renewed her anguish when he said, "No, there hasn't been anyone in a long time."

"Then why?" Raene tried and failed to keep the desperation from her voice.

"He's the right choice. I'm no good for you."

"What does that mean?" Raene asked, thankful her hands were occupied.

When Parson finally answered, she could hear he'd

turned to face her. His voice was low but carried on the wind well enough. Every word sank into her like a stake. "I'll be your husband's brother. I'll be your brother-in-law, and I'll be your friend. You can come talk to me if you need anything, but I can't marry you. I *can't*."

"Why?" Raene repeated. She felt like he'd pointed out she was the ugliest girl in the realm.

"It's hard to explain." The exasperation was clear in his voice, even from so far behind her.

"It has to do with Blossom," Raene answered for him. "Because a Pyro man came into your home and took her away. And when you see me, you think of him, and then you think of her. And you remember that she's gone."

"Yes," he answered, now only a step behind her, his voice little more than a wisp.

To her surprise, Parson pulled his tunic top over his shoulders and handed it to her. It was still damp with sweat and reeked of musk and work, but Raene was nonetheless grateful to be spared more Terra words of disapproval. She gladly covered herself and continued washing.

"I didn't take her from you," Raene couldn't help but remind him.

"I know."

"I thought she was going to be *my* sister." Raene was glad the darkness prevented him from seeing the tears that sprang into her eyes. She kept her hands moving, grinding her soaked shirt against a flat stone. She would do anything to keep from looking at him.

Parson crouched beside her, mindlessly turning his rings. "I'm sorry, I know I'm being selfish, but I can't help it." He dragged a hand across his bearded chin before he said, "Hale is a good man, and he'll be a good husband. He won't hold it against you. He's closer to your age. He's calm and understanding. He's not as—I don't know—grouchy?"

Despite the awkwardness, Raene and Parson both chuckled. "You are rather grouchy," she agreed.

Raene didn't know how she felt about this turn. Parson declining any interest in her didn't feel good, but she was glad to have an answer. There was no reason to be nervous over whether he liked her or not. She knew she wouldn't have to marry him. Now he was nothing more than her future husband's brother.

And she would marry Hale. She'd only talked to him for a few minutes, but he seemed nice enough. Raene's thoughts had only started down that path when Parson interrupted them.

"You know that's never going to come out."

Raene continued scrubbing, her hands shaking from the cold water. "I have to try."

"Is that why Pyros wear red?"

"I have no idea. And it's scarlet."

"What?"

Raene stopped her scrubbing and glared at him, knowing he could see her in the dark. "It's not red. It's scarlet. Or sometimes crimson. But it's not red."

Parson only blinked.

Frustrated and tired, Raene threw the wadded shirt into the creek with a splash. "I'll work on it in the morning. I can't see anything anymore."

"Yes, you can." Parson didn't even hesitate to call out her lie. "But Hale is worried. You should get back."

Raene cringed. "Are you going to tell him?"

"I'm not in the habit of keeping secrets from my brothers."

She could only imagine how that conversation would go. *Oh, Hale. I found your bride in the woods covered in blood and crying her eyes out about some deer she'd murdered.*

Raene took her time wringing the water from her shirt

as best she could, but she knew she was going to have to face him eventually.

"At least tell me if I still have blood on my face." She didn't want Hale to see her so out of sorts. Then again, she was the definition of out of sorts.

Parson stepped forward, and all at once, Raene remembered she was wearing his shirt. His bare arms and broad shoulders caught every bit of the scant moonlight that snuck in between the trees. He put a finger under her chin and moved her face into the light.

Raene kept her gaze on the trees and let him assess her, desperate to get it over with.

"There's a bit here under your eye." His finger skimmed the spot.

Raene turned away and sank beside the creek. She scrubbed the patch of skin raw before wiping her sleeve across it and returning for his assessment. "Better?"

Parson tilted toward her. "Better," he agreed. But he didn't release her chin. Instead, he moved his thumb to her temple and traced the faint line she knew well. "Did he give you this scar?" he finally asked, his brow knit with concern.

"Yes, but he didn't mean it."

"You're defending him?" Parson stood with his lip curled in disgust.

"He's the best man I know," Raene admitted. And now that she had her totem, it was possible to think she understood him better than ever.

Parson's eyes fell to her scar once more. "But he—"

"He didn't mean it." Raene finished, squeezing the water from her ruined shirt. When Parson only stared back in confusion, Raene told him, "It was my fault. He told me to stay away from him, but I didn't listen. I made him do this, and he never forgave himself. I made him lose control. It was my fault."

Raene hadn't meant to say so much, but it felt good to

get it off her chest. Kaide deserved her honesty on the matter, even if he'd never hear it for himself.

"After his transformation?" Parson asked, and Raene nodded.

As if he expected it all along, Parson told her, "Some of us never really get it under control. I killed my fair share at first. A pair of moose and three wolves the first week."

Raene rolled her eyes and pulled away from him. She'd been honest, and in return, he was making fun of her. "I don't need you to make up stories to make me feel better. I know what I did—"

Parson reached out for her waist and yanked her back toward him, but he pulled too hard. Raene crashed against his bare chest as he said, "I'm not making up stories."

Raene let that sink in before she asked, "What did Da say?"

Parson chuckled under his breath. "To keep my totem under control. Like it was as easy as that."

"And did you?"

"Sort of."

"What does that mean?" Raene searched his emerald eyes, desperate for the answer.

"That I hunt small game further from camp. I hunt more often so I don't get to the brink. I stay well away from the cut or anywhere else I might find someone I know. It's not ideal, but it works. It keeps me from lashing out. Most of the time…"

Raene wondered if she could do that, too. Maybe it wasn't so much about controlling her totem as managing it. With her chest pressed against Parson, it was possible to think it might work, but still, she'd have to tell Hale where she went and what she'd done.

She pulled her hand from Parson's grip and collected her shirt where she'd dropped it. In her best elegant tone, Raene said, "Thank you for your candor, Master Frane. I'm ready to go back now."

Parson shook his head, not accepting her words in the slightest.

With her wet, crumpled shirt in her hands, Raene side-stepped him and started toward camp. She could find the way easy enough. Already, she recognized the scents of it—the smoke from a dozen small fires, the sweet fruits and berries, the aged odor of the canvas tents. The walk was longer, as they'd gone out of the way to pass the stream, but Raene didn't mind. She had that much more time to organize her thoughts. She needed to figure out what she was going to say to Hale.

Thankfully, Parson didn't bother her. He said not a word until the camp was in view.

"This way," he announced as he darted to the right. Raene followed him as they rounded the exterior of the camp and arrived behind Lathan's tent. From there, it was easy to slip inside unnoticed.

Lathan and Tasia sat in conversation, each perched on a plump pillow. "Do I even want to know?" Tasia asked with a raised eyebrow and a smirk. She looked back and forth between Parson's bare chest and Raene's shirt wadded in her hands.

"Probably not," Parson answered for her.

Raene ignored them all and crossed the tent, darting behind the partition before the Terras could harp on her lack of modesty. There, she pulled out a fresh Pyro shirt, still saturated with the aromas of home. She stripped out of Parson's shirt and replaced it with her own. Already she felt better.

Once all her straps were tied and clasped, she folded Parson's shirt and carried it back to him. "Thank you," she said, using her most elegant tone, revealing none of what had transpired at the stream. With her hands free, Raene loosened what remained of her braid. It was so tangled, she knew it would take an hour to get it all combed through again.

No sooner had Parson pulled on his shirt than Hale shot into the tent. Locks of hair fell across his forehead, and his chest heaved as he worked to catch his breath. His eyes darted frantically around the tent until they settled on Raene.

"It seems all the Franes forgot their manners today." Tasia laughed with easy amusement.

Raene couldn't find anything funny when Hale closed the distance between them. He arrived before her and cupped her cheek in his hand. The sudden closeness made Raene's pulse pound in her ears. For a long moment, they stood there, eyes locked. Raene nearly buckled under his easy calm, but was saved when, in a low voice dripping in worry, Hale asked, "Are you all right?"

Guilt bubbled up within her like a summer spring.

"Yes, I'm fine," she answered with a false smile. He was sweet and caring, and he certainly didn't deserve her apathy after worrying over her all day.

Satisfied she wasn't hurt, Hale started in on the real questions. "What happened? Where did you go?"

Hale's continued proximity only made her more nervous. She knew it shouldn't—they'd be married soon enough—but it was hard to concentrate on her rehearsed explanation when he stood so close and touched her cheek that way.

Raene opened her mouth to produce an answer when Parson interrupted. "She got lost. I found her about an hour ago wandering around pretty far from the cut. Took us a while to get back."

Hale frowned. "I'm sorry. I should have gone with you."

Raene could only picture the gruesome scene—her in tiger form crouched over the body of an elk, still warm and spilling blood into the Alderwood soil, and Hale standing by, watching. She was glad he hadn't seen her that way. To cover her humiliation, Raene batted her eyes innocently. "I didn't mean to make you worry."

Hale put a trembling hand on her waist. "I'm just glad you're all right. Let me take you home."

Raene's breath caught in her throat. Home? As in, Hale's tent? Just the two of them? If having him stand close made her this nervous, she didn't even want to think about being alone with him in his tent.

"That's not the arrangement," Lathan offered, always so quick to defend her. Raene shot him an appreciative look.

"It's the Mother's will. It's been decided," Hale answered without turning.

Raene glanced at Parson, wondering if he would protest, but instead found the spot vacated. He'd slipped out when she wasn't looking, distracted by Hale.

So much for that.

To her horror and shock, Lathan conceded, offering Hale a terse nod. Raene was frozen as stiff as a board, but that wasn't enough to prevent Hale placing a hand low on her back as he led her toward the tent flap.

A second later, Raene and her future husband emerged in the dark. This time, the urge to flee and transition and kill was lessened, temporarily satiated by her previous outing. But still, she was afraid to be alone with him. She didn't know him—other than he was the brother who hadn't rejected her at first sight.

"I'm sorry about earlier. That shouldn't have happened," Hale began as they walked, his hand still on her back.

"It's not your fault," Raene offered, racked with nerves over where this was going. He was touching her, and they were going to his tent, and soon enough they'd be married.

Raene couldn't help but wonder what he wanted to happen tonight. She did her best to slow her steps.

Oblivious, Hale continued, "All the same, I didn't like it. He shouldn't have pushed you that way." After that, Hale was quiet. Their footsteps sounded in her ears like drums. Her blood still raced from the elk and Parson and now Hale.

All too soon Hale stopped at a tent. Raene hadn't expected them to arrive so soon, but they'd run out of camp. This tent, a large one with a bear painted over the flap, was the last before the edge of the dark and empty Alderwood forest.

Hale held open the flap and bid her entry.

Unwilling to offend him, Raene ducked her head and pushed in. Unlike Lathan's tent, or even Da's tent, Hale's tent was large and filled with items. A dozen candles filled the space with something like daylight. Low cabinets and open boxes lined the perimeter, and on the far side, a small table with two chairs. It was by far the most furnished space she'd seen in camp.

Somehow, it made her feel better. It was nothing like the expensive alder wood furniture or lush carpets of the manor, but at least Hale's tent looked like someone lived here. Someone had a life here. It was more than a tent over a patch of earth.

A pang of nostalgia raced through her. This would be her home, but it didn't feel that way. It wasn't her father's stone house that stank of wine. It wasn't the manor in all its finery, filled with people who loved her. This place was strange, and the man beside her a stranger.

Hale stood at the tent flap and let her take in the sight of it. She could hear his quiet breath as he waited.

"What is all this?" she asked, motioning to the cabinets and boxes.

"Mostly clan records, past cuts and trade accounts. That cabinet there holds all the medical supplies." Hale stepped around her and pulled a wooden bottle from the bottom drawer. With a boyish smile, he added, "And a hidden stash of amberwine. Would you like a drink?"

Raene tried not to nod too eagerly. She would have given anything for a nice, cool strawberry wine. Still, amberwine was a welcome sight. Under the circumstances, she wasn't about to turn it down.

He produced two alder wood goblets from the drawer and set them on the table. Raene took the nearest seat as he poured, strangely missing the comfortable pillows of Tasia and Lathan's tent.

"How are you doing?" Hale collected his cup and sipped the wine slowly.

Raene did the same and replied, "It's good." Not as good as strawberry wine…

Hale chuckled and sat in the other chair, his eyes on her the whole time. "I mean, how are *you* doing? I'm sure this has all been a lot to work through."

"It's all right." Raene wanted to tell him, to let all her turmoil spill out, but she knew once she started, she would explode. Between her last conversation with Kaide, Blossom's disappearance, and her transformation followed by her immediate streak of violence, Raene didn't know where to start. Instead, she fell back on old habits—warm smiles and batted eye lashes.

But Hale sensed her falseness. After a long, deliberate inhale, he said, "You can tell me."

Raene grappled for an answer. When she remained silent, he offered, "You don't have to, though. I know this is all new and strange, but I'm always here. Whenever you decide you're ready."

"Thank you," Raene replied, though her voice fell to a whisper. She wasn't merely being polite; she meant it. Hale was far kinder to her than he had to be.

A long, heavy silence emerged and filled the tent. The

candles danced as the two drank their wine without a word.

"Your birthday was the second of this month?" Hale asked after a while. Raene nodded, and thanked her luck when he didn't ask her anything else. Instead, he told her, "In Terra, the fifth month is the month of the cherry.

"It is said in the beginning, the Alder Mother was alone. She lived in the forest and grew. Her blossoms spread in the spring and fell in the summer heat." Hale's voice was a melody, deep and even, and he recalled the story like a memory. The cadence of his voice lulled her as she listened.

"To share her love and guidance, the Mother split herself into thirteen spirits, and for a time, there were thirteen mothers—thirteen sacred trees. The world lived in peace until, one by one, the spirits fell to weakness." His brow wrinkled in disappointment. "The first lied, and the Mother cursed him with a sugary sap as false as his words. The Maple Tree.

"The second tried to leave, angry at the Mother's treatment of the first, so the Mother coated his branches in long vines. He was weighted to the ground, becoming the Willow Tree. The third rebelled and betrayed the Mother. She turned his wide green leaves into needles as pointed as his actions."

"The Pine Tree," Raene offered.

Hale smiled sweetly and nodded. "That's right. The fourth cast his eye toward a young woman, and the Mother turned his fruit sweet and soft like the flesh of the girl. The Peach Tree.

"And the fifth," he paused for effect. "The fifth killed a man, and the Mother gave him fruit as red as the blood he spilled. The Cherry Tree."

Raene couldn't help but feel he was telling her this story as a warning.

But Hale only refilled her glass and smiled. "They're

just stories. The Mother is more than old tales and fruit trees."

Too late she realized he was teasing her. All this talk of a sacred tree was foreign to Raene, but she liked to learn this little piece about him. The wine did its job, and before she could help herself, Raene curled her lips into a smile.

A real smile.

And Hale noticed. "Ah, there you are. Maybe after a while, I won't have to fill you with wine and tell you lullabies to get you to smile." Hale toyed with the stem of his goblet before his soft, tentative gaze returned to her. He stood in a single, fluid motion and held out his hand for hers.

Raene's nerves returned, as if summoned by his voice, but she slipped her hand in his, feeling the warmth and smoothness of his skin.

Hale pulled her to her feet in the span of a heartbeat. For the second time that evening, Raene found herself pressed against a Frane son, held tight in arms that encircled her. Hale's stubbled chin skimmed the top of her shoulder as he whispered, "You don't have to be nervous. We have a long time to get used to this."

Then, he pulled away, and Raene could breathe again. She'd never understand how he was so calm through all this. Hale didn't have half her troubles, but still, she expected him to at least stumble at the prospect of marrying a stranger. But he didn't. He acted like he'd had years to get used to the idea.

"Let's get you a place to sleep." Hale started toward one of his boxes and produced a thick stack of fabric. Then, as carefully as Norsa, he set to spreading them into a pallet on the floor. He must have thought her quite the delicate princess; he piled the blankets so high they nearly toppled over.

Raene stood as still as a stone as she watched him

prepare his tent for her. It was endearing to see him take such care to make her comfortable, and for the first time since arriving in the Alderwood, Raene thought maybe this might work out. Maybe Parson was right. Maybe Hale was the right choice.

"Would you like something to sleep in?" Hale reached for yet another stack of folded fabrics and handed it to her. "I borrowed these from Gemini. They should fit well enough. I'll step outside." He thrust his hands in his pockets and stepped back before disappearing through the flap.

Raene clutched the stack of clothes, at a loss as for what to do. She didn't want to wear the moss-green clothes of Terra. She didn't want to wear borrowed clothes from someone she hadn't even met, someone who probably hated her for being Pyro. But she didn't want to go back to Lathan's tent to get her own clothes, either. In her panic, she'd forgotten them, but it was too late now. She didn't want to give Tasia the satisfaction.

So, reluctantly, Raene removed her Pyro clothes, folding them neatly before sliding on the borrowed night shirt. The fabric was soft on her skin. The neckline was high, and the sleeves were long—clear down to her wrists. When she saw its hem went well past her knees, Raene wondered how tall this Gemini was. Everyone she'd met in the clan was short—or at least shorter than her. With the exception of Parson and Lathan, she was the tallest person here.

When Hale returned, he put her even more at a loss. He looked at her with a quizzical brow and said, "It's a little short. She's not quite as tall as you, I guess. I'll see what I can find for tomorrow, but that should do for now."

Raene struggled to keep her mouth from falling open. A little short? As in, Hale expected her to wear a night shirt clear down to her ankles? Was that what all Terras wore to bed? Tasia's modesty prevented Raene from even glimpsing her in her night clothes, though now that she'd seen some, Raene couldn't imagine why the Terras were so afraid of a little skin.

It was ridiculous. She would make do for the night, but tomorrow, she'd be sure to get her own clothes from Lathan's tent. Her loose, black shorts and low-cut top were much preferred over this heavy thing.

Hale didn't seem to notice her surprise. Instead, he moved about the tent blowing out candle after candle. The tent slowly dimmed and filled with the acrid scent of extinguished flames. Then, all at once, they descended into darkness.

It took only a moment for Raene's cat eyes to find him in the gloom.

"Don't worry. I'll keep to my side," he teased. Raene could see his shadow change as he removed his boots and shirt and settled into a spot on the far side of the tent.

Raene sank to the pallet of blankets and curled up. It was all so strange: the forest quiet, the over-large shirt, the man only steps away. None of it was necessarily bad, but Raene couldn't adjust all at once. Sleep wouldn't come when her ears perked at every sound and her mind raced with all that had happened that day.

And as much as she hated the cold of Lathan's tent—was overjoyed to have a real blanket—Raene found herself overheated in the mound of fabric. She threw off the top three and still couldn't get comfortable.

"Can't sleep?" Hale whispered. In the silence of the tent, it sounded like a shout.

"No," she admitted. Behind her, Hale stirred, and then, step by step, he neared. A second later, he sat on the ground behind her.

Raene jolted when she felt his hand on her back, such an unwarranted touch. Through the fabric of her borrowed shirt, Raene felt how his fingertips moved up to her shoulders and dipped back toward her waist, then up once more. Over and over again, he ran his hands along her spine in easy, rhythmic motions.

"My mother would do this when I couldn't sleep as a boy," he said, his voice little more than breath. "It's one of the only things I remember about her."

Raene turned enough to face him but not enough to disturb the long strokes on her back. "How old were you?"

"Five. Parson was eight, and Lathan eleven. Blossom was only a week old."

"She died of complications?"

"She started bleeding. I don't remember, but that's what Lathan said. No one else will talk about it. They couldn't get it under control. She struggled for a whole week before the Mother took her back to her grove." The pain in his voice skipped over every word like a stone on a pond.

Raene rolled onto her back, putting a swift end to his comforting motions. "In Pyrona, they're called fire children. A child born to the loss of the mother has the world's fire inside them."

Hale collapsed and lay beside her, his head propped on his elbow. "In Terra, they're called the Mother's children. They lost their mother, so the Sacred Mother watches over them."

"Do you think that's true?" Raene whispered, unable to tell him that she, too, was a fire child, though her mother had struggled for almost a year.

Hale chuckled and put a hand on her shoulder, pushing her onto her side and exposing her back to him once more. He resumed the gentle stroking of his fingertips as he said, "It has to be. How else do you explain Blossom? She's where she's supposed to be. We all are."

Raene squeezed her eyes tight in hopes his words were true—that wherever Blossom was, she was where she belonged. And that Raene, here in the Bear Clan, maybe she was where she belonged, too. Her thoughts and Hale's motions put her at ease in a way she hadn't felt in weeks. Her totem was quieter than ever, so despite the heat of the tent, Raene managed to drift off to sleep.

Until she heard her name shouted through the tent flap.

Raene bolted awake, only half-aware of the sunlight streaming in. Hale lay beside her, an arm's length away, already sitting with eyes wide. He, too, had been startled.

Da didn't seem the least bit surprised as he shot into the tent and announced, "Time to go, Ms. Randal!"

Raene only had a moment to blink before she was dragged from the tent.

TRAITOR

BLOSSOM SAT ALONE at the glass table in her chambers, mindlessly munching at the roast rabbit as she skimmed the Aero files again. The screened device was large enough to show the full chart of Aero personnel—the Syndicate, Vice Syndicates, Commissioners, and Division Heads—the ones Eton insist she learn. Along with personnel, Eton made her practice walking with elegance, talking with a measured tone, and keeping her face pleasant and devoid of emotion.

She'd rather do a thousand other things. When she asked Eton for access to a library, he glared and said, "Books are for those whose minds are empty and need to be filled." He claimed similar useless excuses when she asked about an art gallery, music, or anything that deviated from the 'values of Aero', not that he would tell her what that meant.

Blossom was stuck learning about the branch she hated and the position she never wanted. After a week of lessons, Blossom was finally getting the hang of it, not that it would matter if she never left her apartment.

Earlier than usual, Eton emerged from his room. He wore the same pressed suit as always—this one a slightly dimmer shade of grey—and his hair was smoothed and perfect. Today, the rings in his face were black.

When he saw the Pyro clothes she still wore, he frowned, but Blossom refused to let it bother her. She'd already given up her curls in exchange for the straight hair that fell in her face and tickled her shoulders. He would have to be satisfied with that.

"You have your first assignment," he announced.

"Oh goody," she mumbled. The bits of glazed rabbit meat sat in her stomach like a brick, far too heavy for so early in the morning. She'd much rather have a plate of fruit or nuts.

"That means you get your panel. I've already set it up." He thrust it toward her as proof.

Blossom accepted the slim device, all black and metal as she remembered. "The Syndicate said I was supposed to get this a week ago."

"Yes, I kept it from you intentionally." Eton didn't seem the least bit ashamed of such a betrayal.

Blossom ran her finger across the screen and saw it prompted her to enter a code. "I can call anyone?" She sat up straight in anticipation for his answer. Holding the panel in her hand, she knew she had the ability to call Kaide, and now that she could, she wanted to more than anything.

"Technically, yes. But you should use it sparingly. It's common knowledge the Syndicate has access to all the files and transmissions. Anything that comes across your panel is subject to her review."

That's why he withheld it from her. Blossom's excitement was gone as fast as it had come. "I need you to help me get a message to Kaide." She hated to do admit it to him, but she had no other choice.

Eton lowered his voice to a whisper. "I would help you if I could," he replied as he sat in the metal chair beside her. "But I'm only your advisor. I have certain privileges related to your position, but I can do almost nothing on my own."

To his credit, he appeared genuinely disappointed.

But Blossom wasn't satisfied with that answer. "He has to know where I am. This has gone on long enough." She didn't want to think about what Kaide thought of her absence, but he deserved to know the truth. Blossom knew where he was, knew he was safe, knew he was missing her.

But to Kaide, she had simply disappeared. With absolute certainty, she knew her absence would destroy him, if it hadn't already.

"Blossom, I understand. But there's nothing I can do. We'll figure something out, but be patient. When an opportunity arises, you'll know it."

Ignoring his protests, Blossom pulled the panel into her hand and tried to figure out how to work it. She was just going to have to risk it. Kaide needed to know she was safe, but more than that, Blossom wanted to see him—to hear his voice and see those bright blue eyes of his.

Eton's hand landed over top of hers, hiding the panel from view. "Please, don't. You have to see she's testing you."

"What are you talking about?"

"The Syndicate. She offered you a communication panel knowing you would use it to contact him. She can see everything you do on it, every word you say. It'll be all she needs to ruin you for committing crimes against Aero. She's testing your loyalty."

"That's a test I'm definitely going to fail." Blossom had no more love for Aero than she had for a gnat—maybe less.

Eton recoiled. "Never say that again. Do you understand? Those words never pass your lips. Not in front of anyone. Not even me."

Startled by his sudden seriousness, Blossom only nodded.

"Then let's forget this conversation ever happened."

He snatched a mouthful of meat from her plate. "For now, you have business."

"Am I going to hate it?"

"Undoubtedly."

"Fantastic. What unpleasant task do you have for me today?" She pushed away the plate and let him have the rest of it.

"You have to exile a traitor." Eton motioned to the panel. "Your code is one-nine-one-six. Enter it in, and you'll see your open assignments. Remember, the Syndicate can see everything you do, so make sure to keep your communications professional and loyal to the Aero branch."

Blossom tapped the numerical buttons on the screen and watched as it changed to a virtual folder. At the top, a tab was labeled with an alphanumeric code. She had no idea what the code meant, but as it was the only one available, she tapped it just the same.

Inside, she found a brief description of her assignment:

PERPETRATOR: WERSA HAMMOND
CRIME: DISLOYALTY TO AERO
ACTION: EXILE (TERRESTRIAL)

Blossom looked to Eton for an explanation.

"Wersa Hammond is a trader. He routinely travels to Hydra to buy fish and sell it here in Aerona. He's being charged with sharing Aero secrets with some of his Hydra relations."

"What secrets?"

Eton slipped into his usual formal tone. "I'm not allowed to disclose those until you're given direct access. Aero treats their security and privacy with the utmost importance."

"So this guy knew things that I'm not allowed to

know, and he told them to some fisherman in Hydra?"

Eton nodded. "According to the report."

"What does that mean? That he didn't really do it?" Blossom glared as she waited for the answer.

"His wife, Kiza Hammond, is the sister to Commissioner Thorrow. One could speculate certain political advantages might be gained by her absence."

Blossom looked back to the panel. "But she's not exiled. He is."

"Aero law doesn't distinguish between the two. If one is exiled, the family is exiled as well."

"So this trader and his wife are going to be exiled from Aerona because someone wants to get to the Research and Development Commissioner?" Blossom asked, recalling her personnel lessons.

"Yes, along with their daughter, Helena. They all go." Eton's passivity was clearly a well-practiced guard to stay neutral. He disliked it as much as she did.

"Where do they go?"

When he didn't answer right away, Blossom knew the answer was bad. "Where do they *go*?" she repeated.

Eton set his jaw. "The manner of their exile is listed. Terrestrial. They'll be brought to the surface and sent away."

Blossom didn't see what was so terrible about that. Sure, it wasn't the ideal situation, but they could always make their way somewhere else and start over.

Then she remembered the view from Aero Tower. "The ground is covered in snow."

Eton offered her a half-hearted nod. "Most die of exposure before they get south of the frost."

"They can fly," Blossom realized. "As birds, they could get south—"

"They'd have to leave their daughter behind. Children don't have totems."

"That's awful." Blossom slumped in her chair at the idea of it.

"Told you you'd hate it."

Blossom announced, "I'm not taking any part in this."

"You have to. It's your assignment. If you don't, Syndicate Mercer will punish you in an equally creative manner. And she'll pass this task off to Peppers. You can't save them."

She groaned her disappointment. A moment later, she made her decision. Blossom sprang up and darted to her closet.

"What are you doing?" Eton eyed her as suspiciously as a thief.

"Getting dressed." Blossom found a dozen suits hanging in her closet, each one of the light blues or greys of Aero. Careless as to the color, Blossom grabbed one and threw it on the bed. From her pocket, she pulled out Hale's coin—still bare on one side—and set it on the bedside table. Then, as she promised never to do, Blossom began to exchange her Pyro clothes for Aero ones.

"But why now?" Eton continued, his shock evident in his voice.

"So we can help them." Blossom found Aero clothes to be hysterically complicated, with so many different pieces, she didn't even know where to start. The pants were easy enough, but once she realized she was supposed to wear a pair of slim shorts beneath, she had to pull them off and start over again.

"Would you like some help?" Eton finally offered.

"Just tell me where this goes." Blossom held up yet another fabric puzzle piece.

"It's a vest," he said as he pushed out of his chair. "But you need the shirt on first." Arriving at the bed, he motioned to a long-sleeved shirt with a row of buttons down the front.

The sight of it reminded her of Kaide's cloak—of the buttons he so meticulously worked to remove it just for her.

Blossom shook the thought away and slipped her arms into the shirt.

"I thought Terra girls were supposed to be modest," Eton asked, his head listed to the side.

She only shrugged and continued dressing. "You already saw everything. You and that little old man." She didn't mention that she'd seen the look in Kaide's eye when he looked at her. Blossom knew what it looked like when a man desired her, and Eton had none of that.

"It's my job to accompany you in every way. I can't advise you very well if I don't have all the information."

"Then I hope you consider yourself fully informed on my bare figure." She pursed her lips and shot him a look.

Eton allowed himself a chuckle. "You'll be a formidable adversary if you learn to tame your tongue."

"I have no intention of taming anything. Am I ready?" Blossom held her arms to her side and let him check her over. The fabric touching her skin felt wrong in one hundred ways, but she stood still and waited for his assessment.

"You'll need to take off that ring." Eton nodded toward her hand.

Blossom curled it against her chest. "No." There was no way she would allow this ring to leave her finger.

"It's easily noticed. If Syndicate Mercer sees it, she'll require you relinquish it to her. I'm honestly surprised she didn't take it last time. You're better to leave it here." When she didn't move, Eton took a step forward. "It's clearly valuable to you. If you mean to keep it safe—to keep it at all—then it has to stay here. No one can ever see it."

Blossom's determination to appear Aero fled from her like a candle flame in a windstorm. She wanted to help an innocent family, but she wasn't sure she could part with his ring. Her finger skimmed the engraving, the single word, *Beauty.* She could hear him say it in that voice of his. *Hello, Beauty*, he'd say. Or, *Good morning, Beauty.* And her heart would stop beating and race like a drum all at once.

Horrified, Blossom tugged the ring from her finger and offered it one last longing look before she placed it in Eton's open palm. She might as well have chopped off her whole finger and handed it to him. She felt as incomplete as the wine glass she shattered on Kaide's floor so long ago.

"Now am I Aero enough?" Blossom held out her hands and let him look.

Eton's eyes tracked up and down, from her newly-shaved head to the toes of her pointed white shoes, taking in every stitch.

At last, he allowed a curt nod. "Aero enough, but not a Vice Syndicate, yet." Eton stepped away long enough to collect a floor-length cloak from the closet.

He might as well have brought her a snake.

Blossom didn't want it. The sight of it solidified the reality of her new position. Where the black cloak of Pyro represented the esteem and power of Kaide's position, this white Aero cloak was yet another mechanism to keep her trapped here.

"Go on," Eton pressed, draping the cloak over his forearm to display it for her.

Blossom reached out cautiously and skimmed the fabric with the tip of her finger. It was incredibly soft, as smooth as baby fox fur. Each thread held a hint of shine so the whole cloak seemed to shimmer in the light. Along its midline sat a row of opalescent buttons, lined on each side by delicate filigrees embroidered in matching white.

"I have to?"

Eton nodded and held it up. Blossom slipped her arms in. Wearing this cloak was nothing after she'd already given up her alder wood ring.

As she worked to close the buttons along the front, Eton asked, "Now, what is your plan, exactly?"

"I'm going to exile the Aero traitor so the Syndicate will trust me and let me have my totem."

Eton blinked, clearly at a loss over the unexpected answer. "I thought—"

"But I'm going to do it my way."

"What does that mean?"

"I'm going to buy them enough supplies to survive the journey to the capital. Then, they can make their own way from there."

Eton closed his eyes and sighed. "You can't do that. She'll find out. She always does—"

Blossom put up her hand to stop him. She'd heard enough of his protests for one morning. "This is what I'm doing. I don't care if you like it or not. You don't have to help me. But if you're not going to help me, point me in the direction of the nearest market, and give me some money. Just don't stand in my way."

As she knew he would, Eton caved like a puffed-up pastry. Blossom didn't so much as glance at her reflection in the mirror before she maneuvered her newly dressed form to the door of her room. This wasn't her, not really. This was an Aero abomination of the girl called Blossom. The real Blossom was in Pyrona, reading books in Kaide's private library, listening to jazz, and feeling his fingers rake through her curls.

"What's that?" Eton asked as they filed into the elevator.

"What?" Blossom looked down to see if she missed a button.

"That song you're humming. I've never heard it before. Either that, or you're really bad at humming."

"Probably both," Blossom answered, disinterested in

explaining her experiences with jazz. She'd have to be more careful.

When Eton was certain she wouldn't sway from her plan, he brought her to a small train platform. It was covered in cool white tile from floor to ceiling, and a slender silver train sat with doors open, waiting for them.

"You have a train?" Blossom asked when she saw it. Was it possible she'd been so out of it she'd missed a network of train lines throughout Aerona?

"This is the Robin, a train reserved for Aeros of a certain class, though some are wealthy enough to buy passage. Kind of like the portals."

"Can't we walk?" Now that she had a half-dozen layers of Aerona's finest fabrics draped over her body, the cold tunnels might actually be tolerable. Anything would be better than a train.

"You're a Vice Syndicate now. Walking in the tunnels would be highly unusual."

Blossom sank to the low bench inside the car and gripped the nearest handhold. Her stomach already churned at the idea of sliding through the earth in this metal snake. "I don't have a good track record with moving things," she warned him as the doors pressed shut, sealing them inside.

"I remember." Blossom didn't imagine the experience of dragging her to the portal room, forcing her inside, and holding her against the wall while she threw up on his shirt was a pleasant memory for Eton.

To this day, it filled her with a sick sort of satisfaction. He could have let her have her real totem. He could have let her go. He could have pretended he never saw her land. She could have gone home to Kaide, and they could have figured something out.

But Eton had obeyed his orders. He'd captured her—using force, as necessary—and brought her back to Aerona. The spittle on his crisp, white shirt was a far smaller punishment than he deserved.

The train lurched into motion, sailing down the slim tunnel with nothing more than a quiet clacking as it drove along the tracks. Blossom closed her eyes and imagined herself in the transport, sitting in Kaide's lap, or in a portal room with his lips pressed hard to hers, his hands taking in all he could—anything to still the swirling in her stomach.

"Blossom?" Eton's voice pulled her back.

"What?" she snapped.

"You're humming again. And we're at the Emporium," he said as he motioned to the open doors and the awaiting, white platform.

Blossom huffed and rushed for the door, but Eton caught her by the arm. "No, not like that. In control, even when you're not. Try again."

He released her, but it was too late. She was already angry, her lips pressed in a thin line and her eyes narrowed at him.

"That's terrible. Try again. You can be angry, but don't show it. Even you can do better than that." He smirked when he knew he'd won.

Blossom wasn't one to have her pride wounded. As much as it pained her, she swallowed down her anger and forced her feet onto the platform with slow, careful steps, though she would have much preferred to stomp away from him.

"Better," he conceded quietly.

Had Blossom not felt the movement of the train, she would have thought they were still at the elevator to her apartment. The platform looked eerily the same—though everything in Aerona was that same ugly white. Even Blossom was covered in head-to-toe white.

It made her sick.

But rather than an elevator, this platform had only a small hallway that led to a secure door. Eton scanned his palm to open it and reveal a bustling marketplace.

Storefronts lined the enormous circle—at least two hundred paces across—and in the middle, a railed balcony. Even from where she stood, Blossom could see a dozen food shops with skewered meats, smoked fish, and baked goods. A flower shop overflowed with ruby-pink daisies, gold chrysanthemums, and soft lavender.

"The Aerona Emporium," Eton announced with practiced airs. He stepped to the edge of a balcony, and when Blossom joined him, she saw why he stood there. This was merely one floor of many. There were at least eight, if she counted right, each a ring that sat deeper than the one above it.

From such a vantage, Blossom was tempted to leap. Her falcon wings would spread wide and carry her easily as she soared, flying past shops and patrons as naturally as the wind itself. Her fingers found the edge of her metal bracelet and tugged. She sighed when it remained firmly in place, as always.

For a good hour, Eton led her from shop to shop and let her pick out what she wanted—a pair of large, warm winter coats, and a smaller one for the girl. Three hats lined with elk fur and matching gloves for each. Boots she could only hope were the right size. An oversized bag stuffed full of water bottles, preserved meats, matches, and various other survival gear.

When it was time to pay, Eton produced a slim, white square, no larger than her palm and as thin as the thinnest metal. He showed it to the balding man with a mallard totem before depositing it back in his pocket.

"What is that?" Blossom inquired.

"It's a form of automatic payment. Rather than pay at each store, shop owners will deduct the amount from your account automatically. So as not to inconvenience you by making you wait," he explained.

Blossom remembered that, like Kaide, she was entitled to a considerable salary for her 'service' to her branch. It seemed silly to think someone could have so much money that spending it was an inconvenience. As it was, she couldn't argue. With arms full of supplies and winter clothes, she was relieved to not have to do it herself.

As soon as they left each store, Eton collected the items she'd picked and carried them to the next shop. "I can do it myself," Blossom argued for the tenth time.

"No, you have a position and title to uphold. What would people think if you carried all this while your advisor stood idle beside you?"

"I don't care what they think."

"You should. That's half your problem." Blossom didn't want to know what the other half was.

Her eyes scanned the shoppers moving about their business. Most wore suits like the one beneath her cloak, but others were dressed more plainly, with loose tops and pants not unlike those she wore in the Alderwood. Whether fancy or not, Blossom couldn't decide why she should care what anyone thought of her.

Then again, earning popular opinion had never been her talent.

"Where else do you want to go?" Eton asked as he readjusted the items tucked under his arms.

Blossom looked at the nearby storefronts and pointed to the one she wanted. "That one." Eton followed her gaze to the sign that read, *Ismenia's Arms*. Racks of knives and daggers stood on either side of the entrance, but further inside, Blossom could see bows lining the back wall.

Without waiting for him, Blossom crossed the walkway and navigated past the shoppers who clogged her passage into the store. Most were a head taller and didn't seem to even notice her until she was already gone, but Blossom paid them no mind.

At last, she arrived at the back wall, the one that held a dozen models of bows, though upon closer investigation, they were like nothing she'd seen before.

A child of the forest, Blossom had held her fair share of bows. She'd made her own when she was nine—with Hale's help. After that, Parson had shown her how to make arrows from the cast-off bits from the cut and feathers they plucked from birds he hunted. And if she was being honest, she was pretty good with a bow. Not as good as Parson, but good enough to get her own meal when she wanted one.

But these were something else entirely. Rather than wood pulled into the rounded shape of a bow and tied with horse hair, these were metal—a few of them even glass. The bowstrings weren't strings at all, but instead some sort of metal fibers spun into an impossibly strong cable. Blossom had only begun to trace her finger along the edge of the nearest one when Eton sounded behind her. "A compound bow?"

"For hunting," Blossom explained, though she wasn't sure this was what she wanted after all.

"Why not a spear? Oh, I know. A rock. You should give them a rock."

"What are you going on about?" Blossom didn't even offer him her disinterested glare.

"You want someone to survive using one of these? It's so rudimentary, it's ridiculous—" His voice fell away as the realization hit him. "This is what you used to hunt in the Alderwood?"

Blossom didn't bother to answer. He knew already.

"These are for showmanship competitions. No one actually uses these to hunt for *food*."

"Then what do you recommend?" This time, she turned and crossed her arms. As much as she hated it, she needed him. If she was going to give the 'criminals' a chance at survival, they needed something useful.

Eton nodded toward the left wall of the shop. "A small rifle. And a dagger for cleaning the meat."

"And they'll know how to use that?" She eyed the slender wooden devices with suspicion.

But Eton only chuckled at her ignorance. "Everyone knows how to use a rifle. Especially a little one like this," he said as he thrust his chin toward the bottom row. "It'll be easy enough to handle, light to carry, and quick to reload. That's the one you want."

Blossom collected the one he picked out, but she spent another minute readjusting her grip to his satisfaction.

"It's not loaded, but never point a rifle at anyone you don't want to die."

She tried not to fluster at that particular comment. Instead, she walked to the store front and picked out a small dagger with a serrated edge—the kind that would easily cut through animal fur. Then, Eton paid and walked her back to the Robin.

On the platform, he helped her open up the large bag and fill it with all the supplies. Only the coats, hats, and gloves were left out.

Then, as she'd dreaded all morning, it was time to exile an innocent family. Eton set the Robin in motion, but after only a few minutes, Blossom knew it wasn't going to go well. She searched the train for anything to retch into, but of course, there was nothing but clean white floors and matching white walls.

At the last moment, Blossom thought to turn away and spew her breakfast onto the floor by the door, missing her cloak entirely. The air hung heavy with spoil and sickness, and when at last Blossom righted and wiped a hand across her lips, Eton had moved three full seats away, the back of his hand pressed to his mouth as if he, too, might be sick.

"I'm sorry," she squeaked. What she wouldn't give for a handcloth and a drink of water. Without either, Blossom did her best to remove the spittle from her face and swallow down the dank flavor of her own regurgitated meal.

"Are we almost there?" she begged when her stomach churned again minutes later.

"About halfway." Eton pinched his nostrils shut with his fingers.

"That far?" Blossom tried not to whine, but there was no way she would make it that long. There was nothing she could do but resume the same position and spew again, though thank the Mother it was far less this time.

"Seriously?"

For the last ten minutes, Blossom dry heaved until her stomach ached and her sides began to cramp. Her mouth was horribly parched and coated in retch.

When finally the train slowed to a stop and the doors parted, she didn't know who was more glad to be free. Eton bolted for the platform like the train had caught fire.

Blossom trudged out after him, relieved to be on solid ground, and a little impressed she'd managed to escape the whole event without so much as a stray drop on her cloak to betray her sickness.

All in all, she'd done well. She felt rotten and hated to let Eton see her that way, but it was nothing compared to what she was about to do.

"Where are we?" she asked when the crisp platform faded into a raw stone corridor before opening into the wide lava tube. This time, there was almost no one present, and of the dozen or so who were, they all wore the same plain clothes she'd seen at the Emporium. If she didn't know better, she'd say they weren't in Aerona anymore.

"These are the outskirts, the poorest housing units well outside the city. This is where the Hammonds live."

Not for much longer, Blossom thought sourly.

With the large bag on his shoulder and the coats hung over his arm, Eton led her through the main lava tube to a smaller branch, and another one after that. The corridor became narrower and dimmer with each turn.

An older woman with grey wisps of hair stopped suddenly when she saw them turn the corner. "Bless me, Eton Samina. If I didn't see it with my own eyes—"

"A pleasure as always, Mrs. Ruen." He nodded politely to the woman as he waited for Blossom to pass her—the tunnel wasn't wide enough to fit them both at once.

"Who was that?" Blossom asked when they were around the next bend.

"Just an old woman. Don't worry about her." He waved his hand in the air, as if she was nothing more than a pesky insect.

Blossom was inclined to believe him until another person, this one an older man with a long white beard, stopped at the sight of Eton and began to mumble under his breath as he neared. When he was close enough, he reached out for Eton's shoulder and said, "Glad to have you back, son."

"Thank you, Mr. Grone," Eton replied with a polite smile. Then, he peeled himself away from the man, as if touching him was painful.

"That was your da?" Blossom asked after the next turn.

Eton frowned at her. "Of course not. Here we are." He pointed to an unmarked door in the middle of the impossibly small hallway.

Blossom half suspected he had merely picked one at random to get her to quiet, but then she heard the playful shrieks of a girl inside.

The Hammonds had a little girl, she remembered.

With a hand has heavy as lead, Blossom reached up and knocked, producing a hollow, metallic ring through the hall. The girl's shrieks stopped instantly.

Quiet footfalls grew gradually louder until a woman pulled open the door. Blossom didn't know what she expected, but this pretty woman in her twenties, with soft features and a full head of lovely blonde hair wasn't it. The delicate way her fingers grasped the door and the carefully pinned hair left no doubt: Kiza Hammond was a woman of elegance.

"I'm looking for Mr. Wersa Hammond," Blossom stammered as the woman stood in wait.

With one hand still on the doorframe, the woman turned and called out for him. A few seconds later, her husband's wiry frame appeared behind her. His eyes bounced from Blossom to Eton to Blossom once more, but the way his jaw rippled and his lips went thin, Blossom knew she wouldn't have to explain it.

He knew why they were there.

"Go and get Helena ready," he told his wife. She slipped away and left them alone. "We just need a moment," he explained.

How he was so calm about being exiled with his family, Blossom would never understand. If it had been her, she would have kicked and screamed until the last second.

"Take as much time as you need," Blossom said, trying her best to make this horrible situation that much less horrible, but both Eton and Wersa Hammond openly stared at her.

Kiza Hammond reappeared with a long-sleeved shirt and a bag on her back. Both her hands rested on the shoulders of a light-eyed girl, the one Blossom guessed to be Helena Hammond. She was no more than five years old.

Blossom wanted to kick herself that she hadn't thought to get anything to comfort the girl—a toy or a book or something, anything to distract her, if only for a short while.

As it was, Blossom had nothing.

"You have to tell him," Eton prodded.

Blossom swallowed hard and ran her hands down the front of her cloak, never taking her eyes off the girl. "I've been tasked with escorting you to the surface for exile."

Wersa Hammond plucked his daughter from the ground and held her against his chest. She flopped her head against his shoulder as she had clearly done a thousand times before.

After that, no one moved. "Walk them back to the main lava tube," Eton instructed.

Blossom wasn't sure she could find the way, but it turned out to be easy. As long as she picked the largest passageway, she knew she was moving in the right direction. Behind her, she could hear Eton's careful steps followed by Wersa and his wife. No one spoke, and Blossom didn't turn around for fear of what she might see on their faces.

It would be all right, she reminded herself. She wouldn't be doing this if she thought they would really be in danger.

So Blossom held her head high and navigated the dim stone walkways until they emerged in the main lava tube.

"There's an elevator down there to the left."

Blossom followed Eton's instructions and walked the Hammonds to the doors of the elevator. She tried to ooze calmness as she waited, but she felt anything but. She was closer to explosion than serenity.

At last, the shimmering elevator doors slid open, and the five of them entered. No sooner were the doors shut, than Blossom pulled the coats from Eton's arms.

"We don't have much time. Put these on," Blossom said as she shoved the coats toward Wersa and his wife. He didn't hesitate to set little Helena on the floor as he worked to get the coat over his shoulders. Wasting no time, Blossom collected the smallest coat and helped the girl into it. "Here you are, Helena. Nice and warm, with fox fur here on the collar. Isn't it soft?" she asked in her sweetest voice, desperate to keep from alarming the girl.

Eton handed over the hats and gloves, and again, Blossom helped Helena, frantic to get each of her little fingers into the right spot before they reached the surface.

Then, Eton handed the heavy bag to Wersa and helped him center it on his shoulders. "There's a hunting rifle and ammo, a dagger, matches, warm blankets, water-proof boots," Eton explained, but Wersa only nodded. He reached for Helena as the elevator finally stopped and the doors slid apart.

Blossom was ill-prepared to see the surface.

A horrific, howling wind flew into the metal box, carrying snowflakes and stealing the heat from her lungs. Like being plunged into a frozen lake, Blossom gasped at the sudden coldness. The sky was a grey blanket, far from the crisp-blue hue she'd always known. The surrounding area was nothing more than a snow-filled barren.

Kiza looked back at Eton, her eyes heavy with sorrow, before she said, "Best of luck, Eton. And to you, Ms. Frane." Her hand fell to Blossom's forearm with a light squeeze before she plunged into the knee-high snow.

"Be safe," was all Blossom could think to say as Wersa followed after his wife, their daughter held tight in his arms.

Had she questioned Eton's determination to use the shocking feature of the bracelet, Blossom would have left, too.

With arms clasped tightly over her chest, Blossom watched them fade into the cold, their figures distorted by the snow flying past. The air in her lungs felt like needles, but still she waited. Even once they were out of sight, too far away or hidden by too much snow to be seen, Blossom wouldn't move.

Eton smacked the button to close the doors. The elevator kept the cold air inside as they descended. The resulting quiet seemed so much louder after the howling winds.

"You think they'll make it?" Blossom heard herself ask. It would never sit right with her, what happened to the Hammonds, but at least Blossom could live with the knowledge that she'd done everything in her power to give them their best chance at success.

Eton's gaze became soft as he shrugged. "There's no way to know. You did the best you could. More than anyone else would have."

"I did good?" she asked with a tempered smile.

"You did well," he corrected. "But we never mention this to anyone. Ever. Understood?" Eton's stern words were a direct contrast to the proud smile he wore. No matter what he said, Blossom knew she'd earned his respect.

TRADE

BEFORE RAENE could make sense of what was happening, Da had a hand on her shoulder and thrust her into the daylit clearing in front of Hale's tent. Too late she realized she wore nothing more than someone's shirt Hale had borrowed the night before, and her braid was loose and messed from sleep.

She put an arm over her eyes to shield them from the too-bright morning light, so intense after the dimness of the tent.

"Come along, Ms. Randal!" Da sang as he walked her through camp, either enjoying her confusion or oblivious to it.

Raene could feel every eye find her as she walked, looking her up and down. She heard the whispers as these strangers questioned why she wore a night shirt, why Da was so intent on taking her wherever they were going, why she decided to be Terra.

Tears pricked behind her eyes within seconds, but Raene blinked them away. She wouldn't let them make her ashamed of being Pyro. After Kaide's claws marred her face, Raene had grown accustomed to the less-than-friendly stares of those around her. She'd quickly learned to ignore the comments and keep her chin up, a skill that served her well today. Inside, she was as taut as a bowstring. To everyone else, she was calm and at ease.

By the time she realized where Da was headed, they were already within steps of Lathan's tent. She ducked her head and darted inside, as if dodging a loosed arrow.

Raene thanked her luck when Da remained outside. "Get dressed quickly, Ms. Randal. We're already late!"

Tasia closed in a second later. "Don't worry, he doesn't mean any harm." She held out a clean set of Raene's Pyro clothes and pushed her toward the partition.

Raene was still clasping the ties behind her back when she heard Hale's shouts outside. She hurried to finish tying her shirt and resigned herself to leave her hair as it was as she shot back into the clearing.

"You had no right to do that!" Hale shouted at Da, his cheeks red, and his eyes narrowed in an anger she had never imagined to see from him. Raene realized he was protecting her—from what, she wasn't sure—but it warmed her to see him so up in arms for her sake.

"We're late," Da replied, calm and smiling in the face of Hale's fury. "We have a trade with Hydra this morning."

"I'm going as well. There was no need for that."

"Not today, son. And there *was* a need. We need her. And we're *late*." Da made it sound like the whole deal would fracture without Raene there to make it happen.

But Hale wouldn't hear any of it. He took a step closer and raised a pointed finger at Da. "You dragged her across camp like she'd done something wrong. She's my *bride*," Hale shouted.

"That's enough," Lathan boomed. Raene hadn't even noticed he was standing a few steps behind Da. Hale, too, seemed surprised by his oldest brother stepping in. But as always, Lathan had spoken, and that was that.

It was then Hale saw her standing at the tent flap.

Ignoring Lathan and Da, he rushed over and collected

her hands in his. He squeezed them so tight, the edges of his rings dug into her fingers. "You did nothing wrong. This isn't your fault, got it?"

Raene nodded, unsure of what he meant.

Then she realized how it looked. She'd spent the night in Hale's tent, in borrowed clothes, only to be dragged away by Da in the morning. They had words for such women in Pyrona, though Raene had never thought to have anyone think them about her.

A second later, Hale cupped his hand against her cheek. His sage-green eyes were soft and wounded, like he thought he'd personally offended her. Raene felt her humiliation fade to warmth under such a gaze. She closed her eyes as he whispered, "You will never be treated this way again. I'll make sure of it." Despite the morning chaos, Raene felt her pulse slow and her anxiety slip away, if only a little.

"Time to go!" Da interrupted with an invincible smile. "Let's go, child," he said to Raene.

Raene tried to pull her hands from Hale's, but he held tight. "Just stay calm. Don't let anyone get you fired up. The Mother will protect you. You'll be fine." Then she realized he worried she would transition in anger again.

He couldn't know how she shared that worry.

"I'll do my best," she replied, though it sounded inadequate, even to her. When she could stall no longer, Raene turned to go, but that didn't keep Hale from planting a sweet kiss on her cheek.

Raene tensed in surprise. She hadn't expected such a display of affection from him, especially not after their already tumultuous morning. As always, Hale was calm and confident in himself. He smiled warmly as she left, and she was not at all sure if she should kiss him back.

Following behind Da, Raene put her hand over her cheek, at a loss as to all that had happened this morning.

When she looked up, she saw Parson standing before his tent, watching her pass without a word. Their eyes connected for a moment, and she couldn't help but wonder if he'd seen Hale kiss her.

Raene dropped her hand and continued to hurry after Da and Lathan, both marching through the camp like they were on their way somewhere very important. She trotted to catch up.

On the edge of camp, Da pulled himself up into the driver's seat of an alder wood cart with wheels as high as her chest. At the front, two pairs of horses stood waiting in their harnesses. In the back were boards of rough-cut alder wood, long enough to build a house. Even Raene knew such wood was insanely valuable.

"Up here with me, my daughter," Da said with an amused smile and an outstretched hand. Raene didn't like to be addressed as his daughter, but she knew he didn't mean it unkindly. She accepted his hand and hoisted herself into the seat beside him.

"Today, we meet a Hydra clan for a trade. It'll be good for you to see how our clan works." Da didn't wait for a response as he grabbed hold of the reins and snapped them to spur the horses into motion. "And I thought you could use a day away from *them*." He leaned in and said it like a secret despite how he yelled over the rumble of horse hooves.

Raene kept both her hands clasped on the cart rail to keep from bouncing around so much, but soon enough, the horses settled into an easy trot. Great big alder trees passed one by one, and every few minutes, she'd find a stray beam of morning sunlight that managed its way through the canopy. Even in the shadows, the lovely alder blooms colored the branches so that it appeared they moved under a stunning pink ceiling.

"Parson told me what happened at the cut yesterday,"

Da announced quite suddenly.

Raene's mouth fell open for a half-second as the shock struck her. Parson had kept her transition from Hale only to tell Da? She should have known he wouldn't really keep her secret. "I'm sorry. It won't happen again," she said in her defense.

Da's happy smile faded into a confused look. "What ever do you mean, my child?"

Oh no.

With a cringe, she realized she'd misunderstood. "What did Parson say?" She hoped distracting Da with questions would make him forget the idea entirely.

"That he suggested you choose Hale as your husband."

Oh, *that*.

"Yes, he did." Raene worked to keep the wound hidden. She had no real desire to marry Parson, but it hurt that someone—even him—would reject her so easily.

She was lucky that at least Hale seemed interested in getting to know her.

"You don't know my sons well yet, but you will. And you'll learn they are all good men. Lathan has a bear's quiet presence, and his senses are second-to-none. Parson has the strength and rage of his bear, though he's also fiercely protective. And Hale has a bear's size and keen mind. They are all bears, but they are all so different. You'll have to know them better to see it. I'm sure Parson meant no disrespect. He said it because he thought it was right." Da smiled, as if he was proud of Parson. "But I want to be clear. Your uncle and I agreed, and on this point he was adamant. Your husband is to be of your choosing."

"I understand." It wasn't much of a decision anymore; there was nothing Raene could do about it now.

"Do you? The choice is yours, Ms. Randal. You can have any Frane son you like. Technically, you could even choose Lathan." Da nodded to where Lathan and a half-dozen other young men each rode horses to the side and rear of the cart. "But to tell you the truth, I would absolve the contract before allowing it. Still, the choice is yours."

Raene blinked at him. "Are you suggesting I choose a husband that doesn't want me?" Surely he didn't mean for her to choose Parson after he'd already declared his disinterest in her?

"I'm suggesting you know the specifics of your arrangement before you make your decision. They are both good men. They will both make good husbands. It will be up to you to decide what you want."

Raene didn't know what to say to that, but Da didn't let her sit in silence for long.

"Your uncle must care for you greatly to make such a trade for you. I've never seen such conditions for a marriage arrangement."

"That didn't keep him from sending me away." The words tasted like vinegar, and she regretted them as soon as they passed her lips, but she knew they were true nonetheless.

"Ah, but that's the way of it, my dear." Da's voice turned from amused to soothing, like Olin's would have been. "In the beginning of the realm, when a trade was made, daughters would often steal away to their home clans. To secure their trades, the clans agreed that they would draw up contracts, and the daughters would never see home again. It was the only way to assure loyalty to the receiving clan. The long-distance trades are the most sacred because they are the most secure, as yours is. It is a great honor to have such an alliance, for you and Blossom both."

Raene didn't feel honored. She felt discarded, thrown to the wind without a care. Of course, she knew better, but that didn't keep her from feeling that way.

When Da went quiet, Raene thought she was in the clear, but of course, she wasn't that lucky. "Now, what is it you wanted to tell me, dear?"

Raene groaned inwardly. She was usually so much more careful than this. Since when did she get herself into these situations? All her years of careful practice and coyness, and she'd let it all go to waste after only a few days in the Bear Clan.

"I transitioned at the cut yesterday, after Parson—"

When Da's eyebrows went up in surprise, Raene knew he hadn't heard a word of it from Parson or anyone else. Raene had shot her own damn foot.

For the first time since she'd met him days before, Da appeared genuinely concerned. "Do you see that young man there?" He pointed to the brunette boy riding a sandy mare at the back of their group. When Raene nodded, Da continued, "That's Endel Carson of the Bear Clan. Along with his sisters, he has a beaver totem. He is a talented carpenter, and even at only fifteen, he's been a great asset to us at the cut."

Raene nodded, at a loss to why he was telling her all this.

"That one there is Tanner Grace, a green anole. Do you know what that is?"

"A small lizard," she answered over the trotting hooves of the horses.

Da nodded. "And him, Orren Dean, a possum. Asla there is an elk. Loren is the last of a family of raccoons. The Connors are rabbits. You see, my daughter, within the Bear Clan, there are many totems. Some small, some large, some slow, some fast, but all of them are here for the protection of the bears. They live and work amongst us so that we will keep them from harm. My sons and I each took an oath to protect any member of our clan from danger. As one of the Bear Clan, you must always be the protector, never the predator."

Raene felt shame creep into her chest and settle there.

She killed an elk, and she just as easily could have killed any of the totems with them now. Maybe Olin had been right. Maybe she should have run. Sooner or later, she would kill someone.

Because at her core, Raene knew—she was a predator. She had claws for slicing and teeth for ripping. She had ears that could find any prey and strong, agile legs to chase down any that dared run from her. She was a tiger, a killing machine.

But that wasn't what Da wanted her to be. "I understand," she replied. It would be hard to stifle her urges, but she would do it. She had no choice. She couldn't be a murderer.

Raene could only imagine the look on Hale's face when someone told him that she'd killed a person. Not an innocent in the forest, but a member of his clan. A person he'd known his whole life. Or worse, what if he saw her do it? Not even Hale could be kind to her after witnessing such violence.

"I'm glad to hear it, my daughter. I trust we won't have to have this discussion again." Despite Da's gentle nature, his warning was clear enough.

Simply thinking about how she couldn't transition into her tiger form made her want it more. Da couldn't have known how his words would trigger her desire to run and hunt and kill. Less than a day after losing control, the urge grew within her again. Only this time, she knew how to get it to quiet—the one thing Da forbid.

As Hale suggested, she did her best to stay calm. There was nothing to be angry about, she reminded herself. Da was merely pointing out facts she already knew—she couldn't go around killing everyone.

Raene let herself get lost in the rolling motion of the cart and the rhythmic clop of the four horses before them. Thankfully, Da turned to one of the other boys on horseback beside them and chatted with him a while, leaving her to concentrate on the air going in and out of her lungs.

At midday, Lathan whistled. Like a well-choreographed procession, the horses and the cart stopped. The loudness of their motion became the quiet of the forest. Raene wondered if maybe he'd heard something—some danger, some threat to them. She perked her tiger ears but couldn't discern more than the usual sounds: bird wings fluttering, frog songs, and tiny feet scurrying across branches high above. Nothing out of place.

For a good minute, no one moved. Then, somehow signaled, the six horse-riders dismounted in unison. Raene turned to watch as they each tied their horse to the side of the cart before working to pull the rough-cut boards from the back. In pairs, they put the boards on their shoulders and maneuvered them into the open space far to the front of the cart. Without ceremony, they set them into neat piles before returning to the cart for more.

"What are we doing?" Raene finally asked Da.

"Trading with Hydra," he stated, as if it was obvious.

Raene wondered if maybe Da was starting to lose his senses. Surely this random clearing in the Alderwood wasn't a suitable place to exchange illegal lumber with another branch. Besides, it wasn't like there were actually any Hydras present.

The clan was still unloading the wood when the first glimpses of blue appeared. From the west, a similar procession neared the clearing. Rather than horses, the Hydra men rode camels, and one toward the back was seated high on the back of an elephant. The sight of it only reminded her of the elephant that stopped her from killing Olin at the Syndicate building.

She winced at the memory.

At the far edge of the clearing, the Hydra men stopped

and dismounted. From the sides of their animals, they unlatched bushels of straw, jugs of water, and dozens of other plants lashed into bundles. Like an intricate dance, the Terra men set about collecting the Hydra goods while the Hydra men worked to pull the alder boards onto some sort of sled hitched behind the elephant.

No one spoke until an older Hydra man approached. His facial hair was cut along his jaw line but shaved in the center of his chin. He wore a long, cerulean shirt that somehow turned into wide pants that swished when he walked.

Da climbed down from the cart to meet him. The two stood with shoulders clasped.

"There are shortages—" the Hydra man began before Da put up a silencing hand.

"Not to worry, old friend. Our clans have traded for decades and will continue to do so for decades more."

"Thank you, Argeran. We're working on it, I assure you. Next time will be better." He shot Raene a suspicious glare but didn't make mention of her Pyro attire.

"I have no doubt of it," Da answered with his classic playful smile. They each nodded to the other before returning to their respective parties.

When Da was seated, Lathan approached Raene's side of the cart. "You should tell him we'll have a smaller lot if he keeps this up. We can't trade a full lot of wood for a half lot of supplies."

"Let me handle it." Da waved him off.

"If you don't tell him now, he'll be offended at the next trade. You should give him some warning," Lathan continued.

Raene felt put in the middle of an uncomfortable situation yet again. The two men arguing across her put her even less at ease until she could take no more. She launched herself from the cart and landed on both feet behind Lathan.

When he turned and blinked at her, Raene smoothed out her pants and said, "I'd like to ride a horse on the way back."

"Very well, Lathan can sit here with me. We have much to discuss." Da pointed toward the cinnamon-colored horse tied to the side of the cart. "That one's his."

Lathan only offered Da a cross glare before he climbed into the cart.

Raene didn't waste a moment. She approached the horse and stroked its nose before loosening the reins and pulling herself into the saddle. It had been a few days since her last jaunt on a horse, but already, she settled into the familiar position.

When the men finished loading the last of the Hydra items, Da started their envoy back toward camp. He had to lead the cart in a wide turn before finding the path once more.

Raene was initially satisfied to be atop her own horse and have that freedom. Then, she realized, the cart moved at a horrifically slow pace. The four horses hitched to the cart moved at little more than a trot, and Raene was stuck trotting alongside.

"Did you see Blossom in Pyrona?" asked a voice behind her.

Raene turned to see a boy only a year or two older than her, his hair the same chocolate-brown as most Terras. She pulled the reins back to slow her horse and fell into step beside him.

"A little." Blossom and Raene's time in Pyrona hadn't overlapped by much, and what time they'd had was occupied with Kaide or the festival. If Raene had known their time would be cut short, she would have made better use of it.

When he inclined his head toward a passing alder tree, Raene caught sight of the horned deer tattooed on his neck—an elk. "How is she?" the boy asked.

Raene's mind raced with a thousand thoughts. *Lost in the world. Probably dead. Maybe worse.* But instead, she said, "She was well last I saw her." That much at least was the truth. "You were her friend?"

"No, I wasn't, but Gemini was."

"Gemini?" Raene couldn't recall why the name sounded familiar.

"The woman I'm courting. They were friends since they were young. You were wearing her sleep clothes this morning."

Oh right. "And you are?"

"Asla Brimmen."

"A pleasure to meet you, Mr. Brimmen. I'm Raene Randal." She extended her hand and shook his, feeling comfort in the habit of such a normal interaction. It was a welcome distraction from thinking of how good elk meat tasted.

And then, like it was nothing, Asla spurred his horse to trot away, though he slowed again only steps in front of her. Raene spent the rest of the day staring at his back.

The slow crawl of the procession left her itching to run. Wedged between two Terra boys—one of them an elk—and under the watchful eye of Da seated high up in the cart, Raene had no choice but to weather the dawdling pace back to camp.

Golden afternoon light peaked between the branches by the time they arrived. Raene had never been happier to see the moss-green tents of the Bear Clan. Another hour of slow clomping, and she would have lost her mind. She happily dismounted and handed her reins to Asla when she noticed Parson and Lathan talking—well, arguing.

To Raene, it was clear Parson was going somewhere. He had a quiver of arrows on his back and a large bow slung over his broad shoulders.

"It's not a good time to go running off," Lathan

warned him.

"We haven't had a kill in days. Someone needs to go," Parson replied.

"Go where?" Raene surprised even herself when she interjected.

"No one is going anywhere." Lathan's voice was nothing if not final. He even turned and began unloading the cart, sure the conversation was over.

Parson grunted his frustration and started to stomp away. Raene put a hand on his arm. "Where were you going to go?"

"Hunting. Some of us need *meat*." He nearly spat the last word at Lathan's back.

Raene stepped closer and lowered her voice. She tried not to sound desperate as she asked, "Can I go with you?"

"No, you heard him. I'm not—" Parson stopped and narrowed his eyes as he realized. He glanced once toward Lathan before he said, "At the stream. In an hour."

Raene wanted to ask more, but Parson had already turned to go. Then she saw why: Hale was approaching at a jog. His small smile grew until it consumed his features. "How'd it go?" His hand snaked around her waist as he turned her away from the cart.

"It was fine," she answered. As far as she could tell, nothing about the Hydra trade was out of the ordinary. "We saw some camels." Raene didn't tell him she'd never seen one in person before.

Hale beamed. "They're interesting creatures, aren't they? I'm glad you had a good day. Next time, we'll go together."

Raene didn't realize she'd be going to meet Hydra regularly. For some reason, she thought it would be just the once. Still, she smiled at Hale's insistence to protect her, even if it was only from Hydra traders.

Or maybe it was to protect them from her.

Raene felt that flare of aggression renewed. With Hale's arm around her waist, she worked to swallow it down. She kept her thoughts on her breathing and her steps, one by one taking her closer to Hale's tent.

She had no idea how she would get away.

"I got you something today," he said when they were far enough from the others.

Raene looked up at him. "You did?"

"A welcoming present. You'll see." Raene didn't press him further. Knowing she'd made plans to go hunting with Parson made her feel guilty. Knowing Hale had been picking out gifts for her in the meantime made her feel downright horrible. More and more, Raene felt like a she had turned into a terrible person.

Lying. Scheming. Killing. The old Raene was gone, and this new, awful Raene stood in her place.

At that moment, Raene made up her mind not to go. She couldn't change what had happened with the elk, but she didn't have to keep doing it.

Sooner or later, she was going to have to get her totem under control—might as well be now.

Raene and Hale pushed into his tent, already lit with his multitude of candles. On the table, goblets of wine were already filled, but it was the other items that caught her eye: stacks of moss-green and honey-brown fabrics. Terra clothes. A dozen items, if not more.

Hale pulled her over and let her inspect them up close. "These are shirts, all your size. And the pants had to be altered, but Yaiza finished them this afternoon. They should all fit."

Raene did her best to keep the horror from showing on her face. She knew he meant it as a sweet, welcoming gesture—he'd said as much—but she didn't want to wear Terra clothes—not now or ever. And it would only hurt him to refuse his gift.

"How about some wine?" Raene asked, to which Hale chuckled softly.

"I thought you'd never ask." His hand skimmed the small of her back as he handed her a goblet.

Raene drank eagerly. She gulped the wine but couldn't quench her thirst.

She wouldn't give in so easily. She didn't need to kill. Amberwine was satisfying enough.

Raene refused to give her totem power over her. She was more than capable of sitting in Hale's tent, drinking wine and chatting, without feeling the need to murder anyone or anything. Kaide had learned to keep his beast at bay, and Raene would do it, too.

And as much as it surprised her, she did like Hale. Rubbing her back and telling her stories, Hale had a way of calming her. No one else had been able to accomplish such a feat since her transformation.

"What did you do today?" Raene asked, eager to keep her mind on more civil subjects.

Hale shook his head. "Not much. I thought I'd be at the trade today. I took care of some things, checked on the outliers."

"Outliers?"

"The clan members who live outside of camp. The Grace family houses and tends the horses. The Connors have a garden that supplies us between trades, not that we really need it. Gemini grows some of the finest fruits, so no one's complaining." Hale shot her a smile, but Raene was too stuck on the name.

"She was friends with Blossom?"

"Gemini? She's friends with everyone, but yes. She was close to Blossom." Hale's features darkened in a way she hadn't seen before.

"I'm sorry. I shouldn't have asked." Raene slipped into her old habits of decorum.

"Can I ask who told you that?" There was a severity in his eyes that made Raene afraid.

She sipped her wind and told him. "Asla. Why?"

Hale stood and turned his back to her as he refilled his goblet with wine. "We've made it clear we don't want non-family to mention her."

"Why would you do that?" Raene sat stunned.

Hale turned, and for a moment, he stood in the dancing candlelight trying to find his words. "I'm sure you can imagine we're all rather upset with that particular turn of events. I have faith in the Mother and her plan, but that doesn't change the fact that I love my sister and hate that she's gone."

"Hale—" Raene began, but she ran out of words. Instead, she pushed out of her chair and wrapped her arms around his neck, mortified she'd even thought he might be so heartless. Tasia had warned her not to say anything, and Raene was simply too stupid to listen.

Hale's hands found her waist. "I shouldn't have said that," he whispered. "I trust the Mother. It's wrong of me to be angry."

"How could that be wrong?" Raene wondered how angry he would be if he ever found out Blossom was no longer under Kaide's protection—that she might not even be alive.

Hale pulled away but left a hand on each of her hips. "Did Da tell you I'll be clan leader?" When Raene shook her head, he continued, "Well, I will. And someday, all these people will turn to me for protection and guidance. I can't let myself get so emotional over things I can't change. Blossom was meant to go with your uncle. It was the Mother's will. I need to be better at showing my faith in her."

Hale tilted forward to kiss Raene's cheek. "And this is her will as well. You were meant to be here." Reminded,

177

Hale motioned toward the stack of clothes on the table. "There's a few nightshirts there. Why don't you get changed while I get us some dinner?"

He was gone before she could protest. Raene stood alone in his tent and tried to think of what she could say to him. She hadn't meant to upset him about Blossom, and she didn't want to disrupt this newfound trust he'd placed in her. But Raene couldn't let go of her Pyro roots so easily, not even for him.

Then, she saw the look on his face as he pushed into the tent with two full plates. He wore a deep-set frown at the Pyro clothes she still wore. "They didn't fit?"

Raene sucked in a breath for strength. In her best warm tone, she replied, "I would prefer to wear my Pyro clothes."

Hale set the plates on the table and collected her hands between both of his. "I know this is all new and strange, but it's for the best. Terras value modesty, and these clothes will put you in the best position in the eyes of the clan."

Raene kept careful control of her tone as she said, "I understand your Terra values, but I'm not Terra. I appreciate the gesture, really I do. But I want to wear my own clothes."

Hale sighed and released her. "As you wish."

After that, they talked and ate—bread and roasted vegetables, to her dismay—but an uneasy cloud hung over them. She continued to drink wine, but it did little to quiet the storm within her.

Raene could only wonder if they were having their first fight, but she knew resolution was futile. She wasn't willing to compromise. Hale could try to convince her all he wanted, but that wouldn't change who she was.

If nothing else, Raene was Pyro.

When evening faded into darkness, Hale surprised her and said, "I'm going to go sleep at Da's. Do you want me to get your bag from Lathan's tent?"

Raene's mouth fell open with shock at his refusal to sleep in the same tent as her while she wore her Pyro clothes. It was enough to destroy the last of her resolve. "I'll get it," she replied, seizing the opportunity before she could second guess it. "I could use some fresh air. All this wine—" Raene waved her hand like it was nothing, but she couldn't even fake a smile as she darted out the tent flap.

But rather than turn toward Lathan's tent, Raene didn't hesitate to trot into the forest. In the twilight, her human eyes were less useful, but it wasn't dark enough to give her cat eyes the advantage. She picked her footing carefully, following her nose toward the stream and the man who would take her hunting.

Parson used the edge of his fingernail to smooth out the fletching of an arrow. The lazy, meandering stream gurgled at his back where he sat on a large stone. An hour had come and gone and still she hadn't shown. He should have known she'd bail.

He shouldn't have let himself get excited to see her totem again. It was selfish to want to watch her hunt with his own two eyes, to witness her raw power in action. From the little glimpses he'd seen, Parson hummed with excitement. Only now, she hadn't showed, and his excitement had soured into disappointment.

She was probably curled up in Hale's tent, sipping wine and laughing, enjoying her new, carefree romance with the best man Parson knew. Maybe he was touching her shoulder. Maybe he was kissing her. Maybe worse.

It shouldn't bother him, he knew. He had no right to feel anything but happy for the new couple. He should have been ecstatic for his brother to have earned such a bride.

But Parson had never been in control of his emotions. They erupted like geysers, dissipated like thunderstorms. He was as powerless as a leaf sailing on the current of the lazy stream.

He tried to think of Blossom, of whatever life she was living in Pyrona with her new husband. The thought made him want to hurl. That rush of anger was all he had left of her, but it had lost its edge. Maybe she was happy there— maybe she enjoyed her new home.

If Pyrona produced people like Raene, it couldn't be *all* bad. Could it?

As always, his thoughts seemed to find their way back to the Pyro princess, to the tiger raging inside her.

His bear ears heard her first. The small snapping of a twig. The rustle of shoes on the leaf litter. Her red shirt appeared from a shadow a moment later. No, not red. *Scarlet*.

"I'd almost given up on you." Parson tried to tease her—to pretend like this wasn't as difficult as it was—but when he saw the stern frown that had once been her pleasant mouth, he knew it was no use.

"This way." Without waiting, Parson moved deeper into the woods. Her footsteps appeared behind him in seconds.

She was eager. She wanted this.

"How does this work?" she asked, her voice low, like she thought someone might overhear.

"We go far out, so far we won't accidentally get back to camp. We'll keep in sight of each other but not too close. We'll hunt small game, nothing messy. Only innocents." A moment later, he asked, "Do you know how to tell the difference?"

"In what?" Raene's arms crossed over her chest.

"Between innocents and totems." When she shook her head and looked up at him with those alluring eyes, Parson explained, "Innocents live their whole lives as an animal. They have nothing but instinct. Fear and hunger and survival. In totem form, we have those too, but we also have the human side. An innocent will flee on instinct. A totem will hesitate, their human side will think for a moment before they act. You can see it in their eyes."

"You said we'd be far enough away." There was no mistaking the fear in her voice.

"We will. Why?" And then, Parson knew. "Da said something."

"I don't want to talk about it," she countered. "I'm sorry, I just—"

Parson couldn't hold it against her. "I know. Believe me. I know." He increased his pace, hurrying to put camp as far behind them as possible. His bow jostled against his shoulders as he trotted further into the uncharted depths of the Alderwood.

He took her a good hour out until he knew they were well enough away, and then he took her another twenty minutes past that, just in case. At last, the time had come.

Parson tightened his bow and quiver against his back. "Ready?" When he looked over, Raene had crumbled. From the low hang of her shoulders to the way her eyes never left the ground, Parson could see her fighting it.

He should have stopped sooner.

"Go on," he prompted when she didn't move. "*Go*. Go hunt." Parson had to push her to get her to look at him, but once she did, he knew that was all it would take.

Her eyes blazed. Even in the dark, those blue eyes shone bright as they turned gold. Her pupils elongated into the fierce predator eyes that could see every animal in the night. Russet fur sprang up along her arms, spreading like fire through a dry meadow. Where before she'd been rigid, standing solidly and trying to hold it in, now she was wild, her arms shaking as they rippled with layer upon layer of

181

muscle.

In seconds, she fell forward into her cat stance and stretched her paws. When her tiger eyes caught on him, she released a low rumbling growl.

"Go!" Parson shouted, appealing to what little of human-Raene was still in there. She needed to hunt, to kill, to eat, but he would prefer if she didn't make *him* her meal.

He watched her race between the trees in awe. Parson had never been anything other than the most impressive creature in the Alderwood. In a forest of deer and rabbits and foxes, the bear was king. And now, at last, he'd been eclipsed. Raene was magnificent.

The sight of her made his chest ache.

Parson let her get a full minute's head start. He couldn't keep up with her, anyway. But still he waited those eternal seconds before giving in to his own transition. In his bear form, everything was so much clearer. There was only the tiger he tracked, the growl in his belly, the strength in his legs. No need to worry over his lost sister or the quiet beauty who took her place.

The scent of her filled his nostrils as soon as his transition was complete. Bear-Parson sniffed the area for several seconds, enough to get a sense of where he was and where he would come back to, but after that, he was only hunting.

His strong bear legs carried him between the trees, though it was a sort of clumsy ambling compared to the lean, capable strides of the tiger. *Her. The tiger*, he remembered. He was following a tiger.

Bear-Parson tried to hold on to the idea of her, of hunting *with* someone, after he'd been alone so long. He kept to her trail easily enough, only venturing away to catch his own meal—a pair of rabbits in a shallow burrow, a fox caught outside its hole, even an old badger, thankfully too slow to put up much of a fight.

But quickly enough, he followed her scent again. With his belly less empty, it was easier to concentrate, to remember why he was following her. Bear-Parson kept to her trail, running tirelessly through the dark woods until he heard her ahead.

Her cat feet were too quiet to hear at such a distance, but her hissing growls were loud enough. Bear-Parson raced ahead, eager to intervene if she was in danger, but instead, he found her circling a coyote. The air was thick with the scent of blood, and when they turned, he saw the coyote's mouth coated in crimson.

It had somehow managed to injure her. Without hesitation, bear-Parson flew forward and smashed his hulking frame into the coyote. The yellow-grey dog could do nothing as it was crushed against the ground, smothered and shattered in an instant.

Then came the fire in his shoulder. Claws dug deep into his flesh. Tiger claws.

Bear-Parson howled at the attack. The forest echoed with his sound as he threw her off him and watched her slide across the forest floor.

Tiger-Raene was too quick. She was on her feet and charging him a second later. Bear-Parson stood tall. He waited for her to be just near enough before he swatted her away, using his massive paw like a club.

She landed on the ground and was slower to get up this time. Bear-Parson seized the opportunity. He rushed her and stood over her, pinning her claws under his weight. She may have been quicker and more agile, but she could never beat him in a contest of strength.

He only had to wait for her to tire.

And tire she did, but only after several minutes of fighting him. She kicked and growled and squirmed to get a claw free, but bear-Parson remained. Only when he saw her transition begin, did he let his own occur. Had she been her human form beneath his heavy bear form, he would have crushed her instantly.

But Parson managed to calm himself and slip into his human form as she shrank beneath him. Before she could fight him, he grabbed both her wrists and pressed them hard into the ground.

"Did you eat?" he asked when her blue eyes caught his green ones.

"Let me go," she protested.

"Did you eat?" he repeated, demanding an answer.

Raene scowled deeply at him. "Foxes," she all but spat at him.

"How many?"

"Five."

Parson relaxed, more than impressed. "Five?"

She looked away as she said, "Two adults, three cubs." After that, he released her entirely. If she was human enough to be upset about killing fox cubs, then she wouldn't transition again. Not for a while, anyway.

He moved away, all too aware of how close they'd been just a moment before. His eyes fell to the body of the coyote only steps away. "What was that about?" He pointed, wondering if she knew coyotes were uncommon this far from Terrana, or that this one wasn't an innocent.

Raene sat up and shrugged. "Not sure. He jumped on my back and—" Suddenly remembering, she craned her neck over her shoulder and tried to see the damage.

Parson scooted through the leaf litter to have a look. In the dark, he couldn't see more than the crimson stain on her torn scarlet shirt. "It doesn't look too deep. Just flesh. Ruined your shirt, though."

Raene pulled her knees to her chest and rested her face against her arms. Where moments ago she'd been an impressive tiger, now she was a girl, curled up and scared.

"Raene—" he started, but he didn't know what else to

say.

"He got me Terra clothes," she whispered against her arm. Parson didn't see what one had to do with the other, but she clearly told him for a reason. He was just too dumb to figure it out.

"That's good, isn't it?"

She picked up her head and turned to look at him, her eyes dim and her smile fake. "Yes, it is."

Parson immediately knew he'd guessed wrong. She pushed to her feet and started back in the direction they'd come, never for a moment guessing her whereabouts. He could do little more than jump up and follow her.

"You don't want to be Terra?" As he said it, he saw it clearly. "Because you're Pyro. *Actually* Pyro."

She stopped and pulled her yellow hair away from her neck. There, in the same spot as his, a tattoo, only hers was the word PYRO in red and black in the shape of a tiger. "I'm not one of you. There's nothing I can do to change that."

Raene lowered her hair and resumed her slow trudge through the forest.

"What did Da say?" Something had happened, that much was clear, but how his family of generally well-meaning men had managed to make her feel so unwelcome, he had no idea.

"That I can't be a predator. I have to be a protector."

Parson almost laughed. "He's used that speech on me more times than I can count. Don't let it get to you. He doesn't understand."

She didn't seem to think it was very funny.

"What else?" he pressed.

"Nothing."

"Raene—"

"I said it's nothing!" she screamed in exasperation.

Parson stopped and waited. "That doesn't sound like

nothing. I've seen you covered in blood. What's so bad you can't tell me?"

"I'm *Pyro*!" Again, she shouted her frustrations at him, but he couldn't understand why. Everyone knew she was Pyro. "I *am* a predator. I want to hunt and kill and it's the only damn thing I can think about that doesn't make me—" She stopped and huffed a breath before she continued. "It's the one thing I'm not allowed to do."

"Don't worry about Da. He's trying to be a good clan leader. He thinks that's what you need to hear. Seriously, don't worry about him." Parson tried to express how useless those speeches were, but he knew he wasn't doing a good job.

Raene kicked a leaf with the toe of her boot. "Not just Da."

"Oh." Parson let it slip before he meant to. He should have known. "Hale doesn't understand. He's never—" He struggled to explain it without putting down his brother. "He doesn't have what we have. His totem is quiet. He's always in control, and he only transitions when he means to. He thinks it's easy—"

"It's not easy," Raene said, her voice dripping in misery. She threw her hands out in frustration. "I feel like I'm going to explode!"

It was then Parson understood. She wasn't done. She still had that intense hunger within her. He'd pulled her back to human form before she was ready.

Even in the dark, Parson's bear eyes saw every flicker of her exasperation. He could see every flinch of pain as she fought that urge inside her. She was more than any of them knew.

"Then go," he told her.

"What?" she screamed louder than she needed to.

Parson took a step closer. "Go." He pointed toward the trees lost in shadow. "Hunt. Kill. Whatever it takes."

Her eyes darted from Parson, to his pointed finger, to the woods, then back to him. Her confusion was clear. She thought he was playing a trick.

Parson gripped each of her shoulders and gave her a small shake. With his eyes level with hers, he told her, "Go get it done. You can't do anything until you get it out. So go."

Her jaw clenched tight for a moment before she replied, "The coyote, it wasn't an innocent. It was a totem—"

Parson was more than a little impressed she'd figured it out on the first try. He knew coyotes were almost always agents of the Alderai, sent to monitor or capture or even kill. But Raene didn't, and she figured it out in a matter of seconds.

He couldn't let her hunt alone.

"I'll watch you. I'll stay with you." He released her and thrust her toward the nearest alder tree. "Go," he shouted. When she only stopped and glared, he screamed louder, "I said *go!*"

At last, her totem got the better of her. She transitioned in a flash, her warm skin enveloped in orange fur that looked more tawny-brown in the dark. Her usually lovely features twisted into the intense face of her predatory cat. What once was tall and polite became low and growling.

Parson only let himself admire her for an instant. She was off and running, and this time, he would have to keep close.

And he couldn't keep up with her in his human form.

So Parson forced himself back into a bear. It was less effortless than usual; without his anger or hunger to fuel it, his transition took real work, but he made it happen. His bear claws struck the ground and propelled him through the trees, following her trail again.

At first, it seemed as though he wouldn't be able to

catch her. She was faster, more agile. She could turn around the trees with a speed he could never manage. But then he found her—just in time to hear the crunch of tiny bones and watch the furry body of some mangled creature slide down her throat.

Tiger-Raene offered him a wayward glance as he slammed to a stop a few hundred paces away. Parson wondered if she'd recognize him, if she knew he was her ally and not her enemy.

Thankfully, she chose to disappear between the trees instead. Of course, to bear-Parson, she could never really disappear. He could smell her as if she were standing right in front of him, that smokiness of Pyrona with her signature scent. He could never lose her.

ENVIOUS

RAENE HAD NO idea how many lives she'd ended this night, but as the rabbit sank to her belly, she knew she'd finally had her fill. The heat in her veins subsided, and Raene was able to retake her human form. That urge was quiet at last.

Crouched low, it felt odd to push to standing after so long with all fours on the ground. Without a tail, it took her several moments to regain her balance. Her tiger ears caught every sound around her, including the transition of the bear that followed her all night. On the far side of the narrow clearing, he, too, stood tall.

And then he was moving toward her at a run. His dark chestnut hair had come loose and bounced with each step as he neared. His eyes never left her.

"Get your fill?" he asked when he was near enough.

Raene nodded. "I couldn't eat another bite."

Parson offered her a satisfied smile, and Raene realized she'd never really seen him smile before. "Just in time."

"For what?"

"Morning." He pointed to the canopy, and sure enough, a tiny smear of pale blue had appeared across the night sky.

She'd been out hunting all night.

"We should get back." Raene didn't wait for him as she started toward camp. Then, a second later, she turned back. "Thank you, Parson. Really. I feel much better." It was hard to be open and genuine with the man who had so unceremoniously rejected her, but Raene knew she owed him her gratitude and much more.

In response, he only nodded and fell into step beside her. "Can I ask you a question?"

"No." Raene could only keep her straight face for a moment before she broke into a wide smile. "Of course. What do you want to ask?"

"What are you doing here?" Parson gazed at her like it was the most important question in the world, but Raene was sure he already knew the answer.

Raene giggled as if it was a silly question, but really, she didn't want to bring up that gaping open wound. "Kaide made a marriage arrangement with your—with Da. Obviously."

Parson rolled his eyes. "I mean, why honor it? You have a strong totem. You could literally go anywhere or do anything. And you hate it here. Why stay? Because some guy across the realm said so? A guy you're never going to see again?"

Raene couldn't help but feel he was trying to push her further away. "Look, I get it. You don't like me. But the arrangement was made, and it's my duty to honor it." She steeled herself against the truth and said the words that sounded right.

But Parson only inclined his head as he tried to wrestle through his thoughts. He didn't answer, but instead, he chewed on the inside of his cheek.

"What?" she finally asked.

"I don't understand. But I'm not sure if you're not explaining it or if I'm just dumb."

Raene looked at the ground. "You're not dumb."

Parson only laughed. "I'm not Hale. Or Da. Or even Tasia. I'm not like you." In the dimness of the earliest hours of morning, Raene couldn't decide why he was laughing.

When Raene could stand it no more, she stopped dead in her tracks, her voice falling to a whisper. "He loves her." The three words hung in the air.

Parson spun like he'd been shot with an arrow. His eyes narrowed, and his mouth fell open. "What?" he hissed.

Raene backed against the nearest alder tree, grateful for the support. When he remained speechless and rigid, she was tempted to step away, to shrink from the words, but it was too late now. She'd already started. There was no choice but to finish. Despite how her hands shook, she told him, "Kaide loves her."

Parson shook his head, refusing to believe her. "There's no way you could know that. It's only been a few weeks."

"I know him better than anyone. He loves her, and she loves him back. When I left, he had planned a big wedding and—"

Parson glared in obvious horror. "They weren't married yet?"

Raene shook her head. "He wanted to wait until she was ready. He gave her the choice, and she chose him."

"I don't believe you. Did you even know her? There's no way—"

"I know what I saw. They looked like—like Lathan and Tasia. They *looked* in love. I may be a silly Pyro girl, but I know what it looks like." Raene kicked the soil with the toe of her shoe. Moments ago, she'd felt the bliss of release at satisfying her totem. Now, Parson wanted to drag her through painful memories. He couldn't even give her five minutes of peace before he crushed her.

Without looking up, she finished telling him, "And by

coming here, I'm honoring the arrangement. If I didn't—"

Parson sighed and finished for her. "Da could nullify the trade and take her back."

She swallowed down her nerves and nodded. It wasn't the whole truth, but it wasn't a lie, either. Raene refused to tell him of Blossom's disappearance—or her part in it. For all she knew, Blossom was found by now. Even so, Raene wouldn't be the one to give them that news. Not until she had to.

Parson took one long step to arrive before her, too close for comfort, but with her back against the tree, Raene had no choice but to withstand his gaze. "So, you're going to do all this so Blossom and—and your uncle can be together?" Raene didn't miss the way his words caught at the mention of Kaide, but she nodded her agreement.

It was then he closed the gap between them. He laced his fingers into the thick hair at the back of her neck while the other clutched her waist and pulled her against him. He was so strong, his arms corded with muscle from his days working at the cut. His lips were hard and eager and soft and hungry, and Raene had no choice but to give in to such intensity.

She'd never kissed a boy before. Not in Pyrona. Not the sons of elite houses or her wealthy marriage prospects. In all the times she'd imagined this moment, she'd never pictured it this way—her back pressed to an impossibly tall tree, a Terra man's tongue exploring her mouth as she explored his—even the rake of his fingers in her hair made her tingle with excitement. Her hands grasped eagerly at his neck, desperate to taste more of him.

Parson's calloused hand slid up the back of her shirt, and a shiver of exhilaration raced through her. And when he dropped his hand to her thigh and tugged her leg up around his waist, Raene couldn't help but let out a gasp.

At the sound, Parson pulled away and braced his arm

against the tree, eyes heavy and breaths ragged. "I'm sorry," he said, though it was so low only her cat ears caught it.

Her mouth fell open in shock. To Raene, the words were too unfair and cruel to fathom. What had been a freeing moment of release and excitement was now dashed to little more than a gaping wound. She wouldn't let him see her crushed. Instead, she darted away only to have him lash out and grasp her wrist.

"Let me go," she said as she tried to get free. She cursed his physical strength. Raene had all the speed she could ever need, but Parson would always be stronger.

Parson only pulled her toward him, not minding a bit that she fought him the whole way. "I didn't mean it that way—"

"Let go of me," she insisted, using her free had to pry at the iron grip of his fingers around her wrist.

"Just stop. Raene. Stop!" It was only when he shouted at her that she went still.

Her eyes narrowed in anger and hurt and frustration. "You had no right," she started, and once she had, she couldn't stop. "You already said you don't want to marry me. You don't get to say that and then do this. It's not fair. You had no right!"

Raene felt as mangled as one of her kills.

Her first kiss ruined. Every person she'd ever known gone. Her totem far out of her control. And Parson only made everything worse.

"You're right. I shouldn't have done that. It's just—" His resolve faded a moment later. "I don't know what I'm trying to say." And then he released her.

Raene wouldn't cry. Not in front of him. As soon as she was free, she turned away and marched toward camp, thankful for the little bit of morning light that eased her path. As her vision blurred and tears began to fall, Raene wasn't sure if she was going the right way, but she didn't care.

She only wanted to be away from him.

Hale smelled the blood first. It was unmistakable. Not the putrid stench of a scavenge, but the coppery aroma of fresh blood. It filled his nostrils well before he had her in his sights.

Even in the scant morning light, the apple-red color of Raene's shirt stood out among the trees. Her steps were quick and forceful. She was angry.

Hale saw her tears next. She wiped at them to hide the fact she'd been crying, but it was too late. He marched forward, his steps as quick as hers, and when he was close enough, Hale threw his arms around her, good and strong as she needed.

Hale, too, had had a rough, sleepless night, worrying over her safety but trusting in the Mother's plan. A thousand times he'd thought to go after her—he could have followed her scent easily enough—but the coin had told him to stay, and so he had, though that didn't keep his mind from racing, from questioning every word from the night before.

Holding Raene against his chest was as much a comfort to Hale as his arms were to her. Her ragged breaths slowed, and her grip on his waist turned less desperate, but she didn't let go.

"Are you all right?" he whispered in her ear. She was tall enough he had to tilt his head up, but not much. He hated the slightness of his human form. It would be so much easier to comfort her if his bear size was evident beyond his totem form.

With arms clutched around his neck and her face

buried in the crook, Raene nodded, a subtle motion against his skin.

For several long seconds, they remained entwined, both refusing to let go. "Are you hurt?" he asked, smelling blood mixed with traces of his brother that lingered from the night before and the strange scents of Pyrona still on her clothes.

Raene straightened and pulled away. "On my back," she admitted quietly.

Hale turned her around enough to see a large section of her shirt ripped away, and in the exposed space, a bite mark crusted with blood. It was several hours old, Hale knew right away. "Let's get that cleaned up." He held her hand in his and walked her back to his tent—*their* tent.

Together, they navigated through camp, but neither said a word. Hale could figure out where she'd gone—the blood and injury were clear enough. And however it had happened, Raene didn't seem keen on discussing it. Instead, she wiped at the last of her tears, turning away so he wouldn't see.

Once inside, Hale laid out her blankets. Her injury wasn't so serious as to warrant the use of the uncomfortable cot. "It'll be easier if you lay down," he told her as he prepared the space. He lit a dozen candles and collected the small medical kit from his cabinet.

Raene already lay on her stomach, her head resting on her arms. Hale sat cross-legged beside her and set a tall candle nearby. Getting a good look, Hale saw the tattered edges of her shirt caked with blood. One long strip of fabric was embedded in a deep gash right through the center.

Hale located the forceps from his kit and began the careful process of pulling the tattered material from her injury. He went slowly, limiting how much he had to pull or dig into her flesh, but several times he heard her breath catch from the pain.

"I'm sorry," Hale said after he freed the end of the largest piece. The last thing he wanted to do was make her uncomfortable.

"It's not your fault," she replied, though her voice betrayed her misery.

"What did this?"

"A coyote."

Hale let out a relieved sigh. All innocents carried disease—especially in their mouths—but a coyote was no worse than any other. A badger or wolf would have been cause for concern, but not a coyote. He had antiseptic ointment that could handle it well enough.

Still, it left them with another problem. "We'll send Lathan to kill it. Can't have a coyote so close to camp." Hale had no idea why the Mother had allowed coyotes this far north. It wasn't a good sign. There were too many vulnerable totems under their protection.

Raene adjusted her hands under her chin as Hale peeled away the last of the debris from her wound. "It was far away. And Parson killed it."

Hale froze, not sure how he should feel about that. Parson always had an unpredictable streak, but he'd passed on Raene from the start. Hale had smelled his brother on Raene's clothes but had dismissed it. Now he was unsure. Hale didn't understand why they would be out together in the middle of the night. Killing coyotes seemed an unlikely answer.

At a loss, Hale refocused on his task. "Could you sit up? I need to cut away your shirt so I can clean the wound."

Raene moved to a sitting position, but she cast him a sad glance over her shoulder. "You have to cut it?"

"It's the best way to keep it from getting more debris. I can try to slip it off—"

"No, just cut it. It's ruined, anyway."

With scissors in hand, Hale cut away the remnants of

her Pyro shirt. Each snip revealed more of the angry, blood-crusted injury, and around it, her bronze skin. Hale couldn't help but admire the color, so much richer than the light skin of Terras.

Her golden hair was braided and hanging over her shoulder, though it was messier than she liked. Even in their short time together, Hale knew that much about her: Raene liked to maintain appearances.

With her wound centered over her spine just below her shoulder blades, Hale had to strip away all but the very top of her shirt.

"Just take it off," Raene said. She reached up and unclasped the only remaining strap—the one behind her neck—and let her shirt fall away.

Hale paused to watch her, more in awe than anything. She kept one hand over her chest, but even so, she was far more bare than any Terra girl would be in the presence of a man. He had to remind himself that she grew up in a much different place.

But if she was comfortable in such a state before him, Hale wouldn't argue. Eventually, they'd know each other intimately, but for now, he was glad she could trust him with this.

So Hale continued. He couldn't count how many times he'd done this for his siblings or other clan members—rinsing the wound with clean water, applying one of Gemini's numbing antiseptic ointments, and bandaging it with strips of sterile gauze.

Each step in the process was familiar, yet there was still a quiver in his hands. His knuckles skimmed her smooth flesh a half-dozen times, each one making his pulse race with nerves and excitement.

"Hale?" Raene looked over her shoulder just as he pressed down the last edge of the bandage.

"Did I hurt you?" he asked, though he knew the

ointment would already have begun to numb the wound.

Raene shook her head, causing her braid to flop a bit. "I just—I thought you should know. In the woods—"

Hale dared to put a hand on her bare waist and leaned over so she could see his face. "I don't care what happened. As long as you weren't in danger, and you didn't put anyone else in danger, then it doesn't matter."

Raene kept one hand guarding her chest. Her brow was creased. Her eyes were full of worry, and for the first time, Hale feared she'd done something horrible.

He put his hand over her cheek and offered her a reassuring smile. His faith in the Mother reminded him that everything happened as it was meant to. If it was as bad as Raene thought, the Mother would have required his intervention.

So Hale stroked her cheek with his thumb and waited for whatever it was, ready to dispel her concerns as soon as they were aired.

Raene's lovely blue eyes were tinged and dark as she said, "He kissed me."

Hale blinked in shock. His mouth gaped, and his mind raced to consider if he'd even heard her right. Surely she didn't mean…

Her words tumbled out rapid-fire. "I don't know why, and he said he was sorry. I thought you should know—" She looked at her lap as she awaited his reaction.

Hale was determined not to disappoint her. "I'll talk to him. It won't happen again." Then, another thought occurred to him. "Unless you want—"

The violent shake of her head was answer enough. "No, I don't."

Hale couldn't resist a smile. "Then let's forget about it."

Raene put her hand over his where it rested on her cheek. A second later, she collapsed forward and wrapped her arms around his neck.

Hale didn't miss the fact that her bare chest was pressed to his tunic. "Hey, it's fine," he assured her. "I'm not mad. You have nothing to worry about." He didn't tell her that fulfilling this particular plan of the Alder Mother was the greatest thing to ever happen to him.

Raene didn't move except to squeeze him tighter. She was afraid of whatever it was she had to say, but Hale could guess easily enough.

"Raene, I know you went hunting." The way her grip loosened around his neck told Hale he was on the right track. "It's just one of those things we'll have to work on."

"I'm sorry. I shouldn't have left."

"It's fine. We'll figure it out." Hale filled his voice with as much confidence as he could. He knew the Mother would make sure it all worked out.

Raene pulled back and scanned his face, her mouth tight with apprehension. "You're not mad?"

With her arms locked around his neck and her bare chest hovering so close, Hale smiled and shook his head. "No, a little envious. But not mad."

"Envious?" Raene wrinkled her brow a moment before she used her fingertip to smooth it over. "Because he kissed me?"

"Absolutely." It nearly killed him to force out the word, true as it was, but the Mother wanted this. Hale had to walk the fine line between the Sacred Mother's will and earning Raene's trust and respect. If he went too fast, he could alienate her, push her away. But if he went too slow, she would think he wasn't eager to have her as his bride. So as much as he hated to be so bold, Hale cleared his throat and asked, "May I kiss you, Raene?"

Her eyes widened. Hale momentarily wondered if he'd overstepped, but then she offered him the smallest nod.

A nervous drum took up beat in his chest. Hale

reminded himself he'd kissed plenty of girls—well, two. But he didn't need to be nervous. This was Raene—his bride, his future wife—and this moment may very well be the start of a long and glorious marriage.

Hale forced his hands to quit shaking as he placed one on either side of her face, his palms on her cheeks and his fingers wrapping behind her neck. Then, he leaned forward, pulling her closer until their lips met. He started slow, a gentle pressing together of their lips, until hers parted. Her arms tightened around his neck as she neared to get better access to the recesses of his mouth.

But Hale forced himself back. He had to use both hands to create distance between them. He couldn't go too fast, he reminded himself. He couldn't compromise the Mother's will for his own selfish indulgence. Hale pulled her close again and kissed her forehead, not at all missing the flush to her cheeks or the sweet smile she wore. "Now turn around."

Raene finally released him—for which he was both grateful and disappointed—and turned her bare back to him once more.

Hale collected the tangled lengths of her hair and worked his fingers through it before braiding it as she liked. He'd never had cause to do it for Blossom—her hair was far too curly—but for Gemini, Nyla, and some others, Hale had been one of the few adults not at work or at the cut. His fingers completed the familiar motions and set her braid against her spine.

"Thank you," she said, offering him a shy smile over her shoulder.

She would make a fine wife. Hale could see it already. She was kind and polite and intelligent, and once they got to really know each other, they'd be loyal and devoted to one another. Each moment he spent with her made him more sure.

Hale helped her slip a Terra sleep shirt over her shoulders and convinced her to lay down, all too glad to avoid another conflict over Pyro clothes. He rubbed along her back as best he could without disturbing her bandages, and within minutes, Raene gave in to much-needed sleep.

It was hard not to admire her. She was different and exotic, but Hale was confident that even in Pyrona, Raene had been a cherished beauty. He would have liked nothing more than to lay beside her and rest as well.

But instead, Hale kissed her cheek and stroked her hair before he got to his feet. He had work to do today, and he was already late, but first, he was going to have a talk with his brother.

"Do I have any assignments today?" Blossom asked her devoted advisor over breakfast.

Eton shook his head, though it wasn't enough to displace a single perfect hair on his creepily pale head. "Not so far. Why? Looking for another traitor to exile?"

Blossom pressed her lips into a thin line and glared. "Not at all." She pushed away from the glass table they shared and collected her cloak from the closet.

"Where are you going?" Eton asked, his brows wrinkled more than usual.

Buttoning the front of her cloak, she replied, "To make a *friend*."

Eton scoffed. "There's no such thing."

"Oh, sure. You're the master of making friends. I forgot." Blossom couldn't hide the contemptuous roll of her eyes before she headed for the door. She wasn't about to spend the day in her apartment thinking of things she couldn't change.

"Blossom, really. Where are you going?" Eton was on

her heels in a heartbeat. It was almost cute the way he followed her like a dog. Her own little pet Eton.

She pressed her hand to the cool glass surface of the scanner and waited for the beep. As the door opened, she thrust herself into the circular corridor of the Halo and began searching for the right door. Only when she'd completed a full lap to no avail did she bother to ask him for help.

"Which one is the Apprentice Vice Syndicate Dodd?"

Already, she knew he hated the idea of it. His pale-blue eyes dimmed, and he rubbed his hands together before him. "Blossom—"

She'd hear none of it. "I'll knock on all the doors if you don't want to tell me."

When Eton didn't respond, she turned back down the hall and approached the first door. Only as he she raised her hand to knock did he stop her. "That's Crin Peppers."

Blossom lowered her hand and allowed herself to smile at her victory. A second later, she continued down the corridor to the only door left.

"Be careful," Eton said, his voice low in her ear. She hadn't even realized he was so close.

"Yes, sixteen-year-old girls are so deadly and dangerous. I better watch out."

"She seems sweet. That's her game. She's from an elite family and has been in politics in Aerona her whole life. She knows everyone. She gets whatever she wants. Don't underestimate her." He chewed on his lip piercing for a moment before he added, "And don't trust anything she says."

Instead of answering, Blossom knocked on the door. It made a sad, tinny sound, and she wondered if anyone inside could hear her at all. A minute later, the door finally opened, and a serious Aero man stood in its place.

Blossom couldn't remember his name. She's seen him

once before, standing behind the Apprentice Vice Syndicate Dodd in the corridor. He was her advisor, but Blossom knew nothing else about him.

He stood tall, his shoulders broad and his hair shaved on the right side. A heavy metal hoop hung from his nose. If Blossom had to guess his totem, she'd suspect a crocodile or rhinoceros. Something hardened and careful to match his demeanor.

With an impossibly slow bow, he greeted them and said, "Welcome, Vice Syndicate Frane. Please come in. I'll inform her of your arrival." He held out a hand and bid them entry.

Blossom was less than surprised to see a space identical to her own. The couches were a richer blue and the tables were silver instead of glass, but otherwise, it was the same frozen, white space as her own apartment.

The advisor led them toward the couch and motioned for them to sit before he walked toward the bedroom doors.

"Remember what I said," Eton whispered so low only she could hear.

Blossom brushed him off. She could do this. Having tea with a tiny albino teen was hardly on the list of life-threatening activities. As a Vice Syndicate—even a transfer—she had more sway and power than an Apprentice. Besides, Blossom was going to lose her mind if she had to spend another day alone with Eton.

Right on cue, the lovely face of Yveline Dodd emerged from her bedroom, all glowing and gracious smiles. "Vice Syndicate Frane!" she squealed in delight. "I'm so happy you've come to see me. We have so much to discuss."

Like a butterfly, she fluttered over to the seat facing Blossom, her white cloak as light as a cloud. Delicate, glittering piercings dotted her eyebrow, nose, and both cheeks. When she sat, she crossed her legs and rested an elbow across the top of her thigh. "Can Herson get you something to drink? He makes a lovely lemon lilac tea."

Blossom tried to mirror the girl's gracious smile. "Thank you. That sounds delicious," she lied. Given the choice, Blossom would never consume another drop of tea in her lifetime. Norsa's sour, orange monstrosity had turned her against the idea altogether.

But she couldn't go offending her future friend in the first five minutes.

Yveline nodded to her advisor before turning back to Blossom. Her piercings glittered as she asked, "How are you finding Aerona so far? It must be quite different from where you're from."

Blossom was tempted to be false—to lie and say she loved it here—but she couldn't. Instead, she heard herself say, "I'm still getting used to it. Everything is so strange here."

"Like what?" The girl beamed.

"Well—everything," Blossom said with a small laugh. "The food and the clothes. You have tunnels instead of volcanos. It's always cold instead of hot." It was only when Yveline scrunched her lovely face that Blossom realized her mistake.

She'd been talking about Pyrona.

"But I'm doing my best," Blossom said, trying to hide it. "Eton's been helpful getting me set up with new suits and a panel and this." She pointed to her newly shaved head.

Eton grunted in the seat beside her.

Reminded of his presence, Blossom turned, and, in the most even voice she could manage, said, "Thank you Advisor Samina. I have no further need of you this morning."

Eton allowed himself a rare moment of public shock before he caught himself. With his jaw clenched tight, he nodded and launched from the couch. Seconds later, he was gone out the door.

Without him, Blossom felt more alone than she would have thought. Since her arrival, Eton had been by her side every waking hour. Now, Blossom would have to manage on her own. In the personal quarters of one of the most important people in the realm, she tried not to feel intimidated.

She didn't need Eton. She could do this.

"You grew up here?" Blossom asked, desperate to talk about anything other than her life outside of Aero.

Herson arrived with a pair of transparent glass mugs filled with amber tea. Tendrils of steam rose from each as he handed them over.

Yveline took her tea without a word and sipped it carefully. "My family has been in politics for generations. My father was the Research and Development Commissioner. My mother was the head of the Transformative Analysis Division. My oldest brother now holds that position."

Blossom could see it right away. From the way she kept her eyes down to the large sip of tea she took, Blossom know Yveline's parents were dead.

"I have three brothers," Blossom told her. "All bears."

Yveline looked up and giggled. "My brother is an ostrich. Big, mean old thing, he is." Then, as Blossom would never have expected, Yveline tucked her wrists against her ribs and bobbed her head like a pecking bird.

It was all Blossom could do to keep from spilling her tea as she erupted in raucous laughter. "Are you practicing for when you're an ostrich?" she said between hoots and hollers.

It was Yveline's turn to explode in laughs. "I'm not going to be an ostrich!" she shouted with a wide, consuming grin.

Blossom sobered instantly. She tried to hold onto the merriment of the moment, but she couldn't make sense of it. "You won't?"

"Of course not! Who'd want to be some giant bird that can't even fly? No, thank you. I'm going to request a kingfisher." Yveline seemed awfully pleased with such an idea, but Blossom had no idea what she was saying.

Her confusion must have registered on her face. Yveline retrieved her panel from her cloak pocket and made several quick motions before she turned it to face Blossom. The screen displayed a cobalt-blue and yellow bird with a long beak and a rounded body.

"You've never seen one? Isn't it gorgeous? Such *colors*. I could get lost in them." She put a hand to her forehead as if to swoon. "They're not all that large, maybe this wide." Yveline held her hands a little more than shoulder-width apart. "But they are skilled hunters, and they can live anywhere. Caverns, tunnels, trees. You should see them fly. They can do these amazing long dives and turn faster than a frigate. Not as fast as you, of course—" Her eyes landed on the peregrine falcon tattoo half-concealed by the collar of Blossom's cloak.

Blossom couldn't take it all in fast enough. "It's beautiful," she admitted of the pictured bird, but otherwise, she didn't know what to say.

"I've thought about a peregrine. Of course, who hasn't? Fastest bird in the realm. It's an obvious contender, but I think this is the one for me. Then again, I have two years to figure it out," Yveline continued, oblivious to Blossom's confusion.

"I'm sure you'll make the right decision."

Yveline slid her panel back into her pocket and collected her tea. "That's the hardest part about this job, don't you think? So many complex decisions. I thought it would be easy, but it's so much more than anyone thinks.

Really, it is." Her brows creased with worry, and for the first time, Blossom saw there was far more to the young Apprentice than she let on.

A moment later, they were interrupted by a knock at the door. Herson answered and, as stoic as a statue, Eton walked over and joined them for the second time.

Blossom was more than a little irked he would so clearly disregard her instructions, especially when she was actually starting to like the Apprentice Vice Syndicate Dodd. "I told you, I don't need—"

Eton only held out a large black coin. Blossom accepted it and turned it over in her hand, trying to figure out what it was. The surface was so shimmering smooth, she could catch glints of her own reflection, though it was disturbed by stamped images—a lotus flower on one side, a wide-winged bird on the other. "What is this?" Blossom asked when Eton produced no explanation.

Yveline startled them both when she rushed over and sank onto the couch beside Blossom, so close their hips touched. "It's an offer," she said as she took the coin into her hands. "Did she receive this just now?" Yveline asked Eton, who promptly nodded.

"An offer? For what?" Blossom knew the answer as soon as the words were past her lips.

Yveline rattled off information faster than Blossom could take it all in. "This one here, the flower, that must be you. And this one, the golden eagle with a sun, that's the symbol of the Volstead clan. See here, these initials? FRV. Farley Volstead offers you his hand in marriage!"

"The Commissioner of Aero Security?" Blossom recalled the name from her endless lessons on Aero hierarchy.

Yveline continued turning the coin in her hand, as if she couldn't believe it was real. "One of the highest-ranking officials in the branch, besides us, of course. He'll make a fine match." She placed the coin back in Blossom's hand and grinned ear-to-ear.

"But I've never even met him," she answered, looking back and forth between her advisor and her new friend.

Eton shook his head. "You did. At the Spring Ceremony."

Memories of that night crashed into her with enough force to make her sway. Blossom squinted against the onslaught of images—the Alder Mother, the dance floor, the dark fur of her beast. So many things she could never forget.

But the face of her proposed groom wasn't one of them. She only knew him from the files, the charts, the profiles Eton forced her to learn.

"And you've been summoned by Syndicate Member."

Between Yveline's refusal to look at her and the hard-set edge of Eton's jaw, Blossom knew a summons couldn't be good. She set her tea on the silver table and stood. "Thank you for hosting me, Apprentice Vice Syndicate Dodd. I'll be sure to return the favor in the near future."

The ghostly white girl stood and managed a cinched smile. "I very much enjoyed our talk. And please, Miss Yveline will do fine."

Blossom nodded. "And Miss Blossom for me then." With that, she spun toward the door, ignoring the sweeping circle of her cloak, and followed Eton back into the corridor.

It wasn't until they were alone in the elevator that she asked, "Something's wrong, isn't it?"

"She didn't summon you to sip tea and giggle over boys if that's what you're wondering." As soon as the elevator doors were open, he directed her toward the Robin platform.

"Again?" she fussed.

"Only for a few minutes. Even you can make it that

long."

Blossom took her seat and crossed her arms. "What's your problem?" It wasn't like him to be so cavalier with his anger.

"Nothing," he hissed. Leaning against the wall, he stared out the window as the underbelly of the Earth passed them by. As he said, it was only a few minutes before they reached the elevator that would take them to the top of Aero Tower.

Tucked under the sleeve of her cloak, the silver bracelet was completely hidden. But Blossom felt it every moment of every day. The expansive views offered in the elevator only reminded her of what she couldn't do.

"Maybe she's going to let me take it off," Blossom said, more to herself than Eton, but she'd convinced neither of them.

Eton managed to maintain his silent, angry pout all the way to the Syndicate's office.

"Good morning, Vice Syndicate Frane," the Syndicate began, her usually pleasant warmth nothing more than a cool greeting.

"Good morning, Syndicate Mercer," Blossom replied. Standing in the center of her large office, it was impossible not to feel like a mouse in a lion's den. Jurra lingered at the windows, a silent observer, looking ready to eat her if she made a mistake. Eton hovered along the wall by the door, watching, but never moving. "You wanted to see me?"

The Syndicate ran a hand through her dark hair and motioned toward one of the chairs facing her desk. When Blossom sat, Syndicate Mercer produced a handful of papers from her pocket. A second later, she all but threw them across the top of the desk. They were images, Blossom realized, but as soon as she saw them, she looked away.

On the first, the glazed open eyes of a girl, her cheeks

marred by deep scratches, and below that, her throat was cut with a trio of similar marks. Despite a mere half second glance, Blossom knew the girl was dead.

But more than that, she knew the girl's name. Helena Hammond.

"You violated a direct order from the office of the Aero Syndicate. You violated a direct order from *me*," Audra clarified.

"I'm sorry," Blossom whispered, but she said it to the girl, to the family she hadn't helped. She was so, so sorry she hadn't done more to help them. Blossom had released them to the frozen forests of Aerona, sealing their fates. She just stood there and watched them leave.

"This cannot go on. Insubordination will not be tolerated. You were selected for this position because you possess the ability to make difficult decision and follow instructions. Has that changed?" With her eyes squeezed shut and her head turned away, Blossom could still feel the penetrating stare of Syndicate Mercer. She felt every word like a dagger.

"Is this you?" she continued.

When she had no choice, Blossom looked up. The Syndicate held another image, but this one was a bird's-eye view of Blossom. She was shopping in the Emporium, running her hands along a rack of compound bows. Behind her, Eton stood with arms full of supplies she'd picked.

"Is this you?" the Syndicate repeated.

Blossom nodded. There was no denying it. She was too short to be Aero, her hair too brown.

And the Syndicate knew it, too. She wasn't asking to gain information. She was pointing out that Blossom had been caught. She was rubbing her face in it.

Blossom hated this game. Every last minute of it.

Now that she had Blossom's attention, the Syndicate collected a few of the images that covered her desk. One was an aerial photo of the three Hammonds, all sprawled at awkward angles. Helena still wore the coat Blossom had picked out. One of Kiza's elegant hands was clutched around her daughter's arm, and Blossom knew, even in their final moments, she'd been a protective mother.

Their faces, their bellies, even their arms were a patchwork of deep, angry scratches. Blossom had never seen such gore. They were innocent, unarmed, exposed. How could anyone do this?

Syndicate Mercer leaned over the edge of her desk and lowered her voice. "I am so disappointed in you, Blossom. I expected more from you." After a slow inhale, she pursed her lips and said, "I'm afraid I'm going to have to restrict you from the Ascension Ceremony tonight. You are restricted from all official activities until you've demonstrated your ability to comply. You understand that this is for your own good? And the good of the Aero branch?"

Blossom sat in the chair in a daze. She was full of anguish and pain and guilt. She'd let this happen. Blossom was eaten up with the shame of it. She could do nothing more than sit and withstand the angry words of the most powerful woman in her branch.

"Do you understand?" the Syndicate pressed.

With her head bowed low, Blossom nodded.

"Then you may go."

Blossom couldn't get away fast enough. Eton would fuss at her later, but she didn't care. She wouldn't cry in front of the Syndicate, and she couldn't hold her tears back much longer. Blossom darted for the doors at little less than a jog.

Eton turned to follow her.

"I'll have a few words with you, Advisor Samina."

Blossom's stomach dropped. Behind her, Eton only offered her a sorrowful glance before he reentered the

Syndicate's office.

"Eton?" Blossom couldn't stand to leave without him. It was her fault Eton had helped the Hammonds. She could only imagine what tortures the Syndicate had planned for him.

"Go home." Eton didn't even turn to face her before he marched forward. Blossom moved to join him, but the office doors slammed shut not even a pace in front of her.

There was nothing she could do but wait and hope the Syndicate wasn't too hard on him. It had been her idea, her plan, her decision. The Syndicate had to see that.

Or maybe she'd show him even more images of the family so brutally slain. Maybe she'd show him how Blossom had failed to keep them alive for even a day.

It was those images that made her turn back to the elevator. They would forever be burned into her memory, sealed in a dark place. She'd never forget how it felt to send an innocent family to die.

With all his might, Parson swung the axe down into the wood. The small limb sailed away, along with a few dozen sizeable splinters, but Parson didn't even pause. He took a step forward and removed the next limb with equal fervor.

"Watch it," Lathan groaned.

When Parson looked up, he saw his oldest brother showered in cast-off bits of alder tree, plucking them from where they'd landed on his shoulders.

Parson only nodded and got back to work.

That is, until Lathan sat his axe head on the ground and leaned on it, watching Parson work with that knowing look of his. "What happened?" Lathan asked, his voice little more than a growl.

"Nothing." Parson's axe sank into wood and severed

the next limb.

But Lathan remained, watching, his pine-green eyes darker than usual.

"I messed up," Parson said, caving under the pressure of such a gaze from his brother. In aggravation, Parson brought down the axe again with more force than was necessary. He groaned when the axe remained lodged in the wood

"How?" Lathan asked, watching Parson use his foot to leverage the axe free without success.

Parson answered between labored grunts. "I just did."

"You always mess up. What happened?" Lathan stood stoic and quiet as always, but his words weren't laced with insult. He meant it as a fact. Parson *did* always mess up. Lathan wasn't wrong to wonder what made this time different.

Instead of answering, Parson put his full weight into pulling the axe handle until it freed. He staggered back to regain his footing when he saw a figure approach.

It was none other than Hale. He was at the cut, where he had no reason to be today. But Parson knew exactly why he'd come.

"Damn." Parson cursed under his breath, his hopes of maintaining some level of secrecy dashed when he saw the look on Hale's face. He'd trusted Raene would understand that Hale could never know, but she hadn't. She'd told him, and a part of Parson knew his relationship with his brother would never really be the same. He'd crossed that line, and there was no going back now.

"What were you thinking?" Hale shouted as he neared, his jaw set as stone. He stepped over a few bundles of limbs without taking his eyes from Parson. His unshakable focus rocked Parson to his core.

"I wasn't. I'm sorry." Parson couldn't get the words out of his mouth fast enough. He was so, so sorry. It was epic mistake, a horrible failure. Parson hated that he'd done it.

When Hale was near enough, he put both hands to Parson's chest and shoved hard, his eyes steeled in anger.

Parson had never seen Hale this way. It was Parson who couldn't control his anger. Hale was always so calm, so careful with his words and his actions. Hale was never violent, even when it was warranted.

The look in his brother's eye scared Parson more than anything. "I'm sorry," he said again, knowing it sounded hollow and weak. But what else could he say? Nothing could change what had happened.

"Five years, Parson. It's been *five years* since you've even looked at a woman. And now, all the sudden, you want her? You want the woman *I'm* supposed to marry?" Hale huffed. "Tell me that's not how is. Tell me you aren't playing some game."

Put that way, Parson could see how bad it looked. He hadn't accepted nor made an offer in years. He passed on Raene the moment he saw her, and only once she was aligned with Hale did he interfere. That was never his intention, but Parson couldn't deny how it appeared. "I'm not playing a game," Parson told him, desperate to have his brother's understanding. "It had nothing to do with you. It was—"

"It has everything to do with me!" Hale shouted, his face reddening with every moment of uncharacteristic anger.

"*What happened?*" Lathan bellowed as he stepped between them.

Hale glared for several long seconds before he got control of himself. "It doesn't matter. It's *never* going to happen again." With that, Hale turned back toward camp, and Lathan and Parson watched him leave in silence.

Then, Parson collapsed onto the nearest branch and

sat, rubbing his eyes—his eyes that burned from lack of sleep. Countless times he'd ventured into the woods for a hunt at the expense of his sleep, but never had he stayed out *all* night. His body ached, and fatigue fogged his mind. His thumb traced the two rings of his index finger, reminded yet again of the weight they didn't carry.

Lathan sank to his side, but mercifully didn't say anything. Instead, he leaned his elbows on his knees and gazed out at the cut, their work almost finished. In a week, they'd start shipping loads of lumber to Terrana or Hydrona or even Seraphine City. In a month, they'd be done and on to the next, maybe even move camps.

"I took her hunting," Parson finally told him.

Lathan clasped his hands together and gave Parson a crooked look. "And?"

Parson struggled for the words, "And, she's—she killed a lot of innocents. She had a run-in with a coyote, but nothing serious. She's—" *Magnificent. Powerful. Stunning.*

"Not yours."

Those two words hit Parson harder than a slap to the face. He gaped wide-eyed at his brother. "I know. I'm not trying—"

"Then quit. Or don't. But don't say one thing, and then do another. It's not fair to him." If Lathan was this unforgiving about hunting, Parson didn't want to know what his brother would say about kissing her.

But Parson couldn't say it was a mistake. If anything, giving her to Hale had been his mistake. Letting her think he wasn't interested was the mistake.

Not the kiss.

Parson tried to remember what it had been like to hate her. The Pyro girl. The niece of the cruel Vice Syndicate who stole Blossom. He'd been so consumed with anger, but now, all he could see was a tiger, claws out as she struck down her helpless prey. The two were intermeshed now, and Parson didn't know what to do.

"Give it some time." Lathan squeezed Parson's shoulder in his massive, bone-crushing hand before he went back to work. Parson knew he was right, as always. It was hard to argue with the oldest Frane brother, as stone-solid and wise as he was.

After the first taste of Hale's wrath, Parson knew it was time to end this. Raene wasn't his, and Parson could no longer be selfish. She was elegant and graceful and aggressive and dangerous, but she was seven years his junior and the future wife of his brother. There was no reason to dwell.

Raene was better off with Hale.

As much as it pained his tired body, Parson forced himself back to work.

CAVERN

WARM WATER rained over her. Blossom kept her knees tucked to her chest as she cried, her tears rinsed away by the river of cascading water.

"Blossom!" Eton's shouts echoed across the metal room a few seconds before his heavy feet sounded in the washroom doorway.

She didn't argue when he stepped into the stream of warm water and sank to the floor beside her. His arm appeared around her shoulders, but she refused to move, refused to be comforted. A vast hole of guilt had taken up residence in her chest. Her eyes could see nothing but the look of death frozen on Helena's small face. Angry and horrified, her sobs shook her so hard she struggled to breath. Each motion sent a hammer of pain through her ravaged head.

"I'm sorry," Eton began. "I didn't know she was going to show you—I would have warned you. I promised I would tell you. Truly, I didn't know."

Blossom shook her head. "It's my fault," she squeaked, her voice too damaged by sobs to produce a proper sound.

"No, Blossom, stop, it's not. Of course it's not. There's nothing you could have done to change their fate.

There was nothing you could do. She's punishing you. That's how she works. You defied her, and this is your punishment." When he ran out of words, Eton wrapped his hand around the side of her head and pulled her under his chin, nestled firmly against him. He held her tight, like her brothers might have, in a protective grip she so desperately needed.

Because despite Eton's protests, Blossom knew she could have done more. She should have done more. She should have done whatever it took to prevent them from coming to harm. They put their lives in Blossom's hands, and she failed them.

She had never felt more ashamed.

Eton's hands combed through her wet hair as she cried against his chest. He never let go of her, even when the water turned cool. Instead, he pulled at her legs and angled them over his lap so she could share in some of his warmth.

At long last, Blossom could cry no more. She was too tired. Her sides ached and her eyes burned. The pit of grief in her chest had hardened into something else—into something permanent. Blossom would carry it with her for the rest of her life.

"Come on," Eton told her. "Let's get you out of these clothes. You're frozen."

When she looked at her hands, Blossom saw the tips of her fingers had taken on a bluish hue. Now that her sobs were quiet, she noticed the way her elbows shivered against her sides, the audible chattering of her teeth.

Eton helped her to her feet—a laborious task considering the weight of her soaked cloak and the slipperiness of the too-smooth, white tile of her washroom—and peeled her out of the countless layers of Aero clothes she wore. As each piece fell away, Blossom felt lighter, but nothing would change that feeling in her bones. The intensity of it scared her.

Blossom didn't argue as Eton exchanged her wet clothes for dry ones and pushed her into the unused bed. He pulled the soft, white blankets up to her chin and turned out the lights, bathing her in darkness.

"I'll be back in a few minutes," he whispered before he closed the door.

In a bed she hated, in clothes that felt all wrong, Blossom wanted nothing more than to go home. Back to the manor. Back to Kaide. He would hold her and tell her he would kill whoever had done this to the Hammonds. And he would understand why she felt responsible, just as she understood his hatred for Aero.

It was all so clear now.

Blossom let her fingers search out the familiar warmth of her alder wood ring, but of course, she found it missing. She'd given it up, she remembered. Eton had it. She made up her mind to ask him about it when he returned, but otherwise, she closed her eyes, willing away the images that seemed burned into them.

She had no idea how much time had passed when her door opened again. Without looking up, she asked Eton, "Can I have my ring?"

"What ring?" Blossom jerked up to see the saddened features of Yveline Dodd. "Advisor Samina said you might want some company. I'm guessing it didn't go so well with the Syndicate?"

Blossom shook her head and flopped back onto her pillow, annoyed it was so soft.

Dressed in her fine cloak and her hair done just so, Yveline was elegant and lovely while Blossom felt like a pile of ash, burned and empty.

Yveline's cloak swished quietly as she neared and sat on the edge of Blossom's too-large bed. "Do you want to talk about it?" she asked tentatively.

"Not really." Blossom was too afraid to say the words

aloud. She didn't have the energy to cry anymore.

"Come on then. Get dressed. I have a surprise for you." Yveline rushed to the wardrobe and rifled through the dozen matching suits, searching for what, Blossom didn't know.

"Leave her be," Eton demanded through the open door.

"You asked me to come over, and here I am. So kindly go away." Yveline somehow managed to be stunningly elegant and also unwaveringly firm in the same breath. Blossom was sure she'd never be able to manage such a feat.

Despite how she never wanted to move again, Blossom wanted to listen to them bicker even less. So she heaved off the thick blankets and let Yveline help her put her suit together, each piece in the right order this time, then a fresh cloak.

Buttoned up tight in her Aero uniform, Blossom felt surprisingly better, as if looking put together made her feel that way, if only a little. Yveline reached up and stroked a hand through Blossom's chestnut hair a few times before she was satisfied.

"She's not ready." Eton stood in the doorway, blocking their exit.

"That's not your decision to make," Yveline argued. "Step aside."

Ignoring her, Eton maintained his stance and looked to Blossom. "I made a promise. She's taking you to the Gallant—"

"Shhh!" Yveline interrupted. "It's not much of a surprise if you spoil it." While she stood a full head-and-a-half below Eton, she glared at him with a fierceness that made Blossom nervous.

But Eton wouldn't budge.

Blossom put up her hand to stop them. "It's fine. I'll

go. Thank you, Eton." She looked up at him with genuine gratitude. Where before they'd been uneasy partners, now things were different. And they both knew it. Blossom nodded her thanks to him as she followed Yveline to some place called the Gallant.

Blossom stopped in her tracks in the corridor. Emerging from the far side was none other than Lota Castor, the Terra Vice Syndicate known for his taste in too-young girls. His bulging eyes and sallow cheeks made him one of the least attractive men Blossom had ever seen, but as always, he wore a pleasant smile and held his hands clasped behind his back. In his moss-green cloak with a vine decoration embroidered in walnut-brown thread along the front, Castor looked more like a powerful political figure than a disgusting monster.

"Good evening, my dear Apprentice Dodd," Castor purred to Yveline. His eyes caught on Blossom a half-second later. "By the Mother. Is that Miss Blossom Frane?" He sauntered over with unexpected quickness and took Blossom's hand in his, lifting it to his lips and kissing her knuckles. He scanned her features, lingering on the redness and puffiness from too long spent crying. She hated to be so exposed before him.

"You're a Vice Syndicate now? An *Aero* Vice Syndicate," he corrected, smiling his amusement.

It made Blossom's stomach churn to have his hand on hers, to watch his eyes roam over her figure.

"A pleasure to see you again, Vice Syndicate Castor." Blossom offered him a half-hearted bow. She didn't like him—or any child molesters, for that matter—but she knew better than to insult him in the presence of Yveline.

"What brings you to Aerona?" Blossom asked.

Castor shook his head like it was nothing. "Your compatriot Vice Syndicate Peppers and I had some business to discuss before tonight's ceremony. I look forward to seeing you there." With one more kiss to her hand, Lota Castor entered the empty elevator. Blossom didn't mention that she wouldn't be in attendance. She didn't want to explain any of it, especially not to him.

Blossom and Yveline waited for the doors to shut before they said a word.

"You know him?" Yveline pressed when they were alone again.

Blossom shook her head. "Not really. I've only met him once before."

With Castor gone, the two girls took the elevator to the Robin platform. Blossom entered without complaint, steeling herself against the motion, and forever grateful that Yveline's tales filled her ears for the few minutes it took to arrive.

The Gallant was like nothing Blossom had ever seen—in Aerona or otherwise. The lights were dim and cast long shadows across the dark space. The floors and walls were all black stone. If Blossom hadn't known better, she'd have thought they'd traveled to Pyrona—or at least the Syndicate Building in the capital.

A dozen chairs lined each side of the wide space, and Blossom didn't put up even the smallest fight as Yveline ushered her into the nearest one. The walls were covered in cabinets and shelves, each filled with various devices, jars, canisters, and a myriad of other objects Blossom couldn't name.

A man not much older than Blossom emerged from a hidden black door and approached them. He paused for a moment when he saw them but soon recovered as he neared. He had hair as dark and smooth as ink, and when he was close enough, Blossom caught a glimpse of a tattoo peeking out from the sleeve of his shirt.

He was Pyro once, Blossom realized.

"Welcome, Vice Syndicate Frane, Apprentice Vice

Syndicate Dodd," he said formally.

Yveline shot him a playful grin. "Don't be silly, Mallie. This is Blossom's first time. We don't want to scare her."

Eton's warning came rushing back. *Leave her be. She's not ready.*

But Blossom's anxieties faded as soon as they'd come. There was nothing they could do to her. With Kaide gone, her ring taken, and the Hammonds dead, Blossom couldn't think of anything that could happen in that chair that would make things worse. So she let them talk and waited patiently.

"Close your eyes," Yveline instructed, bent at the waist so her face was even with Blossom's. She wore a beaming smile, so bright and genuine, Blossom couldn't deny her. "This will hurt a bit, but not too bad. Just close your eyes for a moment."

Blossom sighed and did as she was told, trying to picture what was going on around her. Metal clicked and glass containers clanked together. Even when some cold, metallic object was pressed to the side of her nose, she didn't figure it out.

Then, something shot her. A loud noise startled her as pain erupted from the edge of her nostril. Blossom screamed out in surprise and put a hand to the spot. Where her nose had been smooth only moments before, there now sat a cold metal hoop.

A nose ring.

A reward for failing to save the Hammonds.

Her eyes found Yveline, her hands clasped and her smile beaming. "It looks wonderful!" she purred. "Mallie, get a mirror. Let her see."

The Aero man offered her a small square of reflective glass. In it, Blossom saw the shining silver color of the hoop through her nose. Seeing faces so punctured with metal in Aerona, Blossom wasn't all that surpris d, but she'd never thought about having any piercings on l er own face. Seeing and wearing were two entirely different hings.

Yveline extended her white card to the man named Mallie. "My treat," she told Blossom with a smile.

"Thank you." Blossom tried to sound earn st but wasn't quite sure she managed it.

And then, without another word, Yveline and E ossom headed back to the Robin. "I'm sorry I have to rush back," Yveline began, though Blossom hadn't even tho ght to mention it. "Herson will be sour if I don't start getting dressed for the Ascension Ceremony. I hope yo don't mind."

"That's all right. I hope you have fun." Blosson didn't mention how much she was glad to be spared fi)m the evening's event. She wasn't in the mood to pretend 1) enjoy herself.

Then, Blossom realized with a start that Kaide would be there. She would have been in the same room w h him. He would have been there, and he would have see her in Aero clothes, with Aero hair half-shaved, with a rin in her nose but not on her finger.

Blossom was glad he couldn't see her like this It was for the best, she knew, that she stay away from hi n until she had her life under her own control again.

She wouldn't even be able to show him hei totem, even if she wanted to.

For a brief moment, she contemplated asking veline to get a message to him. To tell him she was alive, le was loyal to him, she wanted to go back to him mo e than anything. But Eton's warning sounded in her ear. No one in Aerona could be trusted, not even the sweet Ap rentice Vice Syndicate.

So as much as she wanted to conspire to get ord of her new position to Kaide, Blossom bit her lip until veline dropped her back at her apartment and left to get ready for the ceremony. Blossom was more than happy to strip from her constricting Aero cloak and suit and return to her room, though this time, she opted for the more comfortable rug.

Eton reappeared hours later, a platter of fish in his hands. "Hungry?"

Blossom took one whiff of the fish and shook her head. "Not particularly."

"Suit yourself. Get dressed."

"What now?" Blossom's patience for being dragged around Aerona was quickly waning.

"A surprise you'll actually like," he insisted. "And not the full suit. Just these." He tossed her the light undershirt and the hip-hugging bottoms she wore under her suits.

Intrigue got Blossom off the floor and moving. When she was dressed—mostly—Eton held out her cloak as she slipped her arms into the sleeves. Once buttoned, it was impossible to tell she lacked the full suit underneath.

"You're wearing a suit," she pointed out as they left.

"I don't have a cloak," he reminded her.

Instead of taking the elevator to the Robin platform, they descended to the lowest level of the lava tubes. "Where are we going?" Blossom asked, not at all sure she cared.

"To the caves."

"These are all caves."

"True. But these are different. You'll see." The elevator doors parted and released them into total darkness. Unlike the other levels, this one had no lights whatsoever, not even the dim ones of the outskirts.

"What are we doing down here, Eton?" she asked, her voice exasperated. All too late she wondered if she'd made another mistake. The last time she'd gone exploring with a stranger, she ended up nearly kidnapped in a warehouse. Like with Trean, she had trusted Eton's kind eyes and promises, though she knew it had been a mistake If the Syndicate had told Eton to kill her, he would do it without hesitation. Blossom was as good as dead.

"Going to see the caves. I told you." He produced a beam of light from his pocket and aimed it ahead. Then, he stepped forward and left her standing at the elevator door.

"Wait for me!" Blossom shouted when the darkness came too close. She rushed after him—or the light he held—and planted a firm hand on his shoulder, determined not to be abandoned in the dark. Even her falcon eyes could discern nothing in such pure black.

Eton chuckled and led her further into the gloom. His beam of light cut through it like a sword. Minutes later, a low, bluish glow appeared ahead, but it wasn't until they'd arrived that Blossom could see what it was: a pool of water, tinted a lovely teal color by some sort of light source deep within.

The light reflected across the sloping cavern ceiling, showcasing the slender pillars that punctured the far side. Closer, a low stone ledge met the surface of the perfectly still, clear water. "How does it do that?" Blossom asked of the soft glow produced so far within the Earth.

"These are off-shoots of subterranean rivers. Wherever they reach the surface, light enters, and these cave stones reflect it, bouncing it halfway across the realm until it ends up here." Eton bent and tugged off his pointed white shoes, followed by his socks. Then, he rolled his pants to the knees and sat on the stone edge of the pool, dipping his legs in the water up to his calves.

Blossom followed suit, stripping out of her cloak and leaving it in a haphazard pile on the cave floor, followed by her shoes. She dipped a toe into the water. "It's warm," she said in awe.

"We're far enough down, the Earth keeps it warm." Eton kicked his feet in the water, disturbing the perfect smoothness of the surface.

Blossom took several steps back.

"What are you doing?" Eton asked over his shoulder.

In answer, Blossom ran forward. Her feet pounded the hard stone floor as she gathered speed. At the water's edge, she pointed her arms over her head and dove in, sailing into the pool like a bird through a cloud. It was the closest she'd been to flying in weeks.

Blossom savored the feel of water on her skin, like a warm bath large enough to swim through. As long as she could stand it, Blossom swam, holding her breath until her chest ached, hungry for air. Only when she was desperate did Blossom kick toward the surface.

With her head above water, Blossom sucked in one deep lungful after the other. She looked around and found she'd swum only halfway across the pool. Sitting on the far ledge, Eton looked tiny.

Blossom rolled onto her back and let the water hold her. Her newly punctured nose burned, but otherwise, she was content to swim and never return to the world. She lazily flipped her arms and kicked her legs to move about, but she didn't care where she went. The calm of water on her skin was too good to resist.

Kaide would have loved this. They'd never gone swimming together, or even discussed it, but she knew Kaide would savor the magic of this place the same as she did.

If only she could ever get the chance to show him.

"I didn't know you could swim," Eton said when she drifted near enough to hear him.

Blossom answered without stopping. "Hale taught me." Even saying his name felt strange. It had been so long since she'd seen the person she used to see most often. She'd been closest to Hale of all her brothers, and she hadn't even talked to him in almost a month.

"Hale?" Eton asked.

"My brother," she answered with a nostalgic sigh.

"I thought you were from the Alderwood."

"I am. We moved our camp every few month For a while, we lived in the west near Lake Hydra. I woul sneak off to see the water, and Hale was afraid I would fal in and drown, so he taught me." In her mind, the memory was as vivid as the day it happened. She'd been only s ven or eight, and Hale had been at least twelve. He lif d one skinny arm after the other to show her the motions, now to kick to get the most power, how to lie on her back and let the water hold her if she tired.

She relished filling her mind with memo ies of something so assuredly good. Blossom still had hei doubts about Eton, and knew that Kaide would never acc pt her new position, but her childhood in the Alderwood, h r years of freedom in the trees, that could never be wrong.

For the first time in a long time, Blossom wis ied for the Alderwood. She'd never known how mucl she'd needed it until it was far behind her. She'd cros ed the realm a half-dozen times now, yet still her heart ac ied for the tall trees of her youth.

"I'm never going home, am I?" she heard hers lf ask, her own voice muffled by the water in her ears.

"Probably not, no." Eton's voice was warl ed by water, but his words damaged her all the same. "I won't always be this bad. We just have to get through tl is, and it'll be better."

"What's that supposed to mean?" Blossom pu ed her head up and began to tread, determined to hear his ai swer.

Eton looked at his feet where he kicked thei. "My father was a Syndicate. Did you know that?" He sh ok his head and laughed. "Of course not. No one talks a out it. Syndicate Jasper Samina. I was still a kid w en he ascended."

Getting the idea this was going to be a long story, Blossom swam to his side and rested her forearms on the stone ledge.

"He was really good, really fair. He took me to a lot of the meetings and things, though I'm pretty sure I wasn't supposed to be there. He spent a lot of time out in the Emporium, or just walking the lava tubes."

"Which is why so many people know you," Blossom interrupted. She didn't mention the reverence they held for him, and now she knew his father was a beloved Syndicate of old, everything made more sense than she cared to admit.

With a nod, he continued. "All the Vice Syndicates hated it, that he was so involved with the lower classes, but he didn't listen."

"Someone killed him?" Blossom had been in Aerona long enough to know how this story would end.

Eton nodded. "I was ten. My aunt took me in until I came of age. She nominated me for Vice Syndicate, but I keep getting passed over."

Blossom was thankful for her grip on the ledge. Without it, she wouldn't have had the frame of mind to keep herself afloat. The reality of it hit her like a hammer. "You wanted this position," Blossom said, putting voice to her thoughts.

"As my father's son, I'm an obvious candidate. But because his name was tarnished after his death, and my lower-class aunt raised me, Mercer has enough reason to select someone else for the position. She assigned me as your advisor to rub it in my face."

Helping Blossom was Eton's punishment for being his father's son.

Or maybe there was another reason. "Have you ever disobeyed an order?" She peered up at him from the pool, her legs kicking behind her. She fell still when she saw the shadow drawn across his too-pale face.

Never taking his eyes off his feet in the water, Eton offered her a single sullen nod.

Blossom had not a shred of doubt that the Syndicate—Mercer or her predecessor, Waller—had punished Eton just as creatively as she had Blossom. And like her, it had left its own sort of scar.

She wanted to ask what had happened—what had been worth defying the Syndicate—but she wasn't sure she really wanted the answer. If it had been anything like the Hammonds, she knew ignorance was the better course.

Instead, she asked, "The Syndicate ordered you to modify my totem, didn't she? So I'd be Aero?"

Eton's eyes flashed up with something like shock. His mouth hung open a bit before he recovered. "Yes, she did."

Blossom looked up at him and cringed. She'd known it, but the words impaled her with the force of a spear. "I'll try not to hate you forever." And she would—she would try her best not to hate Eton for following that particular order. But in her heart of hearts, a part of her would always resent what he'd done to her.

"I suppose that's fair." Eton studied her carefully as he asked, "You knew?"

Blossom shook her head. "Kaide told me she would." And in her stubbornness, Blossom had gone to transformation anyway. Stupid, stupid girl.

Eton listed his head to the side and asked, "What happened with him?"

Blossom pulled herself onto the ledge to sit beside him. There was no way she could talk about Kaide and swim at the same time.

And, as much as it gutted her, she wanted to talk about him. It made him feel more real, even if it was only in her head.

She tucked her knees to her chest to ward off the chill, ignoring the water dripping into a shallow puddle around her. "He was wonderful," she began, a description that was entirely true yet still a vast injustice to him. "He was sweet and kind and so strong," she continued, remembering the time he'd carried her up a mountain.

"Really?" Eton asked, his eyes as round as saucers.

"Yeah, why?"

"He's pretty much the jerk of politics. I mean, he's charming and careful and obviously smart to pull off what he does, but everyone knows he's just as calculating as anyone, and worse than most. He might not be cruel like Mercer, but he's just as determined. It's hard to imagine anyone thinking he was *sweet*."

"Well, he is." Opposed to the turn in the conversation, Blossom pushed to her feet and found her cloak, barely visible in the glow from the pool.

Eton appeared beside her, his eyes intent as he asked, "You liked him?"

Blossom didn't know how to answer. There was a resounding *Yes*, that Kaide had made her feel better in their short time together than anyone in the world. But there was also a definitive *No*. Blossom liked climbing trees and swimming and reading. What she felt for Kaide was so much more than that.

"It's hard to explain," she said instead. She finished buttoning her cloak and waited for Eton to take her back to her apartment.

But he stood in front of her with those pale-blue eyes and said, "I didn't mean to upset you. I thought you'd be happy to get away from him—"

"No, not at all." In fact, she'd give anything to be back in the manor with her beast. Not just for his books or his fine things or expensive dinners. Blossom wanted the blue-eyed man who understood her better than anyone. She wanted horseback rides to volcanoes and walks through the market. Blossom wanted her life with Kaide.

"Yes, I can see that now. I misunderstood." He turned and put on his socks and shoes, rolling his pants down to his ankles so he looked put together as always. Only the slight wrinkles in the calves of his pants gave away his previous state. "Ready to go back?"

"Not really," she admitted. If today was any indication of what her new life was going to be like, then she didn't want any part of it.

"I'm doing what I can," Eton said, like he blamed himself for all of it. Then again, he had changed her totem. In a way, he was entirely to blame. "It would help if you'd listen to me. The Aero branch is complex, and there are a lot of rules. I'm trying to help you—"

"I know." Blossom was no stranger to being the problem. "I'll try to do better," she promised for the thousandth time. She hoped she'd be able to do it. She didn't know if she had it in her to fail again. The image of Helena Hammond's body flashed across her vision before she could stop it.

"I'm here for whatever you need. I'll help you be Aero. And when you need a break, we can come back down here." He motioned toward the subterranean lake.

Blossom searched his eyes for an explanation. "Why down here? Why didn't you tell me any of this in the apartment?"

"There aren't cameras down here. No sensors, no scanners. The Syndicate doesn't monitor these caves." Eton licked his lips for a moment before he added. "I don't know whether or not she monitors the apartment, but I know the caves are safe. I won't risk it if I don't have to."

And then, everything about him clicked into place. Eton's coolness, his mood swings, his constant distance broken by quiet moments of worry, it all made sense. He thought he was being watched. And he thought his actions would be used to harm Blossom, just as Blossom's actions had been used to harm the Hammonds.

Eton, like Kaide and Hale before him, had been watching out for her when she hadn't even known it. Like a rockslide, everything she had ever believed about Eton shifted.

I can do this, Kaide reminded himself for the hundredth time.

In the splendor of the Aero Ascension Ceremony, with vibrant white décor, merry music, and a crowd triple the normal size, Kaide was overwhelmed. But standing before the wall-length window centered over the Sacred Mother, Kaide felt some small measure of peace. Her gnarled branches were fully covered in the luscious pink blossoms that marked the spring and summer seasons—and they reminded him of Blossom. Only weeks ago, he stood in this very spot with her, showing her the idol of their realm, the center of their religion, the ancient tree herself. That memory, paired with the general awe he always felt at the sight of the Mother, put him somewhat at ease.

He desperately needed it tonight. His proposal to the Alderai and branch Syndicates went unacknowledged. They would take no steps to address the Prentis. Kaide was less than enthused to spend an evening with those who so blatantly ignored his plan of action against a considerable threat within the realm.

It didn't help that his mind was elsewhere—with the Mother, if she existed, and with Blossom, who had never really been his.

So Kaide chose to sip the bitter rice mead and keep to himself. Any other time, he would have kept moving. Like a wolf on the hunt, he would seek out each target and discern what he needed from them.

But not tonight.

He had no energy for it. Blossom was gone, an l she'd left a hollow man in his place.

"A lovely event, don't you think, Landel?" Kaide lifted his eyes from his glass and saw the sickly fea ıres of Lota Castor. His walnut-brown hair was slicked ba k, and his moss-green cloak was even finer than usual, b t there was no mistaking his vileness.

"Yes, charming," Kaide replied automatically.

"I was expecting to see Ms. Frane here tonigh . Have you seen her?" Lota's brow had creased in a look the might be genuine concern, but Kaide knew that to be imp ssible. Lota had only gotten better at hiding his disgusting g in.

"I'd rather not discuss it." Kaide was hardly e ger to air his heartbreak publicly, even to his secret all. They might share an ultimate goal to see the branch system dissolved, but that hardly made them friends.

Lota shrugged and resumed his usual smirk. "Very well. Have you had a chance to look over the lis I sent you?"

Kaide shook his head. Of all the Vice S ıdicate candidates Castor had recommended for the Terra ıranch, Kaide had no particular leanings toward one or a nother. Castor had offered to let Kaide hold some measure f sway over the position that would soon be vacated by the etiring Vice Syndicate Bartel, but Kaide wasn't interested in any of them. Another ally in the Terra branch would be a major asset to their cause, but Kaide couldn't identify a sin gle one who was suited to the position.

Castor hid his disappointment well. "I'll keep v orking on it." That was the last thing Kaide heard from him When next he looked up, Castor was gone.

That suited Kaide well enough. He was satisfie l in his silence. If Mora hadn't mandated his attendance, e'd be back in Pyrona in his totem form, ending the life c f some criminal. Instead, he was stuck at a festival—an *Aero* festival at that—and all he could think about was how much he missed Blossom.

"Thirsty?" Pruda nearly startled Kaide's drink from his hand. His provocative Pyro Vice Syndicate compatriot laughed and held out a fresh glass of wine, this one a lovely pink color.

Kaide gladly exchanged his half-empty rice mead for a full glass of strawberry wine. "Thank you," he said after several large gulps.

"This rice mead is vile. I don't know how they drink it." Pruda cocked her eyebrow at him and sipped her drink, as coy and devious as her viper totem.

Kaide couldn't help but chuckle. It was such a sorry thing to laugh at, and the sensation of humor felt strange after weeks of agony, but Kaide found a sad smile on his lips and his shoulders shaking with laughter.

"It *is* disgusting," he admitted.

Pruda smiled in return. The plunging neckline of her too-tight crimson dress accentuated her figure in the best of ways, but it was her smile that caught him.

Like most of their political colleagues, Pruda was well-versed in keeping her emotions in check. Her fake smile came more easily than her real one.

Kaide wasn't sure he'd ever seen her real smile until now.

But it was gone a moment later. Her deep, dark eyes narrowed, and she winced slightly as she said, "I was very sorry to hear about your bride, Kaide. I can't imagine—"

Kaide shook the thought away.

"Could I trouble you for a dance?" Pruda set her glass on a nearby table and held her hand out to him, flaunting the flawless tattoo that trailed from shoulder to wrist.

Kaide grudgingly accepted. He was supposed to be showing Syndicate Mora he could still do his job. What better way than to parade about at a festival of his enemies?

Once on the dance floor, Pruda faced him and slid into the formal position—one hand on his shoulder, one hand held in his—but Kaide was struck with the memory of Blossom. How gut-wrenchingly gorgeous she looked. How adorable she was, all stumbles and nerves. How he'd kissed her in this very spot.

"I'm sorry. I can't." Kaide stepped away, crushed.

Pruda grabbed his forearm and held tight. "She's watching."

Those two words were enough to make Kaide turn back and retake his position. He refused to let his eyes scan for Mora, but he knew Pruda was right: she was watching them. She was always watching, observing—even when it didn't look like she was. The woman was far too crafty.

That was half the reason she was so dangerous.

Music filled the cavernous festival space from invisible speakers. All modern songs, all Seraphian of course. Aero didn't even have the decency to play live music. Instead, it was all recorded tunes, sounding hollow as they echoed over the dancing crowd.

Kaide forced his feet into motion. He knew the steps well enough, but his heart wasn't in it. He didn't want to be here. He didn't want to be dancing. He didn't want Pruda in his arms instead of Blossom.

But Kaide could do nothing to change any of it. In all likelihood, he would feel this way forever, and the idea terrified him. What if he never recovered from this?

He'd known that first day in the Alderwood. At first sight—at first scent—he knew Blossom would change everything. And she had, only not in the way he expected. Not in the way he hoped.

She hadn't even gone home. Olin would have detected her had she hid in the Alderwood. His lynx nose was too keen to miss Blossom's scent. She had simply gone off into the world on a new adventure and hadn't bothered to so much as tell him she was going.

"What are you thinking about?" Pruda's question hit him like an arrow, rushing his thoughts back to the present, to the dance.

"Nothing," he replied, refusing to discuss it—unable to discuss it.

"Your eyes give you away, you know. They used to be a lovely peacock blue. Now, they're almost black. Anyone who's paying attention can see you're not yourself." Pruda didn't miss a step as she stabbed him deep in the heart with her words.

"It's a trick of the light," he lied. The white lights Aero so favored would have made his eyes look brighter, if anything. He wouldn't admit it aloud, but Kaide couldn't deny a darkness had grown inside him.

Pruda offered him a knowing smile, and, when the time came to turn her about, she spun elegantly, the black train of her gown sailing around her in a perfect arc. Then, he pulled her back, and she floated into his arms, as she'd been a moment before.

In the last three years, Pruda hadn't been anywhere near the top of his list of targets. She was Pyro, and when he ascended to Syndicate, she'd be under his control, at least publicly. There was no reason for him to go out of his way to charm her as he did so many others.

Kaide wondered if he'd ever danced with her before. If he had, he couldn't remember. But now, he was struck with the smoothness of her motions, how naturally she stepped and spun and followed his lead. Despite the fractures in his heart, it felt good to dance with her.

But soon enough, the song ended, and the speakers boomed out, "Good evening!" Kaide and Pruda both winced at the volume of the announcement, and when the voice continued, it wasn't quite so loud. "Welcome to the

Ascension Ceremony for the Aero Branch. Please gi e your attention to our esteemed Alderai Hamilton."

Kaide groaned and turned to face the middle of the dance floor. At the apex of the Syndicate Buildi g, the Alderai stood tall despite his advanced age, l vingly accepting the deep bows of the realms elite. Rennel Hamilton was at least seventy, maybe eighty. Kaide couldn't remember. His skin was a sagging monstro ity that made him look like he'd already lived thousands of ears— part of the reason he was so respected. There were rumors in Terra that he was immortal—that he had eter al life granted to him by the Alder Mother, a gift for his de otion.

But Kaide knew better. The Alderai, the most p werful man in the realm and supposedly the direct contact l etween the Mother and her followers, was a happy recij ent of Aero's leading medical technology. And duri g his unnaturally long life, he'd done little to prev nt the abduction, molestation, and rape of children t at ran rampant amongst the leaders of the Terra branch Kaide guessed the Alderai was directly involved, and i at his inaction was a defense to prevent interference.

As the Alderai was the single-most power il and influential individual in the realm, Kaide couldn't exactly go around accusing him of anything, particularly st ch sick and depraved crimes. Alderai Hamilton was a sad c ld man who'd kept his position too long, and when Kai le was Syndicate, retiring him would be high on his list of changes to make.

Sadly, no one else seemed to mind him. In f ct, his flawless moss-green cloaked hemmed in go l and embroidered with delicate alder blossoms hung ff his proud shoulders as politicians from every branch lo ked on in awed reverence around him, hanging on every w rd that slipped from his ancient mouth.

"Today, we honor the blessed Mother a d the

ascension of one Audra Mercer into the Aero Syndicate," the Alderai began. "From this day forth, this daughter will stand with the Syndicates in representation of her branch and her realm in honor of the Mother.

"As Syndicate, her duties are to her people, her branch, her totem, and above all others, the Mother. She will select three Vice Syndicates to facilitate her decrees across the realm. May I present to you, esteemed guests of the Mother, your newest Syndicate, Audra Mercer of Aero."

Kaide clapped with as much fervor as the event demanded, and beside him, Pruda did the same. She pushed up onto her toes, leaning closer to him as she whispered, "I wonder how many times that old bag has given this speech."

Together, they hid their snickers in the noise of the crowd.

Ignoring the speech, Pruda continued, "You know, he was once an apprentice for the Terra branch. Or rumor says, anyway. Then, the last Alderai selected him, though no one really knows why. To think we could have had Bartel for an Alderai. Or Castor."

Kaide couldn't hide his cringe. Castor as the most powerful man in the realm? The idea made him want to spew his wine across the dance floor.

But the selection of a new Alderai was one he hadn't considered before. What if Hamilton retired—by some miracle—and selected someone opposed to Kaide's plan to destroy the branch system? It could mean serious conflict if it wasn't handled properly.

His thoughts were interrupted by the arrival of the new Aero Syndicate as she was ushered to the Alderai's side to receive his kisses and blessing. Audra Mercer, the person he hated above all others. The person who had personally destroyed Kaide's totem and left him with this blood-thirsty beast. The person who actively tried to eliminate him from his position, but in doing so, had earned him as her enemy.

And now, she was the Syndicate of her branch. Kaide licked his lips. He would so enjoy destroying Aero. He would relish the look on her face when she watched him incinerate everything and everyone she'd ever loved—if she was even capable of love, that is.

Kaide would have blamed her for Blossom, too, except Blossom had never arrived for her transformation. He knew if given the opportunity to alter Blossom's totem, Mercer would have done it in a heartbeat. He hated her no less.

"As Aero Syndicate, her first order of business will be to pledge her commitment to the latest realm decree." Kaide's ears perked at Hamilton's words. Just when he thought the useless old lump had ignored Kaide's warning about the Prentis, here he was making a public proclamation against them. Or so he thought.

Instead, he heard the impossible words. "Syndicate Mercer will join the Syndicate Dormier, Syndicate Voltez, and Syndicate Mora in actively identifying, neutralizing, and extraditing Alder criminals to Terrana for sentencing."

Kaide fought back a disgusted retch. Alder criminals? That was his concern? Kaide himself was one such criminal, harboring unsanctioned texts in his personal and secret collection of pre-war relics. The Alderai's focus on Alder crimes was so misguided, it bordered on the irresponsible. He'd have his agents out searching for illegal books while rapists and kidnappers continued to run rampant in Pyrona.

It was enough to make him sick. "Is he insane?" Pruda whispered in his ear, her usually calm brow twisted in concern.

Kaide could only shrug in horror and watch the rest of the proceedings.

Behind Mercer stood her always smiling husband and the starkly pale figures of Crin Peppers and Yveline Dodd, the current Aero Vice Syndicates. As an Apprentice, Yveline Dodd rarely attended realm functions, but as this was an Aero event—an Aero Ascension Ceremony, no less—her presence was expected despite her age. Kaide hadn't seen her in many months, and he noted she looked considerably more grown than she had when last he saw her. She stood with a confidence that spoke volumes about her career as a rising Aero Vice Syndicate. Apprentice Dodd would make a formidable enemy if she was ever given the chance. Kaide would have to be sure to squash the Aero branch before Yveline had a chance to ascend, though Mercer was hardly a desired alternative in the meantime.

"Any word on the new Vice Syndicate?" Pruda continued, speaking just under the volume of the congratulations and cheers around them.

Kaide shook his head. Of course, every ascending Syndicate kept their previous Vice Syndicates, a show of solidarity within the branch. As for the newly vacated Aero position, Kaide had a few ideas as to who would fill the position.

Gran Ellis, the Aero Commissioner of Interbranch Relations would be at the top of the list, though maybe a little old. Nowadays, thirty-five was a little late to start a political career. Eton Samina was an obvious choice, except for the fact that the previous Syndicate Waller had liked him, and therefore Mercer hated him. Farley Volstead would be Kaide's choice, if only because he'd worked beside the Aero Commissioner of Security a dozen times and had never found him to be even remotely horrible, a rare trait in the white branch.

Pruda only shrugged when he failed to produce an answer. "Oh well. We'll know soon enough."

HUNTRESS

IN THE LIGHT of the candle at Da's table, Hale stared at the letter, rereading every word over and over again. It wasn't so much a letter—they hadn't received official correspondence from Terrana in years—but a note half-scribbled on a stolen bit of paper. The Amaris clan had risked sending them this message.

The Alderai was searching for them.

While the almighty servant of the Mother had no direct knowledge of the Bear Clan or their activities, he surely recognized the scars they left behind. The wide, severed stumps were evidence enough.

"I told you we'd been too prolific," Hale said once he found the voice to respond.

"It was only a matter of time." Unlike Hale, Da didn't seem worried in the slightest. "We're about finished with this cut. We'll move on and find a new one."

"Or we stop with the cuts for a while. We have enough to last us a few years. There's no reason to put ourselves at risk…" While the Bear Clan lived in relative luxury, with plentiful food and wine and supplies, the majority of their earnings were sent to an account in Terrana. Hale didn't know the precise sum, but he knew it was considerable. They could easily live off such wealth for years.

Sipping a goblet of amberwine, Da meandered about the tent at a leisurely pace. His grey-streaked hair shimmered in the wavering light of the candle. Hale hated when he got in moods like this—like nothing was wrong. Like nothing could ever be wrong.

"This is our purpose, son. If we are not selecting and processing the Mother's gifts, then what are we to do with ourselves? The men will grow bored, and the women will tire of their company."

"But not at the expense of our safety," Hale insisted. Then, as he often did during their more heated discussions, Hale pulled the coin from his pocket and flipped it in the air. A half-second later, he caught it against his arm and stared in awe at the carved image of the alder leaf.

Trust the Mother.

Some days, it was easier to trust her than others. When the Sacred Mother told him to still his hand and let Blossom go, it had ripped his heart from his chest. When Raene pressed her side to his in those small quiet moments in the night, Hale swelled with his trust for the Mother.

Today, trusting the Mother to keep their clan safe from the Alderai's agents was less easy. Raene had already been attacked by a coyote, and now, with news of the Alderai's determination to eliminate operations such as theirs, Hale was more worried than ever. He shouldn't have let Raene leave camp today.

The idea of her in danger set his nerves on edge, but the idea of her putting others in danger made his stomach flop uncomfortably. She was so undeniably lovely, so well-spoken and elegant, and yet lurking beneath that exterior was the aggression of a tiger. It filled him with undeniable dread to think that she was so close to causing so much damage, but he knew it was meant to be. Raene wouldn't cause this incessant pounding in his chest if it wasn't the Mother's will.

Hale's thoughts raced through their morning conversation, trying to remember where she was. She was at Gemini's garden, he recalled at last. It was far outside the edge of camp, but the Connors would protect her. Then again, she might be one to protect them.

But he couldn't think about that. Raene's totem was far too volatile to risk. Hale would have to spend time working with her to get it under control. The day she arrived, he hadn't missed the smell of fresh blood from her traveling companion, the still-bleeding leg wound she kept hidden, though he was less successful in hiding the limp. Hale suspected Raene had caused considerable damage, though he wouldn't be the one to ask her outright. He was supposed to earn her trust, to be the man she felt comfortable with. Accusing her of crimes wouldn't exactly accomplish the Mother's plan.

For now, he would handle the problems available to him. Hale pocketed his coin and used his most decisive voice as he told Da, "We should tighten up the convoys. Keep them localized and in smaller groups. Only deal with established clans we know fairly well. At least keep out unnecessary risk."

Da tossed his head lightly side to side in consideration. "A wise decision, my son."

"We'll need to send a token of our gratitude to the Amaris Clan. They might have news of coyote movement through the Alderwood."

"Send a pair with a case of amberwine."

Hale rolled his eyes. It was far too gracious a gift for such a tiny piece of paper, but Da was never one to do anything halfway. He had his ways, his idiosyncrasies none of them would ever fully grasp, but he'd served them well thus far, and Hale didn't have it in him to voice his doubts. Instead, he answered, "I'll see to it."

"And let's keep this between us for now."

"Da?" Hale was sure he'd heard him wrong.

"There's no need to raise tensions in camp. We're almost finished processing the cut, and we haven't yet decided if we'll relocate in the next weeks. I don't want anyone getting the idea we might be running from this."

Hale sighed as the truth sank in. "We can't afford a loss of confidence." It made sense, he knew. But that only complicated things. How was he supposed to keep his clan safe from an enemy he couldn't even warn them about?

"And these?" Raene pointed to the pear-green leaves emerging from the ground, the ones that curled at the ends.

"Carrots, and these ones are radishes." Gemini nodded down the length of the row. In the sun-baked garden on the edge of camp, Raene sweltered in the summer heat, but her day with Gemini had been one of the best since arriving in the clan.

"So don't pull these?" On her hands and knees, wearing gloves that were entirely too big for her, Raene pointed at the leaves, afraid to harvest the wrong thing.

Gemini stifled a laugh. "Yes, pull them. They're ready."

"How can you remember all these?" Raene asked in awe. There were dozens of crops in the Connor family garden, but Gemini knew them each by sight. She knew when they were planted, what kinds of soil they liked, how much sun they needed, and when to harvest them. She could use her plants to make more teas than Raene could name.

Raene greatly enjoyed learning about plants, but she wasn't sure she'd ever know as much as Gemini.

Then again, she hadn't been farming her whole life, either.

"You know, you really don't have to do this," Gemini fussed for the hundredth time.

"What else am I going to do?" Raene reminded her. "Sit in a tent and stare at the walls?" In her old life, Raene had envisioned lavish parties and fancy dresses. Here in the Alderwood, she was digging plants from the soil to stave off boredom.

Still, she was making a friend. And it kept her away from camp, out of Hale's tent, and she didn't have to think about that night with Parson.

Three days had gone by, and Raene still found her thoughts lingering on that night.

And she hoped keeping busy would help quiet her rising urge, but so far, she'd found no relief. Her stomach growled constantly, always desperate and hungry for more than fruit or nuts or bread. Raene tried not to think about it, to force her mind to focus on the plants in front of her.

"Oh, there's plenty to do. Maybe not anything exciting…" Gemini admitted with a laugh. "That was Blossom's problem. She wanted excitement. There's none of that here."

Startled, Gemini's gaze jerked to the far edge of the garden.

"Speak for yourself." Asla Brimmen emerged from the woods with a smile on his face. His infatuation was evident in the brightness in his eyes and the ease of his smile as he watched Gemini work. "I'm plenty exciting," he teased.

Raene and Gemini broke into girlish laughs. Raene had only talked to Asla once before, but he hadn't exactly given off the impression of being any sort of adventurer. His elk totem was far too quiet for that sort of thing.

Gemini clutched her stomach as she pulled to her feet, laughing all the while. She trotted to Asla—careful to avoid trampling her plants—and offered him a sweet kiss. "I thought you weren't coming by until later."

Asla shrugged and kissed her forehead. "Parson let us go early today. Said he had something to do. We're ahead of schedule, anyway."

Raene sobered at the mention of her future brother-in-law, but she quickly returned to plucking vegetables, wishing a carrot or a radish could silence her totem like a rabbit could. Then, she remembered Gemini's rabbit totem, and doubled her focus on her task.

Oblivious to the darkness of her thoughts or the anxiety in her blood, Asla and Gemini continued their sweet kisses.

"Does that mean you'll get paid early?" Gemini clutched both dirt-crusted hands together and smiled up at him.

Not even Asla could resist such a look. He kissed her temple and laughed. "Yes, and I'll even get you a bottle of amberwine."

Gemini squealed and threw her arms around his neck before Asla lifted her from the ground entirely, turning so that her feet spun wide around him. Gemini's pleasant features twisted in fear. "No, no. Put me down!" she shrieked. Asla let out a groan at her protest, but he set her feet back to the ground, and soon enough, they were laughing again. Even Raene allowed herself a good laugh, hoping such moments could help her overcome the urge to hunt.

Raene would never have thought a small farm would bring so much fun to her life, but a full day of working with Gemini had lessened her anxiety. The fresh air away from camp helped her clear her head. Her nights of fitful sleep in Hale's too-hot tent were taking their toll. Only Hale's company, their wine-filled evenings, and his strokes on her back brought her any peace at all.

If only the itch to hunt would subside. If only thoughts of Parson would leave her be.

This time, it was Raene who heard the footsteps first.

As if summoned by her thoughts, Parson emerged from the woods behind Asla. They froze and gaped at him in unison, wondering why the second son of the clan leader would venture so far out of camp to see them.

Parson side-stepped Asla—still holding Gemini as they stared—and approached Raene, his eyes focused on her. She was suddenly self-conscious, too aware of the dirt on her knees and elbows, the sweat across her brow, the smear she'd left on her cheek an hour ago, the brown color left on the tip of her braid where she'd accidentally dipped it in the soil.

She didn't want him to see her this way.

"I'm sorry to show up like this," he began, standing tall next to where she knelt in the dirt. A second later, he sank to his haunches beside her and continued, "I was wondering if I could talk to you for a few minutes." His hair hung over his face just so, hiding much of his features, but Raene could see he didn't come here lightly. There was an intensity in his features she couldn't resist.

So she nodded and climbed to her feet—her bare, dirt-covered feet. "Just give me a minute to get cleaned up." She started toward her shoes piled beside a tree at the edge of the garden.

"No need. We won't be long." His shirt was dingy with sweat and sawdust, and his hair was clumped with grease. He couldn't exactly hold her appearance against her.

But then she had no more reason to delay.

Raene swallowed hard and nodded. She handed her gloves to Gemini, promised to be back shortly, and then let Parson lead her into the woods.

In the horrible, suffocating silence that hung between them, Raene balled her hands into fists to hide how they shook, but even that didn't work. The last time she'd seen him, he'd kissed her, and as much as it confused her, she wanted him to do it again.

In recent nights, Raene and Hale had taken to sharing sweet, shy kisses. Hale was always so kind, so careful of her boundaries and never pushing her. Raene enjoyed it immensely, but there was a part of her that wished Hale would show a little more passion. If nothing else, she knew Parson had it in spades.

It was all she could do to walk in a straight line beside him, pushing those thoughts to the back of her mind. He didn't want her that way; he'd said as much already. And it would kill Hale to know she harbored such delusions.

Parson's eternal silence only made it worse. They'd walked for ten minutes before he finally spoke. "I'm not sure how to start. I'm not very good at this."

"At what? Apologizing?" Raene avoided his eyes as she waited, though he'd already offered her a sad sort of apology a moment after it happened. She didn't need to reminisce in his regret.

When at last she dared a glance at him, a soft smile played with the corners of his lips. He seemed almost amused. "I guess that's as good a place as any. I owe you quite a few." Parson stopped short and turned to face her, his emerald eyes even with her blue ones. "I'm sorry I blamed you for Blossom's marriage arrangement. I'm sorry I held your Pyro origins against you. And I'm sorry I said I didn't want to marry you."

Raene could only stare, could only listen to the pounding in her chest that was surely audible in the quiet of the woods. Her mouth fell open in shock, and she couldn't force out a response. That hadn't been what she expected at all.

"I don't know how to fix it," Parson continued. "But if I don't at least get it out there, I'll regret it forever. I'd like it if you could give me a chance." His voice fell away before he managed one last bit of strength. "I understand if you don't want—if I've ruined things."

Raene chewed on her lip to keep from hurling words in anger. It wasn't fair, not one bit of it. Because of Parson, she'd been living in Hale's tent, getting to know him, getting to *like* him, and now he wanted to take it all back?

"Why?" Raene lifted her eyes back to his and searched for the answer.

Parson winced as if the question pained him. He kicked the ground with his boot for several seconds before he managed to say, "You're a tiger."

At that, Raene turned around and left. She wasn't going to be some commodity passed between brothers. She had only just started her march back to camp when Parson's grip on her shoulder brought her to a halt.

"I'm no good at this. I'm not Hale. I don't have the words I want to say when I want to say them. I'm twenty-five, and I still can't get the damn words to come out. But please—"

Raene glowered at him as she crossed her arms tight over her chest, but that look in his eye made her soften. He was trying, he was putting himself out there for her. The least she could do was listen. "Fine."

Parson relaxed for a moment before he realized he was actually going to have to explain it to her. He ran his hand through his wavy chestnut locks and thought for several long seconds before he finally worked out what he wanted to say. "I've been in the Alderwood my whole life," he started, and once he had, the words tumbled out one after the other. "No one has what I have. After I underwent transformation, I killed so many innocents. I nearly caught Nyla Connors, but she was too fast. I was a mess. Da and Lathan thought I was doing it on purpose. That I just needed to grow up. I tried and tried to tell them. When Hale got his bear, he was like them. Always calm. It was clearly a problem with me. Something I was doing wrong. Only one person ever understood."

Raene could see where this was going. "Blossom understood."

He gave her a brief nod. "She caught me on a hunt once. You know her, never where she's supposed to be. It was our secret for a long time."

"I thought you didn't like secrets." Too late, Raene remembered the one he still kept for her, that night with the elk.

"I don't, but there was no other way." Parson's shoulders sagged as he let out a heavy sigh. "Your uncle took the one person who bothered to try to understand. There was no one else. It was just me." He sucked in a long, slow breath before he added, "And now you." Parson offered her something like a smile. "You have it. You killed two dozen innocents in a few hours. You hunted and stalked and killed without question. There's no way you don't have it. You're a hunter. A *huntress*. And you—" His gaze fell away with his voice. "I'm not sure how to explain it, but what you did for Blossom—"

Raene only lowered her eyes and replied, "Was far less than she deserved." Even that felt like saying too much, but the weight of it pressed on her heavier than ever. She couldn't withstand his gratitude while hiding what she'd done.

Parson's arm was across her shoulders a second later, pulling her against his chest. There was no way Parson could have known Kaide and Olin and even Norsa had offered her that same comforting motion hundreds of times. There was no way he could have known how the firm muscles beneath his shirt would give her the closest thing to home she'd had since she arrived in the Alderwood.

And unlike the taller Kaide and the shorter Hale, Parson was exactly her height. It was easy to melt against him, to wrap her arms about his waist and linger there, her face pressed to his shirt. Each breath carried the scent of him with it.

Parson's voice was quiet as he continued. 'When Blossom left—I just, I was angry. I'm still angry. I'm never going to be not angry about it." His words skated across her ear where he held her tight. That same hand pushed up into her hair, and his nails lightly raked her scalp, just enough to make her close her eyes and savor the comfort of t. "But she's gone, and you're here. That can't be for noting. It can't be."

Raene didn't know what to say to him. Squeezing tight to Parson, hearing those words, breathing in the rugged sweat-soaked scent of him, Raene felt herself given. She reached a hand under his shirt, running her fingertip along the defined musculature of his torso. She liked being close to him despite how she knew it would complicate her already-messy life.

This conversation had gone nothing like she thought it would. And now Parson was saying things that made too much sense. It would have been easy to turn him away, but now that she understood, she couldn't. She had to give him a chance.

He'd put her in a terrible position.

She stepped back, forcing his hand out of her hair, enough that she could think clearly for a moment. ' can't. Hale—"

"Doesn't have a claim on you—not yet. If you want him, I'll walk away. I won't interfere. But if there' a part of you that wants something else, then tell me. Give me this chance. Let me deal with him."

There wasn't just a part of Raene that wanted something else, there was her entire totem. It had been three long days since she'd gone hunting, since she'd even had a piece of meat. Hale and Gemini were distracting, but there was still that pulsing need to kill, bubbling below the surface. That part of her wanted something else entirely.

"Hale's not going to like it," she finally said. Nothing was official yet, but they had an understanding. Hale wouldn't take kindly to this.

Parson pulled away and grasped each of her shoulders in his big hands, a stupid, happy grin on his face. "Does that mean—"

Raene nodded and started to laugh. She didn't know exactly what it meant, but she was at least going to try it out.

Parson's smile darkened a moment later. "Raene, I want to be clear. I'm not my brothers. I'm not gentle or kind or articulate. I'm a brute with an axe, and I stick my foot in my mouth every chance I get. I—"

"Why don't you let me decide what you are?" Raene put her hands to his chest and pushed. He may have talked her into getting to know him, but that didn't mean she had to let him talk his way right back out of it.

Parson's eyes gleamed with mischief and admiration before he outright laughed. "Whatever you want." And then his hands were on her, pulling her into him with fervor. This time, there was no tree to keep her locked in place, only his strong arms, but Raene didn't fight him. Her mouth gave in to his. She refused to struggle. With already one kiss ruined, she wouldn't let this one suffer the same fate.

So Raene held tight around his neck and dug her fingertips into his shirt, willing him to kiss her faster, longer, deeper—and unlike Hale, he didn't pull back. Parson dove into their kiss with a cavalier enthusiasm, and Raene couldn't help but to return his zeal. Her breath mingled with his until she couldn't tell one from the other. He tasted of sweat and work and wine, and Raene was altogether sure she'd like to kiss him forever.

Without a hint of struggle, Parson picked her up only

to lower her to the ground a moment later. He settled over her, his hips on hers and a hand clutched around the bare strip of skin at her waist. Raene ran her hands through his hair and didn't for a moment apologize for how dirty they were. She could taste his hunger—not for meat, but for her. Raene could have exploded under such energy.

Then a shrill whistle broke the silence of the Alderwood.

Parson pulled away, scanning the periphery for any sign of someone, but there was nothing. They were alone. "Da's calling," he grumbled. For a brief moment, Parson sank against her and kissed her desperately, as if he might not get the chance again. His hand dove into her hair surely a mess by now, before he peeled himself away and rubbed a hand over his stubbled chin. He grabbed her hand, pulling her off the ground and in the direction of camp.

Raene needed several seconds to catch her breath, to get her mind around what had just happened. Had it not been for the whistle, Raene was confident she would have lay entwined with him for hours. It was dumb, it was stupid, and they were going to get caught, but Raene nonetheless knew what she wanted.

"Wait, we're going back now? What are you going to tell him?" Raene was glad to be spared the job of telling Hale of their new arrangement, but she didn't want him to be hurt. Hale had been nothing but kind to her. The last thing she wanted was to have him thinking it wasn't enough.

"I'm not going to tell him anything. Not for a while. It'll only upset him." Each of his fingers slid between hers until their hands were interlaced.

"Parson, no. You have to tell him." Raene pulled on his hand to get him to stop, but he barely slowed. "I'll tell him if you won't—"

"No, you won't. I see the way he looks at you. If

there's a chance this isn't going to work between us, then he doesn't need to know. Not yet."

"Wait, what?" Raene dug her feet into the soil, refusing to take another step with him. "What do you mean? You're not sure? You came all the way out here and—"

It was then Parson stopped. He spun on her so fast, she nearly tumbled back. His emerald eyes shimmered with something like anger. "I'm sure. I'm *entirely* sure. But I'm difficult and moody, and I say all the wrong things. You might find that's not what you want. Maybe you like backrubs and soft beds and going slow, but that's not what I'm offering you. And until you've made your decision, I won't risk my brother getting hurt." Parson ran a hand through his chestnut waves before he said, "You're not the only one who has to make a choice here. You know he won't talk to me? For kissing you the first time…"

Raene withered under his intensity. Anger and protection and devotion all rolled into one impressive gaze that was set right into hers.

"He's not angry about that. We talked and—"

"And he came to the cut and told me to stay away from you. If he finds out about today, then I've lost a brother. Please don't make me do that until you're past the point of doubt." As his anger faded, Parson's features shadowed with pain.

Raene knew then that Parson was serious. He was willing to sacrifice his relationship with Hale for the opportunity to marry her. Raene wondered if anyone had ever risked so much for her.

When Raene could form no response, Parson stepped close enough to thread his fingers low into her hair as he whispered, "Trust me. I know my brother. If he gets word of this, it'll crush him. He won't want anything to do with you after that. And then if we—"

Raene shook her head. She got the idea. She hated it entirely.

"Look, you're doing what the agreement said. You're getting to know each of us and making a choice. That's all you need to worry about. It's my fault about Hale, so let me handle him." Parson tilted his head up and pressed his lips to her forehead. Raene savored the feel of him so close, his hand curled in her hair.

"That's the first thing you've said that has made any sense." Raene knew Parson was right. Kaide had set them up for failure with the specifics of his arrangement. She was responsible for choosing a Frane son, and no matter how this worked out, one of them would be hurt. She might as well wait until she knew which one it would be.

Satisfied this new development would stay between them, Parson led Raene back to camp only to find a celebration well under way. The central fire pit raged, and already most of the clan had gathered with food and drink. "What's going on?" Parson asked Cresta as she passed with a decanter of amberwine.

"Go and see for yourself," the woman replied with a grin. Parson groaned and continued on toward the central pit. He'd given up holding Raene's hand at the edge of camp, so she trotted behind him, intrigued to see what was worth celebrating.

They found Da and Lathan not far from the central pit, toasting their already-full goblets of wine. Parson approached them, but Raene didn't get the chance. Hale appeared at her side and stroked the smear of dirt on her cheek.

"Look at what a mess you are," he teased, his smile warm and bright. His tunic had gold embellishments embroidered along the edge of each sleeve and around the collar. His fingers were even more heavily ringed than usual. Hale was dressed up, she realized.

Raene smiled back to cover her shock. She'd forgotten all about her appearance, and the sight of him shot fear into her gut. Why was he so formally dressed?

Back in Hale's tent, she let him smooth a damp rag across her face, wiping away the muck one stroke at a time. "There, you look like yourself again."

There was that look in his eye that made her stomach churn with guilt. Hale was a good man, and she liked him—they liked each other. There was no reason to mess that up for Parson.

"There are fresh clothes on the table. I'll be outside." Hale leaned in and kissed her cheek before disappearing out the tent flap. Just another small kindness he offered her, never asking for anything in return and never trying to press or hurry her. Hale was content to take his time, to let her keep some measure of distance between them until she was ready.

Guilt churned up anew. She shouldn't have even considered Parson's offer.

Upon inspection, Raene found Hale had left her a matching set of clothes, embellished with the same gold design. He would be disappointed when she didn't wear it, but she wasn't Terra. Someday, Hale would understand she wasn't going to change her mind.

Raene moved to get dressed before she realized the horrible truth of it. She was wearing her last Pyro outfit, and it was covered in dirt. The knees of her black were nothing but big brown patches. She couldn't wear such clothes to a celebration.

Otherwise, she only had the scarlet gown with the beaded bodice—hardly appropriate for sitting around the central pit in her Alderwood clan.

Raene had no choice but to change into the Terra clothes. The outfit was delicately detailed, and far lovelier than her previous borrowed clothes, but still she disliked it.

Her hands and neck were the only bit of her body exposed under the moss-green tarp she now wore. The fabric felt heavy and suffocating, but at least it was clean. She would make sure to wash her Pyro clothes first thing in the morning.

Before leaving the tent, Raene rolled her sleeves to the elbow, granting herself that one small freedom.

She didn't want to do this, to see Parson and Hale together, to be the source of their rift. When she was with Hale, it was easy to find comfort in their relationship. When she was with Parson, she wanted his intensity. When they were together, she had no idea how she'd feel, who she'd be drawn toward. Raene was tempted to rip off her Terra clothes and flee into the woods.

But Raene couldn't run from this. She held her head high and stepped into the clearing. The evening light was already fading, and the central pit threw long amber shadows across the Bear Clan. The same trio of musicians strummed their instruments at the edge of the crowd while the rest of them talked and ate and mingled.

Raene didn't know where to start. There were so many people she still didn't know. And she didn't see Hale. A part of her wondered if Parson had pulled him aside, if he'd changed his mind and decided Hale deserved to know.

But Raene knew better.

Thankfully, Gemini rushed to her side, dark hair hanging loose over the shoulders of her own embroidered tunic. "Look at you, all Terra! And here, you forgot your shoes."

"What's going on?" Raene asked, clutching her forgotten shoes and refusing to acknowledge that she was really wearing Terra clothes out in public.

"Didn't you hear? By the Mother, it's exciting. Tasia's pregnant! They just told us today, and of course, you know Da—"

"Has to have a party for everything," Raene said with a laugh.

"Asla bought some wine. Want some?" Gemini tilted a small goblet toward her, and Raene eagerly accepted. It would never be sweet enough for her taste, but it was welcome all the same.

"Anything to eat?" Raene asked, looking about the clearing.

"Yeah, over there." Gemini pointed and took back her goblet, flipping her dark hair over her shoulder as she did. "I'll be over in a few. I want to find Asla."

Gemini trotted away as Raene went to make herself a plate, ignoring the watchful eyes of the Bear Clan. Everyone stared, though none were obvious about it, and it took all her effort to pretend she didn't notice.

It was all she could do to collect a rabbit leg and some fruits on her plate without eating it all at once. She was starving, and the aromas of roasting meat filled her nostrils. Her mouth watered with anticipation as she found an empty seat and set her full plate in her lap. She had just lifted the rabbit leg to her lips when she heard, "Raene?" Hale stood over her, looking down with concern. "You know that's not a good idea."

Raene dropped the rabbit and nodded. No meat. Hale's cure for a violent totem.

But it smelled *so* good. Not as good as a fresh kill, but it was still earthy, savory meat. And she wanted it.

Raene wanted nothing more than to sink her teeth into it and tear away the muscle fibers, chomping through them with her sharp canines, to fill her stomach with the heaviness of meat, rather than the light, sweet fruit she'd had these last few days.

The wafting smell of rabbit was getting to her.

Before she could argue, Hale collected her plate from her lap. He returned a minute later with a fresh plate of fruit and rolls. "Try that," he offered with a sweet smile as he sat beside her.

Raene filled her mouth with berries to keep from voicing her frustrations. She couldn't say Hale's method wasn't successful—after all, she'd kept to her human form for three full days—but it wasn't exactly comfortable. The longer she went without meat, the more the urge to transition filled her thoughts. And now, with thoughts of Parson swirling in the background, she was more conflicted than ever.

It wasn't Hale's fault, she reminded herself. He'd done nothing but be supportive in the only way he knew how. Raene couldn't ask more from him.

"Better?" Hale asked, his eyes dampened with worry.

"Yes, thank you." She smiled to reassure him.

But Hale could see through her better than that. "I have a violent totem, as well," he reminded her. "The longer you can go, the easier it gets. You'll be able to eat meat again someday. I promise, it won't be like this forever."

Raene nodded, hoping he was right.

"And you look amazing tonight." He kissed the shoulder of her Terra tunic top and smiled up at her with sparkling green eyes.

"So do you," she admitted. His dark hair was smoothed back in a way that made him look more handsome than usual. In another life, Hale might have made an excellent contribution to the wealthy circles of the realm. Here in the Alderwood, his easy confidence and charms were all but wasted. He could have been so much more if he had been born somewhere else.

"Did you know about Tasia?" Raene asked, eager to change the subject.

Hale shook his head. "They've known for a few weeks, I guess. It's good for them." His smile was contagious as he said, "It'll be good for all of us. We haven't had a new baby in years."

Raene had to admire his conviction to his clan, his devotion to giving them a good life. Even if the child wasn't his, Hale was proud to welcome it into his family.

"Why haven't there been any new babies?"

Hale shrugged like it was nothing unusual. "No one of age, really. Lathan was the first to get married. Parson's made no offers in the last few years. Even in the lesser families, there weren't any couples. Gemini and Asla will be next, I imagine." Hale inclined his head to the far side of the clearing where Gemini hung on Asla's shoulders and smiled up at him with those big wide eyes of hers. "And then us."

If Raene had had any food in her mouth, she surely would have choked on it. While she'd been admiring the romance between Gemini and Asla, Hale had been thinking of their future together, a future in which they had children. Raene knew it was bound to happen eventually, but even so, the sudden mention set her on edge.

Hale put a hand to his chest as he laughed at her shock. Raene, too, couldn't help but laugh, but she felt better when he said, "We have a responsibility to set the example for the clan. But don't worry. We have a few years yet."

Raene tilted her head so it rested on his shoulder, though he was so low the angle was a bit awkward. In the last few days, she'd come to enjoy her time with Hale. After she'd told him about the kiss with Parson—the first kiss—it was easier to be open with him, to listen to his stories of the sacred Mother, and ask him about the others in the clan. He kissed her in that slow, careful way, like she was something precious. If only her totem would quiet, Raene would have a happy life with him.

And now Parson wanted to change it. She'd been such a fool to listen.

So Raene sat with her head on Hale's shoulder and laughed with him over who would have children in the next years. Gemini's sister, a young woman named Nya, was well within age and married, though she hadn't had any children, yet. Hale mentioned she might not be able to, as sometimes the Mother doesn't share that gift with all women, but as they'd only been married a few years, no one was too worried.

Raene pushed back the urge, refusing to let it hold sway over her. She laughed and talked and filled her mouth with the flavors of amberwine. She focused on the soothing voice of her future husband and tried to embrace her new life.

THE DANCER

"ELBOW UP. Wrist in. Eyes forward." Blossom felt the snap of leather on her hip, stinging even through the luxurious Aero suit. If the cloak didn't restrict her motion so much, she'd have been tempted to wear it for its cushioning effect.

Blossom kept her face perfectly calm, refusing to acknowledge the pain. It was easier now to keep her mask in place, to keep her emotions buried inside where no one could use them against her. In that regard, Eton was the best of teachers.

Eager to minimize the lashes, Blossom tightened her position. And then, when she was sure her stance was as perfect as possible, she loosed the arrow.

It struck the third ring.

A vicious snap sounded a half-second before the pain in her hip. Blossom put a hand over the spot and breathed the pain out her nose, intent on remaining silent. She wouldn't give the old witch the satisfaction.

Eton was quick to step in. "That's enough for today."

Rissa Drim, Blossom's trainer, glared like a snake. She wasn't used to being undermined. Here, in the archery-competition ring, she was queen.

But even Rissa had to defer to the sheer authority of

Blossom's position.

Grumbling her dissatisfaction under her breatl Rissa made a lobster look friendly. But she was the best tr iner in Aerona, and therefore, the only one worthy 1 train Blossom.

Despite Blossom's previous experience with ι bow, and the fact that Parson—the best archer in the Bear Clan— taught her to shoot, she wasn't as good as Rissa expe ted.

She'd have a good bruise on her hip to prove it.

"I can keep going," Blossom argued. Her hip lready ached, but she was finally getting the hang of the coι pound bow. She got most arrows to hit the target, though o course nowhere near the center.

As she nocked the next arrow and raised the ow to shoulder height, she heard the dreaded words.

"You have a new assignment."

When she turned, she saw the black piercings h d been exchanged for his normally silver ones.

A sign of bad things to come.

Blossom lowered the bow to her hip. Eton's f e was calm as usual, a mask she now knew well. Later, wh n they were alone, maybe in the cave again, she would ε k him what he really thought. For now, she left him to his f çade.

She handed the compound bow to Rissa and ripped off the quiver. With a low nod of respect, she than ed her trainer and walked out the door with Eton.

Neither spoke until they were in the elevator.

"You don't have to let her do that, you know. Υ u're a Vice Syndicate. You don't have to go there at all " Eton enjoyed reminding her of the futility of her compou d bow training. She would never be allowed to ε ter a competition.

But what was she supposed to do? Sit in her rι om for days on end waiting for yet more unsavory tasks f om the Syndicate? Stare at the files of Aero politician she'd already learned? Think about the man in Pyrona who wanted nothing to do with her? Count the black coins in her mounting pile of prospective suitors? No thanks.

Today, she would have to do her job. "What does she want me to do?"

Handing over her panel, Eton showed her the official file as he gave her the overview. "You've been assigned an execution. A child abuser named Orten Lillah."

Blossom lifted her eyes to his to measure his words. Surely he wasn't serious. Blossom wasn't an executioner any more than she was a Hydra farmer. "Don't they have someone to handle things like this?"

"Yes, but the point is to test you, if you'll remember." Eton maintained his false calm, though Blossom knew this assignment burned him up inside. The more stoic his expression, the more severe the emotion he was hiding.

Blossom skimmed the document on her panel. Every word was true.

She was going to have to kill someone today.

Not through negligence let someone die, but actively kill them.

She didn't even know where to start.

"We're going to the tower to get the blade. Then, I'll take you to the cell where he's being held. You can do it there." Eton's eyes were heavy with regret as he spelled out her task.

"He's a child abuser?" Blossom asked, looking through the file. Disgust rumbled low in her gut. She hated to even contemplate such a thing. "Did he really do it? Or is this more rumor?"

"He really did it. There's a clip from the security cameras attached to the file. I'd recommend you don't watch it." The curl of Eton's lip was all she needed to see.

Then the elevator slowed to a stop. Blossom breathed easier for a moment when she realized they wouldn't have to see the top of the tower—or the Syndicate's office—today. She was at least granted that one small reprieve. Eton escorted her to the tenth level, still well within the Earth, where Aero's ceremonial items were housed. There, Blossom signed for a blade.

On the Robin, Blossom turned it over in her hands. It had a hilt that looked to be made of ice, and was just as cold to the touch. Sapphires, opals, and pearls were inlayed into the white metal. The blade was as long as her forearm and sadly not all that sharp. It would be hard to kill with a dull blade.

"Just get in and out. Don't think about it."

Blossom listened the quiet rattle of the Robin along the tracks. "Have you done it before?"

Eton's silence was answer enough.

Sabotaging Blossoms' totem wasn't the worst thing he'd ever done. Still, she couldn't help but to continue to hate him for it.

Then again, who better to help her kill someone than the worst person she knew? Well, second worst.

Her stomach churned by the time they arrived, though she didn't know if it was from the Robin or her upcoming task. Both made her want to retch. With blade in hand, Blossom followed Eton down a long corridor, through a secure door, and down another hall until they reached the holding cell of Orten Lillah.

Eton's handprint was all that was needed to enter.

Inside, Blossom found an Aero man tied to a vertical beam. His platinum hair curtained his face, slicked with grease and caked with what she hoped was mud. A white jacket—or rather its tattered remnants—hung from his shoulders, open to reveal a patchwork of bruises and crusted-over injuries.

At the sound of the opening door, he lifted his head. Both of his eyes were swollen, one of them sealed shut.

Blossom hated the sight of him, hated to think of what he'd already been through.

She looked back at Eton. He only nodded.

Blossom turned the dagger's hilt in her hand several times. "Are you Orten Lillah?"

"I am he," the man replied, his voice as craggy as a mountain.

"You are accused of child abuse and sentenced to be executed." Blossom tried to keep her voice as formal and level as possible. She wasn't killing him. Syndicate Mercer was killing him. She was as powerless as the dull ceremonial blade in her hand.

"I did not do it. He was my son. I could never..." Orten lowered his head once more and began to weep. His shoulders shook and mucus dripped to the floor. He had no shame. Only fear of death.

Blossom winced at the display. He looked so pathetic, so weak. She couldn't kill a man tied to a beam any more than she could kill an animal tied to a tree.

But neither could she risk incurring the Syndicate's wrath.

Orten would die. There was nothing Blossom could do to stop it.

"Blossom?" Eton coaxed from his usual haunt by the door.

Blossom pulled her panel from the pocket of her cloak and scrolled to find the video file. When she tapped it, a corridor appeared on the screen. The camera looked to have been installed somewhere in the ceiling. The floor was a grid of alabaster tiles, and standing on them, a man and a boy. Both were Aero with the ultra-white hair and sleek suit. From above, it was impossible to tell who they were.

It could have been anyone.

"I don't think you should watch it." Eton pushed off the wall and moved to intervene, but Blossom put up a hand to stop him.

She would determine if there was evidence against this man or not. Blossom wouldn't end another innocent life.

As the video played on, she watched the man and boy stop to talk to another Aero man. The two men engaged in conversation while the boy stood idle at their sides. Without sound, it was impossible to know what they discussed, but as soon as they parted ways, the Aero man leaned over and punched the boy square in the face.

Blossom stared in horror as blood splattered the alabaster tile.

The man took a moment to adjust his hair where it had come out of place before he planted his foot on the boy's back and thrust him to the floor. He kicked the child until he no longer moved.

Wider and wider, the crimson pool spread, such a glaring color in the all-white corridor. The boy' small frame lay across it, his arms tucked against his sides, as if he'd merely grown tired and fallen asleep.

Even from a camera planted in the ceiling, Blossom knew the boy was dead.

This wasn't child abuse. It was murder.

Despite Eton's warnings, despite how she knew it would be held against her, Blossom allowed a tear to slip down her cheek.

But as the boy's lifeless body lay prostrate across the lavish tile, Blossom could see no more of the man than the top of his too-blond hair. It could have been any Aero. Maybe trueborn Aeros could tell the difference –could interpret the skull patterns shaved into his head– but to Blossom, he was just one more.

Until he turned his eyes to the ceiling. Frantic, he searched for the camera he knew to be there, and when he found it, he smashed it with his fist. For a full second before the video went black, Blossom saw clearly the face of Orten Lillah.

She slipped the panel back into her pocket.

Then, she took a single step forward and extended the dull ceremonial blade. She had to strike hard to penetrate his flesh, but she managed to open his belly from hip to hip.

A move she'd executed dozens of times cleaning a kill for the clan.

This time, it was worse than expected, but Blossom couldn't muster an iota of regret. Her extra force had sliced the blade through the muscle layer covering the abdominal cavity. Orten Lillah's organs spilled from the opening, and fresh, hot blood spilled onto the already-soiled floor of his cell.

He stopped crying long enough to scream. His fallen intestines steamed in the Aerona chill. He wriggled his shackled hands, desperate to clutch at his slit belly.

No one helped him.

Blossom stepped forward and wiped the blade on the shoulder of his shirt, making sure it was clean before she headed out the door.

She didn't look back.

Eton's footsteps followed her to the Robin, though he never said a word. With the frigidity of a block of ice, Blossom returned the dagger to the keeper of ceremonial items.

Ten minutes later, Blossom and Eton stood in silence as the elevator descended toward the caves. Even once the doors were open and they plunged forward into the darkness, they maintained their practiced silence.

Only when the glow of the subterranean lake appeared did Blossom let herself breathe again. She could finally shed the mask. Tears flowed freely as she stripped away her opalescent cloak, followed quickly by her suit jacket, vest, and every other Aero item she could remove.

Eton didn't stop her from diving into the lake in

nothing but her silk underthings. The water was as warm and refreshing as before, but it couldn't wash the blood from the alabaster tile. It couldn't dispel the image of boy dying at the hand of his father.

By the time she surfaced, Blossom had digressed into full sobs. She couldn't breathe. Her lungs heaved, and her shoulders shook. It was all she could do to make it back to the ledge and pull herself out of the water.

Eton already sat with his pants rolled up and his calves submerged. No sooner was Blossom seated on the ledge than he put an arm across her shoulder and tugged her against his side. "I'm sorry. Hey, I'm sorry. There was nothing you could do. It's never easy to be the one to end a life."

Blossom pulled away. "You think I'm crying for Orten Lillah?" she spat through her tears. "He deserved worse." Had she not been bound by Aero protocol, Blossom could have devised far more judicious punishments for the man.

With a shudder, Blossom realized she was just like them. In her blood, she was Aero.

Eton pulled her to his side again, ignoring the angry tears that continued to fall. "I told you not to watch it. Why can't you listen? You're so stupid. Just listen for once. I'm trying to help you."

"Because you feel guilty." Blossom wiped at her ruined face as she threw her barb. Eton was responsible for her position in Aero. Anything he did to help her now was fueled by the guilt of what he'd already done.

"Then you should trust me more than anyone. I'm the only person in Aerona who has a reason to help you." Eton squeezed her extra hard, and she knew, as much as she hated what he'd done to her life, he was trying to amend it now.

"Do you think it took him long to die?" She despised that her voice was a pathetic croak after so much crying, but she wanted the answer.

"A few minutes at least. Is that what you wanted?"

"That's what he deserved. I can't—I don't know how someone could do that." Blossom tilted her head against Eton's shoulder and sighed as her sadness hardened into something else. She wanted to go on pretending people like Orten Lillah didn't exist. But she'd seen the proof. Every day she spent in Aerona stripped away the false beauty of the world and exposed the ugly truth beneath. Blossom didn't know if she wanted to see anything else.

"I don't know how you could do that to him. After the Hammonds—I didn't think you had it in you. Especially for the first—"

"He wasn't the first." When Eton's face dissolved into confusion, Blossom resigned herself to tell the story. "The second night in Pyrona, I ran away. I was picked up by an agent for a criminal ring. They cornered me in a warehouse. I killed one and wounded another before—" Blossom was surprised how quickly her voice caught. She swallowed and forced herself to finish. "Kaide killed the other two and carried me home."

"So you've killed *three* people?" Eton asked when fell silent.

"You sound impressed." Blossom allowed herself a small smile. It wasn't often she had the chance to prove him wrong.

"I am. Tremendously. It's a little scary, actually."

Blossom gazed across the subterranean lake. She was scary? It made sense when she thought about it. A calloused killer ending a life, intentionally leaving her victim to suffer a slow death.

"What I mean, is that you're learning. You're in control. You can lie when you need to and smile when you hate someone. You're just as ruthless as the Syndicate, but you know when to use it. You could really change things here if you got yourself in the right position."

Blossom shook her head. "I don't want to be like her."

"You're not. That's what I'm saying. You have all the skills but you're not a monster. My father was like that."

"And look how he ended up." Blossom felt the shame creep over her. It was an awful thing to say, but nonetheless true.

"You're right. It's easier to bend to their will and become what they want. My father paid that price but he wasn't half as good as you." Eton sighed when he recognized her resolve. "I know you don't want to trust me, but I really am here to help you. That's my job. Mercer made sure I would stand by your side and watch you implode. But she doesn't know what you can do. She's planning on your hatred, and every time you ignore me, it plays into her strategy."

Blossom pushed off the ledge and slipped back into the water. She didn't want to discuss her role in Mercer's hideous plans, whatever they were. She only wanted to be left alone. She wanted to rip the stupid metal bracelet off her wrist and fly away, back to Pyrona and Kaide. Mercer had already stolen weeks of her life away from him. How much more would she have to give up?

Lying on her back, Blossom let the water support her as she meandered across the surface of the lake. For a long while, she let the water carry her, until Eton's voice echoed across the cavern. Blossom sighed and swam back toward him. "Why don't you ever get in the water?" she asked when she was near enough.

"I am in the water." Eton pointed to his legs. "Cranes aren't really swimming birds."

Blossom propelled herself onto the ledge with such force, a considerable puddle formed. Eton jumped to his feet to keep from getting his pants wet. "You've been reinstated as Vice Syndicate."

"I didn't realize I ever lost it." If she wasn't a Vice Syndicate, why was she sent to kill Orten Lillah?

"You were restricted from formal events after the Hammonds. Since you performed the execution, you've been reinstated. You're expected to attend a Syndicate Council meeting in two days."

"Can't wait." Blossom wrung out her hair and started toward her clothes. She couldn't stay down here forever, as much as she wanted to.

"Blossom?"

"Yeah?" She made no attempt to hide her disinterest. She wasn't sure she wanted to hear anymore news today.

"He'll be there."

"Who?" And then the hammer of realization hit her square in the face. She was going to see Kaide in two days. Kaide was going to see her. And he would know she was Aero.

Sitting beside his bride, Hale felt the glow of joy in his chest, a constant warmth that radiated through him like hot cider on a winter morning. In her fine Terra tunic, with her luscious yellow hair and her charming features, she was everything he could have ever hoped for in a wife.

When Lathan and Tasia came around, Raene was quick to her feet, hugging them both with genuine excitement. Even Tasia hugged her tight, forgetting whatever issues they'd had before. Lathan squeezed Hale in a firm handshake and a rare, wide smile as Hale offered his congratulations. "I can't believe you kept it a secret this long," Hale said with a laugh.

"We wanted to be sure," Lathan answered in that cool way of his.

Hale didn't mind. He knew this was one of the best

days of Lathan's life, even if he wasn't one to show well.

And soon enough, it would be Hale's turn. H could feel the pieces of his life falling to place day by da . Pride swelled within him until he could scarcely keep th happy grin off his face.

As he hadn't dared in public before, Hale put a hand around Raene's waist. Maybe it was the wine mak ig him so bold, or maybe the glow of excitement surr unding Tasia's news. Either way, Raene didn't pull away. istead, she sank against his side and turned to offer him sweet smile.

While Hale still had lingering concerns ab ut her totem, there were so many other things he cherishe about her. The Mother's plan was working perfectly.

Tasia and Lathan moved on, a long night o being congratulated ahead of them, and Raene and Hale re laimed their seats by the fire. The day's warmth hung in the iir, the last remnant of spring before summer fully bloome . Hale let his hand move up and down her back, skimm ng her flesh through her tunic as they talked.

"Do you have any sisters?" Hale asked, reali ing he didn't know. He knew the Vice Syndicate was he uncle, but beyond that, she'd never mentioned anyone else.

Raene shook her head with a sad smile. " o, not unless you count Blossom."

"She hardly counts," Hale teased. In the few weeks Raene and Blossom had shared in Pyrona, they'd clearly become close. Raene's eyes glazed over with mer ory as she sat wordlessly beside him.

"I'm sorry. I shouldn't have asked." When Rae e only continued to stare, Hale ventured another question, hoping the response was less painful this time. "What abo it your parents? What do they do?"

Raene's eyes flashed up to his, their usual vibr it blue shaded. "I don't want to talk about them."

274

"All right." Hale felt it like a punch. He hadn't meant to upset her. "How was your day with Gemini?"

At last, Raene brightened. "It was good. We had a lot of fun. Asla came by toward the end…" Her voice trailed away, as if something else had happened, though Hale couldn't imagine what it would be. Asla was as decent and kind as any of them.

Parson interrupted his thoughts, his hand held out to Raene as he asked, "Up for a dance?"

Hale flew to his feet and squared his shoulders, though it was useless. Parson would always be larger in his human form. Still, Hale wouldn't back down.

Parson had been in the wrong, and he knew it. Hale had addressed it with him. They hadn't spoken since that day at the cut, and not by accident.

Just today Hale had detected his scent lingering on Raene, though he didn't know why. What Parson had been doing out at the Connor gardens, Hale could only guess. There was almost nothing Hale would put past his middle brother, but without anything concrete, Hale kept his suspicions to himself.

There was nothing more to say between them.

"Is that all right?" Parson continued, his hand still outstretched. He looked to Hale for approval but it was clear he was asking her.

Raene sat frozen, looking up between Hale and Parson.

Anger boiled in his chest. If he had his way, Parson would never go near her again. He'd already disrespected her once. Hale had no reason to trust his brother wouldn't do the same again—or worse. Hale swallowed and prepared to air out the fight that had been brewing for days. "No, it's not all right. You crossed a line—"

"It's just a dance," Parson argued. "You'll be here whole time." He nodded toward the open space between the central pit and the trio of musicians. Everyone in camp had a full view of the area.

Hale opened his mouth to answer, but Raene stood and said, "It's all right. I don't mind." She slipped her hand in Parson's and joined him. Hale watched her leave with an unfair amount of hurt. Raene was his bride, and he shouldn't be jealous of her dancing with anyone, but a part of him hoped she would reject him, hoped he would get to see Parson turned away.

But there she stood, beside Parson of all people. Other couples danced around them, but Hale couldn't keep his eyes off his deceitful brother and beautiful bride.

To Hale's relief, Raene and Parson didn't actually do that much dancing—she didn't know any of the steps. Hale watched like a hawk, just waiting for his brother to cross the line yet again, but instead, Parson took the time to show her the moves, failing to touch her even once.

"You like her, don't you?" Gemini appeared and jabbed his rib with her elbow. She waggled her brow with mischief. The clan gossip had new meat to sink her teeth into.

"What?" Hale glowered his impatience at her. He didn't need a distraction. He needed to watch Raene and make sure Parson maintained a respectful distance.

After the last betrayal, there would always be a part of him that wondered.

"You haven't fussed over anyone like this since Blossom. She was your sister. I get it. But Raene isn't. So you must *like* her." Gemini grinned ear-to-ear like she'd puzzled out some great mystery.

"And what of it?" He didn't relish being so transparent. He would have liked to have some measure of discretion, to be someone who had enough control of themselves to keep something hidden. But even Hale had to admit that his heart swelled at the sight of her.

Hale's eyes never left Raene as she repeated the

stomps Parson demonstrated. She was actually pretty good, learning quickly for someone who'd never tried them before.

"I think it's sweet. The ice-cold Hale Frane finally warming up. Who would've thought?" Realizing she'd worn out the last of his patience, Gemini offered him one last beaming smile before she trotted back to Asla. Her arms flew around his neck as he leaned in for a passionate kiss, not caring a bit that the whole clan could see.

It was a little disturbing to watch them so entangled. Terras should have more modesty than that. The Alder Mother had no interest in flaunting such things.

He had half a mind to lend them his copy of *The Mother's Eternal Love*, but Hale knew he might as well thump them on the head with it for all they'd learn from it. When it came time for him and Raene to be so close, they would do it in the privacy of their tent, as the Mother instructed.

Hale gave up his frustrated musings when Raene split from Parson and took her seat beside him. Her cheeks were flushed with motion and music, and her sapphire eyes shone bright. He loved to see her that way.

"You were great," he told her, his hand slipping around her waist as if he'd done it a thousand times.

"Thank you," she said with a smile as she flushed again. "It was actually really hard. Would you show me one?"

Hale shook his head, despising to let her down even in this small way. "I'm not much of a dancer. Never was very good at it."

"You can't be worse than me," Raene teased, but she soon realized he was serious. Hale hated to see her excitement doused, but even Raene couldn't combat twenty-three years without musical inclination.

"Did you dance in Pyrona?" Hale listed his head

toward her in wait of her answer. He could see that she would have been right at home at fancy parties and formal events. She carried herself with all the elegance of class, her motions as graceful as her feline totem.

Raene nodded, regaining some of her previous vigor. "Kaide would never let me go, but I saw all the transmission feeds and heard about it from some of the other women. I'd always help them pick out their gowns. I picked out Blossom's gown for the festiv—"

And then, like a blown out candle, Raene fell silent and stared at the ground, her eyes racing as he knew her thoughts were.

Only Hale didn't know why. "Raene?"

She shot him a weak, half-hearted smile. "Never mind."

Clearly she'd been spending too much time with Parson. After only a few minutes of learning to dance at his side, Raene had fully stuck her foot in her mouth. What was she thinking? Telling Hale of the Spring Ceremony? Of transmissions? Of Blossom that night?

He would want to know more; he would ask questions, and Raene didn't have the answers to those questions. It had been a grave mistake to mention any of it.

She sat frozen beside her future husband, in the midst of a celebration, thinking only of how she could satisfy his inquiries without compromising herself.

Her anxiety was mildly appeased when Hale didn't press her for more. Someday, she knew he would, and she'd have to come up with something. She hated to lie to him, to look in those dark, sage eyes and tell him a falsity. It was horribly unfair to him.

So Raene would avoid the topic of Blossom and

Pyrona as long as she could—forever, if it was up to her.

"Decided to join us after all?" Da asked as he sailed past. In a flash, he grabbed Raene's hand and pulled her toward the other dancing couples.

Raene let out a nervous laugh and tried to remember the steps Parson had taught her. Then she realized this was a different dance, with different steps entirely.

In Pyrona, Kaide had paid for her to take dance lessons from an elderly woman with a bamboo switch. Each time Raene missed a step, she felt the horrific sting at her ankle. Years later, she was one of the best dancers in Pyrona, though Kaide never let her go to any official functions.

Here in the Alderwood, she knew none of the steps. There was no old woman waiting to smack her when she missed. Instead, she did her best and found herself laughing alongside Da. In the whirlwind of dancing, she didn't have to answer any questions. She didn't have to hide anything. She didn't have to make any decisions. She needed only to enjoy the music and holler with laughter each time she horribly missed a step—which was often.

Then, as he seemed to enjoy doing, Parson had to ruin it.

"Mind if I step in?" he asked. Da looked all too happy to hand her over.

"Couldn't wait for the next song?" Raene asked as she watched her feet and tried to keep her movements in time to the music.

Parson picked it up mid-step, an obvious natural. "You looked like you were struggling a bit." Only when he grinned at her did she realize he was teasing her.

"Oh hush. I'm doing great," she joked back. To prove it, she stomped her feet harder for the next few steps, eager to show him she had learned at least a bit of the dance, though, of course, she wasn't nearly as good as him.

"If only you weren't wearing that tunic." Parson's

features shone with hidden laughter, but Raene felt the spear of his words. It took her several seconds to shake them away.

And then, without warning, Parson grabbed her hand and spun her out to his side. In the corners of her vision, Raene saw other couples similarly swirling, but her feet couldn't find the steps fast enough. As if her head wasn't lost enough, Parson tugged her back toward him, so hard she landed against his chest. His closeness rattled her twice as much as the impact.

In her ear, she heard, "Meet me at the stream. Tonight." His emerald eyes blazed with intensity before he spun her out again.

Raene's heart pounded as hard as her steps, thumping out her muddled thoughts until a second later, Parson let her go and resumed the steps of the dance.

It was all she could do to remember what she'd learned, and, thankfully, the song ended not long after. She retreated back to Hale, but her mind raced with thoughts of Parson's whispered words.

What would they do at the stream? Hunt? Kiss? Something else entirely?

For the rest of the night, Raene could think of nothing else. The heat from the fire mixed uncomfortably with the day's warmth and made her brow dot with sweat— at least, that's what she told herself.

An hour later, when Hale stepped away to get more wine, Raene slipped into the dark forest, keeping to the shadows and moving quickly in case he decided to follow. She hated to be so deceitful, but this needed to be handled once and for all.

Minutes later, Raene found Parson at the stream, sitting atop the grey stone, the chorus of rushing water behind him. The gold embroidery of his tunic glittered in the stolen beams of moonlight, but Raene forced her eyes away.

Parson stood as she neared, but she put her hand up to prevent him coming any closer. She didn't want him to stop her.

"I came here to tell you I changed my mind." Raene ground her teeth together, forcing herself to follow through with her decision.

Parson stopped cold, his mouth a stern line. "About what?"

"I don't want to lie to him. I don't want to hurt him. It's not fair." Raene steeled herself for his meteoric anger.

And Parson didn't disappoint. His fists clenched tight at his sides as he yelled, "What about this is supposed to be *fair*? The part where a stranger took my sister? Is it the part where he used you to ruin my relationship with my brother? Or the part where he sent you away? Oh I know, it's the part where you slowly give up everything you know and pretend to be *Terra*." He made it sound like a disease. His scanned her figure, now clad in the moss-green tunic and honey-brown pants, and by the curl of his lip, Raene knew he detested the sight of her.

"I wouldn't be wearing this if you didn't keep ruining my clothes!" Raene shouted, lifting an accusatory finger right in his face.

"Quit trying to be something you're not," Parson said as he stepped closer, keeping his smoldering eyes even with hers. "Quit trying to fight it. You're a *tiger*. So be a damn tiger!"

Raene couldn't believe what she was hearing. How *dare* he blame her for this. Each time, Parson had been the one to instigate, to spur her into transitioning. It was him who cost Raene her Pyro clothes and left her with only one set intact. He enjoyed tormenting her.

The idea of it infuriated her. He was trying to push her over the edge again. He wanted her to lose control, and as much as she hated to give him the satisfaction, the tiger's blood churned too strong in her veins. Before she could get her hand up to smack him across his smug, handsome face, Raene collapsed to all fours. Her hands were gone, replaced by russet paws. Her ears perked to the groaning bear before her, and within a heartbeat, she lunged.

Tiger claws skidded across the thick, fur-covered back of her adversary. He let out a loud growl of pain but it wasn't enough. Tiger-Raene had barely scratched the bear, her feline body sailing over him as he dodged her attack.

By the time she landed and turned, the bear was charging. On instinct, she jumped from his path, but she didn't move in time. The bear's considerable weight barreled into her outstretched legs and knocked her to the ground.

Her tiger claws scraping across the bear's chest made him retreat. He stepped back and growled at her again, a guttural rattle that shook her deep in her tiger bones, but she wouldn't let him scare her.

She refused to lose this fight.

Tiger-Raene lunged again, her sharpened claws outstretched toward the bears thick hide, but an impossibly strong paw clubbed her from the air. Pain erupted across her ribs—at the swipe of the paw, and again when she struck the ground. She hissed out her agony but hadn't even managed to get back to her feet when the bear approached yet again.

This time, he grabbed her neck between his massive, conical, predatory teeth and squeezed. She was powerless, pinned, trapped, terrified. Pain flooded her vision until tiger-Raene could only go still and wait for the final crunch.

In the quiet of those last seconds, Raene's tiger faded. She slipped back into her human form, only to realize her head and shoulders remained inside the mouth of a bear.

Raene screamed, a horrified, haunting shriek.

It was all she could do to scurry away, crawling, clambering across the leaf litter to get as far from the bear as possible.

Only when her back was pressed to an alder root did Parson reemerge. He shook away his bear fur like water and waited for it to cascade to the ground before he moved.

"Are you done?" he asked, his tone weary and tinged with anger.

Raene worked to calm her breath and nodded, knowing it was a lie. Her hands were caked in dirt, and under her fingernails, she found blood—Parson's blood.

"Get away from me," she cried, but he was already close, sitting on his haunches beside her. He put a hand beneath her chin and pushed her face away, revealing the side of her neck.

Where he'd held her between his teeth, she remembered.

"Did I hurt you?" he asked, his eyes scanning.

Raene pushed his hand away. "No, I'm fine."

Parson let out a heavy sigh. "Raene—"

"You could have killed me." She didn't mention the fact that she thought he would have. She thought he *was* killing her. Her heart still raced with that fear.

"I would never. Raene—" He thrust his fingers into her hair, low on the back of her head as had become his habit, forcing her to look at him. "I would *never*."

In that moment, Raene believed him. His conviction, his certainty, his determination. She couldn't doubt him, not when he looked at her that way.

Then, she saw his chest, the shining smear of fresh blood soaking through the slits in his moss-green tunic top. "I'm sorry I scratched you. I didn't mean—"

"Yes, you did." He dropped his hand and added, "It's fine. I earned it."

Raene pushed away from the tree, away from Parson,

and forced her feet back toward camp. She'd done the unthinkable—she transitioned and harmed someone, and she hadn't even gotten the satisfaction of hunting or killing. Her tiger blood churned anew, more eager than ever, yet she'd already erred far more than Hale would ever allow. She had no choice but to tuck her tail between her legs and go back before she did anything worse.

"Where are you going?" Parson called after her.

"I can't do this," she told him again, and this time, she was sure.

"Why did you come out here?"

Raene turned and avoided his eyes as she answered, "To tell you that. I can't hunt with you, or lie to Hale, or any of it."

"I won't ask you to. But—" Parson raked a hand through his hair. "I'm leaving tomorrow. To go to the capital on a trade. You could come—"

Raene shook her head against the possibility.

But Parson continued. "We can get to know each other without anyone else around. Just you and me. We'll be gone for three days. If you're not sure by then, we end it. Hale won't see anything. You won't have to lie to him."

She was still shaking her head when he closed the distance between them. His hands squeezed her waist, and his lips pressed gently against hers.

Raene closed her eyes against him, refusing to give in again. She liked Parson the way she liked getting her totem tattoo. It hurt, but in a good way, and in the end, it would leave a mark. Raene had to pull away before she got lost in him. "You said I could walk away. I'm walking away."

But Parson wouldn't relent. He gripped her shoulders and kissed her again. Breathless, he told her, "I lied. I won't give up."

Raene stepped back, forcing distance between them. "I'm sorry, Parson. My answer is no." It killed her to say it, but someone had to put an end to this.

Parson's mouth fell open as if she'd slapped him across the face. He was hurt and shocked and confused, but that wasn't her problem anymore. Raene had to walk away.

Trudging back to camp, Raene refused to cry. The tears welled up but she wouldn't let them fall. She wouldn't let her face be a mess when she returned to the celebration, when she told Hale where she'd gone.

Never again would she play this game. She was going to marry Hale, and that was the end of it.

ENVOY

RAENE LET HALE pull her back to his tent the second she returned. Ignoring the ongoing celebration, he pushed her into a chair and lit a dozen candles.

Raene didn't breathe a word of protest.

And to his credit, Hale didn't ask her a single question.

He merely brought his chair closer and moved her hair over her shoulder. His features were analytical as he examined the flesh on either side of her neck.

Between his cool, careful fingers and his kind eyes, Raene cracked open. Against her will, a tear slid down her cheek.

"Are you in pain?" he asked quietly.

Raene shook her head and wiped the betraying tear away. She didn't want to tell him, but she didn't want to lie to him, either. Raene had nothing to say for herself, and she wouldn't condemn Parson. Hale deserved better from both of them.

Hale's ringed fingers moved up and down her neck, searching, determining the extent of her injuries.

But Raene knew he would find nothing more than bruises. The aroma of blood was absent from the tent.

Raene reached up nervously and gripped his wrist. Hale's eyes softened, and he stroked her cheek with his thumb. "I'll take care of this. He'll never hurt you again."

Raene could only crease her brow and wonder how he guessed, if he'd known all along.

A sad smile crept across his cheeks. "Even if I didn't know my brother's scent, the bite is clearly a bear. I know Lathan wouldn't dream of hurting you…"

"Parson didn't hurt me," Raene admitted, dropping her gaze in a futile attempt at hiding her shame. "I transitioned. He only did it so I wouldn't hurt him."

But Hale would have none of it. "That isn't how things work here. He could easily kill anyone in the clan. He could have killed you. There are repercussions."

Raene couldn't stand it. "No, there aren't. It was my fault. I should be punished for attacking him." In truth, they were both at fault, but she wouldn't let Parson take the fall alone. Raene would accept responsibility for the sake of the brothers.

In this case, Raene could make a solid attempt at undoing the damage she'd caused.

Hale pursed his lips when he saw she was serious. If he blamed Parson, he would have to blame her, too.

So Hale relented, choosing to comfort her instead. He released her cheeks only to encircle his arms around her entirely. He'd been worried about her. He breathed his relief against her shoulder, and Raene knew it was behind them.

Raene envied that about him—that he could so easily give up his anger. She wondered if someday she'd be less angry about Kaide, or even Blossom. Perhaps once her totem no longer had her life in its grip.

Satisfied she was neither seriously hurt nor in danger from Parson, Hale set up her pallet, and they continued their usual evening of wine and conversation. There was a new edge to him—he sat closer, he touched her arm or her waist more often—and Raene did her best to assure him, and herself, that she was in the right place.

Only two weeks into her month, Raene had already made a decision. It was both easier and far more challenging than she would have ever thought possible. Nonetheless, Raene knew her choice was Hale. There would be no more going back and forth from brother to brother, from hot to cold, from hunting to control. Her mind was made.

Well after dark, Hale left to let her change. Raene hated that she had to choose between Hale and her Pyro night clothes. If she wore the heavy Terra version, he would stay. If she was comfortable in her Pyro clothes, he would sleep at Da's. So Raene conceded.

When they settled in to sleep, Hale maintained his usual respectful distance. He stroked her back in that soothing, calming way only he could manage, and when he lay on the pallet beside her, Raene was less than surprised his hand crept close to find hers.

That simple moment was enough to crush her with guilt. Hale cared about her, deeply she suspected, and she'd been less than reciprocal. He was kind and gentle and devoted. Why had she even considered betraying him?

Hale released her hand for a half-second, and when he found it again, he slid a warm wooden ring onto her smallest finger. "In Terra, rings are symbolic of belief or family or wealth. This one, with thirteen leaves, is the ring of the Terra branch, made of the Mother's wood."

Raene only lay on her pallet in stunned silence.

"This one," he said as he hovered the second ring on the next finger, "is for the Frane clan. You can't see it now, but it's made of iron and has bears carved into the surface."

Hale slid the third ring onto her next finger. "And this is my ring. Terra men are given a ring at transformation. They wear it until they find someone worth giving it to."

Raene swallowed hard to keep from bursting. She

squeezed his hand in the dark and slid close enough to kiss him. Lying on his back, Hale was an easy target. She settled over him and kissed him hard. He put his free hand on her shoulder as if to push her away. Raene smiled against his mouth when he didn't.

"Thank you, Hale," she whispered against his lips. Raene let her hair fall against his chest as she took charge of their first real kiss, the first kiss that wasn't slow or chaste. His hand moved from her shoulder to her waist, pulling her closer.

Raene liked feeling that he wanted her, but she knew his limits as well.

Before she pushed him too far, Raene pulled away. She sweetly kissed his cheek before returning to her pallet.

"Raene?" he whispered, squeezing her hand.

"Yes?"

Hale remained silent so long, she wondered if he'd fallen asleep. Only the drumming in his chest gave him away. After a while, he finally said, "I'm *so* glad you're here."

Raene smiled into her blanket, but otherwise, she didn't answer. She knew he didn't expect her to. She wouldn't say it until she felt it with as much conviction as he did.

Instead, Raene held tight to his hand as he drifted off to sleep. She wished she could sleep as easily as he did, but the blankets were too hot, the Terra nightgown too suffocating. Raene spent the night thinking of her future husband, of the brother she turned down, of the uncle who put her in such a horrible position.

Raene wondered if Kaide had ever expected her to connect with both Frane sons—though in entirely different ways.

Parson appealed to the totem in her; there was no denying that feral connection. But Hale appealed to her human side, the part of her that was refined, elegant, controlled. Raene wanted that life with him, and she let the thought soothe her through the night.

By the time she woke, Hale was already gone. Raene was surprisingly disappointed, but after a few hours of sleep, she was eager to get up and moving.

She didn't mind wearing her soiled Pyro clothes. They were only going to get dirty again. Raene tied off the end of her braid and set out toward Gemini's garden. Hopefully, it would help her silence the incessant urge to hunt, the one that seemed to only grow louder with each passing day. And maybe it would quiet the thoughts of how she'd rejected Parson.

Maybe it would help her concentrate on what a good thing she had going with Hale.

But Da approached her before she'd gone more than a dozen steps. His sly fox eyes glowed as he greeted her. "Good morning, my daughter. I hope I'm not imposing, but I need you today."

Behind him, Raene caught sight of Parson, his hair pulled back just off his neck. She struggled to keep her focus on Da. "I was going to help Gemini—"

Da nodded and cast a disappointed glance at her. "I'm sorry, it will have to wait. I'm sending an envoy to Seraphine City, and you'll need to ride along."

Then, Raene knew what was happening. Parson had asked her to go with him, and she refused, so he recruited Da to force her hand.

"No, I'm not going." Raene stood her ground and crossed her arms, resisting the urge to stomp her foot for effect. She didn't want to look childish. She wanted to look in control, but she wouldn't be coerced into this.

"My daughter—"

"I'm not your daughter!" Raene screamed, the sudden shout escaping her lips before she could hold it back. But with rage fueling her words, she narrowed her eyes and continued. "Blossom was your daughter. Not me. It's disrespectful to even suggest that I replaced her. I'm *not* your daughter." When she'd finally finished, her breaths were ragged from screaming at him.

Da didn't so much as bat an eye at her outburst, as if he expected it all along. He nodded and said, "Blossom is my daughter, but you are, too. I can have many sons and many daughters, and that makes me a greater man, not a lesser one." Da reached forward and placed a comforting hand on her arm. "You are my daughter, Raene. I'm only doing what's best for you."

Raene looked at her feet, mortified that she'd spoken to him in such a manner, in front of whole the clan, no less.

"And I need you to escort the envoy to the capital. I can spare no one else, and your experience there may be needed. I'm counting on you, Raene." His eyes fell to the sides of her neck, and Raene wondered how badly the bruises looked in the morning light.

She pressed her lips into a thin line and nodded. Raene was smart enough to know when she had lost. Da waited as she packed her bag with all the clothes she had. Hale never showed to argue, but Raene knew it wouldn't matter. There was no arguing with Da.

Nonetheless, she wished she could have told Hale she was leaving. After their closeness last night, she wanted him to know that her departure—even if only temporary—hadn't been her choice.

An hour later, Raene found herself in the saddle of a tall, cinnamon-colored mare, riding alongside a cart of cut alder wood, so large and heavy it required a team of six horses to pull it through the shadow-filled forest. Instead of traveling with a half-dozen men, there was only Parson, riding on the cart with the reins in his hands.

"You didn't have to come." It was the first thing either

of them had said since camp. Raene didn't acknowledge him with even a sideways glance. She was too angry. Instead, she concentrated on the rhythmic turning of the cart wheels as they moved along some long-forgotten road. Raene wondered if Parson even knew where they were going.

"Where's everyone else?" Raene finally asked. When she told Da she'd go along, she expected the others to distract her from Parson. She expected Asla and Latian and a few others to keep her company. Instead, it was only Raene and the brother she turned down.

"I don't need anyone else." A moment later he added, "I'm sure you won't believe me, but I didn't ask him to do that."

She ran her fingers over the three rings she now wore. "You're right. I don't believe you."

At least he was smart enough to keep his mouth shut after that. With no real idea of how to get to the capital, Raene couldn't ride at the front of the horse team, but she also didn't want to ride behind the cart, with nothing to see but that back of Parson's head, the squareness of his shoulders...

So Raene was stuck trotting her horse beside the cart, trying her best to pretend Parson didn't exist.

Sometime around mid-day, Parson pulled the cart to a stop and leapt to the ground. From the way he stretched and took each step carefully, he was as sore as she was. Raene peeled herself from the saddle and tried to look like she was in less pain than she actually felt.

"You've got an hour," Parson said, both his hands low on his back as he arched.

"An hour for what?"

"To get something to eat. I figured you'd rather hunt, but if not, you can have some of the venison jerk Tasia made." He reached into the cart and pulled out a leather bag.

Raene's fingers itched and twitched. "What about you?"

"I can survive without for a while. Besides, someone has to keep you from eating the horses." He bit a piece of jerky between his teeth as he grinned. Ripping it off, he added, "Go on. One hour. Don't be late."

Raene had no idea how she was supposed to tell time in totem form, but that was a problem for another day. She couldn't pass up the chance to hunt, to eat, to *kill*.

After last night's disappointment, the urge saturated her more than ever. Without a moment's hesitation, she transitioned and raced between the trees, eager to fill her belly before she had to be back.

Raene had never experienced such freedom. Her nose brought her to one innocent after another, each putting up a meager fight or chase before she crushed and consumed them.

Then she heard a sound, something low and shrill. A whistle, she realized. Someone was calling her. Tiger-Raene ran in the direction of the sound, and before long, she had the scent of horses in her nose. After that, she carved a path straight for them. Her tiger feet carried her swiftly through the trees, and within minutes, she caught sight of the hulking beasts whose scent filled her nostrils.

And then, as it almost pained her to do, Raene transitioned back into her human form. She pushed up from the earth and brushed her hands together. Only then did she notice Parson atop the cart, his bow and arrow drawn, aimed at her chest.

"I'm fine," she groaned, annoyed that he would even think of shooting her. And in truth, she felt better than fine. With her belly full and her hunger satiated, Raene could think clearly for the first time in days.

"It was just a precaution. You never know out here,"

he said as he lowered his bow against his thigh. "Get enough?"

"For now." Raene climbed back in her saddle and collected the reins. "Are you going to go out?"

Parson signaled the horse team into motion before he answered. "I don't need it yet. Tonight, yes. But I'll be fine for a few more hours."

"Did you go out last night? After I—" *Left you alone in the woods. Attacked you. Rejected you.*

Parson nodded, his eyes straight ahead. "I go out every night." It was then Raene believed him. He hadn't asked Da to have her join him on this envoy. After what she'd said to him last night, this trip was as painful for him as it was for her, maybe more so.

Raene had refused him, refused to betray Hale that way, and retreated to the safety of their tent. Hale had investigated the serious bruises on her neck, but they were minor enough. Parson's on the other hand…

"Who cleaned your wounds?" Raene had scratched him and left without even a thought to his injuries.

"I did." His tone was clipped and flat. He didn't want to talk about it.

Because she'd hurt him. Raene knew it with undeniable certainty. "Do you want me to go back?" She wouldn't subject him to three days of her company when he so obviously hated it.

Parson shook his head. His eyes were dark and his mouth was stern and set as he said, "No. I don't."

Raene didn't know what to say after that. Everything with Parson was always so confusing. He was kissing her or yelling at her or ignoring her, and there was never an in between. Hale was even and measured, where Parson was erratic and unpredictable. Hale was cool where Parson was hot. Hale was articulate where Parson spewed whatever came to mind. There couldn't have been two more different brothers if they'd been molded from clay.

The afternoon hours came and went with nothing but the sounds of trotting horses and rolling cart wheels. Neither Raene nor Parson had anything to say to the other, and for a while, the space between them was enough.

Raene was left to mull over her thoughts of Hale. She liked him, and to her surprise, she missed him. This would have been a welcome adventure had she shared it with someone she enjoyed. But unlike Parson, Hale wouldn't condone her hunting, he wouldn't stop to make sure she let off some steam.

He'd be so disappointed in her. Only hours away from camp and Raene had already killed a handful of innocents. She dreaded the look in his eye when she told him—if she told him.

At nightfall, Parson steered the horses off the road and headed into the east woods a few minutes longer before he stopped altogether. One by one, he pulled the horses from the rig and led them to the nearby stream.

Raene wondered if it was the same stream they'd met at so many times before.

When all seven horses were watered, tied to a tree, and grazing on what food he'd brought for them, Parson collected a large green bag and started up the nearest tree. The sight of him climbing the massive tree brought back memories of Blossom. The last time Raene saw her, she was sitting high atop an alder branch. Raene had fostered such hope for Blossom and Kaide. The sudden thought renewed the ache in Raene's chest.

Once up high enough, Parson impaled a long bolt. From it, he attached the bag and let it unroll. All at once Raene realized what he was installing—a tent. It wasn't as nice or as large as Hale's, but it would do for the night.

And then she realized there was only one.

"Ready?" Parson centered his bow and quiver across

his chest and waited.

"I'm not going." It had been a mistake to go before. Hale expected more from her, and she was determined not to fail him again. Raene straightened and lifted her chin, anticipating his response.

But he only shrugged and set his bow and quiver against the side of the tent. "All right."

She blinked when he didn't argue. "You don't have to stay. You can go."

Parson sat and shook his head. "Hale's already going to be furious about this. If he finds out I left you alone to go hunt—"

"But you already let me go out to hunt," she protested. "I was alone for an hour in the woods. You weren't worried about it then."

"No I wasn't."

Raene scoffed, trying not to hit him. "You don't make any sense, you know that?"

Parson's tense mouth transformed into a playful smirk. "Finally figured it out, did you?" He shook his head as he laughed. "I tried to tell you. I'm not like them. I let you go out because you needed it. But I can manage without for a few days."

"And I *can't* manage?" Raene didn't know whether to feel glad or insulted or downright furious.

Parson shot to his feet and met her eyes with his. "No, you were already struggling. They can't see it. They don't even know what it looks like. But I do. I spent a long time doing it your way, and it doesn't work. But if you want to keep struggling, then I won't stop you."

"I wasn't struggling," she argued, no longer sure who she was trying to convince.

Parson ran a hand through his hair. "Then why do you cry? After every hunt, I say two words and you burst into tears every time. Because you're always struggling to hold it in, and once it's gone, everything else breaks loose." His eyes shimmered with confidence. He knew he was right, deep in his bones.

"I didn't cry today." Raene lifted her chin in a pathetic sort of pride. Such a great accomplishment: a whole day without crying!

"No, you didn't. I guess that means you don't need to hunt." Parson seemed almost disappointed. He sank back to the ground in the tent opening and slouched, his eyes on his hands as they fidgeted in his lap.

"You don't need to watch me. I'm sure I can sit in a tent by myself for a few hours." Raene collapsed beside him to prove it.

"You'll tell Hale."

Raene gaped at the insult. "What? No I won't—"

"It's fine. You should."

"So what's your problem, exactly? That I tell him things? Or that I don't?"

Parson's jaw tensed at her questions. He was getting agitated, but she didn't care anymore. He'd flip-flopped on her so many times she didn't even know where to begin.

"Both!" Parson jumped to his feet and paced between the trees. "You lie to him when it suits you. He still doesn't know about the elk, does he?" he shouted before he went off again. "But when it's something that could ruin, entirely *ruin,* our relationship, then that. You can tell him *that.*" Both his hands were on his head, raking through his hair with frantic motions as Raene stared wide-eyed. "You can tell me you want to try this out when you feel like it, and five minutes later he's kissing your cheek, and you've changed your mind. You can hunt when you think you can get away with it, but if you think Hale will find out, you'll suffer for days."

Back and forth he paced, his hands continuing their tracks through his hair as he launched into yet another spew of words at her. "And you can't tell him anything that has to do with Pyrona. You won't even tell him you hate it here. He doesn't know *anything* about you."

And then, Raene had had enough. Like a spring twig, she snapped and rushed to her feet. Parson stopped his pacing long enough for Raene to arrive before him, her eyes boring into his as she said, "And what? You think *you* know me? Is that it? You know me and he doesn't? You don't know the first thing about me!" Her voice was a shrill yell, so unladylike and crass, but consumed with anger, she was beyond caring.

Parson didn't even bat an eye at her uncharacteristic display. Instead, he lowered his voice and speared her through. "I know you can't sleep because you're thinking about a hunt. I know you feel better as a tiger than you ever do as a human. And I know the idea of giving it up terrifies you." Parson's rant slowed to a stop as he realized the effect of his words.

Silent tears raced down her cheeks. She could only stare at him, stunned in silence as her guilt and shame and fear tracked down her face.

Parson covered both cheeks with his hands. Raene slammed her eyes shut, willing him to leave her alone. She squeezed her hands into tight fists and felt the edges of Hale's rings digging into her skin.

"After that, I don't know. You won't talk to anyone. You keep it all locked up. And this is what happens if you don't—" Raene never found out what he was going to say because his lips slammed into hers. Renewed tears fell and struck his fingertips where he clutched her cheeks, but Raene could only think about his kiss.

Then Parson pulled away. His eyes were closed as he pressed his forehead to hers. "Just promise you'll give me a few days. Talk to me. Hunt. Just be who you are, and when we get back, we don't have to ever talk about it again. We never tell Hale or Da or any of them. Just give me these few days," he pleaded.

And like she knew she shouldn't, Raene nodded. She would likely always hate this betrayal to Hale, but Raene was powerless against Parson's intensity.

Three days of freedom hunting in the Alderwood. It was the best she was going to get. Not even Raene could resist such a gift.

When they returned, things would go back to the way they should be. She would tell Hale of all that happened, she would be honest. She could only hope he would forgive her.

Cool air rushed in as Parson hurried away. She watched him collect his bow and quiver, strapping them across his shoulders, before he returned to clutch her hand. He tugged her away from their tent, away from the horses, as he said, "Come on. Let's hunt."

Seconds later, tiger claws struck the ground, and she ran.

Parson collapsed on the padded floor of the tiny tent he'd packed. Had he known Raene was coming, he would have opted for something larger, but now that she lay within reach, he couldn't regret it. After hours of hunting, of filling their bellies with gifts from the forest, Parson brought her back to their temporary camp. And he'd never seen her so relaxed.

In black shorts and a slender top she'd brought from Pyrona, she sat cross-legged beside him, taming her hair back into its usual golden braid. Minutes ago, she'd been a fierce tiger huntress. Now, a pristine Pyro princess sat before him. It was almost unfathomable.

"You have blood on your lip," she said with an easy

smile as she reached up to wipe it away with her thumb. Then, her brows narrowed as she wiped harder. "It s dried on," she said with a pout.

The remains of the fallow deer they shared, no doubt. "Does it bother you?"

Raene smiled again and shook her head.

"Good, because you have a pretty good splatter on your cheek, too." Parson ran his finger across the space between her mouth and ear. Then, without thinking, he tipped forward and licked it off. Parson would never tire of the taste of blood, and with Raene so still and at ease in his hands, he couldn't make himself stop.

When he'd removed every last trace of blood, Parson pulled away to find her eyes shut, her head tilted to give him access, and her skin flushed. She melted into his hand cupped against her cheek.

Her sapphire-blue eyes cracked open and bored into him, as piercing as an arrow.

"I—That was—" Parson failed to form an explanation for his strange behavior.

"Did you just lick me?" she asked in that pointed way of hers.

Parson swallowed hard.

Just when he was sure she would be angry, Raene straightened and tipped forward. He almost pulled back until he remembered the blood on his lip. Sure enough, she pressed her mouth against the very spot, sucking for only a moment before she clamped her teeth down and bit—hard enough to make him bleed.

"Did you just bite me?" Parson pressed a hand to his lip, not needing to see his crimson fingertips to know she'd gotten him pretty good.

But Raene only grinned from ear-to-ear and nodded.

Parson was both horrified and impressed, and in the confusion, he could only stare at her with a gaping open mouth, an idiot before her.

"What?" she asked when he continued to stare, though her smile didn't falter.

Parson shook his head to organize his thoughts. "You just—you're different than you were when you first got here. I thought you were *polite*." He didn't mean it to sound bad, but somehow it did.

But to Parson's relief, Raene threw her head back and roared with laughter. One of the slim, black straps of her shirt slipped off her shoulder, but she was too busy laughing to fix it. "I *am* polite," she purred.

"So biting is polite in Pyrona?" Parson shot her a look.

"I'm sure it is in some circles, but no, not really. But we're not in Pyrona. We're in the middle of a giant forest. Being polite isn't really a life skill here." It was her turn to shoot him a look.

"Good." Parson wiped away the last of the blood from his lip. "It was a little uncomfortable."

"My being polite makes you uncomfortable?"

Parson shrugged. He wasn't trying to offend her, but he knew he was walking that fine line. "Sometimes it does. When you're not sincere, it's pretty awkward. I mean, *Thank you for your candor, Master Frane?* Really?"

Raene giggled and pressed her face into her hands laughing. "I did say that, didn't I?"

He nodded and told her, "When you give up trying to be nice, it's better. What you said to Da this morning, about Blossom being his daughter, that was the first real thing you've said since you got here."

Raene straightened and leveled an even gaze at him. "I shouldn't have said that. He's my clan lead—"

"That. That right there. You meant every word. You *screamed* it. And now you're taking it back. He's not even here, and you're being *polite* about it."

Raene bristled. "And what would you suggest? Go

around saying every damn thought that comes i to my head. That works *so* well for you."

Parson couldn't help but laugh as he stripped off his tunic top and settled his back on the narrow pallet. I is eyes fell to the expanse of moss-green fabric above him and at the very top, a slender opening to the canopies, barely illuminated with some passing ray of moonlight. ' You're right. I'm terrible at hiding anything. I'm an aw il liar. You're too good at it. Neither one works."

"Speak for yourself," she countered. "I'm doing great." Even then, Parson could hear the falsity in he voice. The held-together, confident version of herself was only a veneer of the real one. Parson had been hiding who ie was so for so long, it was easy to see it in her.

"Says the girl who sneaks out to kill inn cents." Parson meant it to tease her, but soon realized he'd ruck a nerve.

Raene's smile fell away, and her eyes darken d with the truth of it. "I don't know how I'm supposed t stop." She pulled her bare legs to her chest—a sight Parson enjoyed immensely—and her eyes went distant as s e said, "It's always there. Even when I'm talking to som one or working. When I'm riding a horse, I'm trying to thin about anything but eating the horse. It's so loud in my lead, I don't know how to make it quiet."

"Does hunting help?" He didn't even need to sk. He knew it. He could see it. Only after sating her tote n on a fresh kill did she open up, speaking freely and can idly as she never allowed herself.

Raene's voice was a whisper as she said, "It's t ie only thing that does."

That, more than anything else, told him he l been right. She had it, she felt it, too. This insatiable urge wasn't his alone. They had it together, and for once in is life, someone understood his struggle. For seven yea ., he'd been alone, and now he *finally* found someone who understood.

And it was a Pyro princess of all people.

"What were you going to do in Pyrona?" Parson propped his head up on his elbow, only able to see her outline with the sharpness of his bear eyes.

"Get married, I guess." Even in the dark, he could see how her features returned to the façade.

"We agreed we were going to talk. You can tell me. I'm sure you had your eye on someone." Parson tried to make it sound like a joke, but he secretly hated the idea of hearing of her prior interests, all too sure he could never measure up.

Raene let out a long, low sigh before she answered. "I thought I was going to be traded to a family with political connections. I'd looked at a few, but they were all for Kaide, so he could have access to a resource or a contact." And then, once she'd started, Raene kept going. "I thought I was going to go to all these parties and events. I took dance classes and fine dining courses and speech training. All kinds of things so I'd make a good wife. And now it's all a waste."

"You're whole life you've been planning to get married?" Parson barely concealed a cringe. "No wonder we're so disappointing."

Raene chuckled. "You're not, it's just different. Did you know the day I left, I thought Kaide was going to tell me who I was going to marry? I brought this gorgeous beaded gown to wear when I met my new husband."

"What does it look like?"

Raene released her legs and lay beside him, turning on her side to face him. Her fingers traced over her Pyro night clothes as she described the deep neckline and the beaded bodice that hugged her ribs, the scarlet skirt and matching train.

"You brought that dress to the Alderwood?" Parson couldn't hide his laughter. "It's the least Terra outfit imaginable."

"And that's why it's still in my bag where it will remain until I die." Raene smacked him in the shoulder to silence him, but it only made him laugh harder.

"You should wear it. Every man in the clan would pluck his eyes from his head and give them to the Mother. I'm sure they'd die if they saw you in this." He motioned toward her revealed legs, her shirt that exposed her collarbones and shoulders. No such garment would ever be allowed in Terra.

Raene shook with laughter. "It's better than that green sack you all wear. For men, it's better," she said as she ran a hand over his bare chest. Parson's breath caught in his throat. "But for women, they really wear that thing all the time? It's so heavy and awful."

"Welcome to Terra. Modesty for the Mother." Parson couldn't keep the snide tone from his voice.

"That's sacrilege," she reminded him.

"Only if you believe in a magical tree." Parson couldn't stand it any longer. He extended his arm and tugged at her shoulders, urging her to come closer. She arrived at his side an instant later, her head cradled in the crook of his arm. "I don't believe in magical trees. I believe in what I can see and touch. Trees? Yes. Magical trees? No."

Raene shook with giggles against him. "You make her sound so silly." In the midnight dark, Raene's finger traced lines across his chest, an absent move that nonetheless left him struggling to concentrate on his words.

When he could take no more, Parson pressed his hand over hers to still her motions, though it didn't help clear his mind as much as he hoped.

"It *is* silly," he admitted. "I literally spend my entire

day cutting up trees. I'm not sure how to reconcile that with some sort of motherly figure in the forest." He didn't mention how the death of his own mother contributed to his disinterest in the Alder Mother. If his real mother was gone, he certainly wasn't going to replace her with a magical one.

"I thought Terras were supposed to be believers. I mean, everyone's a believer, but I thought Terras were serious about it."

"Oh, they are." Parson chuckled as he reminisced about the ridiculous habits of his branch. "All the good little Terra boys and girls saying their prayers before breakfast. Covering themselves so no one might see their *wrists*."

Raene wriggled her hand free from his and shook it in front of his face. "Oh no, my wrists aren't covered!" she said between hearty laughs. "Don't look, Parson! Don't look at my wrists!"

Parson clutched his chest with laughter. He held no small amount of animosity toward the believers in his clan, at their strange and useless habits, but laughing about them with Raene filled him with something else entirely.

And then, as suddenly as a boulder falling from the sky, she stopped laughing. Raene went quiet in the span of a single heartbeat.

"What's wrong?" When she shook her head in protest, Parson pressed her. "Raene—"

"This is nice."

"What is?"

"This. Talking about home and Terra and…" Her voice fell away like it was stolen.

Parson pushed away enough to look at her, desperate to see her eyes. He didn't understand, but in those deep blue eyes, he found the answer. "And now you don't know what to do because it's nice with him, too."

In seconds, the mood in the tent shifted from light to dark. A single thought of Hale crushed any enjoyment he might have hoped to have the rest of the night.

Raene wiped at her cheeks and nodded. It made him smile and killed him all at once. Only minutes after a hunt, she was crying, as he knew she would be. But she was thinking of Hale, and the idea of it made Parson hate himself.

It was far too late, he knew. He'd let her go at first glance, and she'd grown close to Hale. She was wearing his rings and sleeping in his tent. Hale who was everything Parson wasn't. He would never share her need for the hunt as Parson did, but there was so much goodness and honor in his youngest brother. Parson was outmatched in every way.

"I hate it. I hate this." She said it like a secret. Parson momentarily thought she meant him, until she continued, "I don't know what to do. You make me feel one way, and he makes me feel another. And I like both of them. And every time I try to make up my mind, you both do something to make me question everything. No matter what I do, I'm betraying someone. I hate being in the middle of this."

"Hey, it's not your fault. The situation is complicated, but that's not your fault. I'm sure I hold the majority of the blame here." He said it as a joke to hide how true it was. Parson had played no small part in muddling her decision.

"Did you ever have anyone else?" Raene's tear soaked voice was little more than a whisper.

Parson slid beside her once more. He couldn't look at her eyes as he told this story. "Her name was Dars of the Renemy Clan, the Lemur Clan of the Alderwood. For a while, our clans were camped within walking distance. I found her one night, out on a hunt, and we started sneaking out to see each other."

Raene's breath fell against his chest as she asked, "And then you moved away?"

Parson knew he should have agreed. He should have left it at that, but he was so close to getting it off his chest, he couldn't stop now. "She was only twenty, with no real prospects for marriage. It didn't seem like an issue to—"

Raene surprised him and settled a hand on his stomach, moving it back and forth in a comforting motion. She slid her palm up his chest, skirting the edges of the bandages placed over the deep scratches she had given him the night before. Her voice was low as she asked, "Did you love her?"

Parson shook his head. "No. I told Da I did, but I didn't. It didn't seem right to leave her carrying my child. I begged and begged Da to let me marry her, to let her live with us, but he refused. He made an offer out of respect, but it was so low he had to know they wouldn't accept it. He never even said why."

"Did he know?" Raene asked, her fingertips skating across the tattoo inked on his neck.

"He's the only person who ever knew. We moved away a few weeks later and haven't been back since. I still don't know what ever became of them."

"You have a child you've never met?" Raene's breath was warm on his chest, comforting though her question gutted him entirely. Then, she reached up and kissed his cheek. "I'm sorry. Da should have let you marry her. If you wanted it, then he shouldn't have stopped you."

Parson was tempted to write it off as more of her over-polite nonsense, but he sensed nothing but authenticity.

He squeezed her tighter. It felt so unbelievably good to share this with her, knowing she wouldn't tell anyone, one more secret to add to their long list. And she didn't hate him for abandoning Darsa or his child—a son or daughter, he didn't even know that much. But the weight, the horrible heaviness had eased somewhat, and Parson couldn't help but squeeze her in his arms.

Raene nestled into his shoulder. "My mother died when I was little. Not quite a year after I was born. I don't remember her. My father was too full of wine to bother much with me." Raene said the words over his chest like a prayer, like something sacred she'd held inside for too long. Parson lay motionless and listened, refusing to give her reason to stop. "I spent most of my time with Caide's parents, but they were so involved with politics, we didn't see much of them. The staff raised us, mostly."

"I'm sure you miss them." Parson felt like an utter fool. He'd been so torn up over Blossom's departure, he hadn't even considered that Raene had given up far more. Parson had lost one person, while Raene had lost all of hers. And to put him to shame, she'd done it with her head held high, with a grace he couldn't manage if he had ten lifetimes to figure it out. She was eighteen, so young, and yet she was so much more than he would ever be.

For a long while, he held her tight, refusing to let go and refusing to go farther. His chest ached with a low rumbling storm he couldn't quiet. Parson wanted this. Wanted *her*. But getting her was a betrayal to his brother.

Even this stolen moment in the depths of the Alderwood would kill Hale. No matter what he did, someone would be hurt. Parson could give up the only person he'd grown to care about in his adult life, and his brother could be happy with his new, lovely bride. Or he could let this thing grow—whatever this was with Raene— and hope his brother understood, hope Hale had the good heart to forgive him, though even in the depth of his thoughts, Parson knew better.

Either way, one of them was going to lose. One of them was going to get shattered.

So Parson squeezed her tight while he could, feeling the pressure and warmth of her frame against his side. Her breaths fell across his chest, and before he knew it, they were slow and rhythmic, her shoulders rising and falling under his arm. Parson kissed her crown and closed his eyes, waiting for sleep to claim him, too.

STUPID

"**GET ENOUGH SLEEP?**" Parson asked her as he hitched a horse to the cart.

Raene followed behind, bringing the next horse in the line with her. "I'm fine. Did you?" She didn't want to tell him she'd slept more soundly in the tiny tent in the middle of the Alderwood than she had since even before her transformation. In her own Pyro clothes, Parson's warmth warded off the night chill. A day of hunting had quieted her tiger totem to a tolerable level.

A night of sleep had done more damage than all the sleepless ones, as if her body realized what it had been missing. It was almost painful to get up this morning. Raene moved with all the zeal of a sloth.

"You look tired," Parson offered.

"Well your hair is a mess," she retorted, tying off the reins and marching back for the next horse.

Parson caught her by the arm. "I mean, you can sit in the cart if you're not up to ride today. There's no shame in taking a break when you need it."

Raene pulled her arm from his grasp, all too aware he could have used his strength to make her stay. Still, she nodded. The allure of a few extra hours of sleep was too good to pass up.

They finished cleaning up their temporary camp and headed out. This time, Raene's cinnamon mare followed behind the cart.

Raene sat on the cart bench beside Parson. The alder trees towered overhead as always, looming, watching, pressing downward with their ancient wisdom, darkening their path with shadow. Only a few beams of sunlight managed through their dense, summer canopies.

She soon realized the cart bench was much too short to lay across. Parson took up a good third of it, not that it mattered. The bumping motion and thundering hooves prevented her from anything remotely resembling sleep.

Without provocation, Parson reached out a hand and clutched the back of her head. He pulled her against his shoulder and kissed her hair. Raene didn't have the energy to put up even a bit of fight.

His fingers found their usual spot, stroking the back of her head, weaving through her hair. "Lay down for a while. You look miserable."

"You're so full of compliments today," Raene replied, her tone dripping in sarcasm. But the movement of Parson's hand and the burning tiredness behind her eyes made Raene collapse and rest her head on his thigh. It wasn't exactly comfortable—her legs were squashed tight on the too-short bench—but it wasn't enough to make her sit back up.

Parson kept one hand on the reins, easily controlling he six-horse team with little more than the motion of his wrist. The other hand held Raene's shoulder, occasionally stroking down a stray lock of hair. Raene couldn't sleep, but she found herself deep in the trenches of relaxation.

"Was your mother Aero?" Parson's voice broke her from her trance.

"What?" Raene rubbed her eyes, still sleepy and confused.

"Sorry, I didn't mean to wake you." Parson bowed his

311

head low enough to kiss her brow. When she assured him she hadn't been asleep, he finally said, "Your hair isn't dark like a Pyro. Aeros have white hair, but yours is sort of gold."

"My father's father was Aero," she replied with a yawn. "My mother was a well-respected Pyro woman from the elite Tiger Clan of Mount Huntari."

"So you have your mother's eyes and your father's hair." He smiled down at her with such adoration Raene knew he held her appearance in the highest regard.

Raene could only smile back at him. "My father looks Pyro. I guess it skips a generation."

"How come you never talk about them?"

Raene shrugged and rubbed a hand across her face, wishing away her lingering fatigue. "There's not much to say. My mother's parents took me in as soon as she died. I didn't meet my father until I was nine, and only because I snuck out to find him. Once Kaide came of age, he became my guardian."

Parson chewed on that a while before he asked, "Why?"

"To protect me. My father isn't exactly stable, and my grandparents are highly-connected in Aero politics. I think he didn't want them to have access to me."

"Do you think he just wanted to use you for his own gain?"

Raene shook her head. "No. My grandparents disowned us both for it. He knew they would, and he was still willing to risk it to keep me safe. By then, he was Vice Syndicate. He forced them to sell the manor so I could have a safe place to live." Thinking about the manor made her miss its wide open windows and spinning staircases. She'd never see it again.

"So if he's so protective, why send you away? Is there some advantage?"

"There are a lot of clans with more political sway than yours. No offense," she added. "I think he really wanted Blossom, and, I don't know, maybe he thought I would like it here. Maybe he thought it was safer." It had taken Raene a long time to think logically about Kaide's motivations regarding her trade, but Norsa had known all along. He hadn't done it to spite her.

Parson stroked her hair. When Raene looked up at him, silhouetted against the alder blossom canopy, she saw his jaw set firm. After a moment, he asked, "You think she's really happy with him?"

Raene froze solid. It felt so good to talk about home, to relate her old life to the new, but this particular secret was one she couldn't share. "I thought we weren't supposed to talk about her." Raene had to fight to keep her voice neutral, passive, innocent.

Parson wouldn't be persuaded. "I want to know. You said he loved her. Did he make her happy?"

Raene skirted the question. "I know he did his best."

Parson's nostrils flared. "I can smell you lying. What aren't you telling me?"

At that, Raene pushed up to sitting, forcing his hand from her hair. "I don't want to talk about it. Please stop," she begged.

Parson yanked on the reins and pulled the cart to a dead stop in the middle of the road.

That wasn't what she meant, but Raene knew to bail when she had the chance. She launched herself to the ground and rounded toward the back where her horse was tied. She'd barely started untying the knot when Parson appeared on the other side of her cinnamon mare.

Raene kept her eyes on the reins, working to get them free form the cart, but she could feel the anger rolling off him as he glared at her. Heat crept into her cheeks with each passing second under his gaze.

Parson moved around the horse and arrived behind her. With her hands on the reins, Raene was trapped between the horse and the cart.

"I can't tell you," she said without turning, hoping to tide his anger before it got out of control. "I don't know the whole story. I wasn't there, and by the time anyone told me anything, Kaide sent me away."

"Told you what?" Parson was so close behind her, his breath blew strands of hair across her neck.

"I *can't* tell you," she repeated.

"Why?" His hand fell to her hip. In the midst of his anger, Parson still offered her that kind touch. Raene squeezed her eyes shut.

Lower than before, she told him the truth. "Because you'll hate me. And maybe kill me." She didn't know if she could fight Parson's strong totem. In every altercation, he'd bested her easily. The violet bruises on her neck were obvious proof. If he was angry enough to transition, he could kill her in an instant. Not even Raene's tiger could protect her.

"You think I would hurt you?"

"For Blossom? Yes." Raene breathed easier when the infuriating knot finally came free. He put a second hand on her waist.

Raene stilled instantly.

"I told you before. I would *never*." Even behind her, where she couldn't see his eyes or the firmness that was surely set into his jaw, Raene had no doubt Parson meant every word.

But he didn't know what Raene had to say.

Parson wrapped both his arms around her waist and pressed his chest to her back, his chin resting on her shoulder. "I'm not angry, and I won't transition, but you promised to be honest with me, and I deserve to know the truth."

In answer, Raene tied the mare's reins back to the cart, though she made the knot far less tight this time. This would be the end for her and Parson—whatever they had together would be over. Raene reminded herself that this was for the best. She was going to marry Hale. This was simply what it took to get Parson to change his mind about her.

Raene stepped away from him, holding up a hand when he started to follow. When she was at least twenty paces from where he stood by the cart, Raene turned and faced him, trying to pretend this wouldn't hurt.

She clutched her arms over her stomach and called out. "Sure you want to know?"

Parson nodded.

"You won't tell anyone in the clan? I have your word?"

"You always had it."

And then, Raene could delay no more. She was a safe distance away. If she was lucky, she could transition and flee, her speed her only advantage if it came to a fight. He wanted to know. He was forcing her to tell him.

It was Parson's fault she had to do this.

Raene forced her hands to her sides, forced her shoulders back and her chin high. She wouldn't look scared.

"The last day I spent with her was the day before her birthday. She was wearing nothing but Kaide's shirt when she called and asked me to walk the markets with her. Kaide said she was on the verge of a big decision, and I shouldn't try to change her mind." Raene struggled to keep her voice even and strong enough to cover the distance.

Parson stood idle with a crease in his brow.

"We talked about totems. About my tiger and Kaide's monster," she continued. "When she was ready, I brought her back to the manor. She climbed an alder tree and started reading. That's the last time I saw her."

Parson let a nostalgic smile tug at his mouth, but Raene wouldn't relent. She'd started, and now she was going to finish.

"Kaide refused to see me after that. For over a week. When he finally called for me, half his staff was gone. The rest were scared. People I've known my whole life—" Raene's voice cracked at the thought of Norsa that day. She cleared her throat and met Parson's eyes as she said, "Blossom ran away. She went to the capital, but she never underwent transformation. She obviously didn't come home. No one knows where she is."

Raene's pulse pounded in her ears when Parson locked his hands into fists and lunged toward her. "You knew? You knew she wasn't there? This whole time you *knew*?" He rushed her with all the fury of his bear totem.

His anger shattered her. She could have run, but she didn't. Parson was a volcanic eruption and Raene was little more than a tree on his slopes. Motionless, she could only wait for his fire.

This was what she deserved. She'd ruined everything. She'd sent Blossom away. She'd robbed Kaide of his bride. She'd betrayed Hale. And now, she'd ruined her chances with Parson. Raene sank to her knees and covered her face with her hands, waiting for his impact. She didn't want to keep secrets any more.

Parson stopped only a step away, still in his human form. "Why didn't you tell me?"

Shameful sobs clogged her throat.

"Why didn't you tell me?" he repeated.

"Because it's my fault she's gone." Raene's voice dissolved with each word until she could hardly make a sound.

"You're so stupid, Raene. By the Mother, you're the stupidest person I know." Parson sank to the ground beside her and grabbed her shoulders, clasping her against his chest in a single motion. Raene was beyond confused, but as Parson wasn't angry and hadn't killed her, she didn't argue. Like a child, she held onto his chest and cried out her sorrows.

Her weeks of worry and guilt and grief came out in one massive wave of sobs.

Parson only stroked her back and thrust his hand into the hair at the back of her head. When Raene's tears wouldn't slow, he gripped her shoulders and shook her. "Just stop. Come on. You can't honestly think you made Blossom run."

Raene stared at him with red-rimmed eyes that burned from so much crying. Had she been capable of anything more than a pathetic squeak, she would have told him he was wrong.

But Parson continued without interruption. "You could have tied her to a horse and she still wouldn't have left if she didn't want to. You didn't know her very well if you think she'd listen to anyone, even you. Do you know how hard it was to get her to do *anything*?" To Raene's eternal shock, Parson looked at her with an amused smile.

Then he sobered, his smile stolen by darker thoughts. "She wouldn't have given up transformation. It was the only thing she ever really wanted. Something else happened to her. She might be in danger or worse, but there was nothing you could have done to make her run. Maybe your uncle—"

Raene shook her head. Kaide couldn't and wouldn't do anything to jeopardize Blossom's safety.

"Then it was something else." As if the matter was settled, Parson pulled her against his chest again, clutching across her back to hold her tight. Raene melted against him, finally unburdened of her secrets. Her arms encircled his waist, and for a long while, they remained kneeling in the soil. Neither moved. When at last Raene found her voice again, she said, "I'm sorry I didn't tell you. I though you'd be angry—"

"Oh I am. I'm so furious I can't see straigl ." His hands balled into fists at the small of her back. \fter a calming breath, he explained, "But it's not your faul and if what you say about your uncle is true, then someth ig else is going on. I hate that I can't do anything for er. I'll always hate it, but I don't hate you."

Raene could scarcely believe this was the sai e man she'd first met in Da's tent. Since when was Parso Frane reasonable?

When he pulled away, his eyes were dark, bu Raene only glimpsed them before he leaned in to kiss her.

Raene reeled from the insanity of it. He was st pposed to be so angry he never wanted to see her aga n. But instead, he was holding her, kissing her, forgiving her. It was so unfathomable, it bordered on the fantastic.

Raene held tight to his waist, her eyes slammed closed, as Parson's kiss blocked out everything else—h r tear-stained face and aching chest, the morning inlight streaming through the flower-filled branches, th fallen lock of chestnut hair that draped across his eye, the scrape of his beard on her cheek.

When Parson pulled away and let out a long breath, Raene felt robbed. She was far from ready to face t ie day. Fear and relief and disbelief swirled in chaos inside er.

Parson somehow knew. "Come on. I think w could both use a good hunt." He kissed her forehead be ore he helped her up and tugged her toward the trees.

"But the cart—" she protested.

"I'm not going to watch you struggle with it ll day. It's too hot already. Just be quick. We're already la e." No sooner had he released her than he transitioned. [t was impossibly quick. He fell to the ground as a bear in less than a second, faster than she'd ever seen.

Raene watched him go. She'd never seen him in totem before, not with her human eyes. His chestnut fur was a dead match to his stubbled cheeks and the hair so often tied up off his neck. He was huge, with a stocky build and square head and jaw. And, considering his bulk, he was astonishingly fast.

Parson's bear form was out of sight in seconds. Raene gave in to her own transition and followed him, catching up a minute later.

Her tiger's hunger was less intense today, but there was still that edge that needed softening. Between the two of them, the elk buck they found was laughably out-maneuvered. They each ate their fill, tearing off the largest chunks of meat and leaving the rest for the scavengers.

And then, together, they raced back to the cart. Tiger-Raene was by far the quickest, but bear-Parson arrived only a minute later. Raene had already transitioned back to her human form and mounted her horse. Parson regained his human form, shaking off the flurry of chestnut fur, before climbing onto the cart bench.

They were off and moving without a word, though the tension between them was gone. Raene felt the weights of her old life letting go, like she'd been tied and finally the ropes were cut. It felt strange to be so unburdened after holding it in so long. Parson looked refreshed and at ease, like he was years younger.

Raene trotted her horse beside the cart, far more comfortable in the saddle since Parson increased their pace dramatically. She couldn't help but wonder if her breakdown would make them too late for today's trade.

"You're getting better," Parson offered after a while, nearly shouting over the roar of horse hooves. His wicked smile suggested he was entirely pleased.

"It was easier today," she admitted. She hadn't given

over to the tiger as much; she hadn't felt as los to its power. Her transition had been intentional, rather an the result of anger or frustration. And after, she felt calm

"Imagine what it would be like if you went eve day."

Raene listed her head to the side and rolled her eyes at him. "You know that can't happen. No matter what, Da will never allow it."

"Who says Da has to know?"

"Not everyone is as skilled a liar as you." Raene flipped her braid over her shoulder as she landed her barb.

But Parson only laughed. "No, you're far bet r than most. And besides, I don't lie. I just don't tell them. here's a difference. I'm really a terrible liar." They on went another hour before the forest began to thin, th trees becoming narrower and more spread out. Smaller t es and shrubs took up the available space between alder trunks. Raene knew they weren't far from the edge of the Alderwood.

Just as they reached the last and smallest of t e trees where the expansive meadow began, Parson stopped

"What are we doing?" Raene asked, her voice ushed. She felt so exposed here without the trees ahead; it vas the first time she'd seen such a sight since she ente ed the Alderwood over two weeks ago.

So much had changed for her since then.

"We're meeting a Pyro trader. They should e here already." Parson's eyes searched the horizon, looki g even brighter green with the sunlight reflecting off the me dow.

In the distance, the high rises of Seraphi e City towered over the wall that protected the capital. ")o you ever go into the city?"

"Not usually. Once a year, maybe. Why? Do y u need something?"

Raene nodded with a mischievous smile. "A tat)o."

"We'll make another trip," Parson said vithout

hesitation, "when we're not on a trade for the clan. What are you going to get? Where are you going to put it? Doesn't it hurt?" Parson's spew of excited questions only made her laugh. She hadn't thought about specific tattoos with any sort of seriousness—she thought she'd have her whole life in Pyrona to figure it out—but she was determined to maintain her Pyro roots. Permanent ink in her skin would be a good start.

Her tiger ears perked to the low rumble of horse hooves. In unison, Raene and Parson looked to where a cart appeared from the east. Raene held some small hope it might be someone she knew, but of course it wasn't. No elites or wealthy politicians would meet in the Alderwood to trade. Instead, just a pair, a man and a woman, both in Pyro garb that matched her own.

The sight of them brought her back to Pyrona, to the manor, to the shadows of the volcanoes. She thought of Norsa's endless cooking and her father's empty eyes. She thought of Kaide, and how he'd done this to her—sent her across the realm to live in the Alderwood—and yet she found she didn't hate it as much as she once did. There was a life for her here, in one way or another.

Still saddled high on her horse, Raene was pulled from her daydreams when Parson said, "Stay alert. Something's not right." Then, like nothing was wrong, he climbed down from the cart and rounded toward the back. Raene occupied herself with her braid, intentionally looking bored despite how her tiger eyes never left Parson. She marveled as he single-handedly lifted a length of alder wood and carried it to the Pyro cart.

The Pyros observed in silence, both standing to the side as he collected beam after beam of rough-cut wood, each as long as three grown men, and set them into their cart. Parson's brow gleamed with sweat, but otherwise, he didn't seem to notice the impossible weight he carried.

When he collected the last beam, Raene tied off her messy braid and slipped to the ground. She pulled a canteen of water out from under the cart seat, holding it for when he returned. Instead, he lingered at the Pyro cart, discussing whatever business they had. The man and woman each handed him a black bag, one large and one small, before he made his way back to her.

Parson set the bags on the seat of the now-empty cart and accepted the canteen with a grateful smile. Raene watched him drink, watched his throat bob with each gulping swallow. When he was finished, he dragged a hand across his face and said, "Thank you."

Raene glanced toward the Pyro couple as they finished securing their load and started their horses to the east. She wouldn't believe Parson could have moved it all by himself if she hadn't watched him do it. "Was something wrong?" Raene was hardly an expert in Terra trades, but nothing had seemed out of place to her.

Parson kept his eyes on the Pyros as they left. "That's not who I was expecting. They said there was some sort of issue in the clan. They were well-enough informed that we completed the trade, but I'd rather not have surprises like that."

Raene saw shades of Kaide's protective nature in him. Parson was responsible for the trade, a role in which he was clearly comfortable and experienced. It seemed so contrary to his usual mood swings, but at the same time, it suited him perfectly.

Thanks to Parson—and despite Raene—they'd done what they'd set out to do. "Now we head back?" she asked.

He shot her a smirk. "You sound disappointed."

Parson rushed her a second later. His mouth stole her breath, and his hands roved across her back, holding her firmly against him.

Not that she needed it. Her hunger matched his, and

here, so far from Pyrona or the Bear Clan or anything else, it was easy to give in. His unparalleled strength allowed him to grip her hard, and while it scared her, it also excited her.

Parson released her mouth and groaned, as if in pain. His mouth fell to her neck and nipped at her skin. Raene's hand found the bottom hem of his tunic and disappeared inside, stroking his strong stomach muscles with her fingertips, though it was hard to concentrate with his mouth sucking on her neck.

He was so different than his brother. Parson had so much energy when he held her this way. His touch ignited her, but Raene couldn't decide if that was good or not. He made her heart struggle to beat and her lungs ache for air. She felt like she was dying in all the best ways.

Parson's fingers slid into her hair, stroking the back of her head as he often did. Between his one hand resting low on her back, his lips on her neck, and his stomach heaving under her touch, Raene was little more than clay in his capable hands.

She only backed away when she was truly out of breath. Parson's eyes blazed a bright emerald green, and a sly smile erupted across his features. "Come on, we have a few hours left before dusk." She waited for him to pull away and climb into the cart, but he didn't. Instead, he wrapped both arms tightly around her and lifted her from the ground, breathing in her scent in a loud inhale in her ear. She was certain he could feel the incessant pounding in her chest, the haggard breaths she couldn't calm.

And then, all at once, he set her down and released her. Raene watched him climb up and take his seat in the cart, at a complete loss. "That's it?" Once she caught her breath, she would have stayed there with him all day if he'd asked.

He raked a hand through those chestnut locks and smiled. "Yeah, why?"

Raene shook her head and laughed as she climbed back into her saddle. He never made any sense. He was talkative then quiet. He would run his hands all over her before pulling away entirely. He was never the same two days in a row, or even two minutes in a row.

Raene couldn't decide if she liked that or not. Hale was as constant as a river while Parson was a variable as the wind, and she had no idea which was better than the other. How was she supposed to choose? She had thirteen days left to decide.

She tried not to think about it too hard as she rode. Nothing good could come from dwelling on the impossible decision. Instead, she concentrated on the trees growing larger, the thick canopy blocking out the afternoon sun, the way the day's warmth faded into evening cool.

As he had before, after they had come to a stop, Parson tended to the horses before setting up the narrow tent they'd shared the night before. This time, as he unrolled the bundle of canvas, Raene was there to stake the tent to the ground. Their makeshift camp was ready in half the time.

They both knew they wouldn't see it again for hours. Raene hummed with anticipation. She didn't need to hunt— she'd already hunted once today already—but Raene *wanted* to hunt.

Without a word, Parson strapped his bow and quiver across his shoulders, though she'd never seen him loose a single arrow, and approached her. Only the hand at the small of her back urged her into the depths of the forest, but Raene didn't need much prodding. She transitioned to her tiger form, and behind her, the bear companion that never left her side. There was an ease to it now, a comfort, that hadn't been there before. When she followed a trail and pulled away, she found herself circling back, making sure she didn't lose him. They were better, stronger together.

They were sharks of the forest, seeking out every

innocent, killing without hesitation or mercy, before moving on to the next. Tiger-Raene had killed her fair share of rabbits when she caught the scent of something else, something she'd smelled at least once before.

Then she saw the eyes, little more than yellow orbs hovering in the shadow. She knew those eyes.

A coyote.

Last time had not gone so well. The coyote had injured her, and the bear had robbed her of the kill. She wouldn't let it happen again. Tiger-Raene growled low and loud, warning her bear of this new predator. Then, she launched. She had speed and size, and this time, she put them to good use before the coyote had a chance to even touch her.

But no sooner had her feet left the ground than a second pair of coyotes flew from the shadow, knocking tiger-Raene to her side on the ground. She was on her feet and running an instant later, but her back ignited in pain. The coyote weighed on her, its teeth pulling her down as it clamped onto her flesh.

The bear arrived only seconds after the initial attack, and he quickly removed the coyote from her back, biting it hard across its ribs and snuffing the life right out of it.

Ten more appeared where the one had been killed. At least five or six coyotes surrounded the bear, jumping onto his back and latching on with their canine teeth. The bear's groans and growls were lost on the wind as tiger-Raene fought her own attackers in front, behind, and on either side of her. More and more yellow-grey coats materialized from the shadow. She realized her mistake too late: she'd picked a fight with an entire pack of coyotes.

Raene's tiger claws killed one and mortally wounded another before the next managed to leap and grasp her neck between its jaws. She rolled and twisted to shake it, but that left her underside exposed. Pain radiated from her side, her back, her paw. They were everywhere, too many to fight off.

But she couldn't give in. For every bite that pierced her thick fur, tiger-Raene slashed her claws across the throat or belly of a coyote. She was drenched in blood—theirs and her own—and at last, she managed to get to her feet. There were less coyotes around her now, and they picked their footing over the bodies of their fallen packmates.

Raking the ground for purchase, tiger-Raene lunged. She flew through the air toward her target, but she was intercepted. A pair of coyotes each caught her mid-air, one from either side, so that she spun as she landed. She struck the ground far too hard. The entire right side of her tiger form lit with pain. Her front paw hit the ground at the wrong angle and made a horrid cracking sound.

It took her longer than she would have liked, but tiger-Raene managed to get to her feet, circling defensively against the remaining coyotes.

But her front paw was damaged more than she realized. She couldn't put weight on it, and she couldn't use it to strike at the remaining attackers. Somewhere behind her, the bear continued its own struggle. Between the whimpering and growling and barking, she didn' know how he was faring, and when she spared a second to look, she was rewarded with coyote teeth clamped around her neck.

Tiger-Raene was little more than a collection of bites and tears and pain. There was no part of her that didn't scream in agony. There was nothing left but the instinctive urge to fight and survive. Coyote howls and bear growls sounded around her, but Raene couldn't move. She could only lay motionless as the world around her went black.

THE FOLD

TO BEAR-PARSON, a coyote was a menace. Three was a pain. Ten was a challenge. More than twenty? Impossible.

Had he a few seconds to spare, he could have transitioned, positioned his bow and struck them down one by one, each arrow flying true into the heart of a coyote.

But bear-Parson had no such time. He was surrounded.

Trained agents of the Alderai, they were more capable than animals twice their size. In a pack setting, there was no way he could win.

He was relieved to see the tiger had killed at least half already, but the way she lay motionless, streaked with crimson, the blood pooling into the soil around her, made him desperate. He had to end this. Now.

He would kill every last one of them for what they had done to her.

Three coyotes remained clutched onto his back while another four scrambled about his feet, snapping and biting at him if he didn't move them fast enough.

But speed had never been his gift. No, bear-Parson had only strength.

Pushing past the pain and the weight of the dogs on his back, bear-Parson bared down on the two coyotes nearest him. His paws dropped harder than hammers, pounding them into the ground until their bones crunched, and they never moved again.

Five more.

Bear-Parson slammed his mammoth frame into the unforgiving trunk of an alder, loosing two coyotes from his back—one of them dead.

Four.

When the next came to snap at his paw, bear Parson evaded the bite and crushed the coyote a second later. Its skull popped like a melon.

Three.

The two coyotes remaining on his back worked extra hard to tear into his flesh, pulling and twisting to yank out full chunks of fur and skin. He let out a horrific, pain-filled growl, but he wouldn't stop moving. Concern for the tiger fueled his rage. Bear-Parson raced for the nearest tree, his paws thundering on the ground, before he threw his full weight against the trunk. Both coyotes fell away, one dead, the other so injured it never stood again.

One.

But bear-Parson was spared killing it. Alone and in the face of a hostile brown bear, the coyote thought better of his attack. It whimpered once before racing for the midnight shadows that filled the forest. Parson could have easily followed, relying only on scent, but the tiger needed him.

Transitioning to his human form was exceptionally painful given his wounds, mostly on his back with a good bite on his shoulder, but Parson forced himself into a man. He needed to think, to assess her injuries with thought and care. A bear would never know how to keep her alive.

But Raene remained a tiger. It was impossible to see the extent of her injuries through all the blood. The sight horrified him, and he would have been sure the coyotes had bested her if not for the wide arc of carnage around her. She'd fought hard and killed a dozen before she'd fallen—from blood loss, if he had to guess.

Even if she had been in her lovely human form, Parson could do nothing for her. They were a full day's ride from the Bear Clan, and Parson had no supplies to stop the bleeding, had no skill for the medical arts—nothing that could save her life. The bow and arrow strapped to his back were useless in the aftermath.

His jaw tightened. He knew Raene was going to die.

And Parson had let this happen. He had encouraged her to hunt, to leave the safety of the clan.

But more than his guilt or shame, was the knowledge that he was about to lose the only person who understood him. He'd forced his way into her life and was rewarded by getting to know her in return. There would be no more shared hunts. No more secrets or kisses or fights.

Parson was going to lose her.

His chest ached as if it caved under the weight of his anguish. He would never get over this. He would never recover from this loss.

Her striped ribs rose and fell so faintly, he could only tell she was still breathing when he placed a hand against them. She didn't have long.

She would die a tiger.

Death in totem form was never easy. The body didn't know how to decay properly. The transitional energy complicated what should have been the most natural process of all. It would take weeks for her to start to decompose rather than hours.

Parson knew he couldn't see her that way.

"Raene," he shouted in her pointed cat ear, not caring about the cracks in his voice. He had no way of knowing if she could even hear him. But he had to try.

"Come back. Transition back, Raene!" Parson lashed

out his hand onto the meat of her shoulder when frustration got the better of him.

But nothing happened. He couldn't even feel her breaths anymore.

She was gone.

Parson collapsed to the ground beside her, at a loss as to what to do. Hale was going to kill him for this. Da's trade with the Vice Syndicate would be nullified. The Bear Clan would lose their alliance and their tiger totem, and when Da demanded Blossom's return, he would know she was missing.

This night would change everything.

But Parson would never be able to tell them how it affected him. It would be disrespectful to Hale to even suggest she might have had other inclinations, whether true or not. It didn't matter now.

Parson sat frozen in grief and shock. His mind couldn't process it. When he turned back to stroke her fur—to run his hands through those gorgeous russet stripes—he realized the tiger was gone. Instead, the blood-covered form of the human Raene lay in its place.

Her neck was so tattered, even Parson's night eyes couldn't see how much of it had been torn away. Her right arm was obviously broken, the bone jutting out with an angry, pointed edge. The rest of her was covered in bite marks, each missing a sizeable chunk of flesh.

The nearest one, just below her bottom rib, continued to bleed profusely, pumping blood like a river down her stomach.

All at once, Parson realized she was alive. Dead people didn't bleed. The flow of blood was strong for now, but it would wane soon enough.

Except he was too far from anyone who could help her.

He couldn't give up on her—wouldn't give up on her.

She was strong. She'd survived this long. Parson would have to get her the rest of the way.

In less than a minute, he abandoned his bow and quiver, and shredded his shirt into long strips to tie around the worst of her wounds. They were all layered so close and on top of one another, he only needed five strips, pulled tight to slow the bleeding. They weren't clean, and they would produce wounds that festered, but that was hardly a concern at the moment. Parson was all too aware she wouldn't live long enough for it to matter.

Despite how he rolled and turned her to secure the strips around her torso, Raene remained motionless, lifeless. It killed him. It gutted him clean through.

And it was only going to get worse.

So Parson did the only thing he could. He pulled Raene tight against his chest, pressing as much of his body against hers as he could.

"I'm so sorry, Raene," he whispered in her blood-caked ear.

And then he transitioned.

Encased in his transitional energy, Raene folded into his totem in the same way as his clothes or quiver. To anyone else he might cross, they'd never know she was there, wouldn't be able to see her, but to Parson, it was as obvious as anything. She was a natural extension of himself. Her chin pressed against his shoulder, her body molded into his. He felt the energy within her, nothing like her usual strength, but it was there. Deep within his totem self, Parson sensed the life within her. A life that would very likely be over soon.

But he couldn't think about that.

Parson spared only a moment to find his bearings before he broke into a full sprint.

Kaide stood on the front steps of the stone house and adjusted his cloak. He had never before had any reason to visit.

An ancient woman pulled open the carved-iron door, her head bowed so low that Kaide could see nothing but the crown of her smoke-white hair. She bid him entry and escorted him through the lowest level. It was as dark as a cave inside, the volcanic stone soaking up the light. Only a few wall sconces illuminated their route to the formal sitting room.

It was there Kaide found his host. Pruda lounged on a scarlet sofa across from the fireplace. The summer heat was already overwhelming. The fire was for him, for whatever reason.

Kaide stopped in the doorway and bowed his head formally. "Good evening, Pruda. Thank you for having me." He said the words he didn't mean. Kaide was tempted to turn on his heel and head back to the manor, but there was nothing for him to do there. He would only continue to brood in his anger.

An invitation to Pruda's estate was odd enough. Kaide was at least intrigued to see what she wanted. He knew the Alderai wasn't her real aim.

"Oh please, Kaide. Come in. Have a drink with me." Pruda motioned to the wall of wine bottles behind her.

Had he been at home, he might have drank a full bottle on his own and let sleep consume him, no better than the likes of Naiden Randal. Here, he pulled a silver glass from the rack and poured the strawberry wine. Then, he took the seat across from Pruda.

Her hair was down, as smooth as silk and black as ink. The tattoos on her arm danced in the firelight. Her lips were painted, too-red as always, and her dark eyes spent several minutes watching him drink his wine.

Neither spoke. That was fine with Kaide. He couldn't

think of anything to say.

"You really loved her, didn't you?" Pruda's first words were as brutal as a viper's strike.

Kaide tried not to wince.

Pruda's lips formed a pained smile. "You don't have to answer. I can see it. I felt the same about my second husband. Did you ever meet Brill? No, I suppose you didn't."

Pruda was well into her third marriage by the time Kaide was selected as Vice Syndicate. He'd known she had previous husbands, but hadn't bothered to learn their names. They were history.

Kaide shook his head. "I'd rather not discuss it."

"But that's precisely why I've invited you, and why you've accepted." She stood up and carried her drink to Kaide's side. When she sat, she pressed the length of her calf against the side of his thigh.

"I accepted because you said you wanted to discuss the Alderai." Only a half-lie.

"We'll get to that. I have an offer for you first." Pruda draped an arm across the back of the sofa and toyed with the edge of Kaide's collar. He hated to have her so close, touching his cloak that way, but regardless of his disinterest, Pruda was dangerous. He would hardly be the first to die by her hand—or tongue.

When Kaide didn't answer except to sip his wine, Pruda told a story he doubted many had heard before. "My first husband was Winsor Melston of the Hyena Clan of Mount Alkai. He was a Commissioner of Criminal Investigation back before Sangra. He was hard and foul and cruel as anything. I hated that man. We'd only been married a year when I slipped my fangs into his neck and watched him seize."

Kaide wasn't surprised at the words—he'd already suspected she'd done it—but rather, the fact she shared it with him, and in such detail, gave him pause.

"If this is your idea of earning my allegiance, you're wasting your time." Kaide tried to hide the threa in his voice, but there was that edge he couldn't smooth. He had no interest in marrying her, and he wasn't going to be coerced into it. He didn't want to kill Pruda, and he wasn't willing to die.

Pruda's lips curled into an amused grin. "No, that's for later." She even winked at him before she took a long sip of wine and continued. "I married Brill a few months later, sure it would be more of the same. But he was the only son of the Elsor Clan, and I wanted their connections in Hydra. I didn't expect it to last long."

To Kaide's surprise, Pruda's hand fell away. Her gaze sank to her lap, and he couldn't be sure, but it appeared that someone had cracked Pruda wide open.

A look he well recognized.

Pruda's voice barely withheld her grief as she said, "I killed him on accident. He woke me in the night. I still don't know why. I reacted and bit him. He died in three minutes."

Kaide put a hand on her knee, the only comfort he could off her. He was in no position to give anything else.

She cleared her throat and returned to her easy smile. "I tried again after that, but he was so dull. He smelled like rotting leaves. I couldn't take it. It wasn't the same anymore."

Kaide could relate to that sentiment more than anything else. It wasn't the same anymore. But that didn't bring her motives into focus. "Why are you telling me this?"

"Because we can help each other." Pruda's hand snaked back to his collar. A second later, she reached forward and wrapped her lips around his neck, only an instant away from sinking her fangs into his flesh and killing him. But instead, she kissed him before Kaide swatted her away.

It had been a mistake to come here.

Kaide pushed to his feet and set down his wine glass. Smoothing over his cloak, he used his formal tone to address her. "Thank you for your hospitality, Vice Syndicate Swain," he droned as he headed for the door.

Before he'd made it even half a step, her hand was on his arm. "It's not a trick, Kaide. I don't want Syndicate. I just want to see the Prentis burn." Her eyes ignited with that same passion he saw when they discussed Pyro's underground ring of sex traffickers.

Kaide hovered at a loss. "The Prentis isn't the only issue. There are dozens of other matters to address. Why is this one so important?"

"My swine of a first husband used me as he saw fit. Let's just say I have a soft spot for any woman in such a position." She stepped forward and steadied her gaze on him. "I'll help you with whatever you want. You have my full support. Just promise me we destroy the Prentis."

Pruda's face wasn't her usual seductive mask. Her mouth wasn't twisted into a smirk, and her eyes didn't shimmer with vengeance. She was telling him the truth, though Kaide still wasn't entirely certain why. He only knew whatever happened in her first marriage, it had been enough to shape her into the ruthless woman he knew now.

"Just sit down. Let's discuss this reasonably." She tugged him back to the sofa. No sooner was he seated than her legs were draped over his lap and her fingers continued to toy with his collar, but Pruda spilled everything she knew about the Prentis and their leader, the Milton—how she dispatched a trio of private investigators to stage a kidnapping and follow the Prentis, making it halfway across the Alderwood before they were lost.

Kaide sat in silence, listening, absorbing, working

through the information one piece at a time. It was good information—information they desperately needed—but even Kaide wasn't so callous as to condone sacrificing a young woman for it. There was no telling the horror her life had become within the grasp of the Prentis.

And it wasn't enough to change anything. Kaide was powerless to bring the Prentis to light.

"I already approached Mora to set up a Syndicate Council meeting. She denied it." Kaide sighed and told Pruda of his recent failure. "She also denied my request for ascension. She believes me to be *unfit*." He knew Pruda would back out of whatever arrangement she'd sought with him. There was no motivation to be aligned with him when he'd already been passed over.

"She's an old tart. You'll have it. There's nothing she can do to prevent it. I don't want it, and Gould is a bumbling idiot. You're all she has left. Unless she plans on living forever." Pruda had the gall to laugh.

Kaide, too, laughed. "So far, she's doing quite well." Mora's health had been on the decline for years, but she showed no signs of slowing. She was a tough old lizard.

And then, as he sat lost in thought, Pruda's lips landed against his cheek.

"Pruda—"

"Be quiet," she hissed.

"I'm not—" Her lips found the lobe of his ear.

Brusquely, she told him, "I don't want anything from you. I don't have anything to give you, either."

It was then Kaide saw it. She was just as empty as he was, only she'd been empty longer. She'd gotten good at it.

Maybe she'd figured out something he hadn't. Killing hadn't worked. Trying to claim Syndicate hadn't worked. Maybe this would.

So Kaide put his hands around Pruda's waist and centered her over his lap. She was tall, so much taller than

Blossom, but the memory of the Terra girl he loved only spurred him on. Every time he thought of her, he pulled Pruda closer, desperately hoping the woman in front of him could quiet the one who wouldn't quit racing across his thoughts.

Blossom was gone, and he had to go on. He had to move on with his life.

This was the best he could do.

Hale smelled Parson's bear form well before he should have. The wind carried the familiar scent of his brother from the north, but even so, it was too early. A full day too early.

They shouldn't be back yet.

Something was wrong.

Hale burst from his tent and into the clearing in time to see his brother's bear form approach at a full run. His mouth hung open as he panted in exhaustion, and already Hale knew he'd been running for hours. There was no sign of Raene—no scent of her anywhere.

At Hale's tent, bear-Parson stopped. His nostrils flared as he gasped for breath. He shook his head, and then, all at once, he transitioned. But rather than standing in his human form, Parson remained crouched with one arm tight around Raene as he lowered her to the ground. He wore no shirt, and his back was riddled with bites and wounds, but he didn't even seem to notice.

His eyes never left her.

"We were ambushed," he managed through his ragged breaths.

Hale took only a half-second to collect himself. There were so many wrong things happening all at once, he didn't even know how to begin. And then, he saw the dark red color of Raene's usually-vibrant shirt, the streak of crimson from her ear, the bone emerging from her arm.

He covered the distance in a few short steps. Parson fell back and let Hale collect her, pulling her into his arms and bringing her into his tent, laying her on the small cot reserved for more critical patients.

Tasia burst into the tent as soon as he had her laid flat. "By the Mother," she whispered behind him.

Hale didn't bother to turn. "I need clean water. And whatever clean fabrics you can find," he added when he saw the state of his bride. Whatever clothes she had been wearing were destroyed, little more than tattered remnants, and the strips of moss-green fabric were soaked through with blood and grime.

Tasia was gone a moment later.

And Hale was alone with his task. He hated this. He hated the shake of his hands and the way every motion seemed too slow. Just crossing the tent to get his medical kit felt like an eternity away from her.

He didn't even know if she was alive.

Raene's complexion had become a sickly grey-green, likely due to blood loss. She lay so perfectly still, he couldn't tell if she was breathing. He pressed two fingers to her wrist, failing to detect even a hint of a pulse, and her neck was too shredded to even bother. There were no arteries left intact.

Her injuries were grave, but also crusted over with blood—they were hours old. She might have had a chance had she been treated right away, but so long after the fact, there was nothing Hale could do.

The horror of it struck him like lightning, burning its way through him. Whatever had happened out there, she was gone. She lost her.

"Oh, Hale." He didn't realize Gemini was in the tent until she sank beside him, taking in the gruesome site. "Is she—"

Hale nodded. "I can't find a pulse." It shattered him to even say it.

Gemini leaned forward and pressed her ear to Raene's chest, ignoring the considerable slick of blood. Hale was moments from telling her to stop when her eyes widened. "I hear it. It's faint, but it's there. What can I do?"

Hale spurred into action. His medical training guided his motions, as quick and sure as reflexes. Sparing no considerations for modesty, he and Gemini cut away the strips of blood-soaked fabric and exposed Raene's grievous wounds. They were so much worse than he first thought, and to his disgrace, Hale found himself wondering how she'd even survived such injuries.

Tasia returned with a basin of water and joined them. It took a long while to wash away the blood, clean the wounds, and bandage them tight. At least she wasn't losing anymore blood.

Then, Hale addressed the bone protruding from her arm. That would take more time and considerably more care. Gemini held out an alder wood bowl as he plucked the shattered bits of bone from the opening. Then, as it killed him to do, Hale forced the bones back into place. The sickening crunch and snap of tendons echoed through the tent until even Hale wasn't sure he could do it. At last, with one final, horrible crack, Raene's bones settled into place.

Gemini gagged. "Is that really going to work?'

Hale could only shrug. "It'll likely be infected. If not, the bone could regrow in the wrong place. If it grows straight, the muscles may never attach again. More than likely, she'll lose the arm—" *If she lives that long*. He couldn't bring himself to say it.

Ignoring the high likelihood that none of this would matter when she died, Hale bandaged her arm and splinted it to prevent further injury. It was well into the middle of the night when Hale had done all he could. He sent Tasia home—no reason to overwork her in her state.

"Thank you, Gemini," Hale said to dismiss her as he knelt by the cot. He wasn't one to pray in public—his beliefs were between him and the Mother—but instead of leaving, Gemini settled onto her knees beside him. Together, they chanted the Mother's safekeeping prayer.

My Mother of mothers
And tree of trees
Bless us with your light
Grant us passage from the night
We surrender to your might
Guide our darks and our days
Fill us with love in all your ways
Guide our dreams as we sleep
In your grove we're yours to keep
From seed to tree to forest tall
Keep us safe, one and all

Hale sank back on his heels and tried to turn his fears into faith. The Mother would watch over Raene and guide her back to health.

She had to. There was no other way.

Hale could only sit by and wait to see the evidence of the Mother's work. He'd done all he could for Raene. For the rest of it, there were still matters to discuss. He needed to settle things with Parson once and for all.

He left Gemini to watch over Raene as he went to find his brother.

Hale should have known he'd be in Da's tent. Parson sat with the back of the chair between his legs, his arms resting over the top. Behind him, Lathan squinted in the candlelight as he plucked something from one of the many wounds on Parson's back. Only when Hale was closer did he realize it was a tooth.

"My son," Da said when he saw Hale enter. Lathan

and Parson both turned, looking for any sign of grief on his face. Instead, they found only sheer exhaustion.

"She's stable for now. She lost a lot of blood, but there's nothing else we can do. Just have to see—"

So many words remained trapped in his throat.

Hale squeezed his eyes tight and held onto his belief that the Mother had a plan. She wouldn't have brought Raene to him only to rip her away. He was tempted to flip his coin and be sure, but in truth, he wasn't sure. There was a part of him that wanted to hold onto some shred of hope a while longer. He didn't think he could take knowing the wrong answer yet.

"You left her alone?" Parson had the nerve to accuse him.

"Of course not. Gemini's going to stay until she's recovered." Hale didn't exactly like the idea of Gemini sleeping in his tent day in and day out, but it benefited Raene. He'd agreed without hesitation as soon as she'd offered.

Hale pulled up a chair beside Da and his brothers. "So what happened?"

"We've already discussed it. An ambush of coyotes, the Alderai's agents I expect." Da was quick to answer.

But Hale wouldn't be denied his explanation. His bride had been in Parson's protection and she'd nearly come to die—maybe she still would. Hale deserved to hear the truth from him.

And based on the tight jaw and pain-filled eyes of his brother, Hale knew it was going to be a story he disliked.

A long minute of tense silence passed between them. Lathan continued cleaning the wounds as they waited.

Parson released an aggravated sigh. "We were out hunting."

Hale shook his head but declined to react just yet. It wasn't the worst of it, not by a long shot.

"She found a coyote. Just one. I guess she thought she could handle it, but then there were a lot. Too many. She fought them off, killed at least half the pack, but—"

Hale had seen the damage, on both Raene and his brother. He knew what had happened. "And then you brought her back. In your *totem*."

Parson flew to his feet, nearly knocking over Lathan hovering behind him. His fists pumped at his side as he shouted, "That's what you're worried about? *That's* what you have to say to me? I carried her across the forest. I ran for almost an entire *day* so that she might live. And you're going to sit here and scold me on how I didn't do it right?"

Hale was too tired to rise to Parson's threats. "It's dangerous, and you know it. You could have taken the horses." Carrying another person in totem was exceptionally risky and almost always ended in one or both dying. The energies didn't match. The totems weren't compatible. Parson knew his bear form couldn't sustain her tiger totem. He was merely lucky it hadn't killed her outright.

"She was *dying*! What did you want me to do? Walk back? Go an hour in the wrong direction to get the cart? Sit there and watch while she bled out?"

Hale stood to face his brother on his feet. "The Mother has a plan for us—"

"It's a tree, Hale." Parson stepped forward and put his chest to Hale's. His voice was a low rumble, almost a whisper, but every word speared him. "Your beloved goddess is a *fruit tree*. She's not watching. She's not planning. We cut her down to make a living. Get it through your head. The Mother didn't save Raene. *I* did."

And just when Hale was sure Parson would throw a punch, he bolted out of Da's tent.

Hale released a pent up breath, feeling the air in his lungs, all the while wondering if Raene had any left in hers.

342

He couldn't go back yet. It would drive him mad to wait beside her. It was killing him to stay away.

So he sank back into Da's chair and covered his face with his hands. He was drained, exhausted from a night spent working and worrying, and it wasn't over yet.

A hand appeared on his shoulder, so massive it could only be Lathan's.

"I'm fine," Hale lied. He had to be strong. He had to be better than this. If he was going to be clan leader, he would have to deal with worse, though at the moment he couldn't think what that might be.

But Lathan would have none of it. As uncompromising as stone, Lathan squeezed Hale tight in his bear hug, one of the hundreds Hale had endured since he was a boy. And as much as he hated to be reliant, Hale squeezed him back.

His veins teemed with an intensity like nothing he'd ever known. Fear for Raene's life. Anger at Parson's ineptitude at protecting her. Frustration that Hale couldn't comprehend how his life had become such a monumental catastrophe. He'd been nothing but devoted, and this was his reward?

Embraced in the formidable arms of his oldest brother, Hale's anxiety began to fade. The Mother had a plan. Hale would persevere along her path. Raene would survive—he was sure. Maybe this was simply the last test to prove he was worthy of her.

By the time Lathan released him, Hale had relaxed considerably. Without the hum of fear to stay him, his eyelids burned with fatigue, and his body sagged with exhaustion. Hale offered his brother a grateful nod and sank back to his chair.

"Lathan will take a team to collect the horses and cart in the morning, or whatever's left of them." Hale knew Da meant to distract him with logistics—seven horses and their largest cart would be a considerable loss—but Hale couldn't manage to care about it.

Sensing Hale wasn't up for a discussion, Da ... id out an extra pallet in his tent, an open invitation for ... Iale to stay. "This night has been long, my sons. Get so ... e rest. The sun will bring us some answers."

Of all the places in the world Parson wanted to be ... Hale's tent wasn't it. But he'd spent the last of his bandage ... on his injuries a few nights ago. And thanks to Hale's inter ... uption, Lathan hadn't finished dressing the deep puncture ... on his back and shoulder.

Parson was so furious he couldn't see straig ... t. The idea of Hale interrogating him was so ludicrous it n ... de his blood boil. Raene was clinging to life—a life *Parson* saved—and Hale was more concerned with placing l ... ame?

But for the moment, Parson knew where Hale v ... is.

So Parson risked going in.

Gemini lay on the floor beside the cot. She r ... bbed a hand over her tired eyes and offered him a half ... earted smile as she sat up. "I was expecting the other one."

Parson ignored that particular comment. "I ju ... t need some bandaging cloths. And ointment, if you know ... here it is." He didn't want to stay and chat.

Gemini didn't have to look all that hard. The ... pplies were in a box right beside her, and Parson realize ... they'd only recently used them to patch up Raene. "Thistle ... ot and burnt sage," she explained, "for pain and clean ... g the wounds."

Parson nodded his thanks, desperate to leave before Hale returned, but he couldn't help but step forv ... ird, to cross the length of the tent and stand over Raen ... . With considerable bandaging around her chest and to ... o, her shallow breaths were barely discernable. If not ... or the ashen color of her usually-warm skin, she might have looked like she was sleeping, but Parson knew better.

And he would never, ever forget.

Gemini pressed the bandages and ointment into his hands. She opened her mouth to say something, but Parson didn't want to hear it. He clutched the supplies and bolted through the tent flap before she could say a word.

He was too tired to transition and too angry to sit still. He was no good for anyone. He was no good for Raene.

Parson had never been so completely inept at anything as he'd been at keeping Raene safe. He'd messed up with her time and time again, but not like this. He didn't know what he could have done differently, but that didn't change the result. Raene was barely breathing while he was still standing.

It would never feel right.

Tucked into the dark recess of his tent, Parson did his best to smear the ointment over the injuries on his back, though he couldn't reach half of them.

"Need some help?" Gemini asked from the flap, already inside his tent.

He hadn't even heard her approach, but he didn't argue. He simply held the ointment container out to her.

"Here, I brought you some tea to help ward off infection." Much to his chagrin, Gemini lit a candle, illuminating his sanctuary as she held out a small vial of lavender liquid.

Uncaring as to its contents, Parson accepted the vial and drank. "She's not alone, is she?" His strained voice was nothing more than breath.

Gemini pressed the ointment into a bite wound just above his hip. "Hale came back. Said he didn't want to sleep at Da's. I think he blames himself for it."

Parson shook his head in disbelief. Hale blamed himself? He hadn't even been there. He didn't encourage her to go hunting, to run far from the horses and the tent. Hale hadn't selfishly pushed her to embrace her totem simply because he loved watching her kill.

"Be still," Gemini hissed, too bossy for her own good, but Parson listened. Her hands felt good on what skin remained on his back. She was delicate as she treated his injuries, and never once did she cause him undo pain.

"Thanks, Gem," Parson breathed, more relaxed than he cared to admit.

"Sure, Barson." She managed to throw a light punch at the only uninjured space on his shoulder.

"Seriously? We're back to that? Barson?" She'd used the name when she was little, maybe three, and he was at least nine. He paid no attention to her then, of course, but in the years since, Gemini had grown into the clan beauty and a formidable woman in her own right. Asla was a lucky man.

"At this rate, you should be glad. You're going to run out of relatives if you don't watch it." She pressed the first of many bandages to his skin, running her fingers across the sticky edges so it would stay. "You should talk to him. When you're both calmed down. Well, when he's calm." Gemini knew him too well. Parson was never too far from the edge of his aggression.

Parson let out a long, regretful sigh. "There's no point. He's never going to forgive me. And he shouldn't. I messed up." It was the anthem of his life. *Parson Frane, the man who ruined everything.*

Only this time, he hadn't sired a child he'd never see again. He hadn't failed to keep his mother alive. He hadn't let a stranger take his sister across the realm. He'd put Raene in serious danger. She'd be lucky to survive, and even if she did, she'd never be the same. There was such a gaping hole of guilt in his chest, Parson could scarcely draw breath.

"You Frane boys are thick as rocks." Gemini scoffed behind him.

With his face buried in his hands, Parson said, "Bears aren't known for their flexibility." He rubbed at his eyes and found the full day of running catching up to him. He was delirious with exhaustion as his mind raced.

"True," she admitted. "But you saved her life, and for that, he'll forgive you for everything else."

Parson could only think of the words Hale had said, still fresh on his mind from their fight only minutes ago.

It's dangerous, and you know it.

And by all accounts, Hale was right. There was no way Parson should have been able to carry her in totem form. But what choice did he have? She was all but dead anyway. Maybe it had been her weakness, the near absence of life in her that allowed him to carry her. In her full tiger form, all strength and power, they would have killed each other instantly.

No matter how it happened, Parson would never recover—the feeling of Raene tucked into his totem, nestled against him and secured by his transitional energy, the warmth she radiated even in such a weak state—Parson could never hope to erase such an experience, like she'd burned him at his core.

But he didn't want to get into it with Gemini. Instead, he simply said, "I also nearly let her get killed by a pack of coyotes. I'm not sure even Hale is that forgiving." Parson, for one, would never forgive himself.

"Maybe not."

"You sure know how to cheer a guy up. Thanks Gem," Parson replied with a sneer before he gave in to a massive yawn.

"Anytime." She handed him the unused bandages and headed toward the tent flap. "I'll keep an eye on her tonight. Try to get some sleep." Then lower, she added,

"The lavender night tea should help."

Parson frowned. "You said it was for infection."

"You wouldn't have taken it if I told you it was a sleeping tea." Gemini smirked at her victory. Then, he was gone, and Parson was alone with what he'd done.

But despite how he was sure he'd never get his racing mind to settle, he found his eyelids too heavy. Within minutes, he was face down on his pallet, fast asleep.

DAUGHTER

BEFORE SHE WAS even fully awake, Raene felt the pain. Her whole body screamed in agony like she'd been lit on fire. Not aches or sores or even cuts, but sheer, blinding pain. Her head felt as if it had been slowly compressed until her brain oozed out her ears.

Of all the misery she felt, her arm was the only part of her that didn't hurt, but only because she couldn't feel it at all.

Lying on her left side, Raene could barely move. Even a tiny motion reignited the pain, like she'd caught fire once more. She might as well have been crushed under a boulder, her body shattered and pinned in place. There was nothing she could do. Even breathing was agony.

"Raene?" Came a tiny, whispered voice. "I need you to open your mouth. Just a little. Raene? Open your mouth," insisted the voice. Gentle. Female. Bossy.

Raene realized it was Gemini, and though it took her several seconds, she complied, only to have her mouth filled with a strange, cool tea. It tasted of mint and raspberries and something with the sourness of rot. Raene would have gagged it up if she'd had the strength.

"There, give that a few minutes. You'll feel better soon." Gemini let Raene lay in horrible discomfort in silence, but as promised, the pain gradually subside . As if the boulder was slowly raised, Raene regained som range of motion with each passing minute while the tea w ked to silence the worst of her pain.

"Thank you," Raene breathed when she coul stand the sound of her own voice. She dared to crack o en one eye, and then the other. She found her one and onl friend with a brilliant smile plastered across her face. G mini's black hair was pulled up in a messy knot at the bac of her head. Around her, the dimness of Hale's tent.

"You gave us quite the scare. I'm not sure the Franes will ever recover," she teased.

Raene's head ached as she tried remembe what happened. She remembered warmth, a constant dr m, the smell of blood, predator eyes in shadow—all of it a blur. The pounding in her head didn't help. A heavy g had settled into her mind, preventing her from remei bering anything clearly.

"Hale wanted me to let him know as soon as y u were up, but I figured you could use a few minutes to cat h your breath. Want me to get him?"

Raene shook her head and immediately regr ted it. The horrific pounding rhythm only worsened, so painful she slammed her eyes shut again.

"Go slow. The hemhorn tea works wonders but it takes a few minutes to kick in." A cool cloth lai led on Raene's cheek, and only then did she realize the s velling on the right side of her face. A large knot sat on th tip of her cheekbone just below her eye.

Raene tried to lay as still as possible, but h mind raced with questions. "What happened?"

Gemini moved a fallen lock of hair from Raene s face. "Parson said you were ambushed by a pack of coyot s."

Raene remembered the coyotes. Her memory w s slow to catch up, but it was there—the eyes, the yell w-grey coats, the endless snap of teeth. She remembered falling and then darkness. She remembered being deep in the forest, closer to the capital than the clan.

"How—how'd I get back here?"

Gemini leaned an elbow on the edge of the cot and waggled her eyebrows as she liked to do when she had some particularly juicy gossip to share. "Well, it's all so exciting. Parson brought you back *in* his totem. It's terribly dangerous, but I guess since you were going to die, he thought he might as well. Hale's livid, of course, but he's just worried, mostly. He's been here pacing for two days, but Lathan just got back with the cart. Good thing, too. No one needs him hovering about like a vulture."

"And Parson?"

Gemini's features darkened. "He hasn't been by. I'm not sure he's even left his tent."

Raene would have pouted if she thought it wouldn't disturb her tentative comfort. "He hasn't come to see me?" Surely Gemini was mistaken. After all that happened while they were away—the hunting, the conversation, the kisses—Raene was sure he would at least care to know she was all right.

But she'd been wrong before.

Then, Raene realized why he hadn't come. "Is he all right? Is he hurt?"

"He's got a good bite on his shoulder, but the rest should heal up nicely." And then, sensing that wasn't the explanation Raene expected, Gemini pushed to her feet. "Let me get Hale. He can explain everything better than I can. But don't let him stay too long. You'll need some sleep to keep your strength up."

Raene knew she would have to face him eventually. Before Gemini left, Raene called out, "Why can't I feel my arm?"

"Just wait for Hale to explain." And then, she was

351

gone.

Hale burst through the tent flap within a half-second of seeing Gemini's nod, but as soon as he saw Raere, eyes open—though barely—his heart let go a massive wave of relief. She'd slept nearly two days. Two days of anxiety. Two nights of sleeplessness. But it was all worth it to see her awake again.

In a heartbeat, he crossed the tent and sank beside her cot. It nearly killed him to see her inflamed cheek, her black eye, the arm lying motionless across her chest. Her right side was one continuous injury. She worked the blanket up to her chin, trying to hide her appearance from him.

"How are you feeling?" he whispered, running his knuckles across the edge of her jaw, savoring the warmth and life he felt.

"Awful," she admitted, her voice a creaking groan compared to its usual melody. "Gemini wouldn't tell me what's wrong with my arm."

"It's broken," he said, trying to limit her worries. A second later, he changed his mind. She deserved to know what she'd survived. He delicately lifted her arm to show the bandages that stretched from elbow to knuckles. "An open oblique fracture. Both bones were broken clean through. We reset them, and splinted the arm, but there's no way to know if you'll be able to use it again." Hale stroked her hair to provide what little comfort he could. It was the least he could do.

"And my head?"

"Concussion. Probably a serious one. You'll have to take it easy for a while. Gemini's going to stay in camp for a few days to help me. We'll keep you hydrated, and we'll get you a little bit of food, as long as your stomach can take it. When you're ready, Lathan brought some smoked rabbit for you."

Raene's eyes widened. "Rabbit?"

Hale leaned forward and kissed the bridge of her nose. "This is more important. Once you've regained your strength, we'll work on getting your totem under control again. Right now, you need the protein to mend your wounds." He pressed his forehead to hers. "It will take you a long time to feel right again, and it won't be easy, by you have my word. I'm always here with you. Always. I won't let anything happen to you."

A long silence filled the tent, and when Raene closed her eyes, he thought she might have fallen asleep. But then, so low he could barely hear, she whispered, "I'm so sorry Hale."

Hale shook his head. Raene may be misguided in the use of her totem, but these injuries weren't her fault. "You have nothing to be sorry about. Parson shouldn't have taken you so far. I should have told him there was a threat from the Alderai, but I never thought he would venture to the capital on his own."

A silent tear slipped down her nose and fell to her pillow. "I knew not to go," she argued. "I told Da I didn't want to go."

Hale's heart nearly stopped. "What do you mean? Da knew you were going?"

"He made me. He said he couldn't spare anyone else."

A furious anger erupted within Hale's chest. For the three days of the envoy and the two days that followed, Da had sat at his side, discussing trades and cuts and the Alderai's decree, but never once had he mentioned having an active role in sending Raene across the Alderwood. And unlike Parson, Da had direct knowledge of the threat of discovery.

Hale could at least forgive Parson his ignorance. It was

Hale's fault for not telling him. But Da? He knew perfectly well, and he'd done it anyway.

As if summoned by Hale's blinding rage, Da pushed his way into the tent. "My daughter, I'm so glad to see you awake. You gave my sons quite a scare." He smiled warmly at her, like she was really his own daughter.

Raene used her good hand to sit up halfway. "Thank you, Da," she replied before she winced hard. Hale clutched her elbow to help her. Once she was fully up, she pressed her fingertips to her temple to quiet whatever agony she felt there. Even in the midst of some of the worst injuries Hale had ever personally seen, Raene managed a solid attempt at good manners.

Hale's anger surged. He flew to his feet and locked his hands into fists at his side. "Did you knowingly send her with Parson? Did you force her to go?"

"I'm sorry son. We will have that discussion another time. For now, Raene has a decision to make."

"What?" Hale hissed. He was already boiling with anger. Da had already allowed her to come to harm, and now he wanted to distress her further? Hale knew the choice she would make, but she didn't deserve the stress today. As calmly as he could manage, Hale told Da, "She has a concussion. She's not doing anything but sleeping today."

Da put both hands on Hale's shoulders. "I know, my son. I know it. But it must be now."

Raene looked up at him, glaring through her pain. "You said I had a month." Her voice was so weak it sounded like a plea.

"The time has come," Da insisted.

Hale stepped forward. He tried to contain his anger, but it seeped out into every word. "Can I speak with you outside?"

Da shook his head, his eyes heavy with something like

regret. "I'm sorry, my son. This is the way it must be. The Mother uses us all as she sees fit. Your brothers will be here shortly."

It was only mention of the Mother that made Hale keep from striking his Da. Never in his life had he even been tempted, but now, with Raene so injured and Da insisting she make this decision now, Hale was more furious than he could handle.

But it was the Mother's will that he and Raene be married. Announcing their plans was mere formality, and if it gave Hale more say over her treatment within camp, then Hale would let it happen. As his wife, Raene would be under Hale's protection, from Da or Parson or anyone else.

"Gemini, could you come in, please?" Da called over his shoulder. When she appeared inside the tent and nodded with respect, Da asked, "Could you please get Ms. Randal cleaned up as best you can and bring her to my tent? Hale, you come with me."

With Hale and Da gone, the full weight of the situation hit Raene hard. She let a tear slip down her cheek.

"That bad?" Gemini teased, but there was still that edge of concern in her voice.

"He wants me to choose right now." It was too awful to comprehend. Her head hurt. She couldn't feel her arm. Just sitting up sent the tent spinning around her.

"By the Mother, he knows how to make a scene. I swear, that man..." Gemini crouched beside Raene's cot to get a look at her. "First things first: drink this." She produced a glass vial of some sort of scarlet liquid.

Raene didn't hesitate to drink it. While it tasted far worse than the last one, it wasn't nearly as bad as Norsa's teas. "That'll help to clear your head. As for your hair, that will take more work."

It was all Raene could do to sit still and let Gemini's fingers work through her hair. "I washed it last night while you were sleeping, but I couldn't braid it with you laying on it. At least it's not still full of blood and dirt, right?"

Raene tried to laugh, to find the humor in any of it, but she was paralyzed with fear. What was she supposed to do? Who was she supposed to choose? There was no easy answer, no clear winner. Raene was as lost as the day she arrived.

When Gemini finished her hair, helped her into a fresh Terra tunic—complete with fine gold embroidery—and declared her ready, Raene's head only swam a little. She was much improved over her state only minutes before, but even that didn't quiet the consuming anxiety of what she was about to do.

With a hand cupped around her elbow, Gemini helped Raene walk to Da's tent. She probably could have made it on her own—her steps were sure, and her vision didn't bounce as much as before—but Raene was grateful for the assistance, if for no other reason than to combat the staring clan members.

"Go on. Back to work," Gemini fussed, offering pointed glares to the ones who didn't rush away.

Raene kept her eyes on the ground, refusing to acknowledge anyone who took interest in her appearance. Purple cheek. Broken arm. Terra clothes. She was certainly a sight.

And then, all too soon, they'd arrived at Da's tent. A single flap of fabric hung between her and the reality of her decision. Raene's feet froze and refused to move.

"You can do this. It's what you came here to do. And you can't go wrong. We're talking about Frane boys here." Gemini chuckled and squeezed Raene's only working hand. "I'll be at the garden later if you want to come by, or escape, or something."

Raene let out a single nervous laugh. "Thank you, Gemini." She wanted to say more. *I couldn't have done this without you. I owe you forever. I'll find a way to return your kindness.* But the words stuck in her throat.

When Gemini lifted the flap, Raene knew she could stall no longer. She ducked under—ignoring the sudden pounding in her head—and when she righted herself in Da's tent, she was met with a formidable sight. The three Frane sons stood in a line, from oldest to youngest, all in fine Terra tunics, their hair slicked and handsome.

From behind them, Da appeared. He rushed over and kissed her unbruised cheek. "I'm sorry for this, my daughter. If there was another way, I would choose it. But it has to be now. So, please, do not be angry. Do not let circumstance govern this decision. Once made, you can't take it back. Choose wisely."

Raene didn't understand. What difference would ten days make? Why couldn't she have time to talk to both Parson and Hale? Why this sudden rush? Why did she have to choose now when her head was still so frazzled?

Ahead of her, Raene looked upon the three sons of the Frane Clan. On her left stood Lathan, taller and broader than his brothers, with that same quiet he always had. His thick beard hid his mouth, obscuring any hint of distress. He didn't seem even remotely nervous, but rather bothered, like he had better things to do than be here.

Raene realized he probably did. They were giving up a day at the cut for this, and Lathan already knew he wouldn't be chosen.

Parson stood in the middle with his arms crossed over his chest and his gaze on the floor, so all she could see was the mop of chestnut hair on his head. He, too, wore fresh clothes and bore no signs of injury that she could see.

And on her right, Hale. He was shorter and leaner than

his brothers, but he had such an easy confidence despite being years younger. Even now, he had more confidence in her than Raene had in herself.

"Are you ready, sweet girl?" Da put a hand low on her back, though she could barely feel it through the bandages.

A lump formed in her throat. A sickening pain emerged in her gut, and Raene couldn't help but wonder if she suffered some hidden internal injury. But no, it was just her anxiety.

It was just her punishment for her indecision.

Da looked to his oldest son. "Have you anything to say, Lathan?"

"That this is absolutely ridiculous. Look at her, she can barely stand." Raene had never heard such angered words from him.

Da took it in stride. "Then let's not waste her time. Have you anything to say?"

In silence, Lathan shook his head.

"Please, Da. Lathan doesn't need to be here." Raene needed no further witnesses to this spectacle.

Then, without waiting for Da's approval, Lathan stepped forward. He leaned over and wrapped his bear arms around her, far gentler than such a man should have been capable. "You don't have to do anything. He can't force you. We had an agreement, and you can make him stick to it."

Raene had never heard so many words from him in the same breath. Nor had she heard such protectiveness or kindness in his voice. He sounded like Kaide— like a brother. She nodded her understanding and tried to hold back her tears when he tenderly kissed her forehead. A moment later, he was gone.

She thought it would be better without him, but left with only Parson and Hale, she felt a renewed surge of sickness. No matter what she did, no matter who she chose, someone was going to leave here broken.

"Parson, anything you'd like to say?" Da continued the proceedings as if Lathan had never said a word.

Parson shook his head. "Lathan's right. She doesn't have to choose today. And it doesn't matter. She chooses Hale. This is pointless."

Da shook his head sadly. "It's not pointless. She has a husband to choose and an alliance to honor. That's very important, my son."

"Then honor it and let us get back to work."

Raene felt the words like a slap across the face. She could only stand in shock as they argued. On weak knees, she wavered, trying to remain upright, to keep what little piece of dignity she had left.

At her side, Da continued to press for her decision. "Have I ever given you reason to doubt me? I say this is the Mother's will, and so it falls to me to fulfill it. Raene will choose today. There is no other way."

"What is that supposed to mean?" Parson glared at his father, his brows drawn and his jaw clenched tight.

"It means I am your father and clan leader. And this is the way."

"Just let her choose," Hale said, putting up a hand to calm them, though it hardly worked.

Parson all but screamed, "She doesn't need to choose. I withdraw my name. Hale is the only one left. Let me get back to work."

Raene gaped at him, wondering if her mind was more fractured than she thought. Had Gemini's teas made her hear things? Surely Parson, who worked so hard to earn his chance with her, surely he wasn't the one saying he didn't want her. The one who took her hunting and stole kisses in the woods.

Like nothing in the world, Raene hated this. She *hated* it. More than watching her father drink himself sick or that look in Kaide's eye when he glimpsed the faded sca on her face. She hated it more than the crushing loss of E ossom and the last time she sailed over Pyrona in a tr nsport. Raene hated this decision more than she'd eve hated anything.

But Raene knew she couldn't let it affect her. S e tried to comb through her thoughts, her memories of t e time spent with each, to think logically despite the ach in her head.

Parson was chaotic while Hale was constant. Parson pushed her away and pulled her close while H le had worked to steadily build their relationship. Parson aid all the wrong things while Hale said mostly right ones.

Parson took her hunting while Hale forbade it.

Hale spoke calmly while Parson yelled.

Parson taught her to dance when Hale refused.

Hale stayed by her side all day and night a er her injury while Parson hadn't even come to see her.

Parson carried her back while Hale dress d her wounds.

Hale kept her safe while Parson let her come to arm.

They were as different as two people could p ssibly be, and both had traits she loved and hated. There vas no obvious choice.

But when she looked at Parson, he avoided h r gaze. He looked at Da or Hale or the floor, but not her. W en she looked to Hale, he stood quietly waiting, his hands lasped, not shaking, not nervous. As he'd been all along, H le was confident in her and in their relationship, as n w and budding as it was.

"Have you made your choice, my daughter?' Raene heard Da's words, but she still couldn't answer. She looked back and forth between the two Frane sons who h d both gotten to know her in different ways.

Finally, she looked to Parson. "Do you mean ? You

withdraw your name?"

For the first time since returning to camp, Parson met her eyes with his. They were burning bright green with that ferocity she'd come to know from him, but they were filled with more pain and anguish and regret than she'd ever seen. "Yes. I withdraw my name. I told you the first time. I can't marry you."

"Why?" Raene tried to keep steady, to hold her head high.

"I don't have to explain myself."

"Yes, you do. You owe me that much, at least." Raene lifted her broken, useless arm, knowing it wasn't fair. But she needed an explanation. She needed to hear the words from him.

Parson inhaled a sharp breath as if she'd struck him. "Hale wants you. He can have you."

Raene could have crumpled to the ground in a pile and never gotten up again. She couldn't make sense of it. In the depths of the Alderwood, Parson had teased her and made her cry and taken her hunting, but never for a moment did she question his intent. Up until the arrival of the coyotes, Parson had acted like he wanted her for himself. Either he was a skilled liar or something had changed.

But Parson was anything but articulate. He couldn't fake it even if he wanted to. And that left only one explanation.

"Are we settled then?" Hale asked, growing impatient.

Da shook his head. "She has to say it. I won't abide any breach of contract. The decision is hers." He glanced up at her. "Raene?"

She could have smacked Da for his relentless insistence if she'd had the strength. Still, she nodded. No matter how her head spun or her arm hung heavy at her side, no matter how her heart beat loudly in her ears and her palms slicked with nervous sweat, Raene had made her decision. There was a certain peace and satisfaction i that.

No matter what else transpired today, Raene had at least accomplished that small feat.

Her eyes drifted to Hale, where he stood with sweet smile, like this wasn't difficult, like no one else wa there, like she wasn't some shattered girl barely stitched together with bandages and tea.

It took every ounce of her wavering strength Raene squared her shoulders and held her head as high as p ssible. She wouldn't back down. She wouldn't change he mind. She wouldn't let her injuries keep her from voic ng her decision. With her eyes on Hale, she forced out the words. "I choose Parson."

Parson's eyes slammed shut against the words. Thre little, impossible words. He must have misheard her— misunderstood her—but when Da asked her to say i again, she did.

"I choose Parson."

The second time, there was only anger. The sort of sheer, explosive anger that blurred his vision and bo led the blood in his veins. "Are you insane?" Parson shoute .

The words were unfair, but he couldn't hol them back. Parson couldn't marry her. He didn't deserve l er.

Her cheek was a purplish-black mar that loc ed all wrong on her stunning features. Her broken arm hu g limp at her side, but otherwise, her tunic hid her injurie . Only the dullness in her eyes spoke to her pain and frai y. She was strong—always the huntress—but Parson r d her struggle easily. She was alive and standing as he hadn't dared hope, but a part of him would always ha what happened to her, hate his role in it.

"It's my choice." Raene pulled her eyes from Iale to

glare at Parson.

Parson felt like a flame, and with nothing more than a single look, she'd extinguished him, simply wiping him from existence. She emptied him in an instant.

Hale shot Da a frantic look. "Let's save this for another day. She's had a serious head injury. She needs—"

They all stood dumbfounded when Raene squeezed her eyes tight and screamed, "*It's my choice!*" The sound of her shrill voice froze the air in the tent.

And then, all at once, she opened her eyes and looked to Hale again. Her voice was more even as she said, "I'm sorry, Hale. I know this isn't what you wanted. I know there's nothing I can say. It's not my head or the tea or anything else. This is my decision. And I choose Parson." She stepped forward and handed him the three rings—one of them his.

Hale was entirely and understandably crushed. His shoulders sank further with each passing second. His hands clenched at his sides as he tried to comprehend what she was saying, what it meant for him.

Parson couldn't stand it. He couldn't watch his brother's heart get broken. He had to stop it. "I said no, Raene. This isn't going to happen. We're all in agreement. Hale—"

Raene's bright blue eyes blazed with renewed anger. "Hale will make a fine husband. But he won't be mine. I'm not going to ask him to be second choice. If you won't marry me, then send me back to Pyrona. Nullify the agreement. I did my part." Raene attempted to cross her arms indignantly, but too late she realized one of them didn't work. She ended up awkwardly cradling her broken arm in the other, but it had none of the effect she surely intended.

"Why don't we give them a minute?" Da approached Hale and steered him toward the tent flap. And to Parson's shock, Hale put up not the smallest fight. He, to o, was empty.

And then it was just the two of them. The a r hung heavy with tension, palpable and dense so that it nearly smothered them. Parson buried his face in his hands letting himself breathe, letting his anger calm into so ething manageable. When he had control of himself, he lo ked at her and asked, "What are you thinking?" Parson c uldn't even fathom how seriously her head was damaged at she thought this was a good idea. "He's a good man. H ll take care of you and keep you safe. You have no re son to dismiss him that way."

Then, Parson saw the way she shattered ben th the weight of his words. She already looked awful—b daged and bruised and struggling to stand—and now he made her feel even worse. He rejected her yet again, o ly this time there would be no going back.

He was at a loss. He didn't know what to do, ow to salvage the situation.

"Raene—"

"No." She shook her head as the first of man angry tears rolled down her cheeks. With her good ha d, she attempted to wipe them away, but the effort wa futile. More and more tears streamed down her face, drip ing off her chin and staining the moss-green tunic she wore Parson could only watch her with profound guilt, each fal n tear an arrow through his heart.

"I know you didn't come see me because y u feel responsible." She spoke to the floor, hiding her ce. "I know you think you'll let me get hurt again."

Parson stood still, impaled by her words. He id feel responsible. That guilt *had* kept him away. And e *was* terrified of failing her again. But he couldn't tell h r that. She had to change her mind. Hale deserved that muc .

"I didn't come see you because Hale is a go d man

and—"

"Stop saying that!" Her gaze was as pointed as a spear. Her mouth was tight with fury. Every ounce of her shook with it. "You say that like I don't know him. I *know* he's a good man. But you are, too. I was given the responsibility of choosing, and you're my choice. So you can either accept it or not. That part is up to you." And then, exhausted from yelling, Raene wavered.

Parson was barely there in time to catch her by the arm, lowering her to sit on the floor. She was a mess of tears and bruises and screams, but still she managed to captivate him. In the face of Hale's heartbreak and Parson's rejection, she continued to fight, to voice her decision despite the consequences. Had the roles been reversed, Parson didn't know if he could have done it.

He had to give her credit for that much at least.

Sinking beside her, Parson put a hand on her head and stroked her hair, willing her to calm before she injured herself more. "I'm sorry. I shouldn't have encouraged you to go hunting. I shouldn't have taken you so far from camp. I shouldn't have tried to interfere with you and Hale. But you know this can't work. All we do is fight and hurt each other, and last time you nearly died. I'm no good for you."

Raene listened, and when she had better control of her voice, she said, "You're not going to change my mind. If I wanted Hale, I would have said his name. If you don't want me, send me back."

Parson sat in stunned silence. In her state, barely able to stand, she was giving him an ultimatum. To have her as his wife or not at all. He'd never see her again.

Like his mother and Blossom before, Parson was going to lose her.

He could choose the certain loss of Raene, or the probable loss of Hale.

It would never be the same after this. They would

never recover. Maybe in months or years they coul find a new sort of trust, but either way, Hale would alwa s hate him for this.

It was a risk he was going to have to take.

With his hand in her hair, it was easy to pull her against his shoulder and kiss the crown of he head. "You're entirely too difficult, you know that?"

And then, in an instant, she spun. Her arm s were around his neck and her chest was pressed to hi as he clutched her as tight as he dared. Her elbow dug into the wound on his shoulder, but he didn't dare push her away now. He'd only just now gotten her.

She was his—entirely, completely his. No more arguing over who she would pick or wondering if ie was interfering. Her mind was made and the rest of the could only deal with it.

Parson's heart thumped out its excitement loud and fast. He tried not to squeeze her too hard—there was almost no where he could touch her without finding an inju y—but Parson couldn't help but hold her against him. The last time he held her this way, she was nearly dead as he tuc ed her into his totem form. Now, she was alive, real, his.

He could have exploded with the joy of it.

"Are you sure? Entirely sure?" he couldn't help but ask. It was too surreal, too impossible.

She didn't answer, but instead, she continued squeezing his neck, and Parson let her, completely willing to let her melt against him. They could sort the est out later.

"I guess that means we'll be having a celebration tonight?" Parson had no idea when Da had appeared inside the tent, but he stood there with an eager grin.

Raene pulled away from Parson and laughed, wiping at her tear-stained cheeks yet again. Parson had to help her to her feet, but once up, they both agreed.

"Then, Ms. Randal, I think it's time we make you a Frane."

Raene cringed and laughed all at once. She felt awful, and probably would for several days, but there was the relief of having made her choice—the right choice—coupled with the excitement of getting married.

Sure, her wedding would be nothing like she'd pictured. There would be no lavish party, no wealthy guests, no elite political connections to impress. She wouldn't wear a scarlet dress with beads and embroidery. Her arms wouldn't don rubies or diamonds or onyx. She wouldn't sip the finest strawberry wine from long-stemmed glasses.

Battered and bruised and clad in Terra clothes, she had envisioned a thousand likelier possibilities, but this was the one she would have. She couldn't have been happier.

Only the mention of her new name gave her pause. She would be a Frane.

Mrs. Parson Frane.

Raene Frane.

And she'd thought Corson Porsten was bad.

"I'll make the arrangements. For now, let's make it official." Da produced a folded slip of paper, sealed with Kaide's mark. Without ceremony, Da popped it open and spread it across his table. The writing was Da's more slanted script, but the words were Kaide's. There was an undeniable formality to them, a recognizable cadence he used when he was putting on his best airs.

And it was so incredibly long. Raene had never seen a marriage contract before—her own or otherwise—but there were so many conditions, she didn't have time to read them all. Kaide had put great thought and care into this document.

It made Raene's heart bubble with happiness.

Da handed Parson a quill to sign his name at the top, and Raene did the same. Then, Raene watched in awe as Da produced a knife and cut Parson's thumb. Beside his scrawled name, Parson left his bloodied thumbprint.

A second later, Da held out his hand for Raene's. When she hesitated, he said, "It seals the contract with the most secure of bonds. So there is no question."

Raene extended her broken arm and watched with sick amusement as Da punctured her thumb. She didn' feel a thing, a bad sign, she knew. Still, Raene worked her thumb up toward her name and left her mark beside it.

It was done.

"And now, for the good part." Da smiled as he folded the document and took his place at the center of the tent. "Raene, my child, you'll be here on the right. And on, on my left." Da pointed to their positions.

Parson grabbed her good hand with his as they stood before Da. Her hands shook as the reality settled in. She was getting married. To Parson. Who drove her mad. And she was so ecstatic, it didn't seem possible. If not for Parson's hands holding hers, she might have thought she had simply imagined it all.

And when she looked up at those burning emerald eyes, when she saw the consuming smile he couldn't hide, Raene knew she'd made the right choice. She ached all over, and her head swam, but in all the mess, this one thing was really, truly right.

From his pocket, Da produced a small alder wood box, inlayed with lighter oak and darker walnut, depicting the sacred tree and her many branches. When he opened it, he held it out so she could see the dozen rings inside.

"For our new daughter," Da explained, his voice dripping with pride.

Raene covered her mouth as she took in the sight of so many rings. Surely they weren't all for her?

But as she soon learned, they were. Parson held the box with a sweet smile, his eyes glistening, as Da slid each ring onto her fingers. "The first is for the Mother, may she guide and protect you." Raene received a ring that was identical to the one Hale had given her. The sight of it shot her clean through with guilt, but she forced herself to nod and wait for the next.

"The second is for the spirits, so that we remember their sacrifice." He showed her the thirteen tree carvings before he slid the alder wood ring onto the middle finger of her useless hand.

"The third is for the Alderwood, the Mother's gift to her devoted children." Raene bit back a groan and nodded. On and on it went, a ring for the Bear Clan, a ring for being a daughter of the clan leader, a ring for her future children. Raene watched her fingers fill with wood and iron and silver, but only the last ring gave her pause.

"And this one, my daughter, is the first of its kind. Traditionally, daughters receive a ring in honor of their home. For you, I commissioned this one of lava stone, and here," he pointed to a tiny carving, "the black griffin of your clan." Da had barely slid it onto her finger before she threw her arms around his neck.

"Thank you, Da. Truly. It's perfect." Da stiffened at her unexpected embrace, but he melted a second later. In all her life, Raene had never felt more like a daughter.

Raene returned to her position after the breach in protocol and admired her hands, as full of rings as they were. Individually, they were light, but all together, the rings felt heavy. Their different surfaces caught the light in a dozen different ways, each beautiful in its own right. Had she not known better, she'd have thought they were the hands of a Terra.

"And now, for Parson's ring." Da held out his hand to Parson in wait. "Terra men choose one woman to receive their ring, and that woman wears it as a sign of their alliance."

Parson shook his head, a deep regret in his eyes

"Very well." Da smiled but the hang in his shoulders told her that wasn't the way it was supposed to go. Still, Da made no mention of it again. Instead, he pulled a long moss-green ribbon from his pocket. It looked to have once been a shimmering satin, but age and wear had dulled it considerably. He held it as if it was the most precious thing in the world.

"This ribbon was first used to bind the hands of my wife and I under the Mother's grace. It was used for Lathan and Tasia, and now, for you."

Da pulled the ribbon around their clasped hands and began to weave it around their forearms. Raene was grateful it was her good, unbroken arm, free of bandages.

Then Da stood back, arms crossed as he admired his handiwork.

"That's it?" Raene whispered to Parson.

But he only laughed. "Not exactly. There's still the walk." A second later, Da held open the tent flap as Parson and Raene emerged into the clearing. She blinked at the sudden brightness, but once she could open her eyes fully, she gaped in awe.

Where before the clearing had been all but empty, now it was full. Lining either side of their path were the clan members, each and every one of them, and in their hands, a ribbon—some green, some brown, some old, and some never used.

"We're just supposed to nod. Don't saying anything. It's bad luck," Parson whispered.

Standing nearest Da's tent, Lathan stepped forward with a ribbon and tied it around their already-bound hands.

He looked a little misty-eyed as he said, "May the Mother guide you."

Tasia arrived at his side and placed a loving hand on his arm. A moment later, she held out her own ribbon and tied it around their hands. "May the Mother keep you."

Gemini was next with her beaming smile and a scarlet ribbon. "For the Pyro princess," she whispered. "May the Mother watch you."

Beside her, Asla held a muddy-brown ribbon. Tying it around the growing knot, he said, "May the Mother defend you."

On and on they went, receiving ribbons from Endel, Tanner, Loren, and all the other young men she'd met at the trade. After that, Yaiza, Cresta, and every other face Raene had come to know—and a few she still hadn't. Each blessing secured their hands in yet another knot until Raene knew it would be quite the task to get them all off.

But Raene cared not a bit about it. She was walking beside Parson, her hand squeezed tight in his, and they were married by the laws of Terra. She fulfilled her duty to Kaide and Blossom, but more than that, she had a husband who cherished her.

He was a bumbling oaf who said the wrong thing at every opportunity, and he could drive her mad like no one else, but he also made her laugh harder and run faster and dig deeper into who she was than anyone ever had. He saw past her demure smiles and batted eyes. Parson wouldn't let her live a quiet life. He would keep her challenged, and Raene was excited for that more than anything else.

At the end of the line, Raene's excitement faded into nerves, regret, and guilt. Hale stood tall with a brown ribbon in his hands. As if she hadn't ripped out his heart only moments before, Hale tied his ribbon around the considerable bunch of knots and said, "May the Mother protect you."

Raene wanted to stay, to tell him how utterly sorry she was, but Parson pulled her toward his tent. It wasn't the time or place for that conversation, she knew. Those wounds would take years to heal, if they ever really did.

For the last stretch, Raene and Parson walked alone. He looked at her with such emotion in his eyes, Raene's cheeks flushed with color.

Then his features darkened. "I'm sorry I don't have a ring to give you—"

Raene tilted forward to kiss his lips, silencing his futile apology. When she pulled away, she told him, "I know you gave it to Darsa. So your child would have something to know you by."

His mouth fell open so fast she burst out laughing. "Besides, I don't need a ring. I have *all these*." Raene chuckled as she held up her bandaged hand, revealing a half-dozen rings symbolizing all sorts of things she couldn't remember.

Parson rolled his eyes and kissed her forehead. "It should be a perfect day for you. I'm sorry I can't give you more than this."

Raene softened under his gaze, apologetic and adoring as it was. "It's just right. I wouldn't have it any other way."

Parson kissed her cheeks sweetly. She smiled through her nerves and kissed his shoulder as they arrived.

For the first time, Raene entered Parson's tent a dark and mostly-empty space with a floor covered in linens and blankets from the usual Terra color pallet. No sooner were they inside than they were ambushed by a tiny creature.

"Sorry, this is Fig," Parson explained as he scooped up the slender rodent, rubbing a thumb over its tiny head.

"What is it?" Raene had never seen such a creature, like a stretched-out mouse with strange little hands. It was cute in an odd sort of way.

Parson set the animal on Raene's shoulders as she

laughed, his feet tickling her as he walked. "A ferret. He was Blossom's…" Parson collected the animal and set him back on the floor. "Sorry, I should have warned you. Well, uh, this is it, I guess." He held out his hand toward the interior of his tent.

A few candles sat around the edges, none of them lit, and between them, a few boxes of clothes and food. On the far side, a half-dozen bows leaned against the canvas, along with a handful of quivers already full of arrows.

"It's not much—" he started.

"Let me guess, you've been too busy hunting to decorate?" Raene's laughter was sucked clean out of her when Parson spun and kissed her. His free hand clutched at her head and held her near as his lips consumed hers. With one hand tied to his and the other entirely useless, Raene could do nothing but stand idle and kiss him back. The motion and excitement and sheer joy of it sent her head reeling.

And then it was over.

"Let's get you down. Come on. That's enough excitement for one day." Like she was nothing more than a child, Parson lowered her to his pallet on the floor. It wasn't as comfortable as her bed in the manor, but it was better than the ground or the cot or anywhere else she'd slept recently. As before, she lay on her side, keeping the worst of her injuries off the floor.

With their hands still joined, Parson lay in front of her, his eyes even with hers. There was a smile, a glow to him she was sure hadn't been there before, and it made her want to bask in it forever.

"I can't believe you did that." Parson's free hand skated across her cheek. His fingertips were warm and electric, and Raene couldn't help but close her eyes at that little touch. "I never thought—I mean, I wanted it. I wanted this, but—" He gingerly skimmed the swollen purple lump on her cheek before moving to the thick bandage on her neck, and down to her arm. It wasn't tied to his, but it was no more useful. Raene couldn't feel it, move it. She could only watch as he touched what little tips of her knuckles that stuck out from the end of the bandaged splint. "It just seemed impossible."

Raene tilted forward and kissed his cheek again. It really was sweet to see him try to talk, utterly failing as he was. "Obviously not impossible," she teased him.

"Raene, even before we were attacked, you were with Hale. You wore his rings, you slept in his tent. I knew what I wanted, but I knew I was too late. And then when you were hurt—" Parson paused with his eyes distant, his brow furrowed. "You were so brave," he whispered.

"I just defended myself." Raene didn't feel brave. She felt like an idiot. She'd provoked a coyote for no reason and paid the price for it.

Parson pressed closer, so close his breath warmed her cheek. "Raene, you have to see how incredible you were. If you hadn't fallen—" His hand moved from her shoulder down her arm, or at least she assumed it did. She couldn't feel it, she couldn't peel her eyes from his to look. Raene was unwilling to miss a single moment of those eyes.

Raene pressed her forehead against the soft skin of his neck and basked in the warmth of his embrace. She didn't want to talk about all the ways they'd wronged each other or all the things that could have gone better or worse. "It doesn't matter. You brought me back, Hale and Gemini patched me up, and here we are."

Parson groaned. "It matters. I never meant for you to get hurt. We were set up by the Pyro traders." He sighed, long and slow, as he worked to get his words out. And once he did, they haunted her. "I'm going to kill the Alderai and any coyote that sets foot in the Alderwood. I swear, they're going to pay for this." His pulse thumped loudly in her ear, and all at once, Raene realized she'd heard that same racing, rhythmic pounding before.

"Gemini said you brought me back in your totem."

"I had no choice," he said in a clipped tone.

"I didn't know you could do that."

In answer, Parson's fingers crept into her hair, curling in and massaging her scalp, a move he knew would calm her. "It's not supposed to work. Sometimes with kids, a parent can transition to keep them safe, but sometimes it just kills them. You were—I thought—"

"You thought I was going to die, so it was worth the risk." Gemini had told her as much. She would have given anything to have a single working hand to stroke his rugged cheek but instead, she was left to try to explain. "I'm glad you did it. I remember—" But that wasn't it. She stopped and tried to figure out what she was trying to say. "It felt like this. I could hear your heartbeat. You were warm—"

"I was running," he said, like that explained everything. "I had to—"

Raene nodded against his neck. "I know." And then lower, quieter, she whispered, "I know."

BONDED

"**Y**OU SHOULD EAT," Eton fussed.

Blossom shook her head. She couldn't eat. She wasn't hungry. Any food she ate would immediately come right back up.

She had never been more nervous or terrified or excited in all her life. She was in freefall, spinning toward the ground, waiting for the inevitable, terrible impact.

Today, she was going to see Kaide.

Blossom had no idea how long she'd get to see him, if she'd get to talk to him or not, but in the span of a second, he would see what she'd become.

He would know she was alive.

He would know she was Aero.

But he wouldn't know that he still occupied her every thought, both asleep and awake, and that she wanted nothing more than disappear with him to the manor and never see Aerona again.

That was her mission today. Find a way to tell him. He could work out the rest on his own.

"Seriously," Eton continued, his endless fussing more grating today than usual. "The meetings can last a whole day. If you don't eat now, you might not get another chance."

Blossom pushed up from the table in response, and Eton followed her to the door. They were both perfectly polished and put together. They wore their masks of calm serenity, but Blossom knew they were both apprehensive about what would transpire today.

For Eton, it was the first time he would be present during formal Syndicate affairs. For Blossom, she was going to show the man she loved that she had become one of his enemies.

She couldn't think about it. She could think about nothing else.

"Would you like to ask the Apprentice Vice Syndicate to walk with us?" Eton offered.

"Yes, thank you." Blossom had to work extra hard to maintain her measured formality. She stood aside as Eton knocked and discussed their travel arrangements with Herson.

Five minutes later, Yveline Dodd emerged with a luminous smile. Not a hair was out of place, and her cloak fit her every curve. "Miss Blossom, I'm thrilled we'll be attending the Syndicate Council together." Yveline gripped both Blossom's hands in hers and squeezed, the only indication her sentiment was genuine.

For the first time, Blossom saw Yveline's mask. In her apartment, she'd been open and vibrant. Here, she was all smiles and manners, but these niceties were fake.

Everyone was a false version of themselves today.

"I'm so looking forward to traveling to the capital city," Blossom purred, mirroring Yveline's easy cadence.

Together, Yveline and Blossom filed into the elevator, each flanked by their advisor. They chatted happily as the made their way to the Robin—thankfully the ride was brief, for her stomach was already in knots—then to the portals. Only there did they separate.

Eton and Blossom entered one portal room while

Yveline and Herson took the next. "I don't suppose you can refrain from soiling my shirt this time?" he asked when they were alone in the too-small room.

Blossom forced a smile as he inserted the coin. "I didn't eat, remember? You should be thankful I'm at least kind enough to do you that small favor." She closed her eyes and leaned against the wall, picturing Kaide standing over her, one arm planted on the wall on either side of her. He would hold her, kiss her, run his hands over her figure—whatever it took to keep her distracted during the awful spinning.

"Seriously? Again?" Blossom opened her eyes to find Eton kneeling beside her. She was sitting on the floor with her back against the wall, knees pulled up to her chest.

She didn't remember sitting down.

"Are you back now?" Eton asked, his brow creased with a rare display of worry.

"I didn't go anywhere," Blossom argued, pushing him back so she could stand. She ran her hands over her cloak to smooth out any wrinkles.

"Are you that nervous?"

"I don't know what you mean," she lied.

"Yes, you do." Eton was quick to call her bluff. "Are you sure you can do this?"

"I'm fine. Stop fussing."

"I'll stop fussing when you stop drifting off. You can't afford that kind of slip up in there. The Syndicates and Vice Syndicates will all be there. Even the Alderai. You need to be focused."

Blossom nodded and took a good deep breath for strength. Eton was right. Regardless of her feelings for Kaide, she needed to be alert. Mercer was only one of the critical players in the realm's politics.

Satisfied she was ready, Eton opened the door and led her out into the lobby. The last time she saw those shimmering alabaster tiles, she was in Eton's grip, being manhandled all the way to the portal room. She'd been a falcon only moments before, the last time she'd let her wings spread wide.

So much had happened since then.

Yveline and Herson stood waiting in the lobby. "There you are!" Yveline cooed, linking arms with Blossom once more.

Blossom focused on her breathing. She tried to calm the horrible pounding pulse in her ears and soothe her stomach as it threatened to claw its way out her throat. She was an elevator ride away from seeing Kaide.

She was really going to pass out this time.

Eton slipped a hand around her elbow, squeezing too tight for comfort, but it was just enough to keep her grounded. She'd have to remember to thank him later.

With the warped clarity of a dream, Blossom walked the long hall arm in arm with Yveline. Eton released her elbow at the massive metal doors that stood taller than three men and were engraved with a delicate pattern on their shimmering surface. Such doors had all the weight and presence of the Syndicate.

This was it.

Ignorant of her apprehension, Herson pulled open the doors, producing an ominous groan. With all the elegance demanded by their positions, Yveline and Blossom entered the Syndicate Council Chamber, a circular room broken into four quadrants. At its center was round table with four chairs, one for each Syndicate, though only the Hydra and Terra Syndicates were already seated. At the next level, a few steps higher, were three chairs for the branch Vice Syndicates. Behind them, chairs for the five branch Commissioners, though Blossom knew they wouldn't be in attendance today.

Illuminated screens ringed the perimeter of the room,

and on every one, the topic of today's meeting: The rentis.

Blossom's stomach dropped out from under her

She turned to Eton long enough to know he saw it. When she looked to him a moment longer, he sh ok his head ever so slightly. They would discuss it later. F r now, they were on display for the realm's most power ul and influential politicians.

Eager to keep her emotions hidden, Blossom ried to look like she was merely admiring the general s ze and splendor of the space—truly it was magnificent—bu really, she was looking for Kaide. He was taller than mo t, with dark hair and a perfect black cloak. It should ha e been easy to spot him, but Blossom couldn't. She breathe easier at being spared his hatred a few moments longer.

Blossom could only wait.

At least Yveline didn't seem to notice her dist action. Blossom stuck close to her friend as they moved al ut the room, reintroducing her to the Vice Syndicates she h d only met in passing at the Spring Ceremony. Eton and Herson maintained their positions a few steps behir l, but otherwise, they didn't interfere.

The two young women formally greeted Jin N na and Zuni Bartel, both older Vice Syndicates of the Terra ranch. After that came Unsel Gould, the only Pyro Vice Sy idicate currently present, and one of the few Blossom hadn't already met. She forced a smile to the Hydr Vice Syndicate Tead Iolla as she wondered if his wife was at home tending to the injuries he often inflicted. The made sure to offer Syndicate Mercer a public greeting as her position demanded, a show of allegiance and suppo in the midst of representatives of the other branches.

Together, Blossom and Yveline made the r way around the room, plying the realm's leading litical figures with their fake smiles and batted eyes. And to Blossom's amazement, it wasn't as awful as she e ected.

She kept her mask on, pushing back thoughts of Kaide, working to stay focused on her current company. Only one managed to compromise her practiced calm.

"What a lovely pair you two make," Castor offered with the warmest of smiles.

Blossom choked back the urge to gag. He was so eager to fill her ear with compliments each time they met.

Two could play that game.

"How fortunate to see you again, Vice Syndicate Castor. How are you finding life in Terrana? I'm sure it's lovely this time of year." Blossom had never personally visited Terrana, but as the home of the Alderai, she knew it would have alder trees aplenty. This close to summer, they would be in full bloom, a luscious pink canopy. She envied he should get to see it while she was stuck in the underground of Aerona.

"Not half as lovely as you, Vice Syndicate Frane. I hope you'll accept my invitation to visit later in the season. I'm sure you'll be due some sunlight after so much time in the dreariness of those tunnels." Blossom managed to smile. Not a fake one, but a real one. Even for Lota Castor, the lowest of the low. He seemed the only one who understood her imprisonment.

A loud groan sounded.

Castor's eyes shifted to something behind her. Someone.

Blossom turned in time to see Kaide entering the Council Chambers. At his side, the other Pyro Vice Syndicate, Pruda Swain. A viper, Blossom remembered.

But she had no time to think of the woman. Instead, she could only see Kaide. He wore his usual Vice Syndicate expression, as solid as stone. His hair was perfect, as it always had been, and his cloak was smooth black luxury. Even from across the room, Blossom could see his mouth move as he whispered to his colleague. His eyes scanned the room, taking measure of each and every person.

His gaze sailed right over Blossom and kept moving. A half-second later, he stopped walking. He stopped talking. He only stared at her. Frozen. For an eternal moment, he took in the sight of her, from her straight, half-shaved hair to the metal piercing in her nose, from the opalescent cloak to the absence of his ring on her finger.

Kaide saw it all.

Blossom covered her mouth with her hand to keep from saying the words she so desperately wanted to tell him. This was a snake pit and she was a mouse. Her eyes welled with tears as she saw him go rigid with anger. With disgust.

It was as bad as she feared.

So long she'd clung to that dire hope that somehow Kaide would see past the color of her cloak and still want the woman beneath. Now she knew it had been a fool's dream.

His eyes seared her with their hatred.

Blossom felt her cheeks go hot with disappointment and shame. Rejection cut her like the edge of a too-sharp knife.

Kaide lowered his gaze at last, his eyes focused on the floor in front of him. His hands clenched into fists, and all at once Blossom realized what was happening.

Just the sight of her had pushed Kaide to transition. He collapsed forward as muscles erupted across his shoulders. His legs and spine lengthened until he stood well above the others, even on all fours. The dark grey fur she so loved sprouted across his every surface. His lovely bearded face elongated into the snout of a wolf with teeth bared.

Eton appeared before her in a flash, positioning himself between Blossom and her beast.

The crowd hushed in an instant. Kaide's beast form silenced the most powerful people in the realm. They all stared up at him in horrified awe, waiting to see who he would kill first.

Castor was only a few steps to Blossom's right, Yveline a half-step behind her. Mercer and the Pyro Syndicate Reva Mora stood at least twenty paces to the left. The Pyro Vice Syndicate Pruda Swain was alone behind Kaide, frozen in fear. She had no idea what to do.

None of them did.

There was no telling who Kaide would strike first. But Blossom refused to let Kaide become a murderer, to give up his life and his career. She stepped around Eton only to feel his iron grip on her wrist. "Let me go!" she protested.

Eton would have none of it. He squeezed her tighter. "He's going to kill someone. You have to get back."

"He won't hurt me," she argued, hoping it was true. There was a time she knew it with certainty. Now, she couldn't be sure.

But Eton wouldn't release her.

A long, angry howl resounded off the stone walls of the chamber, near-deafening in its intensity. In his beast form, Kaide sniffed the air, searching. They had mere seconds.

"I need you to trust me." Blossom glared at Eton with all the fire she possessed. At last, his fingers loosened their grip.

She didn't hesitate. Blossom lunged forward, planting herself between beast-Kaide and the realm's politicians. She was only steps away from him, close enough to feel the warmth of every ragged breath from his beast mouth.

She'd almost forgotten the enormity of his totem. Her head didn't even reach his shoulder. As she had the first time, Blossom stood in awe. How she had missed him.

"Get back!" someone shouted behind her.

"He'll kill her," another screamed.

Hisses and growls sounded over her shoulder where

some of the braver elites had transitioned, ready to pounce if he should take so much as a step near them.

But Blossom had no time for them. She was here for Kaide. She'd always been here for Kaide.

"Hello, Beast," she said, her voice low. She knew he could hear even that small sound with his wolf ears.

Beast-Kaide lowered his head and flared his nostrils, sniffing the air around her, measuring her. She wondered what he could smell. The chemical in her hair that stole her curls? The metal bracelet that kept her from transitioning? The nervous sweat trickling down her back?

Taking his inaction as a good sign, Blossom dared a step forward. This time, he growled, baring his teeth, but she wouldn't be dissuaded. If he was going to kill her, a few steps wouldn't make a difference.

Blossom neared enough to dip her hands into the rich, thick fur along his neck. Had she a blade, she could have killed him then. Maybe that's what the others thought she was doing. But Kaide and Blossom both knew better. She melted against his charcoal-grey coat and breathed in the ashy scent of him.

"I'm so sorry Kaide," she whispered, unsure how much would get through in his totem form. "I'm with you. I'm always with you." She cherished such proximity to the totem form of the man she wanted to marry. These weeks of absence had only made her want him more.

The low, rumbling purr in his throat almost made her think he understood her. Then, she realized he wasn't purring. He was growling.

Before she could say another word, he pulled away. His fur fell away in a thick cloud and his shoulders shrank until only the human form stood before her.

Kaide's deep blue eyes drank her in. He was close enough to reach out and touch her, but he didn't. Instead, he turned on his heel and marched right out the massive metal doors.

Eton's hand was on her arm before she could move. "You're mad, you know that?"

Blossom could only nod. It probably looked that way. They probably all thought she was crazy and Kaide was dangerous, but they couldn't have been more wrong.

"Please let me go," she asked him quietly, her eyes still on the space where she'd last seen Kaide. "I'll come back. I'll do the meeting. I won't be gone more than five minutes. But please, let me go."

To her everlasting shock, he did.

Ignoring the crowd of eyes that never left her, Blossom maintained her decorum long enough to slip through the doors. Once out of sight of the Syndicates, she broke into a full run. Bypassing the elevator, Blossom bolted down the stairs—all eleven flights of them. When she reemerged in the lobby, sweating and out of breath, she managed to catch sight of him entering the hall of portal doors.

And Blossom knew just which door he would take. She hitched up the heavy cloak and ran as fast as her feet could carry her, stopping long enough to throw open the door to the hall before she jogged to find the portal room. Number 413. The only one he ever used.

Blossom pulled open the door. This was it. She had so much to tell him.

But her heart sank when she saw the empty portal room. He was already back in Pyrona, on his way to the manor.

She was too late. She didn't have a chance to explain.

The entire Syndicate council had just watched her run to him, watched Kaide transition and threaten them. There would be no going back after this. Blossom and Kaide had sealed their fates. They'd both exposed themselves horribly, and it was all for nothing.

Kaide was gone.

She'd lost him.

Parson laid in his tent beside Raene—*his wife*—and savored his new reality. With his hand still tied to hers, he could do nothing more than watch her sleep, listening to the light inhales and exhales that matched the warm breaths she cast across his chest.

She needed the sleep, he knew. A head injury of that caliber would take weeks to fully mend, not to mention the wounds on her neck, her arm, her back. Unwilling to disturb her, Parson was trapped there. Not that he minded. He chalked it up to one of the top three best experiences of his life.

And he needed that time. It had all happened so fast, it was so impossible. Parson had never allowed himself to really believe she would choose him. She was too invested with Hale, and he with her. So Parson spent those precious hours next to Raene letting it all sink in. The stunning Pyro girl who appeared in his clan in exchange for his sister was now his wife. She had the most powerful totem he'd ever seen, and it radiated out of her even in her human form. She had that energy and fire that kept him drawn to her, even when he tried to keep away.

His mother had been right all along. Blossom was gone, but something strong had grown in her place. Parson was just too dense to see it right away.

Despite his bliss, there was so much left that ate at him. Thoughts of how he would deal with the Anderai's attack. How he would deal with Hale's understandable hatred. How he would help Raene heal from her injuries, particularly the arm she still couldn't feel. Even Parson knew that was a bad sign.

But Parson pushed it to the back of his mind. Today

wasn't a day for such thoughts. It was his wedding day, and while it was a far cry from what anyone would have expected, he wouldn't sour it for her. Raene deserved to have a good day—or as good as possible, given the circumstances.

She finally woke sometime in early evening, breathing in a big yawning inhale before batting open her sapphire eyes. Already, he could see she'd improved. Her eyes were brighter, her skin less dull. On reflex, she tried to move her hand but found it tied to Parson's. A sunny smile erupted across her features. "Did you lay here all day?"

"Couldn't exactly escape," he teased, pushing back a stray lock of golden hair. "Ready to get these off?"

Raene nodded and let him help her sit up. Her eyes darkened with momentary dizziness, and Parson remembered the vial in his pocket. He opened it and held it out to her. "Gemini brought this by. Said it would help clear your head for a day or so."

She attempted to grasp it but couldn't manage it in either hand. Instead, she opened her mouth and let Parson pour it in. Then he set to work on the bundle of knots. Traditionally, the new couple would work as a pair to remove the ribbons, but with Raene's broken arm, it was left to Parson to do it. He didn't mind, but a part of him felt like she'd been robbed of that experience.

The first to come off was the brown one bestowed by Hale. Parson was all too happy to remove it, eager to leave thoughts of what he'd done to his brother behind. There would be a time to deal with that, but not now.

"I'm assuming these have some sort of symbolic significance." Raene watched his fingers work though the next knot.

Parson nodded, not really sure he wanted to explain it. When she shot him a look, he knew he wouldn't get out of it. "They represent a bond—" He tried to remember the words his mother had told him so long ago, when h 'd tied a knot around the joined hands of a couple at only s < years old. "They bind us together until we are bonded be ore the Alder Mother."

"Bonded?"

"Consummated." Parson kept his eyes on the ri bons.

Raene smiled an amused little grin. "So ever one in the clan knows when new couples have—"

"That's the idea." Parson chuckled at the absu dity of it.

Raene's cheeks flushed with color. "In yrona, wealthy families display the blood stain on the shee . A lot of them don't do it anymore, but technically you're supposed to."

"Is that what you were going to do?" Parson c uldn't imagine someone as refined as Raene subjected t airing her soiled bed linens.

Raene only shrugged. "I don't know. Depends n who I married, I guess. Some of the families were pretty traditional."

"Well here in the modesty of Terra, you're sp ed the bedsheets," Parson offered dramatically. "But you o have to deal with this mess of ribbons."

"Well either I slept a lot harder than I thought, Raene replied, mirroring his tone. "Or you really shoul n't be taking them off."

Parson managed a low chuckle. "I didn't tou h you. And I'm not going to until you're ready. A few ays at least. I think you deserve a little leeway after what I ut you through." He was lucky she was alive and that she as his, and he wouldn't push his luck asking for more. He efused to mention the torture of sleeping beside her evel night until then and *not* touching her.

Raene squeezed his fingers where they re nained intertwined with hers.

Parson shook his head and refocused on his task. "No." It wasn't up for discussion. She might as well ask him to kick her in the face or light her on fire. It was simply not going to happen.

"Parson."

"I said *no*."

"Parson," she said louder this time.

Again, he shook his head. "I'm not going to hurt you again. You're still healing—"

"You're not going to hurt me," she insisted.

Parson huffed out an aggravated sigh. "Raene. Listen. It will hurt. It always hurts the first time. That's why there's blood on the sheets." Between her previous status as a Pyro princess and his certainty Hale would never try it, Parson was confident Raene was pure. And he wasn't going to put her through even an ounce of pain. Not today.

Raene remained silent while he finished removing the ribbons, sparing him yet another argument. They'd been married less than a day and already they were disagreeing. At last, Parson untied the last ribbon, the moss-green one that had bound his parents together. Raene pulled her hand away and flexed her fingers, feeling the stretch and movement in them for the first time since their wedding hours before.

Then she lunged at him. Raene struck him so hard he fell over, his back striking the ground painfully. Supported only by her one good hand, Raene centered her face over his and grinned a wicked, salacious grin at him.

Parson could only stare up at her wide-eyed, his heart pounding. The desire to touch every ounce of her and his determination to keep from hurting her put him in grave conflict.

She straddled his hips and hovered in glory above him, silhouetted by what little evening light slipped through the tent flap. When she collapsed over him, it wasn't to kiss him. Instead, her lips fell to his neck, nipping at the soft flesh under his ear. Parson groaned against her assault.

"Raene—" he managed to croak, but her hand was on his chest, her nails sinking into his shirt and offering just a hint of pain.

"Just shut up for once," she purred in his ear. Then she sat up again, and tugged at the bottom of her tunic top, working with her one good hand to yank it over her head.

And to his shame, Parson helped her do it. That green monstrosity never suited her anyway. Bare-chested above him, Parson couldn't help but let his eyes catch on the bandage on her neck, the pair on her right shoulder, the edges of white gauze that curled around her sides. He didn't want to see her back. The left side of her torso was little more than a continues purple contusion, marred with black or sickly yellow in some places. But on her bruised face, she wore a playful smile. She was excited but nervous, too.

Parson knew he had lost. She was too stubborn, too brave, too insatiable.

He wouldn't disappoint her yet again. He placed a hand on each of her hips, rubbing his thumbs across her smooth flesh. She couldn't have known how he had imagined this moment, always as an impossible dream, and now it was here, actually happening. She was really his.

He didn't deserve her.

That didn't stop him from pushing up and catching her mouth with his, bracing against the ground with both hands. He wanted nothing more than to throw her to the floor and have his way with her, but she was still injured, still too frail for such an endeavor. So Parson let her go as fast or slow as she wanted, as she could. He didn't pull her against him. He didn't pin her to the ground just to watch her squirm. Instead, he helped her remove whichever article of clothing she deemed unnecessary. He supported her weight when her arm grew tired. He kissed every ounce of flesh that came close enough. And in the eyes of the Alder Mother, Parson made Raene his wife.

Hale could think of absolutely nothing he'd rather do less than attend a celebration for Raene and Parson's wedding. Literally nothing.

On the outside, he was the same Hale as always. He made sure of it. He was calm, collected, maybe a bit more lost in thought than usual, but he refused to let his wounds show on the surface.

He wouldn't lash out like Parson. He wouldn't run.

Hale had more integrity than that. He had put on a brave face and tied the ribbons around their joined hands as was expected of every clan member, Hale included.

But there was no denying the tempest raging inside him. He'd been shattered, trampled by a stampeding herd or hung like a carcass to be bled dry. There was nothing left in him. A gaping wound of the gravest kind.

For the life of him, Hale couldn't figure out where he'd gone wrong. He'd done what the Mother asked. He welcomed her into his clan, his tent, his life. He rubbed her back when she couldn't sleep and helped her cope with her violent totem.

Hale did everything in his power to keep her safe. And Parson had done everything to put her in danger. Sneaking off. Hunting. Leaving camp. Parson failed to protect her, and for that, he was rewarded with her selection. Parson had her as his wife, and Hale had nothing.

It didn't make a damn bit of sense.

And worse than that, he'd been wrong. For the first time in the five years since his transformation, his coin had failed to convey the Mother's plan. It was Hale who should have her for his bride. It was the Mother's will.

Hale didn't know what to believe, what to feel. He was so overcome with emotion he couldn't feel anything. He was numb, in shock, frozen, burned from the inside out.

None of it made sense. Not one shred of it.

With hands clasped tight at his chest, Hale lowered his head and prayed. The Mother had never led him astray. She had his undying faith and devotion, but Hale couldn't help but ask her why. He knew she wouldn't answer, that it was selfish of him to ask, but the temptation was too great. He clung to the hope that there was a simple explanation, a misunderstanding perhaps, but there was only silence, another test of his faith.

Midday came and went, followed by afternoon, and then evening. No one asked for his help setting up the celebration, and Hale didn't leave his tent to offer. How was he supposed to face them?

The entire clan knew. Every person he'd ever known had watched him court Raene. And now that they'd tied ribbons around Parson and Raene's hands after their wedding walk, the clan knew that Hale hadn't been chosen. Everyone knew Hale was second to Parson.

It was more humiliating than he could endure.

Hale worked to bury his pain, to tuck it away where it hardened and festered, out of sight but still sucking him dry from the inside.

By the time all traces of daylight were gone, festive music radiated from the central pit. They were the same songs he'd heard all his life, but now he couldn't stand to listen. Hale sat in his chair with his head buried in his hands, praying for it to end.

"I'm so sorry, Hale." Gemini's voice sounded inside his tent flap, but he didn't look up.

"Leave me alone." He didn't need to be anyone's spectacle.

"You look like you could use some company."

Hale flew to his feet and glared at her. She'd been a staple in his life for no other reason than Blossom. Hale had known Gemini since the day she was born, but never had he had reason to harbor anything but tolerance toward her. Now, he spewed all his pain and frustrations at her. "Get out."

He should have known she wouldn't listen.

Already clad in her ceremonial tunic, Gemini crossed the tent and stood before him, too close for comfort, searching his face. Hale didn't know what she wanted, but he let his gaze fall away. He didn't want her to see the pain in his eyes.

Gemini's arms were around his waist a moment later. She squeezed him so tight she all but forced the air from his lungs. For several seconds, Hale stood tall, unyielding, but he couldn't deny the appeal of what little comfort she could provide. So he buried his face in her black hair and breathed deeply, trying to stay the storm in his chest.

When she pulled back, she offered him a sad smile. "You deserve better."

They were precisely the words he needed to hear, the one thread of hope to which he could desperately cling. For a moment, it felt as if his hardened pain might have cracked, if only a little.

Hale pulled her in and kissed her temple. "You're a good girl, Gem." While the rest of his clan—including his family—spent the day celebrating the new couple, only Gemini had looked back toward Hale. Out of all of them, only Gemini thought of Hale. Even in his grief, Hale wouldn't fail to show his gratitude.

"Oh, I know it," she teased with a playful wink. In the dimness of his tent, Hale almost missed the redness under her eye.

"What happened here?" Hale gladly shifted into his medical mind, evaluating the injury for cause and

393

treatment. It was raised and red, like she'd been struck, but there was no laceration, so the object hadn't been sharp. The swelling indicated it was several hours old and hadn't been properly treated. Had she come to him sooner, he could have pressed a cool cloth to it to keep the swelling down.

Gemini put a hand over the spot. "Just being clumsy. I'm about to go get some wine and get even clumsier." A warm smile spread across her cheeks. "Will you be all right? Want me to bring you some?"

Hale shook his head. He didn't need to have his thoughts muddled any more than they already were. Prayer would guide him through this, not drink. Gemini knew she couldn't sway him. She offered him one last quick embrace before she left to join the celebration.

A part of him envied her simple life, her simple garden, her simple suitor. Nothing in Gemini's life was complicated, and when her friend was married, Gemini was happy. She celebrated with an open heart.

For Hale, it was more complex. He wanted Reene to be happy, but he thought it should be with him. He had no idea how he was supposed to go on with his life now that he'd failed so spectacularly.

He settled back into his chair and clasped his hands in front of his heart. And for the rest of the night, Hale prayed.

AMNESTY

"**Y**OU'RE GOING TO make us late to our own celebration," Raene teased, one hand held over her eyes as Parson insisted. She sat fully nude in his tent listening to the sounds of him rustling through one thing or another. She had no idea what he was up to.

"It'll be worth it, I promise," he said for the third or fourth time.

Raene only beamed in wait for her surprise. Gemini's tea had worked a small miracle. The pain in her head was all but gone, though that didn't help her other ailments. Her back ached from so much movement in the last few hours, and while her arm was no longer numb, a dull pain had taken up residence in her wrist. As time passed, it spread into her fingers and up toward her elbow. She knew by the end of the night, it would bother her considerably.

But for now, Raene was satisfied waiting for her husband to present her with whatever it was he had for her. When at last he said, "Open your eyes," Raene looked up at him with profound awe.

In his hands, Parson held a full Pyro outfit. A scarlet top with all the ties and a pair of wide-legged pants. None were shredded or stained or cut. They were perfect.

Tears pricked her eyes as she stared up at them.

"Where did you get those?"

"From the Pyro traders. Since all yours were ruined. Lathan just brought the bags back this morning. " He sank to the floor beside her and showed her the items up close. They weren't the fine clothes of the wealthy and elite of Pyrona, but they were Pyro clothes nonetheless. Raene had never received a greater gift.

"You'll have to tell me how to work this thing," Parson said as he laughed and held up the shirt by one of its many straps. "Unless you'd like to wear the ceremonial Terra tunic." He tossed his head in the direction of the moss-green bundle by the tent flap.

"Never." Raene had to rely entirely on Parson to get her shirt positioned and strapped into place appropriately. He held her pants out as she stepped in one foot at a time before he cinched in the waist strap. Already Raene felt better, felt more like herself. The strip of bare skin across her stomach was a welcome relief from the heavy Terra clothes she'd worn all day.

And she glowed with the idea of it. Even before they were married, before they were attacked by coyotes. Parson had actively sought out Pyro clothes for her. He didn't want her to be Terra any more than she did. With him in his ceremonial garb, with gold embroidery at his wrists, and Raene in a more common version of Pyro clothes, they looked quite the mismatched pair. But he was fire and so was she, and together they burned brighter.

"Are you ready, Mrs. Frane?" Parson picked her up by her waist and set her by the tent flap, a playful grin on his cheeks all the while.

"Why yes I am, Mr. Frane." Raene bowed low with respect as was expected of a lady of her birth. And, as she'd hoped, Parson laughed at how ridiculous she looked.

Then, as they had when they entered, Parson and Raene grasped the other's hand and strolled out into the dusk.

Already, music rode the wind, echoing between the trees and filling the Alderwood with festive energy. The lustrous flames of the central pit illuminated a large swath of the canopy overhead. As they neared, sounds of chatter and laughter emerged over the songs, and by the time they were within sight of the celebration, Raene knew it would be a good night.

Da was nearly drunk already, dancing wildly with a trio of eager middle-aged ladies. Gemini and Asla spun and giggled, and even Lathan was on his feet twirling his wife in an elegant maneuver. Raene squeezed Parson's hand with excitement.

"Just remember to take it easy," he reminded her. "You're still recovering."

Raene looked up at him and smiled. "Then let's have a dance before I'm too tired."

Parson looked decadent in his Terra tunic. His hair was the same as always, his chestnut locks falling into his eyes, as uncompromising as he was. Still holding her hand, he easily led her to the crowd of dancers and joined in.

Raene held out the side of her wide-legged pants to get a better view of her feet, but it hardly helped. Her mind was a mess, and even under the best of circumstances, she couldn't learn a new dance in a single song. Nonetheless, she let Parson lead her around, laughing and spinning, and this time, when he pulled her close again, he kissed her, good and long in front of everyone. Raene's head spun more than she did, but she wouldn't quit. Her injuries were grave and the pain grew with each passing hour, but this was her wedding night, and she had the right man beside her. Raene glowed with the sheer, raw happiness of it.

Within two songs, Parson insisted she rest. He pushed her toward a low alder wood bench and handed her a plate of roast badger. Raene dug in eagerly, filling her belly with the smoky flavors of the meat.

Raene had a full mouth when Gemini sailed over and sat beside her. "Is it the happiest day of your life?"

Without needing to think about it, Raene nodded. She was no longer under pressure to make a decision, to pit one brother against the other, and while she would always regret how things turned out for Hale, she couldn't let it impede her happiness with Parson. She caught sight of her new husband across the clearing talking with Lathan, and when Parson's eyes caught hers, a beaming smile warmed his face.

"Good!" Gemini replied with a sloppy laugh. She'd had too much wine already, but the two only giggled. "It would take a tiger to tame the supreme grouch that is Parson Frane."

"He *is* a grouch," Raene admitted between laughs. "An insufferable grouch! But he's so sweet, too. You'd never know it, but he is."

Gemini reached an arm across Raene's shoulders. "As long as he's good to you." Her words slurred together in more than one spot, but Raene only tilted her head against Gemini's shoulder and admired how she'd come to such a place. She had not only a husband she adored, not only a good friend, not only a safe place to live, but a real family for the first time in her life. Raene would never have known what she was missing if she hadn't been there to experience it herself.

"Are you feeling all right?" Gemini asked after a moment. "You feel warm."

"We're sitting next to a huge fire," Raene reminded her with a hearty laugh. She refused to mention the throbbing in her arm. There was too much good to spoil it with even one little bit of bad. "And what's going on with your eye here?"

Gemini rolled her eyes and laughed. "I walked into a

tree."

Raene tilted back and hooted with laughter as she pictured her friend walking into such a massive thing. Gemini smacked her arm but chuckled as well.

They chatted and laughed until Da appeared and grabbed Raene's only good hand. "I better get a chance to dance with the bride before it's too late!" he said as he pulled her toward the dancing couples. Raene only had time to hand her plate to Gemini before Da had her stomping and spinning and smiling wider than she had in years.

"I'm so proud of you, my dear. My sons are hard to know, and rarely do young people know what they want. You've done so well. I couldn't be more pleased for you, my daughter." Da's glassy eyes shone as he held her hand and spun her around during the height of the song.

Raene thought of reprimanding him for his continued use of the term 'daughter', but now, as strange as it was, it was true. She was a Frane. She was a daughter to the clan leader. She was married to his second son. And as he said, she'd found the right son for her despite their best attempts.

Mid-song, Parson interrupted and stole her from Da. Rather than hand her over easily, Da kissed her on each cheek and gripped her shoulders in each hand. "I know you'll continue to make me proud." And then he was gone into the crowd.

Parson collected her good hand in his and picked up where Da left off. "What was that about?"

Raene shrugged and laughed. "A little too much amberwine, I'd guess."

Where Parson held her good hand, his fingers grazed over the top of her knuckles, a move she knew no one else could see as they spun in the dance, but to Raene, it was a sweet sign of his devotion. She was nearly tempted to beg him to head back to his tent early, but the dance was interrupted.

A fleet of grey-clad men emerged from the shadow and filled the clearing around the central pit. The music stopped instantly, the last note hanging in the air like a noose. On and on they came, at least three or four dozen Terras in tunics with a silver wolf embroidered over their hearts—no, not a wolf. A coyote.

The threat of their presence sent a chill through the camp. Raene stiffened at the sight of them. She despised what happened the last time she encountered coyotes, and now here they came, row after row, far more than an envoy. They wanted something, and they were here to take it by force.

Parson reflexively positioned himself between the strangers and Raene. She had to peek over his broad shoulders to see them streaming in. By the time they were done, the strange Terra men outnumbered the clan three to one.

A tall, lithe man stepped forward from the rows. His walnut-brown hair glistened amber in the glow of the central pit. His pointed nose crooked to the side like it had been broken one too many times. "Argeron Frane," he announced, his voice echoing through the quiet woods.

Raene's breath caught in her throat.

"I am he," Da said as he stepped forward. He offered his best warm grin, as if welcoming a long-lost friend rather than a fleet of enemies.

The man nodded to him. "You are under arrest for crimes against the Mother. You will be escorted to Terrana to await your trial."

Raene marveled that Da could remain so calm. She gripped tight to Parson's hand, forcing herself to remain quiet as she watched. There was nothing she could do. There was nothing any of them could do.

With hands outstretched like a gracious host, Da said, "Thank you for taking the time to travel all the way here.

But unfortunately, I have been granted amnesty. If you will." Da motioned in the direction of his tent, and to everyone's surprise, the man followed. Though no one was more astonished than Raene when Da searched her out in the crowd. "Come, my daughter. I need you."

Raene swallowed back her fears and ignored her pains as she nodded and stepped forward. Parson was only a half-step behind her.

Inside Da's tent, a series of candles already glowed. On the table, Raene and Parson's marriage contract sat open in full view. The Terra agent stepped forward and read it from top to bottom.

Raene and Parson hovered nervously at the flap, unsure what was happening and unwilling to interrupt to find out.

"This contract was signed only today," the man finally said.

"Yes, my daughter had an unfortunate run-in some days ago. We were delayed as she recovered." Da looked over to Raene as he winked, as if this was somehow fun.

"According to this contract, the marriage grants you amnesty from alder crimes by one Kaide Landel?"

"He's a Pyro Vice Syndicate and the uncle of my newest daughter," Da offered.

Even Raene's tattered mind could put the pieces together. He'd planned this all long. How he knew, Raene could only guess, but Da had forced her decision today so she could protect the clan.

Her and Kaide.

But the man threw the document on the table.

"The Vice Syndicate Landel has no jurisdiction over Terra matters. You are charged with destruction of the sacred Alderwood, evading arrest, and assault of the Alderai's personal guard. You will be escorted to Terrana or executed."

It was then Raene knew this was all going to go horribly wrong. Da's shoulders slumped too low. His eyes were dim, and his usual playful nature had been snuffed out entirely. He'd planned on this moment, but he hadn't planned on losing. Da nodded his acceptance and let the agent lead him back into the clearing where the clan lingered, desperate for an explanation.

Parson and Raene followed behind them, too stunned and shocked to even move. They stood outside Da's tent flap with hands clasped as Da begged the agent to let him have one minute more.

When the man conceded, Da turned and searched the crowd until he found Lathan. "Guard the clan," Da instructed. A second later, he looked over his shoulder at Parson. "Keep her safe." And then he turned to the far side of the clearing where Hale stood with his hands in his pockets, awaiting his father's words. Da had to nearly shout to get his voice to carry across the camp. "Serve the Mother," he told his youngest son.

Raene's vision blurred with tears as she heard Da's cryptic words and watched him leave with the crooked-nosed man. Da squared his narrow shoulders and held his head higher than Raene had ever seen, a move she easily recognized. He was scared and nervous, but unwilling to show it before his clan.

Beside her, Parson stood taut, waiting to transition, to spur into action, but even he knew better than to fight so many. Together, they watched the man clasp some sort of metal loop around Da's wrist and lead him away from the clearing. Only when they were at the far reaches of the fire's light did the crooked-nosed man turn back to them. "This man is a ward of the Alderai until his trial. Should anyone interfere, we will be forced to execute him. Then, like he hadn't just sucked the breaths right out of them, the man took Da and disappeared into the shadows. His dozens of guards stomped and trotted behind, leaving a quaking echo long after they were gone.

The last guards hadn't been out of sight for more than a few seconds before Parson took off. Still gripping his hand, Raene raced behind him, but she was in no position to be running. Her head pounded, but she wouldn't let go. She couldn't let him leave. If Parson left, he would fight, and he would lose. And they would kill Da just for trying.

"Parson!" she shouted when she could manage.

Remembering her state, Parson stopped cold in his tracks. "I'm sorry, Raene. I have to go. I can catch them before they get too far." He kissed her cheek before jogging to his tent.

Raene tried to keep up, but by the time she arrived, Parson already had his bow and quiver strung across his back.

"You're not going anywhere!" Lathan's voice was an ominous boom that froze the blood in her veins.

Not even Parson could ignore such a command. He stood in place as Lathan's boots stomped toward him. Behind the mountain of a man came Tasia, Asla, and a dozen other young men eager to take action. They should have known Lathan would be the voice of reason. "You heard the Commissioner. Anyone tries to go after him, they execute him."

Parson narrowed his eyes, seething anger rolling off him. Both fists were clenched tight at his sides. "What do you want to do? Let him go? Go back to our festival and pretend we never had a Da? He gave himself up for us! We *have* to go get him."

"Weren't you listening?" Hale surprised them all when he stepped forward. He didn't shout or scare them with volume. Instead, he was almost quiet. Raene had to strain to hear him. "We have our instructions."

"Instructions?" Parson nearly spat at him.

Lathan neared enough to put a hand to Parson' chest. "If Da thought this was the last time he was going to see us, he would have said the words. But he didn't. He told us what to do. And you're supposed to keep Raene safe. That's your job. Honor Da, and do your damn job."

Raene saw the moment he wavered, considering the words of his brothers and the action in his heart. And Raene knew she would have to be the one to pull him back. Forcing down her pounding head, Raene slid between Lathan and Parson, looking straight into the eyes of her husband.

His mouth was pressed into a determined line but he let her speak, and she knew he measured her every word. "We can do nothing tonight. Tomorrow, we'll leave for Terrana. I can contact Kaide and get this worked out." For the moment, she pushed away thoughts of contacting Kaide and all she had to tell him. This wasn't about her. This was about Da, and keeping Parson from getting them both killed. Raene did her best to maintain the calm she knew her husband needed.

"I can't just sit by and let them take him." Parson's voice was quiet, his words just for her. Raene knew all too well how Parson would take the loss of yet another beloved Frane.

The welled-up tears in her eyes flowed freely, but she didn't care if he saw. She didn't care if any of them saw. "Trust me, Parson. This is the way. Let me talk to Kaide. You just have to be patient and take me to Terrana."

"He's not in Terrana. He's in Pyrona. We don't have enough time—"

Ignoring the pain in her broken arm, Raene clutched his neck, and in his ear, she whispered, "I need you to trust me."

Parson finally gave in, melting against her, squeezing hard around her waist despite the still-raw wound there.

Behind her, Raene heard the shuffling of boots as the rest of the crowd dissipated. And then, when it was quiet, Parson whispered, "It should be me. I cut down the trees. I made the trade. I killed the Alderai's men. It should be me."

"I killed them, too." Raene released his neck and kissed him hard. "This is what I'm here for. A Pyro princess with political connections. Let me get Da back."

Parson lowered his eyes and nodded. He knew she was right. When he put aside his anger, he could see the truth of it.

"Let's go home. We'll get it sorted in the morning." Raene breathed easier as Parson walked her back to their tent, helping her sit on the pallet and finally lay down for the night. He curled around her, needing her comfort as much as she needed his.

Raene kissed his forearm where it crossed over her chest. Parson squeezed her and buried his face against her neck, breathing in her scent and savoring her warmth. Lying there with her husband, it was possible to think it would all work out. If only her stomach would quit its nervous twisting.

End of *Raene and the Three Bears*.
Continue Raene's story in
Hale and Gemini (available Spring 2017).

WORKS BY RS MCCOY

The Sparks Saga
Sparks
Spirits
Schism

The Luminary Chronicles
The Lightning Luminary
The Sea Shade

The Alder Tales
Blossom and the Beast
Raene and the Three Bears
Hale and Gemini
The Snow Owl

The Extraction Files
The Killing Jar
The Lethal Agent

ABOUT RS MCCOY

Rachel McCoy is a Texan living in New Jersey. Between binge watching MTV reality shows and baking gluten free treats, she writes paranormal fantasy and science fiction novels.

She is the self-published author of the *Sparks Saga* trilogy, *The Alder Tales* series, and *The Extraction Files*. Back when she lived in the real world, Rachel earned a degree in marine biology, which contributed to her die-hard love of manta rays.

To connect with RS McCoy (or swap recipes), visit her on her website (www.rsmccoyauthor.com) or check out her Facebook page (www.facebook.com/ AuthorRSMcCoy). You can also join her newsletter to receive release updates, free stories, and bonus extras (http://eepurl.com/YItp1).

CONNECT WITH RS MCCOY

Friend me on Facebook:
https://www.facebook.com/AuthorRSMcCoy

Follow me on Twitter:
https://twitter.com/RSMcCoy1

Visit my Author Website:
http://rsmccoyauthor.com

Sign up to Receive Emails:
http://eepurl.com/YItp1